# THE LAST P

**Vows are made to be ke**

With Marco Morelli seemin ... being, Zane is determined to ensure ... stable and that he's financially secure in orde ... for Erin and what the future will bring.

There's a lot riding on that - firstly he needs to quash the rumours doing the rounds about his ability which threatens to derail the lucrative deal with Diego Delgado. Zane is relying on that deal to remain to ensure his foothold back in London.
But Diego's wife has plans of her own.

As does Colt Shoreham, who has returned to take up the offer that his brother promised him many years ago, should he ever need it. However, Tiger has issues of his own to deal with: one, his past and two, in the shape of a young woman who Marco treated so badly.
But out of all of them, who will be the one not honouring their promise?

**Also by Edie Baylis**

***Scarred Series***

*Mirrors Never Lie (Scarred #1)*
*The Price of Betrayal (Scarred #2)*
*Trusting Blood (Scarred #3)*
*The Hard Truth (Scarred #4)*
*The Last Promise (Scarred #5)*

***Allegiance Series***

*Takeover (Allegiance #1)*
*Fallout (Allegiance #2)*
*Vendetta (Allegiance #3)*
*Payback (Allegiance #4)*
*Judgement (Allegiance #5)*

***Retribution Series***

*An Old Score (Retribution #1)*
*Finders Keepers (Retribution #2)*
*The Final Take (Retribution #3)*
*The Retribution Series Box Set*

***Hunted Series***

*The Status Debt (Hunted #1)*
*The Family Legacy (Hunted #2)*
*The Target of Lies (Hunted #3)*
*The Hunted Series Box Set*

***Downfall Series***

*Until the End of Time (Downfall #1)*
*Escaping the Past (Downfall #2)*
*Vengeful Payback (Downfall #3)*
*The Downfall Series Box Set*

# THE LAST PROMISE

SCARRED #5

EDIE BAYLIS

ATHAME
press
- LONDON -

First published in Great Britain in 2025 by Athame Press.
This paperback edition published in 2025 by Athame Press.



Front cover photography: fxquadro/depositphotos.com; majdansky/depositphotos.com; stetsik/depositphotos.com; maliy/depositphotos.com; chrisdorney/depositphotos.com
Back cover photography: Stefan.Dzalev/depositphotos.com



Paperback ISBN 978-1-916977-09-9
e-ISBN 978-1-916977-08-2
Large Print 978-1-916977-11-2
Hardback 978-1-916977-10-5

Athame Press
Unit 13230 - PO Box 6945 – London – W1A 6US

***For Max***

# PROLOGUE

**1995**

*I REMAIN STANDING exactly where I am. I always stand during meetings, especially important ones because even in my brother's absence, the hierarchy of being the second son relegates me to little more than a runner.*

*My hands curl into fists underneath the cuffs of my pressed Savile Row shirt, but my face reveals nothing of the rage inside me.*

*Yet again, I count for nothing in my father's eye.*

*I cannot stop myself from sneaking a subtle glance in his direction.*

*Oh yes, Guiseppe Morelli - the big shot; the head of the Morelli empire - the empire that should be* mine *now Zane is no longer able to stand as our father's second-in-command, finally has the chance to put this right.*

*And he's got no choice about that now Zane has caused the firm and our family gross embarrassment after I successfully framed him for murdering that stupid bastard our father had an unspoken truce with. Now the golden brother languishes in jail awaiting trial for his crimes and it's only a matter of time before he's sent down.*

*That's the whole point of this meeting and the only reason I'm keeping my temper under wraps. Today, I will finally get recognition and be awarded what's rightfully mine. Christ knows I've waited long enough to be afforded the respect I wholly deserve.*

*A twitch of a smirk flickers over my mouth and I quietly chase it away, instead shifting my weight onto my other foot.*

*Finally, finally,* finally, *my father has deduced that I have plenty to offer. More importantly, he now knows he's been wasting time on Zane.*

*For instance, the coke deal that I've single handedly brokered with the South Americans is of the size London has never seen. That's down to* me. *Zane never pulled anything of this size off and nor will he because whilst he's in nick, it's* my *turn to shine.*

*That also includes getting the prize which Zane didn't want...*

Sofia.

*I focus harder on the conversation going on around the large mahogany table. If I don't concentrate, I will regret missing one second of my father apologising. The concept is so pleasurable it's almost orgasmic.*

*'All I can do is apologise once again for my son's unexpected actions of going against my strict instructions. He has both disappointed and embarrassed me, along with our entire family.'*

*Guiseppe speaks, his baritone voice only holds a slight trace of the thick Sicilian accent I remember so well as a child. But that was a long time ago. And this is now.*

Now *is the time I come into my own.*

*I move my eyes towards Franco Buscemi, his imposing figure intently studying my father sitting opposite him.*

*I can sense my father internally cringing as he waits for Buscemi to speak. This is crucifying him. He never apologises. It's wonderful.*

*I remain nonchalant and perfectly composed, but secretly I'm itching to hurry Buscemi along.*

*'It's a sacrilege, Morelli.' Buscemi's leans on the table and knits his long fingers together. 'Sofia has waited years for your son. I agreed to the arrangement over thirteen years ago now and I do not randomly promise my daughter's hand.'*

*'I appreciate that, Franco, but...'*

*'But Guiseppe, it was agreed they would marry when Zane reached twenty-five years of age. That, you said, would ensure he was fully fledged and able to offer my daughter the expected standing.' Buscemi shakes his head. 'But when your son* did *come of age, there were excuses after excuses for...' he snaps his fingers, 'three further years! And now he's in prison!'*

*'But Zane was out of the country on business for much of that time and then there were huge deals to broker....'*

*Seeing a bead of sweat trickle from the back of my father's hairline and run under his collar, I feel a laugh brewing. My father's standing his ground, but he can't fix this one. He knows what he has to do. He should have seen this coming.*

*Zane didn't want to marry Sofia in the first place. Even after I removed that pointless English bitch, Shirley Wilson, from the equation, Zane wasn't interested in Sofia. But would father listen?*

*I offered. Several times I offered to step in, but he stood firm that it had to be Zane.*

*More fool him. He's just wasted time because now I'm getting Sofia anyway.*

*'Guiseppe, surely you must realise I will never allow Sofia to marry Zane now, even if he is released from prison without charge.'*

*I watch Franco Buscemi smile - one of those smiles that doesn't reach the eyes. This situation is better than I imagined. And Zane won't be released without charge. I've worked extremely hard to ensure he's going down and will never come out.*

*'I understand.' Guiseppe nods. 'That's why I'd like to*

*propose an alternative solution.'*

*'I'm all ears, Morelli.'*

*My father glances at me. Here it is - here it comes...*

*My palms are sweating. I'm not nervous, just exhilarated. I've waited so,* so *long and now Sofia is mine.*

*'Marco has recently arranged an extremely lucrative arrangement with the Delgado family. I'm sure you've heard of them?'*

*Seeing Buscemi's small nod, I flinch. What the fuck has* my *deal - the one I've single handedly swung to supply London with cocaine, got to do with this?*

*'Firstly,' Guiseppe continues, 'as a goodwill gesture for the inconvenience of Zane's actions, I'd like to offer you ten per-cent of all forthcoming profits of that deal.'*

*My blood thunders in my veins. I'm sure I'm scowling, but I don't care.*

*I feel sick.*

*Why is my father giving this man ten per-cent of my profits as an apology for Zane getting banged up?*

*No, no and fucking* NO*!*

*Did I say that out loud? If I did, I'm about to, yet I don't get chance.*

*'Fifteen per-cent and I'll accept,' Buscemi says, his voice cold. 'But this gesture doesn't change that because of your son, my daughter remains on the shelf. The association alone may have already damaged her viability for other suitors.'*

*Pushing aside the rage at a chunk of my profits being handed out, I straighten my shoulders. Now they're getting around to it.*

I'll *ensure Sofia doesn't remain on the shelf. I'll wed her straightaway. That's fine by me. There will be a kid by the end of the year too if they ask nicely.*

*My heart pounds as I wait for my father to put me forward as Sofia's replacement suitor.*

*'I fully appreciate the situation Zane's unavailability has placed your daughter in and I've already given that some*

*consideration. I think I have found the perfect solution.' Guiseppe smiles. 'Now we have a relationship with the Delgados, I took it upon myself to speak to Emiliano Delgado and he has offered Diego to marry Sofia.'*

*'The eldest son?' Buscemi asks, looking thoughtful.*

*I blink.* What the actual fucking WHAT? *'Erm... father... I...' I'm silenced by a flap of my father's hand.*

*'Yes, Diego is the eldest.' Guiseppe leans over the table towards Buscemi, 'Of course he will inherit the Delgado empire in its entirety, offering Sofia full reassurance for the future. So, what do you say?'*

Oh my God! I hate him. I fucking hate him!

*My legs shake inside my tailored trousers. I'm not sure I can remain upright. In hideous slow motion, I watch a huge shit-eating grin form across Franco Buscemi's face. I might kill him too.*

*'I will give your proposal some thought, Guiseppe, but let's just say, I think it sounds like it could be a reasonable alternative solution.'*

*I watch my father and Buscemi shake hands, the image jerky behind my eyes. I'm melded to the spot. I cannot move nor function.*

*Neither can I believe that I've been bypassed.*

*Again.*

*Yet. Another. Fucking. Time.*

*Sofia is mine. MINE! She should pass to me by default, yet she's going to Diego Delgado, along with fifteen per-cent of my profits?*

*Fucking no bastard way can this happen!*

*Watching Buscemi leave my father's office, looking a hell of a lot more pleased than when he arrived, I realise this* is *happening and as usual, I can do fuck all about it.*

*This shit I get handed is going to have to change.*

# One

**14th August 2001**

ERIN LANGLEY swallowed a giggle at the absurdity. Zane Morelli becoming a dab hand with DIY was something she didn't think she'd ever see. He was far from domesticated, but since the meltdown which almost cost them their entire relationship, she couldn't fault him for the effort he'd put in, day in day out.

Her hand came to rest on her belly where their baby slowly grew. Giving up on Zane was never something to consider. True to his word, after that day when he'd drunkenly questioned the child's paternity, driven crazy with grief after finding out the daughter who he'd been led to believe was his, was Marco's, he'd put his heart and soul into putting his demons to rest.

Erin glanced around the penthouse they now lived in. It truly was a beautiful place, even if Marco had tainted it by taking ownership without Zane's consent. But Marco was gone and being as Zane owned this place and they needed somewhere more permanent with a baby on the way, the decision was made to bite the bullet and move back here. She knew being here made Zane uneasy, but he'd done it. As well as taking a backseat from his business over the last few weeks to give himself - *both* of them, breathing space, he'd reverted the penthouse back to the way it was before Marco pimped it out with his ostentatious, tacky alterations like the hideous lighting and garish cinema screen complex to watch his disgusting films.

She also knew Zane discovering Marco had sold off the collection of fancy motors which had filled the large underground car park of the penthouse was a huge blow. Zane had amassed that collection of over the years and ploughed a huge chunk of money into the prestige machines, many of which were rare, limited-edition models - their value only increasing with time.

It was a nest-egg Zane had mentioned several times and one she believed he'd secretly harboured getting his hands on during the years he'd been absent. Even his beloved Ducati bike had gone and Erin suspected that alone upset him the most. That, and the loss of his father's prized Bentley.

However, Zane being Zane, he'd shrugged off the loss, stating it was a small price to pay to keep Marco off the scene. As for the sentimentality of his father's Bentley, maybe it was best to retain no reminder of the man who it seemed Zane hadn't known at all.

Nevertheless, whenever Marco had taken or sold those cars was further salt rubbed into the deep wounds, adding to those he'd already inflicted.

Erin shook away the rising anger against the man who had inflicted so much pain to Zane, herself and everyone around them. This was now *their* fresh start. No more dwelling on the past and the grief it had caused. The aim was to look forward and concentrate on the good things to come.

She smiled aa Zane unscrewed the concealed plates of the air conditioning vents, looking every inch the sexy handyman in a black sleeveless vest top and jeans, a belt around his hips holding a selection of tools. Although it was strange living in this exclusive and elite penthouse in Battersea with panoramic views over the Thames, she was gradually getting used to it. And it would be even better when they got to the bottom of what that goddamn awful smell was, which was getting progressively worse.

The sickening stench was sometimes so bad that it made her heave.

Convinced a dead animal was trapped in the walls or under the floorboards, Zane had looked just about everywhere, refusing to let workmen become involved. *'No one's digging around in my place,'* he'd said, insisting he would solve the mystery origin of the disgusting smell himself.

But if he didn't locate the cause soon, Erin would insist he called the professionals in. What if the water supply was tainted or there was a sewage leak? Wasn't that kind of thing especially dangerous when pregnant?

Getting up from the new sofa they'd purchased, she walked over to the ladder Zane had propped against the wall and craned her neck to look up at him. 'There won't be anything in those ducts, surely?'

'There might be a squirrel or something. It's the only bloody place I haven't looked!' Zane unscrewed the final bolt on the plate. 'Don't stand underneath ladders. It's unlucky.'

Chuckling, Erin wandered across to the window, the amazing view over the London skyline never failing to enthral her. This really was a lovely place and once every last trace of Marco ever being here was erased, it would be perfect. Aside from the mental and emotional implications, of course. Those were things they both had to learn to live with.

It had been especially fraught the first couple of weeks after Zane allowed Marco and Skye to walk away. He'd fully expected retaliation. But that was before they heard that Skye had been gunned down.

Erin's usually unlined forehead creased with a frown.

Skye's death was a strange, bittersweet moment. The papers reported the motive of the drive-by shooting by an unknown biker, yards from Green Park station as a 'wrong place, wrong time' incident. Others billed it as a case of 'tragic mistaken identity'.

*But they knew better.*

Marco's 'broken-hearted father' statement in the news didn't fool them. There was no doubt he was behind it.

Erin shook her head with contempt. Skye being Marco's daughter was neither here nor there as far as he was concerned. In his eyes, she'd done her job and therefore surplus to requirements. And as much as Erin dismissed the girl, it was sickening.

*Sickening, but unsurprising.*

Zane took the news surprisingly well. Erin knew he still harboured a lot of stuff deep down but was holding it together. And with Marco stepping into the background in what appeared to be a silent truce, there was hope.

She glanced down at her virtually flat belly and smiled. There *had* to be hope or everything was pointless.

Suddenly hearing a clang as Zane finally dislodged the air conditioning vent panel, Erin was assailed by a stronger than ever blast of foul stench.

'Jesus Christ!' Zane clattered down the ladder, his hand clutched over his mouth and nose.

Desperately trying to keep her breakfast where it should be, Erin rushed to open a window. 'Urgh! That's horrific! Can you see where it's coming fr…' Turning to see Zane's face, she stopped, worry flickering. 'What? What is it?'

'A woman's body!' Zane gasped, gagging for the second time. 'A fucking rotting, stinking body!'

• • • •

'THAT WAS SOLENZO.' Standing in the room off the back of the warehouse in the Thames Canning Works, Tiger Shoreham shoved his mobile back in his jacket. 'Apparently, Alyson Read is well enough to be discharged.'

He shook his head in dismay. The girl they had removed from the penthouse when they'd faced Marco off had been drugged, used and abused - even *filmed* as part of Marco's sick money-making ventures. She'd been in a right state, the poor cow. Only young, too.

Alyson's absence to her parents had been initially explained by letting them know that she'd gone out of the country for a while with her devious bitch friend, Skye. But that hadn't sufficed for long. Once Alyson became compos mentis enough to talk, the horror of what she'd been put through sent her spiralling into a breakdown, leaving her adamant she couldn't return home. Not now - not *ever*.

Because of this, the idea to e-mail the girl's parents saying she was remaining in London to work and would be in touch seemed like a half-decent plan at the time. The risk of having anxious parents sniffing around had to be deleted and the e-mail seemed to do the trick. But none of them had weighed up what they'd do with the girl once she was well enough to leave Solenzo's private clinic.

Maybe they'd all presumed that by then she'd be in a better place in her own head and return back to where she came from. But no one had bargained on her point-blank refusal remaining as strong as it always was.

And that left them with a bit of a problem.

Tiger looked at Leo Holland - the man he'd worked with for as long as he could remember. Both being Zane's trusted inner circle men, there was little they hadn't seen or done, but dealing with the welfare of a teenage girl in this sort of situation wasn't one of them. 'What the bloody hell are we supposed to do with her?'

Leo ran his thick fingers over his short, cropped hair and grimaced. 'Find somewhere for her to stay, I suppose. But it has to be a place Marco won't dare to go. He's still out there somewhere and if he finds out Alyson has remained in London, he'll want to silence her.'

'But Marco's gone to ground, He'll have better things to do than chase after shutting one young bird up,' Tiger reasoned.

Even as the words left his mouth, he knew that wasn't the

case. No one knew what Marco was doing, where he was or what his plans were. The general consensus was he was giving Zane a wide berth and had stepped out of the game, but the risk remained that he was biding his time instead. And anyone, such as Alyson with the means of bringing the authorities sniffing on his tail needed to be deleted.

Tiger frowned. 'What if she comes here? The place is heavily guarded, therefore secure. We could put together a room for her.'

Leo shook his head. 'Dumping a fragile young girl in the middle of a cocaine warehouse isn't a great idea, mate!'

Tiger laughed, despite the situation. 'You're right. Okay, so how about Shirley or Fiona Bolt? They must be settled by now.'

'Nah, that's too close to home for Alyson.'

'Then what about the penthouse with Erin and Zane?'

'They need time out,' Leo said. 'Why do you think we've been overseeing most things? Plus, Alyson was Skye's friend, or at least she was *supposed* to be, had that little bitch not set the poor cow up for Marco to ruin. And that won't help Zane by having a reminder around.'

Tiger folded his arms across his wide chest. 'Where do you suggest, then?

'She can't stay at mine. I've only got a studio apartment.' Leo looked at Tiger thoughtfully and raised an eyebrow. 'But she could stay with *you...*'

'No. Fucking. Way!' Tiger cried. The accusation Zane's pseudo-daughter made about him attempting to molest her, not only lost him some teeth, but almost ruined his career and the family of Zane's firm that he'd been part of for so long. The insult that people he'd known most of his life; that he'd willingly die for, had contemplated even for a split second that he'd do such a thing, had hurt and hurt *badly*. Never again would he put himself in a situation to become a target of vindictive lies.

'Look,' Leo pressed. 'I know what happened before, but you have two-bedrooms. This girl isn't Skye Wilson and she'll be safe with you. Marco won't risk coming so close, so even if it's only for a short time, surely you can consider it? What other options do we have? We can't abandon the poor cow.'

They may not know Alyson, neither owe her a damn thing. It hadn't been *them* who had drugged her up or screwed her for the purpose of porn films, but diminishing the damage Marco had already inflicted was also important. 'Out of principle, I feel we should step up.'

'But it's not *you* who'll be doing that "stepping" though, is it?' Tiger grumbled. He stood up, the plastic chair in the makeshift office at the Thames Canning Works scraping across the lino floor. 'Besides, before we even think about dealing with Alyson Read, we've got things to do here.'

Pulling his ringing mobile from his pocket, he frowned. 'It's Zane.' He pressed the phone to his ear. 'All right, mate? What? You found *what* in the air con shaft?'

# Two

SOFIA DELGADO glanced at her diamond-encrusted Rolex and crossed her shapely legs over one another, allowing the red sole of the Louboutin stiletto on her right foot to dangle provocatively, just the way Diego liked it.

Taunting him with sexual allure but rarely delivering on it anymore, was a never-ending mode of enjoyment - something that made the long years she'd spent in this unwanted marriage just that little bit more bearable.

And thanks to Diego's stupidity, along with the strange, inherited trait from his prehistoric father that a wife should be treated like a queen, the last few months had been even easier.

But Sofia knew she was pushing her husband to the limit and she had to control herself. Diego had a line and it was one which was relatively easy to cross. Sofia didn't want that happening - especially not at this late stage in the game.

Getting up from the pink velvet chaise longue was becoming increasingly difficult whilst this charade continued. Furthermore, it would be impossible to maintain a smidgen of the sex appeal men always drooled over if the plan didn't pull off soon.

Standing up straight, she ran her hand over the bump that

made her feel, as well as look like a whale and reminded herself that it was doing her a favour.

Appearing behind Sofia, Diego's hands ran over the stretchy, silky fabric covering her belly to down between her legs. 'How am I supposed to keep my hands off my wife when she looks so hot?'

'Stop it! You know what the doctor said!' Sofia snapped, pulling her husband's hand away. 'You want a heir, don't you?'

Diego stepped back, his swarthy features darkening. 'First time I've heard of pregnancy stopping a man from fucking his wife!'

'Clearly you know very little about placenta previa!' Sofia barked, her cheeks flushing. 'Do you want me to die or go into early labour?' She dabbed her eyes with the silk handkerchief she kept to hand for instances such as these. 'This pregnancy is stressful enough without you making me feel like a bad wife!'

Besides, it wasn't like Diego wasn't getting any anywhere else, Sofia thought with an inward scowl. He'd never hidden his string of mistresses - it was part of the territory. But she didn't care. The less she had to do with him the better, the greasy, South American bastard.

It was only down to her meticulously governed contraception that she hadn't fallen pregnant long before now. But once Diego started making noises about getting her examined for lack of fertility had she made the decision to act.

But it wasn't supposed to go on *this* bloody long.

'When have I ever made you feel like a bad wife?' Diego asked, the glint in his eyes showing Sofia that she'd crossed his line.

Moving forward, he pulled her close, his lips inches from hers. 'You want for nothing, give little in return, yet think you can make sarcastic, offensive comments? You might look hot, but I will not put up with lack of respect, disobedience or insults. That you are finally producing a heir is the only reason I honour your requests.'

Sofia flinched as Diego's hand moved once more to the

swollen mound of her belly and prayed it moved neither higher nor lower because by the look in his eyes, he would not accept her pushing him away for a second time. She lowered her eyes submissively. 'I'm sorry. I'm feeling fragile at the moment. I appreciate everything you do and for your understanding.'

Her hand also moved to caress her belly and, in the process, subtly dislodged his hand. 'I only have three months to go and then I'll make it up to you,' she gushed, knowing that time would never come to pass.

'Good!' Diego smiled coldly. 'You are my wife and should remember that.' He snatched up his jacket. 'I'm going out now. I have some business and other things to do. I will not be back until morning.'

Sofia kept her well-practiced smile in place as Diego walked down the tiled hallway of their Kensington townhouse. She knew what 'business' and 'other things' consisted of. He was welcome to both of them. But what he didn't realise was that he was on borrowed time. Had it not been for things screwing up, Diego Delgado's end would have already arrived.

As the slam of the front door echoed through the house, followed by the roar of the Maserati roar away, Sofia wasted no time in rushing up to her bedroom.

Unable to bear it any longer, avoiding glancing in the floor-to-ceiling mirror at her whale-like appearance, she tugged the merino dress accentuating her blooming shape over her head and slung it to the floor. She then unfastened the myriad of concealed hooks and straps sitting seamlessly underneath her bra and knicker line.

After what seemed an age, Sofia removed the custom-made, film-worthy prosthesis and with a satisfied grunt, dropped it on top of the merino dress. Only now did she turn to the mirror and admire her perfectly toned washboard stomach and tight, trim waist.

In a couple of weeks she would have to upgrade to the eight-months-pregnant prosthesis and that was not happening.

Lifting the silicon and foam contraption from the floor, she opened the wardrobe and shoved it in the lockable partition behind her many clothes rails to join the three, four, five and six-month prostheses, made to order from Marco's film industry contact.

Sofia had devised this plan when Diego had started talking about infertility specialists. She'd had to do something. If he'd found out she'd been having contraceptive injections behind his back for years whilst pretending to try for a much-wanted heir, convincingly sobbing every time her period arrived, he'd have grounds for divorce. And *that* wasn't happening either.

But she'd never intended for this fake pregnancy to go on so long to actually have to *look* pregnant.

It had all been going to plan - Marco's wife had been removed and Diego was next.

Then it had gone wrong...

For fuck's sake, walking around like a whale was bloody dreadful. She'd refused to even go out for the past three months.

But she was not waiting much longer.

Locking the cabinet, Sofia snatched up her burner phone and dialled Marco Morelli's number. 'I'm coming to see you. Yeah, tonight.'

And tonight was the night she would get a date for completing their plan set in stone.

• • • •

'FOR FUCK'S SAKE!' Leo gasped. Holding his breath, his lungs fit to bursting, he held the heavy-duty bag open as Tiger and Zane pulled the last parts of the decomposing corpse out of the vent shaft.

He knotted and double knotted the bag, then pulled off his disposable gloves, carefully putting them in another bag along with Zane and Tiger's gloves. All three men stood in silence and stared at the bag containing the rotting flesh.

Zane wiped the sweat from his forehead using the back of his arm. 'I might have known Marco would leave something extra special behind for me.' It also raised the age-old question which never stopped needling him: *How long it would be before his brother resurfaced to do something else?*

Tiger remained looking at the bag, his chiselled face devoid of expression. 'Who the hell is she?'

'I guess we'll never know,' Zane muttered, pulling on another pair of disposable gloves. 'Someone who came to see Marco and never left.' He glanced up at the void in the ceiling. 'Now I need to clear out that duct and make sure there's no trace lurking.'

The smell hadn't yet dissipated via the air conditioning network into any other apartments in the complex. At least, he hadn't heard any complaints. The smell of rotting flesh was obvious to him, but most people wouldn't be acquainted with knowledge of decaying human *bodies*. If anyone suspected *that*, the police would definitely be involved.

'That bastard's done me up like a kipper again,' Zane muttered. Despite not having lived here for years, it was *his* name on the deeds. If the shit hit the fan, could he prove Marco was here? Either way, he wanted the police involved with nothing. Once they stuck their beak into something they'd be over everything and with a warehouse stacked with several million pounds of street-worthy cocaine and more on route, that was not a good idea.

'It will be difficult to find out who this woman was,' Tiger said. 'There's not much left of her face that's recognisable.' The image of the slushy, decomposing flesh where that woman's face had been was enough to put him off his dinner for eternity.

'We *have* to find out because we need to be ready for any missing person alerts.'

Everyone turned to Erin. 'What are you doing here?' Zane gasped, attempting to cover the stinking bag on the floor. 'I told you to stay in the bedroom and let us deal with this.'

'I'm pregnant, Zane, not deaf and blind!' Covering her mouth, Erin moved further into the room. 'I hardly need to be shielded from what that bastard brother of yours is capable of!'

'Yes, I know, but...'

'Would Alyson know anything about this?' Erin glanced around the group of men. 'She was here with Marco and might have seen another woman. Or seen Marco do something. We should go to Solenzo's and ask her.'

'No need.' Leo scowled. 'She's been discharged. We were making arrangements for somewhere safe for Alyson to stay, being as she's still adamant she won't return to her parents.' He then shot a glance at Tiger. Landing each other with the least favourable jobs was a long-standing joke between the two of them. It injected a bit of humour into their days, but this one stood to force Tiger from his hang-up over having nothing to do with women because of that bitch, Skye. 'Alyson's going to Tiger's flat on a temporary basis until we find somewhere more suitable.'

Tiger's jaw clenched as his usually neutral face delivered Leo a death stare. *He'd made it clear that he wouldn't be put in that position.* 'I don't think th…'

'Excellent idea!' Zane slapped Tiger on the back. 'Thanks, mate! That's good of you. We need to ensure Alyson's protected and she'll be safe at yours.'

'It is really kind of you, Tiger.' Erin placed her hand lightly on Tiger's arm. 'When are you collecting her?'

Tiger shifted uncomfortably from foot to foot. *He'd kill Leo for this*. Ignoring the jubilant grin on Leo's face, he took a deep breath. It wasn't like there was much choice now without appearing a selfish arsehole. 'I'll collect her sometime later on today, I guess,' he mumbled.

'We may find she won't speak about anything that occurred here. Christ knows she's been traumatised enough, but see what you can do, eh?' Zane readied his bottle of disinfectant and steadied the ladder. 'I'll give this a go now. Erin, can you dig out some incense, air fresheners - anything to get rid of the fucking smell in here? And Leo, being as everyone else is busy, you've won the job of getting rid of the bag!'

Leo's jubilance of setting Tiger up to deal with Alyson dissolved. *Great. He was on body duty again, then?*

# THREE

'I BARELY RECOGNISED you with that wig on.' Marco trailed his fingers down Sofia's naked body in the afterglow of sex. Usually, he had no wish for further contact after shooting his load, but with Sofia it was different – it always had been. 'You should have left it on!' he added, a wicked grin on his face.

Batting Marco's hand away, Sofia propped herself up on her elbows. 'Are you saying you prefer me blonde?'

'No way!' Marco pinned Sofia back on the huge bed and moved his body back over hers. 'You're perfect just as you are.'

Sofia would normally be desperate for round two with Marco, but his comment rattled her. *Everything* rattled her lately. It was all very well jumping into bed the second they set eyes on each other like they always did, but this situation was getting untenable.

Ignoring Marco's scowl as she pushed him off her, Sofia got out of bed and strutted naked across the room. She picked up the solid silver straw she'd bought him as a present years ago and helped herself to a line of cocaine. 'I suppose this is Diego's coke too?' she sniped, hoovering up the coke and then delicately wiping powder residue from under her nose. 'When is he going to die, Marco? I can't keep this up much longer.' Her manicured fingernails dug into the soft flesh of her palm. 'Keeping him at bay is getting harder too. If he discovers the heir he's so desperate for is a lump of silicone, then I'm dead!' Her eyes narrowed at Marco spreadeagled on the bed, his muscular form displayed in all of its glory. 'It was never part of the deal for me to walk around looking like a whale!'

Marco's eyes trailed over every beautiful inch of Sofia's lithe body and grinned. 'I can't imagine you ever looking like a whale, babe.' *But he'd like to.*

One day, Sofia's perfectly flat stomach would swell for real when he put *his* baby inside her. He'd show the world that Sofia Delgado was no longer Sofia Delgado, but Sofia Buscemi once again. And then she'd become *exactly* who she should have always been - Sofia *Morelli.*

Marco ran his hand down the length of his erection, the ache for further release relentless.

'You haven't seen me wearing that fucking strap-on belly!' Sofia snapped, the colour in her cheeks heightening. 'Do you find all of this amusing? Diego should have been dead months ago. You promised!'

Marco bristled. Just thinking of that Dago twat having the right to openly touch this woman - *his* woman, injected his blood with antifreeze. 'Well, if the cunt hadn't been so fucking stupid to move his cocaine supply business away from me to my bastard brother, then he would be dead by now!'

And he hadn't expected *that* getting chucked into the mix. The last person Marco believed Delgado would accept as a successor would not only be anyone but another Morelli, but the very same one who had initially been promised to wed the woman *he'd* married? The greasy wanker must have rocks in his head. But that didn't change Sofia getting arsey about the delay. 'You knew that after Diego pulled that thing out of the bag with Zane taking over the deal there was no choice but to let the dust settle for a while.'

'Actually,' Sofia sniped. 'If *you* hadn't made Diego

suspicious in the first place by looking at me "salaciously", as he put it, then he wouldn't have cut your arrangement at all!'

'I'm not allowing your prick of a husband to make *us* argue!' Swinging his legs out of bed, Marco moved across the room and pulled Sofia into his arms. Just the sensation of her velvet skin against his pushed his cock to bursting point. He slipped his hand between her legs, feeling the wetness. This woman was as hot for him as she always had been and she'd remain that way - he'd make sure of it. 'Don't stress. It will be done. And soon. My brother's laying low, playing happy families. His concentration is not on his business anymore and your shit-for-brains husband will quickly realise this and pull the arrangement between them. *Then* the job will be done.'

Marco sucked in his breath as Sofia expertly wrapped her hand around his engorged cock. 'Then I want the date I will be free set in stone right now!'

Careful not to let Sofia's present advantageous position influence him into blurting out 'anytime you like', Marco instead swooped her up and threw her onto the bed. She was the only woman he'd ever met who liked things as hard, fast and twisted as him. 'It'll happen within two weeks,' he growled as he shoved himself home. 'Two fucking weeks, babe and you'll be mine.'

'I'm already yours,' Sofia gasped, raising her hips to allow Marco deeper inside. *And she couldn't wait.*

• • • •

DIEGO DELGADO hadn't announced his arrival. He preferred it this way. It gave him the benefit of seeing things how they really were, rather than the glossed-up, best behaviour showcase his presence usually warranted.

*But not here.*

Sitting on a cheap plastic chair in the room which counted as Morelli's 'office', he looked around. The Thames Canning Works was a shithole – a dilapidated Victorian factory that hadn't seen much, if any, updating since its original time of construction. But that was kind of the reason he liked it. Frills and fancies distracted from what was *really* going on behind the scenes and usually served as a front for incompetence. This place was a refreshing change and that, he liked.

As well as, despite not expecting to, liking Zane Morelli.

The guy was on the level and did what he said on the tin. At least, he had so far. And although from what Diego had seen whilst being led through the shop floor by a rather worried looking foreman, this place being used to house millions of pounds worth of cocaine might be a dump, but it was running like clockwork. And that was good.

Diego glanced at his watch. Almost half an hour he'd waited for Zane to show up. The frightened foreman told him Zane had been notified of his arrival, so where the hell was he? People didn't usually fuck around dragging their feet, making Diego Delgado wait.

But surprisingly, he didn't actually mind that either.

He swilled the whisky around in the dubious looking glass he'd been handed 'whilst he waited' and sipped it. A shit glass, but good whisky.

He frowned. Zane was a bit of an enigma - not the normal sort he dealt with, especially after the experience with the slimy piece of shit brother.

But when push came to shove, and no matter his personal likes or dislikes, Diego was here because of what he'd heard.

What *everybody* had heard.

The whole of London had heard about Zane Morelli's daughter turning out not to be his daughter, but *Marco's*. Diego had also got wind of the speculation about the fiancée getting kidnapped and injured. A child on the way too, by all accounts.

None of that fazed Diego. Why should it? It was none of his business. But what *was* his business and what he'd also heard via his vast network of eyes and ears, was that Zane Morelli had all but retired.

Absent from his territories, no one had seen the man. Word had it that he'd moved back into his flash pad on the Thames and stepped away from the game. Some stories even hinted at a breakdown and a drink problem...

That Morelli nor any of his main men were anywhere to be seen here today was also a red flag.

Diego lit a cigarette, his heavily lined forehead creasing further.

If any of what he'd heard was true, then he'd have no choice but to pull their association. He needed a reliable outlet to move cocaine. This place might be running effectively, but the deal was that Zane ran the gaff, not some muppet following orders in his absence.

With another container load of coke due any day now from his farmers in Paraguay, it was vital he found out how things stood. And if he didn't like what he learnt, he'd be nipping the whole operation in the bud.

# FOUR

THE WHOLE WAY BACK from Harley Street, Alyson remained as far away from the driver as possible, attached to the side of the car door like a sideways stalagmite. The journey was taking forever. Each second was a horrifyingly long, drawn-out moment in time, giving each revolting, disgusting memory of what had occurred further opportunity to plough through her brain in an unending tumult of desperation like it had done over the last several weeks.

The pills she'd been prescribed weren't working. Unfortunately, there was no respite and she had not been spared from the memories constantly forcing their way into her head. Each time the clamouring demands for explanations how or why any of those things had occurred in the first place made themselves known, they remained answered.

And Alyson had no reason, nor excuse why those things which had always been at the root of her morals in life, had failed to mean anything during that short, yet ruinous period of time.

Her fingers gripped the plastic of the car door inner, her knuckles whitening.

She'd had no end of time to revisit the things haunting her.

And there were lots of them. Hours passed slowly when confined to a bed in a clinic full of strangers with no company, save the torturous knowledge that everything she'd ever deemed sacred had been ripped away. All that remained was shame, regret and despair.

It would have been better to have awoken with amnesia, rather than be condemned to live with the aftermath of what she'd done.

It made no difference how many times she'd been told that she had been drugged with a powerful psychedelic and muscle relaxant; that she'd had no conscious control or power to govern or make decisions; that she'd been rendered malleable by chemical means and abused against her will whilst in a helpless state.

She'd been told that a thousand times by the doctors or whoever they were in that clinic, but it fell on deaf ears. It didn't matter what they said.

The familiar rise of bile moved up from the region where Alyson's stomach once was. Referring to *'once was'* meant she now truly believed that her body harboured only an empty space. Her physical outer casing was a mere shell containing nothing - no organs, blood, nerve endings - *nothing*. A void of emptiness, save for poisonous memories and hideous realisations that she was not in any way, shape or form the person she had been.

She was a ruined, trashed and hollow version of herself. Nothing but a traitor. And if she had no time for what remained, then nor would anyone else. How could she blame them?

Realising a sob escaped her mouth, Alyson pressed harder against the passenger side window, away from the occasional glance shot in her direction by the man driving this car. She couldn't look at him. Didn't *want* to look at him.

He was another one of *them*.

Another person who had witnessed her lying like a whore in Marco Morelli's bed. One of many who had seen *exactly* what she was...

Why anyone bothered removing her from that place to try to help her, she didn't know. She wasn't worth it.

How could anyone who deemed it acceptable to lose their virginity to their best mate's father; to allow another woman to perform sex acts on them; to take drugs - be worth anyone's time?

The most crucifying thing of all was that she'd *enjoyed* that out of this world feeling which a man - someone she didn't even know had, with his hands, tongue and body, brought her higher, higher and higher until she'd reached a peak and exploded, drowning in never before experienced pleasure.

Alyson squirmed in the car seat, the throbbing and aching in her most private place starting again, along with that dreadful wetness between her legs. She must be dying. Whatever she had done to herself – what she'd *allowed* to be done to her, had permanently changed her. It had surely damaged her insides because this wasn't normal.

Just thinking about how Marco had made her body feel caused those strange feelings to start again. And that showed that she must be seriously wrong in the head.

*Or just plain evil.*

Those Solenzo people called it 'abuse'. She'd seen their horrified expressions, so how could she tell them that she'd enjoyed it? At least, it had felt good and she'd wanted more.

How could something be abusive if she'd got pleasure from it?

It couldn't, so the truth must remain her dirty secret - her cross to bear. She couldn't handle anyone knowing that she'd got a weird, perverse pleasure from illegal and strange animalistic actions.

Now she'd never marry; never have children... How could she ever look at a man now, let alone a potential husband, when she knew the truth about her sickness?

Unable to help it, a whole-body shudder ricocheted through Alyson as the enormity of what she'd given away and the fate she was condemned to, avalanched over her.

'Are you all right?'

Alyson jumped at the deep voice of the driver. Before she could stop herself, she looked at him for the first time and almost died on the spot. *He looked terrifying. Was he going to kill her?*

The horizon began spinning. 'I… I…'

Why had she got into this car? She couldn't remember doing it. *Oh God...*

'We're nearly there.' The man's eyes returned to the road ahead. 'My place isn't all that special, but you'll be fine once you've settled in. I'll make sure you're safe.'

Alyson wasn't sure whether she was crying, shaking or both. Or even whether she was screaming. Her breathing was short and laboured. She felt like she was drowning. She'd been sold to another nutter and would die. There was no end or salvation for sinners like *her*.

With her vision reducing to a black-edged tunnel, she grasped at the door handle, pulling and tugging. She had to get out. She had to get away from here and away from this man – away from herself.

Her head pounded and the screeching noise in her ears got louder and louder. The light began to fade in her mind as her hands, slippery with sweat flailed, desperate to grip the door handle.

*Must get out. Must get away...*

Suddenly the car screeched to a halt and she was pinned her against the seat. The man was talking. His words made no sense because she was dead and therefore didn't matter.

• • • •

ZANE DID AN IMPRESSIVE job of acting like the back of his T-shirt wasn't drenched with sweat and that his lungs weren't short of air like he'd run a marathon. Outwardly, he appeared unperturbed and calm, but inwardly, he was stressed to the hilt.

Although only a short distance from the penthouse to the canning works, the traffic was abysmal. He'd have been better off running rather than taking his motorbike. The unexpected ad-hoc visit from Diego Delgado didn't help matters - especially when Zane was convinced his jeans were covered with the stinking bodily fluids of a decomposing corpse. He was also sure he must reek of bleach and disinfectant too, but if he did, Diego didn't appear to notice.

So far there had been the standard polite small talk between them, but Zane knew this man's mere presence spoke volumes. He suspected he knew the reason behind the visit and had half-expected it, yet hoped it wouldn't happen. Still, nothing for it but to get it over with. And that, *he* would instigate, rather than wait and give Delgado the upper hand.

Casually topping up both his and his visitor's whisky, Zane placed the bottle down. He leant on the table between them and clasped his hands together. 'I'm guessing the reason for your visit is to see whether I'm running a tight ship? I've heard what's being said about me on the grapevine.'

Zane looked at Diego intently, waiting for an answer, but Diego returned his stare before speaking. That was okay – Zane knew how this worked. He'd do exactly the same.

'I am concerned with what I've heard, yes,' Diego agreed, his eyes still focused on Zane. 'Like you say, many things are being said and I'm sure you understand I need to ensure my business and our arrangement is stable.'

Zane took a sip of whisky and remained silent. *Let the man say what was required.*

Diego nodded at the whisky glass as Zane placed it back on the table. 'Word has it you have a drink problem, amongst other issues…'

As he reached for his cigarettes, Zane couldn't stop his short burst of cold laughter. 'If getting pissed as a rat and smashing my shit up after discovering the girl I thought was my daughter, was in fact, my brother's – the result of him raping my then girlfriend nearly twenty years ago, then yes, I had a drink problem!' He offered a cigarette to Diego before lighting his own.

Zane didn't miss the flash of shock behind Diego's eyes at his words. Everyone knew he'd been duped over Skye's paternity, but the rape was a different story. 'I'd appreciate it if you kept how the conception occurred to yourself. The girl's mother has already been through enough. That is the reason and the *only* reason I'm refusing to publicly comment on anything that is circulating.'

Seeing Diego nod, Zane continued. 'I won't lie, discovering all that knocked me sideways, but I've dealt with it now - in as much that I won't allow Marco to ruin any more than he already has.' He slowly blew out a long, thin line of smoke. 'But it raises questions: Why did I not notice Marco setting me up for this fall? How did I believe this pretend "daughter" of mine's lies? How could I be so slack in not preventing my fiancée from being kidnapped? I expect all this is going through your mind too?'

His eyes narrowed as he leant forward. 'You'll also be wondering whether I'm capable of running my firm any longer, which includes dealing with your cocaine. You and others may be questioning whether I've lost my grip.'

Diego had the good grace to look uncomfortable as Zane succinctly summed up much of what he'd thought. 'You are correct, Morelli. It also concerns me that you were absent from here when I arrived. Absent from all your territories lately, apparently. It is said that you're retiring, but our arrangement was that *you* ran this, not your lackeys.'

Zane bristled. His men, even ones low down in the hierarchy were not 'lackeys'. He respected each member of his workforce, regardless of level. Without them there would be no firm at all. Furthermore, he would not put anything before Erin right now. Everything else took second place until he knew how the land lay. 'Courtesy of my inbuilt belief that family is everything, my fiancée almost died when she was kidnapped, Delgado. But in answer to yours and everyone else's questions, I believed Skye's lies because I *wanted* to. She was the daughter I hadn't known existed - at least that's what I thought. And for that reason, I wanted to make up for my absence in her life so didn't treat what she said with suspicion, like I would if it had come from anyone else.' He cleared his throat as anger and hurt prodded. 'Leaving myself open was a mistake and something which will never happen again.'

Zane snatched up his whisky and took a long swig. 'My firm is running well. I'm on top of everything and will continue to be, regardless of what people believe. That includes our arrangement. It is true that I have taken a few weeks out to ensure my fiancée is well and to put myself back on an even keel, but I have *not* retired. Erin is pregnant and therefore my main and immediate concern. Marco has gone to ground, but I am waiting for his reappearance and will be ready for it, so if anyone thinks I'm incapable or have "lost it", they are very wrong.'

Diego smiled. 'My wife is also pregnant. I understand how important keeping them safe is - especially in our line of work.' He stubbed out his cigarette in the cheap ashtray. 'I appreciate your honesty, Morelli, and I suspect that had I been in your position, I would react similarly. You have given me all I need to know to see that I am correct in wanting to continue our arrangement. You are the kind of man who will see things through to the end.'

'That's how I'm built, Diego,' Zane muttered, the irony that his father had instilled such high values in him whilst covering up what Marco did to Shirley, was something he had still not come close to reconciling.

'It's a shame your brother doesn't share your morals and values,' Diego said. Seeing the flash in Zane's eyes at the comparison to Marco, he quickly moved on. 'I think perhaps we should become better acquainted. Come to my house for dinner and drinks with me and my wife.' Being out of his own territory and with his own woman, Zane would be more relaxed. And that would enable Diego to give a fully transparent appraisal to ensure he was making the correct decision. 'Bring your fiancée. Shall we say the day after tomorrow?

Zane blinked in surprise. *He hadn't expected that.* 'That would be nice,' he smiled, unsure whether it was a good idea or not. He wasn't exactly a fan of dinner parties or even if he had a suit, but it wouldn't hurt to cement their business arrangement further. It would also be good for Erin to get back out again.

• • • •

SWEATING FROM CARRYING a kicking and screaming Alyson into his flat, Tiger was relieved she'd now passed out. The racket she'd been making, her wild eyes darting around and the nonsense coming from her mouth, as well as her fingernails flailing precariously close to his face, was doing his head in.

He wouldn't lose sleep about complaining neighbours - they wouldn't dare. But this was far from good. He didn't get paid for this sort of shit.

Listening to Solenzo down the other end of the phone, Tiger gritted his teeth. He'd had no choice but to call after the mad bitch attempted to launch herself from his car. He didn't have the knowledge to deal with that sort of crap and hadn't known what else to do but call the man who deemed Alyson 'well enough' to leave the clinic.

As much as Mr Solenzo deserved the vast amount of money paid to treat anyone connected to Zane with guaranteed secrecy, as well as earning their respect and trust, on this occasion Tiger was unable to swallow what the old man suggested.

'You said she was well enough to be discharged, Solenzo,' Tiger growled, almost sensing the scowl on the old surgeon's face at being questioned.

'As said,' Solenzo continued, 'it sounds like she's had a psychotic episode. This is disappointing. For that to happen at this stage suggests the damage done to her brain from the psychotropic drugs forcibly administered by that lunatic is permanent. I'll arrange to have her sectioned.'

'*Sectioned*?' Tiger blurted. 'You mean put her in a mental hospital?' His eyes tracked to Alyson Read on the bed, her pale face streaked with dried tears. Even after exhausting herself into unconsciousness, her small hands remained tightly clenched.

A combined pang of guilt and anger resonated somewhere within Tiger's heart. It stirred up a mixture of something he'd managed to keep packed in a compartment for many years. 'She is not being sectioned,' he found himself saying, perhaps *shouting* down the line. 'Yes... yes, I do insist... Yes, if I have to, I will.'

His pulse ramping up to a thunderous pace, Tiger forced himself to concentrate on what Solenzo next said. 'Okay. That will have to do. I'll look out for him.'

Abruptly ending the call, Tiger chucked his mobile to the side. His anger was thoroughly unexpected, but he wasn't being responsible for *another* person's downfall by allowing a decision to section. At the age of eighteen, he'd been in the exact same position, with the difference of okaying a doctor's suggestion to section his own mother. *'It's the best place after a breakdown,'* the man had insisted.

Tiger's jaw clenched, his rage growing. How he wished he hadn't listened to that doctor. How he wished he'd killed him stone dead. How he wished he'd succeeded tracking the bastard down after his mother endured being pumped full of drugs which turned her into a zombie; trapped with no means of escape, surrounded by crazy people who bit themselves, shouted, groped one other. How she'd put up with being strapped to a gurney and sedated if she dared resist the electric shock 'treatment' or endless drugs forced upon her. How he wished that one day she hadn't saved up her 'medication', downed the lot and then slit her wrists because she'd seen no other way out.

Tiger swallowed the lump in his throat. How he wished he'd known what he knew now: a breakdown was different to a permanent mental illness, like schizophrenia.

He found himself looking back at the inert form of Alyson.

After everything that had happened to that girl, what would sectioning do, apart from make it worse? And he wasn't shouldering that burden of guilt and responsibility for a second time. She wouldn't be getting sectioned and Solenzo could send his courier with tranquillizers for Alyson as a 'temporary measure' too, but she wouldn't be taking them either.

Tiger would sit here all night and see her through. Tomorrow was another day. He'd treat her like he'd do for someone on a bad LSD trip. If Alyson was the same in the morning, then he'd have to rethink, but his instinct was telling him to go with it.

Because if he'd done this for his mother all those years ago, then maybe she'd still be here.

# Five

SOFIA GLANCED over her shoulder once more, making sure there was no hint of Diego making a move to leave his home office.

He'd returned from whichever tart he'd spent the night with first thing this morning, yet she'd had to leave Marco's last night. There was no way *she* could risk the luxury of staying overnight with her lover.

She shoved her hand into the sweetheart neckline of her pink chiffon dress. Her botoxed forehead strained with blank concentration as she delved between her breasts and behind the skintight join of the silicone prosthesis. With a final burst of effort, she dragged her burner phone out. *At least the bloody fake monstrosity was good for something!*

Knowing she had little time, she rapidly tapped out a text to Marco:

D has arranged Z and E to come for dinner here tomorrow! Let me know how I should play it. Don't text back yet as D is around.

xxx

Biting her lip, Sofia pressed send and waited for the delivery receipt, deleted the message and then struggled to shove the phone back into its hiding place. With one hand wedged down her top, she squirmed uncomfortably. *Christ, this was ridiculous!*

'What on earth are you doing?'

Sofia's stomach lurched at the voice. She turned to see Diego in the lounge doorway and silently chastised herself for not being more alert. She must remain on top of this - there was no room for mistakes.

Making sure she looked suitably put out, she frowned as much as her rigid forehead allowed. 'My breasts are uncomfortable. They are too big for this bra. Pregnancy has a lot to answer for!'

Diego moved into the room and stared curiously at Sofia's chest. 'They don't look any different to me.'

Sofia's cheeks flushed crimson. 'They might not "look" any different, but they are and it's unpleasant,' she lied. *Fuck, fuck, fuck! Was he suspicious?* 'Don't stare! I feel enough of an ugly barrage balloon as it is!'

'It will be worth it in the end, mon chéri.' Diego grinned, leaning over to rub Sofia's belly. 'My son will be worth every second. Besides, "ugly" is something you'll *never* be.'

Sofia forced a smile. *Son?* Diego wanted this baby to be a boy? How disappointed he'll be realising it's nothing but padding. *Priceless.*

Stopping the urge to laugh, she instead pretended that he'd made her feel better with his compliment. But what was with this fake French shit? *Mon chéri?* What a prat!

It was true that she felt like a barrage balloon. And ugly. How could she possibly feel anything else looking like *this*. Wearing this contraption day in, day out - even under her nightclothes, was driving her crazy. Now Diego expected her to entertain visitors? And *those* particular visitors...

Diego sat opposite on the luxurious cream sofa. He crossed his ankles and studied Sofia. 'Are you not looking forward to this dinner? You've barely seen anyone these past few months. It's unlike you to be so unsociable. You should be pleased I have thought to include you.'

'I'm just surprised at your choice of guests.' Sofia raised an eyebrow. 'I didn't realise you would continue working with a Morelli.'

*Oh yes, she did.* Diego swapping allegiance to Zane was the only reason her bloody husband was still alive. Plus, him delaying the natural course of her plan was why she was lumbered with donning *this* thing.

Her eyes tracked down to the offending bulge under her dress. Chucking it in the bin couldn't come soon enough, yet now Diego was pushing things to the limit by inviting the guy who'd avoided marrying her years ago to dinner? Where was the logic in that?

'Zane is nothing like that waste of shit brother and that's why he's got my custom,' Diego snapped. 'Do not question my decisions, Sofia. I do not talk business with you!'

'I didn't mean to,' Sofia sniffed, put out. 'It's just with the history between me and Zane... Well, I thought that y...'

'Are you trying to antagonise me?' Diego barked, immediately riled. 'Marco was the problem, not Zane. Marco openly gawped at you - undressed you with his eyes - *my* wife! No one has the right to do that apart from me! I should have killed him on the spot, the piece of shit!'

Seeing the shock on Sofia's face, Diego reined in his temper. He had to allow concessions whilst she was pregnant. Getting this baby here safely was the most important thing. That she infuriated him and had never acted much like a 'proper' wife was something he would deal with after the safe delivery of his heir but not before. 'Zane is different to Marco. Besides, if you remember, Zane is not interested in you and never has been. That is why *I* married you.'

Sofia glowed with humiliation and resentment. *Like she could forget why she'd had to marry Diego Delgado.*

She hadn't wanted to marry Zane either. Regardless of what

her father had planned, it had been Marco she wanted and still was. They were alike, but despite his and Zane's physical similarities, Marco was the sexiest brother. So no, it hadn't been a horrific prospect not to be betrothed to Zane. But to be passed to Diego instead was the worst thing ever.

*Still, not for much longer...*

'If you have no problem with it, then neither do I. Plus, I haven't seen Zane for years, so it will be nice to see him and meet his wife.' Sofia smiled brightly, wondering if the woman was the same bitch he'd picked over *her* all those years ago.

'Erin is his fiancée, not wife', Diego corrected. 'She's pregnant too, so you'll have plenty in common to chat about.'

'Yes, we'll chat about that,' Sofia repeated dutifully. *Great. What an absolute bonus. Not...* 'I hope I have something suitable to wear.'

'You've got enough clothes to stock Harrods, so I'm sure you'll find something!' Diego snorted. 'Of course, whatever you wear you'll look stunning.'

Sofia smiled blandly like she was supposed to after another of Diego's shit, afterthought compliments. It would be a tall order looking 'stunning' in anything with this monstrosity strapped where her waist should be, but then again, being as Zane's fiancée was also pregnant, with any luck the ugly bitch would be in a worse state than her.

Besides, regardless of not holding a torch for Zane, it was good practice to ensure the man who'd made the unwise decision not to take the prize offered in her all those years ago was reminded loud and clear what he'd missed out on. Whatever happened, fake belly or not, she'd ensure she looked absolutely drop dead fucking gorgeous tomorrow night.

Sofia smiled once again at Diego, feeling like her face may crack under the strain. 'I'll call the caterers and give them a menu to prepare. I'm looking forward to it.'

She was also looking forward to this dinner hopefully offering an opportunity to glean information to help expedite her and Marco's plan.

• • • •

TIGER STIFLED A YAWN and shifted position in his seat. Sitting up all night ensuring Alyson didn't attempt more stupid stunts was not what he'd had in mind. Having her here at all was not what he'd had in mind either, but it was better than Solenzo's solution.

But what would he do if she remained so frighteningly unstable? *That* wasn't something he wanted to think about. And she was hardly in a fit state to be questioned whether she remembered Marco killing some woman and shoving her in an air duct!

For fuck's sake, this might have seemed like a fitting way for Leo to force him to ditch the resentment and paranoia about Skye Wilson's wrongful accusations. He knew her words and what they could have brought should not still be affecting how he reacted or lived his life, but being dumped with Alyson Read had done something, that in a way was worse.

The resurfacing of the decision he'd made years ago over his mother's mental health had knocked Tiger off kilter and he didn't like it. The guilt and anger over what stemmed from the decision he'd felt at the time the right thing to do, had swarmed forward. He'd almost forgotten how much it fucking hurt.

He thought it gone – buried along with his mother. But the strength of his feelings of doing the exact opposite of Solenzo's suggestion showed that his fear of making the same mistake was alive and well and had purely sat dormant for a long time.

This young girl here was too sweet, too beautiful, too precious, to end her life in such a depressing and horrific way and he'd do everything in his power to...

Sudden movement pulled Tiger's attention to the girl in his charge. Stiffening, he readied himself for the onslaught, but there was none.

'Have you been there all night?' Alyson asked, her voice small. She looked at the mountain of a man sitting on the chair in the corner. Seeing him nod, she felt her eyes brim with tears.

She wouldn't cry - she'd already embarrassed herself too much. Now she had to find a way to somehow redeem herself. It was the only thing left to give her control over any future she may have if she was to succeed in learning to live with what had happened.

She looked around the room. It was sparsely furnished with the bed she lay on and a small cheap chest of drawers, but it was clean.

She then noticed her clothes were intact, her shoes neatly placed by the side of the bed and a wave of guilt moved through her. Had she presumed this man would have ripped her clothes off and done what he wished?

Alyson's time in the clinic had taught her that not everyone was like the animal who had put her there. She'd been beginning to get to grips with what had happened, but now she'd gone and spoilt it by taking those stupid pills.

Alyson's hands began wringing together, then she remembered to utilise the deep breathing techniques she'd been taught to use at times when panic set in. *If only she'd done that yesterday...*

She owed this man an explanation. Through her crazed mind last night her body had shut down, but once in this flat and in between lurching through crazed, manic dreams and thoughts, she'd heard his voice. She'd heard enough to know that if it wasn't for him, she'd be in a secure hospital by now. 'I shouldn't have taken those pills,' she whispered.

Tiger's eyes rested on Alyson, but he remained silent, so she continued. 'I was panicking about being discharged, so I took the antidepressants Mr Solenzo prescribed me.' She swallowed drily. 'Except I took... I took several... I… I thought they would help relax me, but... but they didn't. They made me crazy.'

'Pills are no good,' Tiger growled.

Alyson nodded. 'What I was like last night wasn't good either. I'm... I'm sorry if I said... If I did anything that...' She sucked in a deep breath. 'I heard what you said. They wanted to section me and you wouldn't let them.' She studied the big man's chiselled features. He didn't look friendly, yet he'd been so kind. 'You don't even know me. You could have let them just take me away. Why didn't you?'

Tiger stared at Alyson. He didn't want to discuss that. Didn't *ever* want to discuss that. He didn't even want to be here, for God's sake. 'It didn't seem right, that's all,' he muttered, getting to his feet. 'There's a spare towel for you there. The bathroom's down the hall. I'll leave you to it and go to see if I have anything for you to eat.'

'Why are you doing this?' Alyson whimpered. 'You're being very nice to me.' *The complete opposite of what she'd expected.*

'My boss instructed I must look after you,' Tiger growled, promptly leaving the room.

Shutting the door, he stomped down the stairs. Why the fuck *was* he doing this?

Except he knew, really. It was his chance to make up for his past mistake. He couldn't make things right for the person he'd let down, so doing this for someone else was better than nothing, wasn't it?

# Six

'YOU DID *WHAT*?' Erin gasped.

Zane looked guarded. 'Returning to hands-on work is sooner than I planned but there isn't much choice. From what Delgado said, the crap on the jungle drums is worse than I realised.' He'd heard most of the speculation, but 'retiring' and 'not fit to run the firm', was not something he could allow to continue circulating. 'I can't risk Marco, wherever he is, believing he has an advantage. My priority is keeping him at bay.'

Which in real life, translated to keeping the risk of Marco's resurgence to threaten the safety of Erin and their unborn child, covered. And that threat plagued him every second of every waking hour. Plus, most nights.

Zane's skin tingled with anger once again for allowing Marco's bombshell to derail him enough to make the ludicrous decision to allow the bastard to walk away unscathed. And if he'd needed a reminder that it was unlikely his brother would keep his head down forever, it came via the body left for him to find in the vent ducts.

He took Erin's hand. This woman and their unborn child were his priority. Short of his loyal men, they were his only family. He had no brother - not one that counted, no daughter and certainly no palatable memories of his father.

It was a good job that man was dead and buried because now knowing that Guiseppe Morelli ordered his first girlfriend's rape, Zane would put the man six foot under himself if the man who'd once been his father still walked this earth.

Anger threatened to overflow but Zane shoehorned it back into place and smiled at Erin. 'You know I'd rather be here with you.' His hand moved to her stomach. '*Both* of you.'

'It's not you returning to things that I'm worried about,' Erin cried. 'It's tomorrow! A formal dinner at Diego Delgado's house? What on earth is that about?'

'It took me by surprise as well,' Zane admitted. 'Delgado was rattled about my absence with the cocaine arrangement. It was part of our deal I'd oversee it, so although I think I've convinced him I'm not doing any of the things on the grapevine, I reckon he wants to weigh me up on his own turf.' He shrugged. 'I get that. I'd do the same.'

'But what will I talk about?' Erin moaned, the prospect a nightmare. She was more of a steak and chips girl than a Pâté de fois gras or a Salmon En Croûte chick! 'What will I wear for a start? What do I say to his wife? I need to know what she's like because undoubtedly I'll be left making polite conversation with her...'

Zane couldn't help but chuckle. Despite Erin's steely ability to deal with things that would floor ninety-nine per cent of men, she retained the all-female trait of fretting about clothes and etiquette. 'Stop worrying! You'd look hot in anything! As for his wife, I haven't a clue who she is, but you'll manage. Unless, of course, she can't speak English... How's your Spanish, Portuguese or whatever it is the South Americans speak?'

'Oh my God, don't!' Erin gasped. 'What if she *can't* speak English? Oh no! It will be dreadful. I can't believe you're doing this to me!'

'Just stop!' Zane laughed. 'She'll speak English - they all do. Anyway, she's pregnant too, so swap notes about that.' The flustered look on Erin's face made him want to laugh harder, but he didn't want her thinking he was ridiculing her. He wasn't. It was her little quirks that made him love her more if that was possible. He pulled her close. 'Seriously, it will be fine. It has to be because I need this deal with Delgado to continue.'

'That reminds me,' Erin said, grateful to move away from the subject of the unexpected dinner. 'How do you feel about me returning to the Starbright Centre.' Sensing Zane ready to shout her down, she quickly continued. 'Like you said, we need to push home that it's business as usual. And before you flap about security, the Starbright is heavily guarded and you were happy for me to be there before. Neither of us wants to see Hazel's good work go to waste. The temporary manager is doing a good job but...' She patted her belly. 'I do need time to find a suitable permanent replacement manager for when I've had the baby.'

She ran her fingers slowly down Zane's stubbly cheek and grinned, knowing she'd won this particular argument.

• • • •

LEO EYED THE MAN waiting in a side room at the Thames Canning Works. *This had better be good.*

Having been called back to Mayer's crusher due to the man's demand for extra payment for disposing of the contents pulled from Zane's air conditioning shaft, he wasn't in the best of moods. He'd been due at the Starbright Centre to check on things and because of the shit with Mayer, was already late. Now he'd been lumbered with *this*?

Zane would go tits when he discovered Pete Mayer had pulled this stunt. Mayer had previously been advised of the contents of that bag, so demanding further cash twenty-four hours after accepting the task wasn't part of the deal.

But what choice did Leo have? It was either pay up or take back the 'goods'. *That* wasn't an option, so he'd had no alternative but to shove another wedge of brass in Mayer's greasy, grasping mitt.

Fucking Marco and his bullshit games. Leaving the rotting corpse of one of his unfortunate women in the fucking ceiling was designed to aggravate or incriminate, but then receiving a call from one of the guards to say that there was a visitor who wouldn't take no for an answer, Leo had no choice but to rush back.

*Where the hell was Tiger? He was supposed to be manning the place.*

Lumbering his big frame into a room made tiny by his size, Leo's face was a mask of displeasure. It had crossed his mind that the waiting man might be from the Delgados. After all, Delgado himself had turned up unannounced yesterday, so it was plausible someone else belonging to that lot had decided on a second viewing.

But, Leo thought with a scowl, *this* man didn't look like part of the Delgado bunch. This bloke looked a sandwich short of a picnic. 'You asked to see me?'

'You Zane Morelli?'

Leo tensed, his senses on red alert. His eyes ran over the man's build and height equal to his own, wearing a full-length leather coat with large wing collars. What the fuck was the Gestapo look about? It was mid-August, for fuck's sake! On top of that, the guy had a head the size of a breezeblock, hands like dinner plates and a nose obviously broken multiple times, one strangely devoid eye and… was a piece of his head missing? 'I'm not Zane. What do you want with him?'

The big man awkwardly moved his weight onto his other foot and cleared his throat. 'I heard he might be looking for extra men.'

Now *all* of Leo's hackles rose. *Was this guy one of Marco's?* He folded his arms across his barrel chest. 'And where did you hear that?' *The fucking abattoir by the looks of it*. Then again, it was more likely the result of gossip within underworld circles. A chancer trying his luck.

Sighing, he pulled the door open signifying he was done. He'd rushed back here for *this*? 'No offence, mate, but I ain't in the mood, so off you fuck.'

As the man's ravaged face morphed into a weird-looking grimace, loosely resembling a smile, Leo's irritation grew. *This joker was winding him up, right?* 'Did you not hear what I sa…

'You must be Leo Holland.' The man's shovel-like hand extended in Leo's direction. 'I've heard about you.'

Jaw tightening, Leo ignored the proffered hand. 'It's none of your business who the fuck I am.' This was getting past the point where he could pretend to be civil. He moved to grab the man's arm, sure that with full force he could shift him outside alone.

'You *are* Leo, aren't you? You're just like my brother said.'

Leo paused, his hand mid-grab. 'Your brother? Who's your fucking brother? I don't know your brother!'

'Yes, you do!' The man grinned, his mouth exposing the smashed remains of his front teeth. 'Lyndon Shoreham. You probably know him as Tiger?'

This time it was Leo's turn to look vacant. This was Tiger's *brother*? He didn't realise Tiger even had a brother! And wait - Tiger's real name was *Lyndon*? He'd never thought to ask Tiger what his real name was. No one thought about stuff like that. Tiger had always been Tiger. But *Lyndon*? What sort of a name was that?

None of this added up. Leo had known Tiger for decades and okay, they'd never delved deep into each other's personal stories, but never had a brother been mentioned.

'I'm Colt. Lyndon always said if I ever needed work to come and see him and he'd speak to Zane. That's the bloke Tiger works for, ain't it?' Colt's breezeblock head turned to peer around like there might be someone else concealed in a room the size of a broom cupboard. 'Where is Lyndon? I heard he was based here.'

'I tell you what,' Leo said, pulling together what was left of his rational thought. 'I'll give him a call, shall I?' He tugged his mobile from his pocket, half-expecting Tiger's alleged brother to exhibit a flash of panic at the threat of his lies being exposed, but there was nothing.

• • • •

ZANE DIDN'T KNOW why he found himself on Swain's Lane, but found the magnetic pull towards the cemetery, strong.

Gritting his teeth, he pulled back on the throttle and sped past the turning to the car park. If he'd gone in there he'd have dismounted and picked his way through the gravestones only to ask the same question which had revolved around his head since discovering his father ordered the rape of Shirley Wilson, covered up Marco's deed and paid off Shirley's family to leave London and never speak about the wrongs inflicted on their daughter.

The question was simple:

*Why?*

But Zane knew he'd never get answers with his father lying six feet under.

His jaw clenched harder, the sting of the wind through his open visor enjoyable compared to the stabbing within his heart. He felt like ripping his father's corpse from the ground and tossing it to one side to be picked off by scavenging predators. He couldn't comprehend that his father - the man he'd spent his life idolising; the man who'd painstakingly instilled strong morals in him, was a figment of his imagination.

The man Zane had known did not match the one Marco unveiled. It was impossible to quantify, yet Shirley had corroborated the facts, so whether Zane liked it or not, it had to be true.

Zane accelerated harder, needing to put maximum distance from where the body of the man who he'd never really known, lay. He couldn't think about it. Not yet. *Maybe never.*

Taking that on board on top of everything that had happened lately would be too much and he would not risk losing his grip on logic or sanity. His meltdown after Skye was one too many and he was better off concentrating on the future with Erin and their coming child. Making sure his place in London and business was firmly established, putting the rumours of his mental demise to bed to show Delgado he was still by far the right choice to trust with the cocaine supply, was vital. It would ensure Erin and his growing family would be financially stable and everything around them, secure and established.

He'd go and see Shirley to make sure she was doing okay, but not yet. There was nothing to bind him to her now they did not share a daughter. Skye's murder had severed any link they might have retained for sentiment's sake.

Giving a wide berth to reminders of what had recently occurred was the best plan.

He'd previously called Shirley to apologise for unchivalrously throwing her out of his house in Dalston. But that was water under the bridge now – she'd said so herself. Shirley was free from her demons and was doing well, but he'd touch base with her again at some point once everything was on an even keel.

Doing *this* was of the greatest priority: his presence *here*.

Pulling onto the concrete expanse at the front of the Thames Canning works, Zane yanked his Yamaha FJ1200 onto the centre stand and removed his helmet.

He stared at two other parked motors. *Both Tiger and Leo were here? Wasn't Leo down for checking the Starbright today?*

Confused, Zane dismounted and strode towards the doors.

# SEVEN

'I TAKE IT you bought this courtesy of *my* money?' Sam Whittaker said, busily appraising Marco's Mayfair townhouse. 'This must have set you back a good percentage of what I gave you. It's a bit fancy!'

Marco's non-committal smile concealed his irritation. 'Ah, but you didn't "give" me the money, Whittaker. You were lucky enough to purchase a host of top-of-the-range, limited edition and irreplaceable cars.'

He wouldn't let on that he hadn't purchased this luxurious gaff at all. No fucking way would he shell out a million and a half quid for a four-bedroomed house with tall Georgian windows, chandeliers, original open fireplaces and enough marble to floor the Sistine Chapel. It was all very swish and fancy and he especially liked the twin vault rooms on the lower ground floor, but he preferred modern, contemporary places, not olde-worlde grandeur. Plus, the five flights of stairs didn't half knacker his legs, so give him a penthouse apartment any day.

*But all in good time...*

Having an address in the road behind Park Lane was useful in spreading the word that he was back in business and coining it in. Renting this place for a song from a rich Arab who he'd 'convinced' was the preferable choice, rather than 'risking' the bloke's fondness for young boys being exposed, was an opportunity coming along just at the right time.

This place wouldn't be needed for long, anyway - just until Delgado was out of the picture. And now he'd set it in stone that the task would be completed within two weeks that was what would happen.

He puffed his chest out in self-importance. Marco Morelli did not make vague promises - he *delivered.*

Pulling a crystal ashtray towards him, Marco sparked up a thin white menthol cigarette, deciding they were more refined than his usual Marlboros. He was even using an ashtray whilst living here to keep in line with his newly designed persona.

*Now on to business...*

Marco looked at Sam Whittaker over the other side of the desk in the home office and smiled. Whittaker had the advantage in the last few 'arrangements' they'd made but now it was long overdue for the tables to be turned.

The shots would have to be called cleverly though. He needed Sam to make things run seamlessly, so he'd do things in a way to appear that he was offering a favour.

Putting his hands together, Marco steepled his fingers. He'd practised in the mirror and reckoned the gesture accentuated a businesslike, powerful look. 'The reason I've invited you here is because we're friends.' *No, they weren't!* Whittaker was a greedy cunt and he hated the man, but he'd fall for this hook, line and sinker. Marco knew him too well. He'd always kept on the right side of the bloke for fear of jeopardising further favours - and he'd had to ask for a fair few of those. But now guaranteed success was around the corner, Marco could afford to abandon caution. In two weeks' time, he'd never need anyone's help again.

Just the thought of the coming payout made Marco hard. That and having Sofia to himself. 'Like I was saying, because we're friends and go back a long way, I wanted to give you first refusal on my latest venture...'

Sam studied Marco. The man was a sly one, that was for sure, but he was a canny bastard and clever to boot. He glanced around the expensively furnished office - the antique furniture in perfect proportion with the size of the room. There wasn't a speck of dust or one thing out of place. The house was indeed exquisitely decorated and filled with tasteful pieces - a far cry from the garish mess at Marco's penthouse.

Sam thoughtfully ran his thumb along his bottom lip. Marco must have invested a packet in the purchase of this property, plus the cost of furnishing it. That wasn't something one would do unless the future was assured. It also showed Marco's tastes had shifted away from seedy adult films and his sights were clearly now set on more palatable and financially lucrative ventures.

And *that*, Sam was more than interested in.

However, not wishing to appear over-eager, he relaxed into the wing-back Chesterfield chair and crossed his ankles. 'Like you quite correctly say, Marco, we go back a long way, so I'm happy to listen to your proposal.'

If it was any good and stood to make a decent return, then he'd jump on it before some other fucker reaped the benefit.

• • • •

IN A BACK ROOM away from Leo and the unexpected visitor, Zane stared at Tiger curiously. 'Why didn't you say you had a brother?'

'The subject never came up,' Tiger shrugged. 'No one talks about life before the firm.' And neither would he. There were too many things in his past that he'd prefer to leave where they were. *Colt included.*

Zane paced the room, unsure how to call this. He could sorely use extra muscle and Tiger's brother possessed an abundance of that. But although he made the call on who worked for him, it was only right to give Tiger a say as to whether Colt was offered collar.

He sparked up a cigarette, something he couldn't quite put his finger on vying for his attention. 'You know I don't take on men who aren't personally known to me, but I know *you*, so do you want your brother here or not?'

Tiger's face remained expressionless, but inside he was in a quandary. There had been little option but to immediately come here once Leo called. He'd planned on leaving the canning works in the capable hands of the foreman, just whilst he made sure Alyson was settled. Not that he understood why he was so bothered. The remit was to give the girl a secure place to stay and his place was that, but he didn't have time to babysit the woman.

And Colt's presence here proved that.

He'd always promised his younger brother that if he needed work to come and see him. It was what brothers did. But thankfully, in his and Colt's life, it was also one of those things which was unlikely to be called upon. And in Colt's case, impossible.

Yet here he was…

'Mate?' Zane frowned. 'What's your call on this?'

In a rare show of emotion, Tiger dropped into a chair, the spindly metal frame creaking under his bulk. He ran his hand over his head. 'I don't fucking know.' He sighed. 'Colt... Well, I never expected to see him again.'

'Is there an issue between you?' Zane frowned. 'I could do without more one-upmanship or payback between brothers. Christ knows I've had enough of that shit!'

Tiger shook his massive head. 'It's not like that. It's just... well, Colt can be difficult… Don't get me wrong, he's good at his stuff. At least, he was. But that was a long time ago...'

'What aren't you telling me?'

Tiger paused. He didn't want to betray Colt's personal information, but Zane's firm was at stake here. 'You can't have failed to notice his...' He indicated his own face.

Zane nodded. It was impossible to miss Colt's 'war wounds'. It was obvious the man was blind in one eye and the dent in the back of his head was another unusual feature. 'What happened?'

'Colt's heavy duty - some would say, *too* heavy duty. One day he got set up and attacked with an axe... After that he was worse. And, well… I didn't expect him back on the scene.'

'How come I haven't heard of him? Which firm did he work for?'

'He didn't.' Tiger cracked his knuckles. 'Colt was freelance. He refused to be beholden to one firm.'

'A gun for hire?'

'Something like that...'

'What's he been doing if he hasn't been "working"?'

Tiger eyed Zane. 'As far as I was aware, he was still in prison.' *With no possibility of release…*

Zane wracked his brain to whether he'd heard Colt's name mentioned during his own stint at Her Majesty's Pleasure. Colt was an unusual name and being as it was common for lags to talk of who else was banged up and where they were, he'd have thought he'd remember it. 'I don't recall hearing of him. Which nick was he in?'

Tiger inwardly groaned. *This* was the question he'd been dreading. He took a deep breath. 'Broadmoor. Colt was sent there for the foreseeable. I don't understand how he's out.'

Zane blinked. *Broadmoor?* 'Seriously psycho, then?' He rolled his shoulders, freeing the building stress. The criminally insane weren't people he'd usually touch with a bargepole, but perhaps someone like Colt was exactly what the firm needed right now?

A small smile formed at the corners of his mouth. 'Despite my shit family, if you're okay with your brother coming on board, I'm willing to give him a chance. But you'll have to ensure he remains under control.'

Tiger nodded. *He'd guessed as much.* The problem was he was unsure whether Colt had improved or worsened in the gulf of time that had passed since last seeing him. If his brother was more unhinged than before, it would be difficult, if not impossible, for *anyone* to control the man, not to forget the long-standing blame Colt had harboured towards him.

And Tiger did not relish the prospect of dealing with either of those things.

# EIGHT

FOR A MAN'S FLAT and from what Alyson gathered, a man involved in criminal activities - probably *violent* activities, the place was unexpectedly neat and tidy.

But then there were *several* unexpected things she'd noticed about Tiger. And not bad ones, either.

*Like these...*

Alyson padded across the kitchen in a pair of slippers and glanced down at the fluffy pink slip-ons which had appeared by her bed this morning.

Realising Tiger must have bought them for her, a giggle escaped her mouth and she paused, realising it had been a long time since she'd smiled, let alone laughed. She'd only been here a day and already felt a thousand times better.

Being out of that clinic helped and although nothing could detract from what she'd experienced at the hands of Marco Morelli, and it would be a long time before she could face her parents - if ever, she now felt more equipped to handle the mess in her head.

Despite Tiger and his people having seen her in the most vulnerable and quite frankly, humiliating situations *ever*, no one had judged her. Her parents, however, would immediately know by her eyes alone that something had happened - and that 'something' was not anything she could ever relay to them. The idea of emailing, saying she'd found work with Skye in London and was spreading her wings, was a good one. Surprisingly, her parents had accepted it and she'd succeeded keeping them at arms' length. It wouldn't last forever but she'd worry about that as and when she had to.

Perched on a kitchen chair at the small kitchen table, Alyson looked from the window onto the street below. This flat wasn't in a terrible area, but very different from the large country house she'd been brought up in.

And right now she was grateful for that.

Alyson glanced at the clock. It was early and Tiger's bedroom door was still closed. She hadn't seen him this morning so he must still be asleep, which made sense because he'd returned very late last night. She'd pretended to be asleep when he'd opened her bedroom door a crack, peered in and then promptly left.

Alyson smiled to herself. Tiger checking on her to make sure she was safe was a sweet thing to do.

Strangely, she didn't feel nervous being here. She'd thought she would, but she didn't – even when Tiger had to go out. She couldn't imagine anyone causing problems for this man. He seemed a terrifying adversary to have.

But there was one thing which still bothered her.

Alyson frowned. There was still no word from Skye. She'd texted her several times over the past few days, yet received no response. Surely Skye would know she was staying at Tiger's flat, so why hadn't she been to see her or got in contact? Skye hadn't visited when she'd been at Mr Solenzo's clinic either. They were friends, so why the no show?

Skye had come to the penthouse though. That, Alyson remembered, but the details remained sketchy and she wanted to tie up the loose ends in her head.

Alyson had asked Tiger about it several times, but he'd deflected the questions. Suddenly a wave of dread thundered through her. How had she not guessed?

Skye must have discovered what had happened with Marco!

Cold sweat beaded on her brow.

Skye must either be furious with her or furious with Marco, gutted about her own father's behaviour. Maybe Skye felt responsible? After all, it was Skye who'd invited her to the penthouse in the first place. But she shouldn't feel like that. None of this was Skye's fault.

Refusing to dwell on negativity, Alyson got up from the chair. She'd talk to Skye and get everything out in the open. The clinic said that was the best way to deal with facing up to, accepting and releasing what had happened, so that's what she'd do.

But first she'd cook Tiger breakfast. It was a small way of thanking him for his hospitality. If would also give her the chance to ask about Skye again.

Alyson headed to the fridge to see what she could rustle up. She tugged at the stiff door of the tall fridge freezer. Giving it a hard yank, the door opened but the jolt dislodged something.

She flinched as a bunch of paperwork fell from above, narrowly missing her head. Chuckling, she grabbed a packet of bacon from the fridge and shut the door, then bent to scoop up the mess, deciding that Tiger wasn't quite as tidy as she'd believed.

*Look at the state of this! Receipts, a Chinese takeaway menu, newspapers...*

Alyson stacked the paperwork on the small table, doubting whether she'd reach to put it back where it fell from, when the headline of a newspaper caught her eye.

***Young Woman Shot Dead In "Wrong Place, Wrong Time" Tragedy Near The Ritz***

*How awful*, Alyson thought, glancing at the paper's date – 3rd July. That was weeks ago!

*Typical man, keeping old newspapers!*

As she absentmindedly scanned the article a name jumped out and her hand flew to her mouth. Sobbing, Alyson dropped back onto the hard, wooden chair.

• • • •

SAM WHITTAKER strutted through the vast, high-ceilinged lobby of the building housing his offices. His patent leather Gucci dress shoes clacked on the marble floor as he approached the turnstiles. Flashing his security card at the sensor, he made his way up to the thirty-seventh floor in the lift.

His mind buzzed. Doing this for Marco may not make sense, but it would acquire a coveted tick on his list of elite connections. Everyone knew *who* someone was associated to or on speaking terms with was what brought prestige.

After all, it was on that which Sam had centred his entire career.

Reaching the most sought-after floor of One Canada Square, Sam waltzed through the huge glass doors of his offices, the gilt plaque of *Whittaker Inc* never failing to remind him of the success he'd achieved.

*This* was what it was all about: an entrepreneur with fingers in just about every pie. Sam was almost as well known as the people he'd fawned and grovelled over in order to be included in their circles. His diligence had brought him invites to countless A-list parties and gatherings, as well as a fortune so vast to even recall its exact worth.

Smiling acknowledgement to the reception staff – all personally handpicked for their sycophantic tendencies, Sam hurried to his private office. He pressed the button setting the glass expanse to glide soundlessly open and walked through, leaving the sliding door to close behind him.

Shrugging off his handmade suit jacket, he hung it on the coat stand in front of the floor-to-ceiling window and glanced out at the stunning view of Canary Wharf, as well as half of London.

Settling himself at his pristine glass desk, he pulled out his gold-edged notebook and tapped the end of his fountain pen against the leather of the pad's cover.

A smile cracked Sam's smooth face. Being as Marco pressed home the urgency, he'd better make this call. The sooner he got this in motion, the faster he could add a particular person to his list of acquaintances. And this elusive person was one whom he'd sought an introduction to for a *very* long time. The man in question was the crème de la crème, so having anything to do with *him* would bring bundles more kudos and money by association alone.

Fancy not being aware that Marco had a close relationship with Diego Delgado! Sam usually heard of all collaborations, but then again, both Marco and Diego were involved in dealings well over the other side of the line that *he* had knowledge of, so it wasn't altogether surprising.

But how gratifying was it that Marco should deem Whittaker Inc to have enough influence in high society circles to include him in this new venture? That he - Sam Whittaker - should be seen as the go-to for spreading the word of an investment opportunity within his vast range of circles showed just how far he'd come.

Diego Delgado and Marco Morelli indeed.

*Wow! This was special!*

Not to mention the extremely generous percentage the two men were offering him to reach successful investors. *Brilliant!*

Sam then frowned, not entirely understanding why Marco was so insistent that neither his, nor Delgado's names should be mentioned to anyone in association with this venture once it launched. Neither did he understand why he shouldn't reference Marco when he finally met Delgado. But then, these types of people worked in ways that Sam didn't pretend to understand, so if that's the way it went, he'd say nothing.

In fact, selling the Bentley to Delgado as per Marco's remit, now made sense. It offered a genuine reason to be 'acquainted' with the man and hence spread the word about the venture when the time was right. *Very clever.*

Anyway, there was no point in overthinking it.

Sam clasped his hands together, the thought of the financial bonus the connection would bring better than any orgasm.

How good he was. How literally *fantastic*. One day a film would be made of his life: *'Charting the Success of the World's Most Successful Man'*. Or something like that...

And that was something he was well and truly on his way to achieving without doing much, if anything, for the privilege.

*Oh yes, life was good.*

Thanks to his stunning acumen in homing in on the correct people, his success could only continue to grow.

He flicked through his Roladex - a limited edition of the rotating contacts book presented to him by a grateful Sheik, then picked up his phone and dialled the London Evening Standard.

'Good morning. It's Sam Whittaker from Whittaker Inc here,' Sam said, his chest puffing out hearing the grovelling voice down the other end of the line. 'Yes, I'm good, thank you. Look, I have an advert to place. Like now. Yes, now... It must be in tonight's edition. Oh, and tomorrow's too.' He then frowned. 'I'm sure you'll find a way to delay the print run to ensure it *does* go in tonight's edition, Trevor. Yep... good. Put the bill on my account. I'll fax the wording over now.'

Tearing a letterheaded page from his memo pad, Sam scrawled down the wording for the advert:

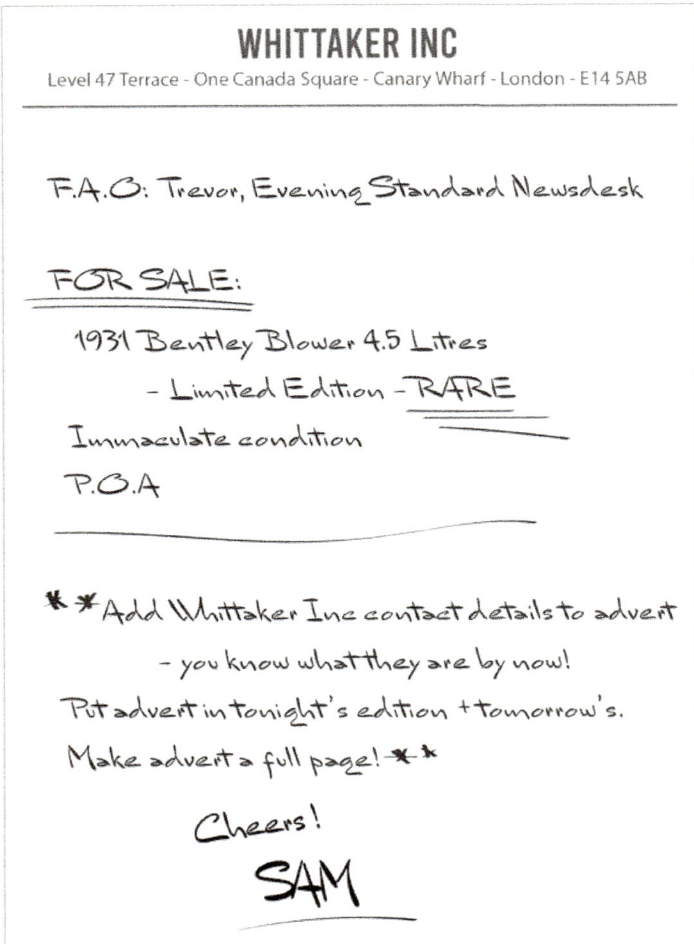

WHITTAKER INC

Level 47 Terrace - One Canada Square - Canary Wharf - London - E14 5AB

F.A.O: Trevor, Evening Standard Newsdesk

FOR SALE:

1931 Bentley Blower 4.5 Litres

- Limited Edition - RARE

Immaculate condition

P.O.A

**Add Whittaker Inc contact details to advert

- you know what they are by now!

Put advert in tonight's edition + tomorrow's.

Make advert a full page!**

Cheers!

SAM

Sam then pressed a button on his desk phone. 'Rachel, I need an urgent fax sent.'

He didn't know how to use the fax machine and nor did he want to. That's what he paid bimbos for. *Beautiful* bimbos, mind you. No mingers here.

Within seconds, his office door opened and a blonde with a sprayed-on blue dress sashayed over and pincered the handwritten paper off Sam's desk with her long pink talons. 'This one, sir?' she gushed, her glossy lips pouting.

'Yes, that's the one.' Sam's eyes lingered on Rachel's ample chest. 'Fax it to the London Standard straightaway. They're expecting it.'

'Yes, sir.' Rachel turned on her sky-high heels, not batting an eyelid when Sam's hand brushed her backside.

Sam's eyes remained glued to Rachel's stunning figure until the door shut behind her. If she was lucky, he'd do her later but first he had the rest of the day to plan.

And to start with, he'd do *this*.

Pulling out his private mobile, Sam brought up Marco's contact details and tapped out a quick text:

`Advert placed. It will run tonight + tomorrow as promised.`

Pressing send, Sam sat back. God knows how this could work, but Marco insisted it would. Sam hadn't asked how or why. He rarely did.

If Marco believed Diego Delgado would spot the advert and buy the car, then Sam had to trust that.

If he sold whatever that old claptrap was to Delgado whilst the man was in residence at his London property, that would be a *mega* tick on his scorecard. Everyone had heard of the South American drug kingpin, but rarely did anyone have personal involvement.

And selling the man a car did just that, didn't it?

Either way, it was a fabulous opportunity and one Sam only hoped that for the sake of the boost to his already skyscraper status, paid off.

# Nine

TIGER RARELY SLEPT through the night, but Colt's reappearance had mentally exhausted him. After Zane offered his brother a job, he hadn't hung around. He didn't want to get into conversation and face the age-old accusations and questions.

Tiger knew he wasn't responsible for putting the knew which helped kill their mother into her reach, but Colt thought otherwise because he'd never *ever* tired of throwing that accusation around, nor that it was his fault she'd been in that hospital in the first place and he didn't want that brought up again. Neither did he want to think about the burden he now shouldered of keeping Colt in line.

He could only hope that over the years, his brother's mind hadn't deteriorated further in the wrong direction, but Colt wearing that trademark trench coat in the height of summer didn't bode well in thinking there was any marked improvement in the general functioning of the man's brain.

Admittedly, Tiger felt guilty turning down Colt's request to stay at his flat. Mainly because he was *relieved* that he couldn't offer it. He couldn't provide Colt with a bed with Alyson there, so he'd have to make do with crashing at the canning works. If his brother wanted work enough, he'd take whatever was offered.

But the nagging questions remained as to *why* Colt wanted the work, *why* he was here and *how* he'd left Broadmoor...

Tiger had voiced none of those questions. He'd prefer not to know. With any luck, Colt would only hang around a few days - he'd never liked being tied to any one place and it was doubtful that had changed. Still, Tiger thought, swinging his muscled legs out of bed, he must get his arse into gear. Now Zane was back in the helm, there would be changed to who was responsible for what and he needed to find out what was expected.

Strolling towards the door in his boxers, Tiger grabbed some jogging bottoms. He mustn't forget Alyson's presence removed the ability to walk around undressed. The thought of being accused of something untoward again was enough to make him sport a hazmat suit.

Pulling on his joggers, Tiger paused.

*What was that?*

Frowning, he homed in on the strange noise. It sounded like crying.

*Alyson?*

Bolting from the room, he dashed in the direction of the pitiful noise, ignoring why he felt so panicked. Rounding the door to the kitchen, he found Alyson with a newspaper clutched in her hand, tears pouring down her face.

'Why didn't you tell me?' Alyson sobbed, her grey eyes staring accusingly at Tiger. 'You knew all along, so why didn't you say Skye was dead? I asked you where she was and why she hadn't been to see me, yet you said nothing. *Nothing*!'

'You went through my stuff?' Tiger snatched the newspaper from Alyson's hand. 'Never do that!' As the words left his mouth, he realised how cold he was acting, but the relief that this woman was unharmed had an odd effect.

'It fell off the fridge...' Alyson whimpered. 'I wasn't... I wasn't snooping... I...'

Tiger then saw the packet of bacon on the worktop. Had she been about to make him breakfast? Guilt pounded but it only deepened his scowl. He didn't have the first clue about sobbing women and didn't want to. 'Forget it and don't waste your sympathy. Skye was a bitch!'

Alyson's mouth fell open and she jumped up from the chair. 'Skye was *not* a bitch!' she yelled. 'She was my friend! My very best friend. I... I loved her and now she's… she's dead!'

'Skye was your fucking worst enemy! You have no idea!' The words came from Tiger's mouth before he could stop them. 'That bitch set you up. She was a cunt and I'm glad she's dead!'

'You bastard!' Alyson yelled. 'I stupidly thought you were nice!' Suddenly, the rage drained from her body and she sagged against the table. 'You... you should have told me she was dead. You should have told m...'

Tiger clocked Alyson's knees giving way before she realised herself. His quick reactions didn't fail and he caught her before she hit the deck.

About to deposit her back on the kitchen chair, he instead found himself supporting Alyson's shaking body as she sobbed, her tears flowing down his bare chest.

• • • •

SOFIA SCOWLED AT the collection of beautiful, expensive dresses, shoes and matching accessories that she'd picked from her many walk-in closets.

The clothes that she'd insisted on being available at their London residence, as well as their place in Miami, mirrored the range she also had at their mansion in Bogotá. The clothes in all locations were identical, short of a few items in her London wardrobe which reflected the ghastly drop in temperature in this godforsaken country during certain times of the year. But aside from those, everything was the same.

Sofia's wardrobes were updated with every season and then mirrored three times. It was the least she expected. It wasn't like Diego couldn't afford it and there may as well be *some* enjoyment taken from this awful, arranged marriage.

The worst part being stuck with seeing Marco so infrequently, governed by their visits to London.

Aside from *this*. That might be the worst thing to date…

Sofia glanced at the jutting mound of her pretend baby bump and seethed. She knew exactly which dress she wanted to wear tonight - one to rub Zane Morelli's face in the shit for his unwise choice years ago, as well as making his wife-to-be resemble a cow pat in comparison.

Just the sight of the Valentino dress made Sofia tingle with goosebumps. It had the same effect since she'd seen it earlier this year at the Milan fashion week. Amazing what her husband's connections could achieve in gaining her the coveted entry, she'd ordered the stunning, backless red number which dripped around her flawless figure like liquid. It was a showstopper. Make no mistake - that dress was what she wanted to wear. *Needed* to wear.

Whatever Erin-Whatever-Her-Name-Was looked like clearly couldn't be a patch on *her* because nothing and nobody could compete.

But she couldn't wear the dress thanks to this thing...

Sofia stuck her long, pointed nails into the firm but pliable mound strapped to her, digging deep into the silicon, the urge to rip chunks out of the despicable thing overtaking her.

It was only the buzzing from her mobile which stopped her. That, and knowing that if she ruined the monstrous contraption, she'd also lose the singular thing guaranteeing her escape from this whole setup and further delay sending Diego on his merry descent to the bowels of the earth.

Sofia reluctantly brought her phone to life and half-heartedly glanced at the screen. It would be the hairdresser. She was due to arrive shortly. Normally, the prospect of pampering and being made to look even more beautiful was something she enjoyed, but lately even *that* failed to have the desired effect.

*Wait! It was Marco!*

Sofia rushed to open the text.

Advert is placed.

Go ahead with plan tonight.

xxx

A glimmer of hope sparked, pulling Sofia from her self-indulgent misery.

Ok but what do I say?

xxxx

Chewing her lip, she glanced in the illuminated mirror in front of her - one of many in the room, to make sure her concentrating expression was on point. It paid to look perfect, even when no one was watching.

Marco's reply arrived quickly.

Exactly what we discussed.

xxx

*Easier said than done*, Sofia thought.

Tonight during dinner in front of all of them?

How will that work?

xxx

Wouldn't it seem odd to read a newspaper at the dinner table? She *never* read newspapers – the print left dirty marks everywhere.

Her phone pinged again.

Just do it like I said. It will work. Don't worry how.

Soon, babe.

xxx

Seeing the words 'soon, babe', made Sofia's heart flutter. *She couldn't wait.*

A smile formed. Somehow, the prospect of not being able to wear the red Valentino dress was less depressing now.

Ok

xxx

After sending her final text, Sofia carefully deleted the received and sent messages and shoved her phone back into its usual place.

With renewed vigour, she jumped up from her velvet chair and returned to the walk-in wardrobe. *Now to find something else equally stunning that would fit over this thing.*

Trawling through the rails, Sofia didn't notice Diego step away from the bedroom door that she'd stupidly left ajar.

• • • •

'WHAT THE FUCK are you doing?' Leo yelled. Rushing into the cocaine bagging area at the commotion, he'd expected to find one of the machines broken. He hadn't bargained on Colt smashing his fist into the face of one of the workers.

With some effort, he grabbed Colt by the shoulders of his trench coat and yanked him off the man on the floor, trying not to focus on the concave dent in the back of the man's head as he did so. 'Fucking leave it! What the hell are you doing?'

Colt swung around, his one seeing eye wild. 'This cunt was pocketing coke!'

'I wasn't!' the man gibbered, his nose smashed flat to his face and his eyes streaming.

Leo stared at the spilt bags of cocaine; the bashed-up face of the worker and the horrified silence of the other packers in the room.

*Fuck. If this got out the shit would hit the fan.*

Colt lurched towards the man again. 'You slipped it into your fucking pocket, you wanker! I saw you. I hate thieves!'

Leo jumped in front of Colt, the man's wild-eyed fury disconcerting. 'There's been some kind of mix-up.' He glanced at the man scrabbling up from the floor. 'Jimmy here has worked for this firm in one way or another for years. He ain't no thief.'

'I've taken fuck all!' Turning out his pockets, Jimmy glared at Colt, anger now outweighing his shock. 'This bloke's a nutter! He just stormed in here and kicked off!'

A general grumbling consensus rumbled around the room.

'What did you just fucking say?' Saliva flew from Colt's mouth as he lurched forward once again. 'You called me a paedo? Is that what you said?'

'For fuck's sake!' Leo grabbed Colt's arm. 'Come with me!' He turned to Jimmy and the other men. 'Clear this mess up. I'll be back shortly.' The floor looked like someone had launched flour over it. Loads of money wasted. It would also be a shit smoothing this over. No one wanted to work with nutters - *himself* included.

Not a happy man, Leo pulled Colt from the bagging room and down the corridor. He'd voiced his concerns last night to Zane about taking Colt on. No one needed the hassle of an ex-Broadmoor resident adding to their problems, but Zane was adamant Colt's 'tendencies' could be useful for dealing with Marco when the time came.

But that didn't include the loon exercising his 'tendencies' on the fucking staff, did it?

And where was Tiger? The condition of Colt getting a chance here was Tiger taking responsibility of keeping the man in check, so where the fuck was he?

Out of the packing room, Colt's previous calm demeanour returned. 'Sorry, mate. I don't know what happened. I was convinced I saw that bloke stuffing coke into his pocket.'

'Well, you didn't!' Leo snapped, punching Tiger's number into his mobile. 'Jimmy's a good bloke. Now you've wasted thousands of quid of coke and pissed off the workforce. You've also pissed *me* off!'

He glared at his phone as it went straight to voicemail. *Was this a fucking wind up?* 'Tiger,' Leo growled into the mouthpiece. 'Get to the canning works. Your brother's kicked off and you're supposed to be here!'

Hanging up, he turned to find Colt leaning against the wall, his oddly shaped head hanging in shame.

'Please don't get me binned off. I don't know what came over me. I thought th…'

'Save it,' Leo muttered. 'Explain to your fucking brother, now fuck off away from me into one of the back rooms and stay there while I go and sort out the mess you've made.'

There was no point bothering Zane with this. He was at the Starbright this morning, then he had dinner with Delgado lined up. He didn't need shit diluting his concentration.

Tiger could bloody well sort this out and, while he was at it, explain why the hell he wasn't here in the first place.

# TEN

FORCING HIS THOUGHTS to centre on his brother rather than the soft body pressed against his bare chest, Tiger let Alyson cry, but wet eyelashes fluttering against his skin and the smell of freshly washed hair made it difficult to ignore.

He pictured Colt's mangled face in his mind's eye - anything to deflect the reaction threatening to stir within his jogging bottoms.

That couldn't happen. The embarrassment, let alone the implications of getting aroused by this young woman would be disastrous and he sorely regretted putting joggers on rather than jeans. At least jeans would make things less obvious.

What the hell was the matter with him? Alyson was eighteen, for Christ's sake! Barely a woman and young enough to be his daughter!

Getting horny over a chick like this was unthinkable, wasn't it? What did that make him? Some sort of pervert? A cradle snatcher? People might think there was truth behind the accusations Skye made about him forcing himself on her after all!

Tiger's chiselled face creased into a grimace. He hadn't touched Skye. Nor had he wanted to. Plus, he most definitely wouldn't have forced himself on her or *any* woman. But getting a huge boner over a young, sobbing woman who had recently been drugged, used and abused and who he was tasked to protect, was inexcusable.

His big fingers twitched but remained unmoving, holding Alyson steady as she cried. He hadn't moved a muscle, but he wanted to. He wanted to run his hands down her face, along her arms, feel her velvety skin and then…

*Think of Colt. Think of Colt. Imagine his smashed head and concentrate on how much he could screw things up if left to his own devices...*

Alyson looked up at Tiger, her tear-stained fear face beautiful. Feeling the increasing ache of warning in his groin as more blood rushed in, he rapidly realised his efforts were in vain...

Holding Alyson at arm's length, he made sure she was steady on her feet before letting go and turning away. 'Now you're okay, I'm going for a shower,' he grunted.

'Wait!' Alyson grabbed Tiger's arm. 'Thank you. I needed that.'

'No problem.' Tiger hastily shook Alyson's hand from his arm and strode out of the kitchen towards the bathroom. *He needed something too. Something he couldn't have...*

Whether it was Alyson's vulnerability, her innocent beauty or whatever it was, she had an effect which shouldn't happen.

His brow creased. This was Leo's fucking fault for pushing her onto him. But he hadn't expected to feel something for the girl.

He wasn't sure what it was, but it was there. And there it must remain safely under wraps. But first, he had no choice but to relieve himself of this relentless arousal in the privacy of the shower otherwise it would return full bore the second he saw Alyson again.

Christ, she had to go. Alyson couldn't stay here any longer. It was too dangerous. He'd arrange somewhere else for her to stay the second he got to the canning works.

Grabbing a towel from the airing cupboard, Tiger snatched up his phone on route to the bathroom, frowning at the missed call from Leo.

His scowl deepened further listening to the voicemail, the urge to empty his balls taking a back seat.

• • • •

IN THE ROOM used for group therapy at the Starbright Centre, Zane looked between Erin and Alicja in confusion.

Reluctantly agreeing to Erin returning to run this place, he'd been busy catching up with the guards, reaffirming the instructions to let no one enter this building, no matter who they said they were.

He didn't like it, but being as he was back to hands-on working it was only fair to allow Erin the same courtesy. Plus, she'd be guarded better here during the day than remaining in the penthouse without him.

But now Erin had requested he listen to what one of the women wanted to say. And what this woman was saying was bizarre.

'You expect me to consider this viable?' Zane couldn't get his head around what was being asked.

'Just hear Alicja out and then think about whether it's an option.' Erin lightly touched Zane's hand. 'Doing this, we can ensure the women's safety and prevent them from being exploited. Surely that's the most important thing?'

Zane turned to Alicja. 'I thought you ladies were happy here?'

'We are, Mr Morelli,' Alicja said, her Polish accent strong. 'But we cannot stay forever. We need to, how you say it, support ourselves and get on with life, yes?'

'But a *strip* club?' Zane cried. 'You women were rescued from a fucking container where it was planned to use you in porn films against your will and exploited as sex slaves, yet you want to do *this*?' Marco illegally bringing that container into the country was the reason he'd bought this building and set up the women's refuge in the first place. 'Half of the women accompanying you were shot dead! You all could have been killed!'

'Yes, and we're grateful for what you did to help us, but...'

'Many of the women feel they've healed sufficiently now and want to move on,' Erin said. 'The Starbright Centre is vital, Zane. I saw paperwork this morning showing we've had to turn several women away due to lack of beds, so if some of the ladies are ready to leave...'

'But doesn't a strip club defeat the bloody object?'

'Many of us worked as strippers before we were brought here in good clubs with no trouble,' Alicja interjected.

'Women *do* choose this job sometimes, Zane,' Erin pushed. 'It's when they *don't* choose it's exploitation. With someone like Marco running a place is when there's problems. If *we* set up a club, pole dancing or whatever, we can ensure women are protected and pay a good wage.'

'Exactly!' Alicja smiled. 'Not all the women are ready to leave but the ones that are will go anyway. It not right for us to take another woman's place here that we no longer need.'

'It would be another legitimate business,' Erin pressed, praying Zane would agree. 'If we don't do it, these women could end up working for someone who *will* exploit them.'

Zane frowned. A strip club was a legitimate business, but he'd never wanted to go down that road. It had too many similarities with Marco. But Erin was right about one thing: it was better these women worked somewhere safe where fair treatment was assured. He rubbed his hand over his jaw. 'Okay, I'll give it some thought.' But he couldn't do that until everything else was smoothed over and right now, his mind was overtaken by reestablishing his reputation with Delgado. Unless he got the rumours doing the rounds about his ability quashed, he could do nothing. 'But,' he continued. 'I want you to promise me that no women will leave in the interim.'

'Okay, that is deal!' Alicja cried, then frowned. 'Is that right way to say it?'

'Yes!' Erin laughed, then smiled at Zane. He looked far from convinced, but opening a club might be a good idea.

Zane rose from his chair. 'I've got a few things I need to do now, but Erin, don't forget, we need to leave at 5.'

Erin nodded. How could she forget? Alicja's unexpected request had pulled her focus onto something else, but now her mind was thrown back to the dread of tonight's dinner. And she was not looking forward to it.

• • • •

SATISFIED SHE LOOKED a million dollars, even with a beach ball figure, Sofia moved into her huge kitchen, irritation glimmering. She was unable to sashay like usual, but instead, forced to adopt what could only be described as a waddle. It was a disgusting concept, but one that after tonight was on borrowed time so she'd concentrate on that.

She watched the caterers putting everything in order. Both gleaming stainless steel ovens were in use and there were trays of covered food everywhere. She was glad they were doing this. She'd never used those ovens and had no idea how they worked. She rarely used *any* oven and couldn't remember the last time she'd prepared a meal, let alone cooked one. 'How many staff are serving tonight?' She spoke to a man who, as she'd heard him barking orders, presumed him to be in charge.

'There will be ten waiting staff in attendance, Madam.' The man nodded with the expected reverence. 'Is that acceptable to you?'

'It sounds adequate.' Sofia inspected her newly painted fingernails. 'Are the drinks and canapés ready?'

'Yes, Madam.' The man gestured to a host of covered silver platters on one of the long granite worktops.

'Good,' Sofia muttered, her lack of interest obvious. These people were getting paid handsomely so there was no need for niceties. Those would be saved for dinner.

She stalked out of the kitchen, her deep red lips curling into a sneer. How she was looking forward to Zane Morelli's face when he clapped eyes on her. Whether he was aware Diego had married who *he* should have, she wasn't sure but suspected he wasn't. Either way, it would be amusing.

Hearing Diego coming down the stairs, Sofia breathed a sigh of relief. If he wasn't here to greet the guests on arrival, she wouldn't be happy. He'd organised this, not her and now it was time to start *her* plan...

Hurrying into one of the five reception rooms her house boasted, Sofia grabbed the *Evening Standard*, careful not to let the paper touch the silk of her dress. She rushed to locate the page the advert was on, annoyed that she'd have to wash her hands again now.

Diego strutted into the high-ceilinged reception room. It was his favourite room housing the Steinway and bookcases where he kept his collection of first editions. It was a quintessential English room and he liked the way it looked.

His eyes moved over his wife's form as she posed alluringly on a chaise longue. She looked every inch the elegant hostess and was undoubtedly beautiful, but to him, the mainstay of that beauty was her incubating his longed-for son. Because it *had* to be a boy to inherit his entire empire. The minute the child took breath, Diego's worldly goods would transfer and bypass the black-hearted woman who was his wife. And it couldn't come a minute too soon.

He walked over to Sofia, a cloud of aftershave following in his wake. 'You look nice,' he said, placing a hand on her shoulder. 'I knew you'd find something beautiful to wear from all your clothes.'

'If you must know, there weren't many which fitted,' Sofia sniffed, inching away from Diego's touch.

'Ah, well, we shall rectify that and buy more.' Diego nodded to the newspaper in Sofia's hands. 'Why are you reading that? You say newspapers are dirty!'

Sofia pulled on a well-practiced excited face. 'They are dirty but forget that for a minute. I picked the paper up whilst waiting for you and I'm glad I did.' Holding it out, she batted her eyelashes. 'Look at this! Oh, Diego, please say I can have it! I've always wanted one!'

Frowning, Diego took the paper and scanned the advert. 'A Bentley? Since when do you like Bentleys?'

'That shows how little you know about me! I've *always* loved Bentleys,' Sofia lied, scowling. Remembering her plan, she softened her look. 'I especially love *this* one. I haven't had a car for ages, so can I have it?'

'We're only in England occasionally, Sofia.' Diego rolled his eyes. 'What would you do with it? Import it back to Columbia?'

Sofia shrugged. 'I don't know but I want it all the same.' *Diego was taking his time.* Normally he'd say yes to whatever she asked for. She'd thought this a stupid idea, but she had to press on regardless. 'Please. I really want it.'

Diego laughed. Sofia always got what she wanted, the greedy bitch, but it was enjoyable making her beg. 'I'll think about it, but that will have to be later because our guests will be here shortly.'

# Eleven

'YOU'LL GET ME INTO SHIT,' Tiger growled, eyeing his brother. 'If you keep pulling crap like that, you'll have to go.'

Colt stared at the floor, his massive frame sagging like a heap of potato sacks. 'You promised you'd be there for me when I needed you, so don't make me leave. I only reacted to what I thought I saw.'

'You're here, aren't you?' Tiger glowered, not impressed with what he'd found on responding to Leo's terse voicemail. Thousands of pounds of coke wasted; the workforce up in arms and even if he'd tried, Leo couldn't have given him a filthier look. 'Are you still taking your medication?'

'I don't need those pills anymore. They fucked with my head. Pills do that,' Colt mumbled.

Tiger didn't miss the veiled dig behind Colt's comment. His hands curled into fists. He knew it would only be a matter of time before the blame game started and he wasn't going down that road. He'd had enough reminders of that the last day or so. He had to get off this subject, so the questions he himself wanted answering could wait. 'Whatever, but you can't randomly kick off like that. If you screw up, it's my neck on the block.'

'I know what I saw,' Colt grumbled. 'But I'll apologise to the bloke I lamped if it makes you feel better.'

Tiger sighed. Nothing would make him feel better. Colt being here was not a good omen. Pissing Leo off and potentially risking Zane's plans was not what he wanted. Having Alyson Read mess with his head was not on his list either.

'You don't seem yourself,' Colt said suddenly. 'Is there something wrong, Lyndon?'

'I'm fine, just don't call me that!' Tiger snapped. Lyndon was not a name he'd used for decades and he wanted it to stay that way.

'It's me, isn't it?' Colt's massive body contrasted sharply with his contrite attitude. 'I don't mean to cause problems. You said to come to you if I needed to. I didn't have anywhere else to go and...'

'Just keep your head down. I don't need any more shit. There's a lot going down at the moment,' Tiger said gruffly. Colt didn't know him, the same way he no longer knew Colt. Too many years had passed for *either* of them to hold that accolade.

And he'd cut his brother's words off for that very reason. Colt was angling at something and he could have used that opportunity to push as to why his brother had suddenly turned up here, but even *alluding* to it would spark accusations.

'What's going on, then?' Colt watched Tiger intently. 'By the amount of powder in this gaff, you've obviously hit the jackpot, so what's the grief?' He banged his huge fists together in anticipation. 'If you're getting shit then I'll sort it, you know that.'

'Just wait for instructions,' Tiger muttered, not about to go into the details of anything with his unstable brother. 'Don't do anything off your own back.'

'Yeah, okay. But this place doesn't help.' Colt's huge arm gestured around the room. 'Confined to a tiny space in the back end of a fucking factory isn't the best after years of being locked up an…'

'There may be a bed available at mine shortly,' Tiger said. 'I'll let you know when you can have it, but just do me a favour and don't rock the boat more than you already have. Right. I must get on.'

'Ah, I get it now!' Colt grinned, the remains of his smashed teeth ghastly. 'That's your problem – you've split up with your bird!'

Tiger froze, his hand on the door. 'I haven't got a bird! What the hell are you talking about?'

Colt folded his arms across his chest. His brother didn't trust him to level on anything, but that was okay. 'The reason I'm not staying at yours is because of your woman. She didn't want me there, right? Hey, you haven't split up because of me, have you?'

'No!' Tiger cried, getting more frustrated with his brother's paranoia. 'And she's not my woman. She's merely someone who's staying at my place for a while for her own safety.'

'That's what they all say...' Colt winked.

'Oh, fuck off!' Tiger stalked from the room and stomped up the corridor, hoping the burning of his cheeks wasn't visible. He didn't do relationships. He rarely even did women! Any involvement with anyone - no matter how vague or short-lived, diverted concentration.

He'd taken a vow of abstinence on relationships and the feelings that came with them many years ago. That sort of stuff weakened a man's resolve. Getting involved, caring and the concept of actually *loving* someone was not something he could comprehend. Being detached, feeling nothing and functioning was what he did. It was a conscious decision he'd made a long time ago and what he intended to keep going forward.

He was married to his job and did not play away.

'OIH! Are you blind?'

Tiger swung around to find he'd walked straight past Leo who now moved to block his path.

'What's the deal? You haven't been where you should be several times now. I can't reach you when I need you.' Leo eyed

Tiger intently. 'You're not being *you* and I've known you a long time, mate, so are you going to tell me what the fuck is going on?'

Tiger's eyes narrowed. 'Try thinking about that yourself! Considering you thought it amusing to dump some silly bird on me and phoning the second my brother turns up or every time he acts like a prat, why don't *you* deal with things? Even I can't be in three places at once!'

Leo remained speechless as Tiger stomped off down the corridor.

• • • •

HOLDING ZANE'S HAND, Erin walked up the short path of the imposing Kensington townhouse. Even though she now lived in a property deemed by many as 'elite', it wasn't like *this*. This was London grandeur at its finest and despite her resolve to treat this dinner as just that - a meal, her nerves jangled.

She bit down on her lip, pre-empting what she would say to Diego Delgado and his wife.

Whether it was pregnancy hormones playing havoc with her brain or not, Erin was jittery and uncharacteristically nervous. Thank God that Zane was here. She'd never be able to do this on her own.

But there was *one* good side to it...

Stealing a sideways glance as Zane reached to press the doorbell, Erin didn't think he'd ever looked so gorgeous. Since being in that horrible relationship with Anthony Walker, determined to wreak revenge on who she'd thought to be her father's killer, smartly dressed men were her nemesis. But that period of her life was what had led her to Zane and wouldn't change it for the world. But still the concept of suited and booted always turned her cold.

However, not in *this* case.

She took in the tailored dinner jacket which accentuated Zane's wide back, the cut making his figure more imposing and muscular than ever. And the way the soft material of his trousers encased his legs...

*Stop!* she thought. She must concentrate on what she was here to do. Even so, she'd never seen Zane in a suit, let alone a dinner jacket and she liked it. 'You look hot!' she whispered, a mischievous smile on her face.

'Not as hot as you...' Zane's hand trailed over Erin's buttocks in her elegant teal cocktail dress. 'When we get home, I'm going to...'

'Ah! Zane!'

Erin's head whipped towards the voice to a man standing in the now open doorway. She smiled nervously at the figure of whom she presumed to be Diego Delgado and came to the conclusion he wasn't what she expected.

'Evening, Diego.' Zane shook Diego's outstretched hand.

Erin watched the two men greet and wondered exactly what she'd expected Diego Delgado to be like.

She wasn't sure. Perhaps an older man; sour-faced, a little paunchy? She didn't know, but Diego was immaculate - almost as good as Zane. Well-built and of a similar age to Zane, his beard accentuated his sculptured swarthy features. Slicked back, dark hair complemented his strong grey eyes and a wide smile was in the place of where she'd expected a thin-lipped scowl. He was an attractive man with what she presumed, an equally attractive wife.

'Meet my fiancée, Erin.'

Erin heard Zane but was unable to function. Her nervousness returned full bore, along with a heavy dose of inferiority. Knowing how important the relationship with Diego was for the future, she hoped she wouldn't embarrass herself or Zane by being socially inept.

'Erin!' Zane hissed.

'P-Pleased to meet you,' Erin stuttered, internally chastising herself. *Pull yourself together*.

'The pleasure is all mine.' Stepping forward, Diego took Erin's hand and raised it to his lips, at the same time leading her into the house leaving Zane to follow.

Erin found herself in an immense square reception hall where an antique side table showcased a Tiffany lamp and a chandelier holding an uncountable number of crystal drops cast a beautiful light onto the Milton floor tiles.

*Should she say something else? Oh God, she didn't know!*

What did someone say when meeting an infamous narcotic kingpin for the first time? Zane was at ease, so why wasn't she? 'What a beautiful house!' she exclaimed before she could decide whether that was an acceptable thing to say or not.

'We think so, don't we, darling?' Sofia glided from a room on the left to slip her hand through the crook of Diego's arm. 'Zane!' she smiled, barely able to contain her amusement. 'How lovely to see you again!' *He looked good. Still, not a patch on his brother.*

And there it was - the flash of recognition followed by shocked horror. Sofia thought Zane did well to conceal it so rapidly, but it was there nevertheless and it was wonderful.

'Sofia!' Zane cleared his throat. 'This is a surprise! Wow! You're looking well.'

'My wife is indeed beautiful, is she not?' Diego smiled, resting his hand on Sofia's bump. 'And *this* triples her beauty, which you too will experience in your lovely fiancée shortly.'

Sofia brushed Diego's hand off. Wasn't her belly sticking out ten feet obvious enough? But now it was time to inspect the creature Zane had chosen.

'And you must be...' Sofia slowly glanced in Erin's direction, making it obvious acknowledging her presence was secondary. 'Ah, yes – Erin!'

Sofia hoped her smile looked natural. She also hoped she'd hidden her shock at Erin's perfect figure that showed no obvious sign of a growing baby. The woman's shimmering dress clung to all the right places and her face was stunning: naturally fine-boned, framed with thick golden hair. *This couldn't be happening.*

'It's lovely to meet you.' Erin smiled as much as she possibly could. 'I only hope I look as amazing as you in a few months' time.' She nodded to Sofia's huge bump, quickly realising by the woman's hostile expression it was the wrong thing to say. *Fuck.* 'And I love your dress...'

Bullshit, but she'd been forced to talk this kind of talk many years ago in situations such as this, so she must relax and let her memory take the brunt because there was something else taking centre stage. *Sofia had said how lovely it was to see Zane 'again'. They knew each other? How?*

'Introductions done!' Diego steered Zane towards a room to the left. 'Let's get drinks before dinner, shall we?'

Erin mechanically followed, her head spinning with questions. Sofia hated her, she could tell that straightaway. But why? She'd also spotted the shock on Zane's face when laying eyes on Sofia.

With a sudden rush, cold flooded Erin's veins. Hadn't Zane been promised to a Sicilian woman called Sofia to join their two families? Zane's father organised it when they'd been children, but Zane had refused to marry the woman because he'd been with Shirley. Zane had told her about it and how difficult it was to go against tradition.

Erin stole a quick glance at the woman next to her. It couldn't be *that* Sofia, could it?

• • • •

TIGER WALKED INTO HIS FLAT. Shutting the door behind him, he leant against the wall and expelled a long breath. He'd toyed with grabbing chips and going to the pub, but he was bound to bump into someone and wasn't in the mood for questions, whether it be from the barman or the punters. There were few venues he could go where someone didn't dig for information on Zane: Zane's firm, Zane's brother, Zane's state of mind, Zane's everything... *On and on and on.*

Why didn't people come straight out and ask the question rather than hint for information or skirt around the edges?

It got on his tits.

Shrugging off his jacket, he placed it on a coat hook, only

for it to fall off. Normally, he'd pick it up, but tonight he couldn't be arsed.

Things were shit. He'd ripped Leo's head off, shouted at his brother, spent the day sorting out crap left for him to deal with at the canning works and spent an absurdly long time procrastinating about where to go tonight in order to spend as little time as possible in his own fucking flat.

And the reason for *that* was because he felt bad about asking Alyson to leave.

Maybe Leo was spot on with what he'd said: it was time he let go of what Skye had said about him. He knew the truth, so why should he let her bitterness affect the rest of his life? Why should her lies make him tread on eggshells around the opposite sex? Furthermore, why should Alyson pay for her alleged 'friend's' actions?

He'd said some hurtful, unnecessary things to Alyson about Skye earlier and shouldn't have. Sure, those things were true, but he could have been more sensitive with how he'd gone about it. But sensitivity wasn't one of his strong points. Nor did he want it to be. He preferred being a machine which fired on all cylinders.

But the hard truth was that his head was messed up. Alyson's unfortunate experience and that stuff with Solenzo had dredged up memories better left buried. And then Colt turning up out of the blue...

Couple those with the unfamiliar attraction he'd begun to experience for Alyson brought him to the conclusion he'd be better off keeping out of everyone's way until he reset himself. But he still needed to tell Alyson he'd find somewhere else for her to stay because his brother needed to stay here. Convincing himself that was the reason was better than admitting that he didn't trust himself not to act on his desires.

Besides, even if he *did* act on it, what made him think that someone like Alyson would reciprocate? It was ridiculous.

Tiger paused halfway along the hallway. It was very quiet. Maybe she'd gone to bed?

Continuing, Tiger shrugged. Oh well, he'd speak to her about it in the morning instead. It was probably best, rather than tackling it whilst in such a strange mood.

He pushed the kitchen door open. Sod dinner. He'd just grab a beer and then hit the sack. He wasn't particularly hungry and... *What the...?*

Alyson held out an open bottle of chilled beer. 'I was beginning to think I'd have to keep dinner warm in the oven! I hope steak is okay? I wasn't sure what you liked.'

Tiger stared at the kitchen table set with cutlery, salt and pepper, sauces and two delicious looking plates of steak, chips and peas. A nerve in his jaw twitched. There was even a candle on the table... *Fuck.*

How could he sit here with her like this? How had he returned from work to find a lovely dinner on the table, ready and cooked for him when he had to tell her to leave?

He stared at the ice-cold beer in Alyson's hand and felt like screaming. 'You shouldn't have bothered. I'm not hungry,' he lied, immediately feeling like a Grade-A bastard as her face fell.

'Oh!' Alyson smiled weakly. 'I should have checked with you first. It was silly of me.' She moved to clear the plates. 'I just wanted to thank you for letting me stay. I appreciate it's awkward having me here under your feet. Maybe another time when you're less...'

Just as Alyson was about to tip the first dinner in the bin, Tiger grabbed her wrist. 'Being as you've gone to so much effort, don't waste it. I can probably manage it.'

*She was too close now. All he had to do was bend his head and if she raised hers, then...*

He rapidly released his grip, but Alyson remained where she was, staring up questioningly into his eyes.

Time paused and Tiger's breath hitched. Then like someone had flicked a switch, Alyson turned away. 'I'll put this back on the table,' she said brightly. 'Let's sit and eat.'

# TWELVE

NEXT TO DIEGO at the ten-seater dining table, Erin tried to catch Zane's eye to give him a hint that she needed to urgently speak to him, but for most of the meal the two men had been deep in conversation discussing subjects centring around work.

No details were mentioned. The unspoken rule was that 'shop' was not discussed with other halves, however Zane included her with all goings on these days.

At least she *thought* he had...

Erin continued picking at her Bouef en Croûte and glanced at Sofia as the woman replenished her wine. She'd tried her hardest to make small talk, but Sofia's abruptness made it difficult to sustain any topic for long. Along with the disapproving looks thrown in her direction, it was clear Sofia didn't think much of her.

Erin beseeched Zane to notice her internal screams, but his face remained a mask of concentration as the topic of import tax continued. The food and surroundings were lovely - even Diego, from the small amount of interaction she'd had, seemed pleasant, but Sofia's presence lowered the temperature by degrees. It was *dreadful*.

As Sofia reached for the wine bottle yet again, Diego

looked up. 'Do you not think you've had enough?' he said, his voice sharp.

Sofia rolled her eyes so dramatically it could have been mistaken for a convulsion. 'A few glasses won't hurt, Diego,' she said, her voice unnaturally high. 'I'm sure Erin drinks when she feels like it without being chastised!'

Erin finally made eye contact with Zane, only to receive a warning glance. She hadn't drank alcohol since discovering she was pregnant. She glanced uncomfortably at her glass of iced water. She could feel the burn of Diego's glare towards his wife without even looking and was loathe to take sides. 'Erm, well, I...'

'Actually, since Erin became pregnant, she's gone off the taste of alcohol. She's the same with tomatoes at the moment,' Zane said quickly.

'Yes, it's really strange,' Erin agreed, grateful for the intervention.

'Are you *sure* you're pregnant?' Sofia frowned. 'You don't look it. It's not just a ruse to get Zane to marry you, is it?'

'Sofia!' Diego barked. 'What an absurd thing to say!'

Seeing Erin's cheeks burn, Zane gave Sofia a cold stare. 'I'd marry Erin any day, regardless of whether she's carrying my child or not.'

'Don't be such a misery! I was joking,' Sofia laughed, the noise irritatingly loud. 'I'm bored to death with you two talking work!' She then leant across the table towards Erin. 'I saw an advert for a wonderful car today.' Sitting up, she batted her eyelashes at her husband. 'Diego's buying it for me, aren't you, darling?'

Giving Zane one of those 'here we go' looks, Diego sighed. 'Sofia's got her heart set on an old car she saw in the paper. There's no point. She can barely drive and it's not like we're in this country often.'

'Barely drive?' Sofia cackled. 'I can drive perfectly well! And it might be "old", but it's a limited edition, rare model. It's beautiful.' She turned to Zane. '*You'd* appreciate it because from what I remember, you like cars.'

Erin stiffened. *There it was again - a reference to the past.* She must be the same Sofia. Oh God, this was awful. Was Diego aware of the connection? It could ruin everything for Zane.

'It's a Bentley,' Sofia continued. 'It's like one of those cars Penelope Pitstop had. Do you remember that cartoon, Erin? The one with the Ant Hill Mob?' Her laugh reached new heights. 'Ha ha! I could put Diego and Zane in the back of the car and shout "HEEEELP!" like Penelope!'

Erin pretended to laugh, but she was sure Sofia must be drunk. Why would she ramble this rubbish?

'Bentleys are nice cars,' Zane said unexpectedly. 'My father had one.' His voice was normal, but Erin detected anger behind his eyes.

'When will you buy me the car, Diego?' Sofia continued, her voice whiny.

'For Christ's sake, Sofia! I'll get you the bloody Bentley, okay?' Diego snapped. 'Now do you mind if me and Zane continue our conversation?'

Sofia pushed her chair back, the legs scraping loudly against the floor. She'd done what she was supposed to do, even if maybe she'd pushed things a bit far. But it was now time to play games with this loser bitch and see just how clever she was. 'Let's leave these two to it, Erin. Let's go into another room and chat.'

Erin clocked Zane's slight nod and got up from her own chair. *Great*. Now she had to sit alone with Sofia who may or may not be the woman Zane was supposed to marry, who was either drunk or mad and who disliked her for reasons yet unknown. *This would be fun. Not.*

Cutting Zane a look, Erin dutifully followed Sofia from the room.

• • • •

MARCO GLANCED AROUND the Burgundy Cellar wine bar.

Not that in real terms it was an actual 'cellar' being as there were steps up to it from outside. Still, that was neither here nor there. And even though he didn't much like wine, nor wine bars, this one was his favourite out of the vast choice around here, helped somewhat by the useful 'agreement' he had with the manager.

Marco did his usual double check of the clientele to see if anyone was paying attention to his unusual companion. Thankfully, his usual booth shielded him to an extent. And so it should! He paid the manager enough to be left alone.

Still, he didn't know why he entertained the thought of there being a problem. Soon London and everyone in it would treat him like a king, falling over themselves to do whatever was required.

Whittaker would set things up perfectly. What a stupid bastard the guy was. The prick fell for the 'new venture' bullshit, just like expected - tripping over himself in his greedy rush for the over-generous percentage on offer. Not that the fool would get *any* benefit. Namely because there was no venture. But providing the cock followed his strict orders not to namedrop him into the conversation when with Delgado, it would work brilliantly.

And *this* guy was the additional ace up his sleeve.

Marco turned to face Colt Shoreham, wincing at the mound of leather of the man's strange coat crammed into the already cramped space of the booth. Did this cunt think he was in the fucking Matrix or what? 'How did you know where to find me?' he asked, an eyebrow cocked. 'I thought I said to do everything via that mobile I gave you.'

'I have ways of finding out most things and I thought it would be amusing to see this bunch of stuck-up cunts' faces when I walked in asking for you.' Colt placed his meaty fists on the table with a jolt which tipped the glass votive candle holder in the centre to one side. 'And it *was* amusing. Fuck me, this lot don't half believe their shit don't stink!'

'It's called money, dear man, *money*!' Marco clicked his

fingers and precisely two seconds a waiter hurried over. 'Another Chateaux Lafite and...?'

'Lager,' Colt snarled, not looking up. 'Pint of.'

'Erm, we don't serve pints... sir,' the waiter stammered. He then fished an embossed drinks list from the black apron around his waist and held it out gingerly. 'We have a range of bottled beers that y…'

'I want a fucking pint, not a gay bottle!' Colt glared at the waiter, baring the freaky remains of his teeth for added effect.

'I'm sure you can arrange a pint, can you not?' Marco smiled smoothly at the terrified waiter.

Nodding, the waiter scurried off leaving Colt to burst into loud abrasive laughter. 'Fucking classic!' he roared. 'See his mug? No way I'd be seen dead sipping from one of those fucking bot…' He stopped abruptly as Marco's fingers dug into his wrist.

'Don't push things!' Marco hissed. 'We still need to be careful.' He leant closer. 'Best not to forget the "unusual" circumstances that achieved a rare release from your previous "residence". It wouldn't take much for that to be revoked, so don't draw attention to yourself.'

*Or to me*, Marco thought. But despite Colt's less than helpful behaviour, it was a genius idea getting him on board. Whatever people said about his failing memory, he'd remembered *this* guy.

Oh yes, he'd made sure to keep tabs on everyone and everything ever associated with his 'family' and with a bit of effort – okay, a *lot* of effort, he'd located the very person to give him that extra 'something' to ensure no stones were left unturned.

*Everyone was available for a price...*

Marco's scowling face changed to a congenial smile as the waiter returned to deposit more wine and a pint on the table.

'Sorry,' the man gibbered, rushing to dab up the splash of beer his shaking hands spilt from the glass as he laid it down. Purposely averting his eyes from the psychotic looking man in the booth, he hastily backed away.

Marco stared at the pint glass and then at Colt. 'Better?'

Colt's enormous head bobbed up and down as he greedily slugged the pint, then let out a loud belch.

'Christ!' Marco muttered under his breath. *This had better be worth it.* One million pounds he'd promised this nutter for the work and he'd already handed over half of it as a retainer. 'You'd best not let me down, Shoreham,' he spat, his eyes resuming their ice-like quality. 'Tell me what you've got so far.'

Colt glanced around to see if he could spot that dweeb waiter for a refill, but there was no sign of the twat. He pulled out his cigarettes and lit one, blowing smoke slowly through the space where his teeth should be. 'It hasn't yet gone the way I hoped.'

Marco sat forward, tense. 'What do you mean? You're in there, aren't you? You said you'd...'

'Yeah, yeah, I'm in there.' Colt cracked his knuckles. 'But I'm stuck living at that crummy factory where they bag their coke, rather than my brother's flat.'

A nerve twitched in Marco's jaw. *His* coke, to be correct. It was *his* coke - *his* deal - *his* arrangement. It had all been his until Delgado got his knickers in a twist. Reminding himself that it was only temporary, he took a deep breath. 'Okay, well you're in the factory, so that's good. Any questions over your unexpected return?'

Colt shook his head. 'Nope and I doubt whether there will be. Lyndon knows what he's done.' *And what Lyndon had done he would never forgive.* 'I get the distinct impression I'm not wanted though. If it hadn't been for your bruv I don't think I'd have got the time of day and would have had to revert to other means.'

'Zane is not "my bruv",' Marco snapped, his eyes glinting. 'He's someone who owes me and will pay. With interest!'

'Yeah, whatever,' Colt muttered uninterestedly. 'But I'm not happy to be kipping in a shit factory.'

'So, what happened to staying at your brother's flat?' Marco frowned. 'I thought you said you'd stay there as well as working at the factory? I need you living at the flat - in the centre of things.'

Colt's massive shoulders moved into a shrug. 'I've been told there will be room for me soon. Lyndon and his tart have just split up. I made out I was upset that she didn't want me there. He's a fucking joke and thinks I came down with the last branch! He told me the woman was only there for her security and wasn't his bird at all!'

'Who is she?'

'Dunno. Some slag called Alyson. I'll find out if you want?'

Marco tensed. *Alyson? Fuck!* He'd thought the last shot he given that girl would have been enough to finish her off like the dead hooker he'd left as a present for Zane to find. *Shit. Fuck. Shit.*

If Alyson was still alive and under *their* protection, she might decide she had the clout to go to the Old Bill.

Colt saw Marco's expression. 'It'll only be for a few more days, if that. If that bird's moving on, then I'll move in - no stress!'

'Yes, yes, you're right.' Marco reinstated his neutral face. He needed to weigh this up and decide whether to take evasive action as priority. Alyson would be dealt with - no doubt about that because whatever happened, he couldn't afford to have *her* living and breathing to remain a constant threat. But maybe he didn't need to deal with that immediately. 'Keep me posted as to what's going on with that bird of your brother's.'

'What's with the interest? What the fuck does she matter?'

'She doesn't,' Marco lied. 'It's just that... Oh, hang on! This could be important.' Pulling his phone out of his suit jacket, his pulse ramped up seeing a text from Sofia. *She'd better have done it. She'd better have stuck to the plan.*

He opened the text with surprisingly sweaty fingers.

Mission accomplished. D is buying car

xxx

Marco expelled a rush of breath, a wide grin splitting his face. *Thank fuck for that! Stage one complete.*

Now the stage was set for an opening where he would know the exact date and time when Delgado would be standing outside, just waiting to be gunned down. All he required now was to get this bozo here to find out the date and time of the next coke delivery due in for Zane from Paraguay. And Marco knew it was around now because *he'd* been the one to organise the original schedule.

Diego's death, plus a brand-new load of coke would be achieved in one go. *Perfect.*

Colt watched Marco with interest. 'Good news?'

'Yes, it is,' Marco said, now in a much better frame of mind.

'When are you going to tell me exactly what you've got planned?' Colt fixed Marco with a steely stare. 'I might look demented, but I'm far fucking from it! If I don't know the ins and outs, it will make things difficult and possibly less successful.'

Marco laughed. 'It will make *nothing* less successful because if it does, you'll get paid fuck all!' He finished his glass of wine, grimacing at the taste. He hated the fucking stuff, but drinking wine in a wine bar was expected, wasn't it? 'You'll get the finer details once you prove you're not setting me up and feeding everything back to your goddamm brother! The first thing to do is keep me abreast of impending deliveries. *Large* ones…'

Colt snorted, his flared nostrils making him look even more sinister. 'Think what you fucking like! The last person I want to help is the wanker who got my mother put in a fucking loony bin! I've waited years for revenge and I'm having it, so if you don't pay me, I'll fucking kill you and take double!'

Marco grinned. Threats aside, he'd got a good one in Colt Shoreham. A psychopath with an 'in' to the one place *he* could never have. A cunt with even less morals than himself. And one hell bent on destroying his own brother.

The similarities were astounding, therefore things would work like a dream.

He was almost there and by the time this fell into place, he might give Colt *ten* million for his troubles rather than one. It wasn't like he couldn't afford it by then.

Furthermore, if this man was as good as he believed him to be, then he might find himself with a new second-in-command of a firm that would rise from the ashes any day now.

# THIRTEEN

SOFIA LOUNGED into the leathered luxury of a cream armchair situated in the furthermost reception room from where she knew Diego would retreat to with Zane.

Making no attempt to conceal her scrutiny of Erin, she crossed her long legs, remembering just in time to cross at the ankles only. This bulk put paid to crossing her legs in the proper way.

Deciding to make a show, she fidgeted in the seat and stretched out, closing her eyes with mock relief. 'Urgh! You've got all this to look forward to!' she said, inwardly gloating that Erin's svelte figure would soon be ruined for real, unlike *hers*...

Erin smiled, relieved that the strange behaviour Sofia exhibited at the dinner table had passed. 'It will be worth it in the end.'

'I doubt that,' Sofia scoffed. 'Why anyone would choose to ruin their figure is beyond me!'

'But surely you want this baby, don't you?' Erin blushed with her forwardness. 'I mean, I... I'm sorry, that's none of my business. I...'

'I'm sure you're aware that men like ours expect heirs produced. If you're not aware, then you will be...' Sofia's eyes glinted with spite. 'You must be concerned though… Zane's hardly the most reliable of men and hasn't married you yet, has he?' She arched a finely plucked brow. 'You don't belong to a relevant family, so there's no honour to go through with marrying you. No doubt you'll end up with nothing, short of a brat and stretch marks!'

Erin didn't know how to react to this and for once, was glad Sofia's shrill laughter made a response impossible.

'I don't expect Zane told you that *I* was the one he was due to marry, did he?' Sofia continued, her eyes alight ready for the shock on this stupid bitch's face. *The thick cow didn't have a clue and the revelation would screw them right up. Ha, ha, ha!* 'Unfortunately for him, he didn't but that's his loss!' She laughed, thoroughly enjoying herself. 'I'm sorry, I suppose I shouldn't have said anything.'

Finally looking in Erin's direction, a percentage of her self-satisfied grin disappeared. *The stupid tart didn't look particularly crestfallen.*

'I knew about the arrangement between your two families, but not that you were the same Sofia here tonight,' Erin admitted. 'Does Diego know about… about your "history"?'

A sly smile inched unto Sofia's face. *Trying to insinuate threats now, was she?* 'Of course he does! He has no issue with Zane. Why would he? Diego won and Zane has to live with the loss. Although...' She raised her finger to her glossy lips in mock-thought, mindful not to smudge her lipstick. 'It must be hard for you knowing you will always be second best...'

Resenting the burning flushing her face with heat, Erin knew she should swallow the dig. It was important to keep things sweet for the sake of Zane's deal, but this woman was an abject bitch! 'Zane and I have a great relationship and I've never felt "second best", as you put it.'

*Not entirely true*. There were times in the past when Erin had felt exactly that. But that was through her own insecurities and she wouldn't allow this spiteful diva make her bite the obvious bait.

'No, I'm *sure* you haven't,' Sofia said sweetly, her eyes mocking. 'Maybe Zane will get around to marrying you eventually... Hopefully, anyway.'

'So, how's life with Diego?' Erin consciously steered off the loaded subject. 'He seems a lovely man.' A man which, from the interactions between them at dinner, was a little tired of Sofia's high maintenance needs. 'He's buying you that car too! Wow! You lucky thing!'

Something about Erin's tone hit a nerve. *Was that sarcastic? A fucking dig?* Sofia didn't mean to allow it, but it caught her off guard and ignited the touchpaper constantly hovering near an open flame where Diego was concerned. 'Lucky? Diego has *me*, doesn't he? And because of that, I get exactly what I want!'

A flicker of amusement passed over Erin's face, her eyes flicking to Sofia's swollen belly. 'I can see that…' *If one could have a dig, then it was game on.* 'Except perhaps to drink whenever you want...'

Sofia opened her mouth to retaliate but the door opened, thankfully preventing her from slapping this little whore.

Entering the room, Diego walked over and placed his hands on Sofia's shoulders. 'Have you ladies finished chatting? We thought we'd have a game of cards and you're welcome to join us.'

'I'm not feeling well and need to lie down,' Sofia whined, her bottom lip trembling.

Diego paled, his hand immediately falling to Sofia's belly. 'Do you wish me to call the doctor?'

'The baby's fine, darling.' Sofia incorporated in a wince of pain as she smiled lovingly at her husband. 'I think I overate at dinner, that's all.'

Making a big deal of needing help out of the chair, Sofia leant weakly against Diego and turned to Zane who had followed into the room. 'I'm so sorry to desert you. This pregnancy is taking it out of me.' She stroked her bump. 'Hopefully we can do it again soon.'

'Please don't worry,' Zane smiled. 'We understand, don't we, Erin?'

'Perfectly.' Erin's mind was running at ten to the dozen. She'd seen the flash of irritation on Sofia's face when Diego touched her. She'd masked it, but it was there. Sofia was good, Erin would give her that, but what was her game?

'Apologies, my friends.' Diego smiled. 'I will be in touch soon.'

'Not at all. Thank you for a lovely evening.' Zane shook Diego's hand, then took Erin's as she stood up.

'It was nice to meet you, Erin,' Sofia said sweetly, clinging to her husband's side.

'You too.' Erin returned the smile but knew her eyes were as cold as Sofia's, harbouring the strong sense that the Delgados were not in a good place. And Sofia was the one driving it.

• • • •

'THAT HILARIOUS!' Alyson giggled, thoroughly enjoying Tiger's stories. Tonight had turned out a little like Tiger himself - unexpected.

Judging by how the evening started, she'd thought she'd want to finish eating as soon as possible and retreat to her room. It had been obvious Tiger's acceptance of the meal hinged from guilt, but after an awkward start and a drink or two, they'd both relaxed and conversation flowed. In fact, Alyson would go as far to say she didn't think she'd ever had such an enjoyable evening. Tiger's anecdotes had her in stitches. 'At the risk of laughing my makeup off, dare I ask what happened next?' she asked, eager to hear the outcome.

'Well,' Tiger grinned, his stone-like face alive. 'After I chucked the geezer down a flight of stairs and straight out of the club's door, I discovered he was the father-in-law of my boss!'

Alyson roared with laughter. 'Oh my God! You chucked your bosses father-in-law out? What happened afterwards?'

'What do you think? Aged fifteen and the first day of my very first proper job as a bouncer at this crap club in Streatham and I get the tin tack!' Tiger's weathered face creased with amusement. 'I was gutted!'

Alyson's mouth fell open. 'You worked as a bouncer at fifteen years old?'

'Things were different in those days. It was a long time ago! Not wishing to point out the obvious, you're a lot younger than me!' Tiger laughed - another rare occurrence.

'Not that much younger, I bet!' Alyson said, silently wondering exactly how old Tiger was. *Not that she cared...*

'Trust me, you are. God, in those days everyone was pissed as farts! Happy Hour! Two pints of Snakebite for 30p or two doubles for 50p was the culprit! Half the punters in clubs ended up getting chucked out halfway through the night. I got launched out of a few places myself for being off my head back in the day. You know what it's like!'

The change in Alyson was immediate as a needle came from nowhere to puncture her balloon of happiness. She'd almost forgotten for a minute, but now it was back. *It would never fully go, would it?* 'No... no, I don't know what it's like... I… I never got off my head before... Until…'

'Shit!' Tiger rubbed his hand across his face like the action could retract his words. 'I'm so sorry… I should have thought...' How could he have been so bloody stupid to rattle on, knowing Alyson was innocent of most things?

His rage built. She *had* been innocent of most things until Marco Morelli ruined her.

Even though it was the last thing Alyson wanted, she was powerless to stop the landslide of memories crashing into her brain. She'd been having such a fantastic evening. This big, strong man intrigued her. He frightened her, yet was so kind to her and he'd been the *best* company. She'd wanted to impress him - dared to hope that perhaps he could see past how he'd first met her and that maybe she could show him she wasn't a sad, gullible little girl, frightened of her own shadow. Perhaps she'd prove that despite her backfiring plan of self-medicating herself that day which had only achieved the opposite, he'd made the right call by not getting her locked away in a crazy ward. She was okay and stronger than she looked...

But most importantly, Alyson realised she wanted Tiger to *like* her. Maybe *more* than like her…

She'd even lost it again this morning; shouted at him; cried about Skye's death – refusing to believe that her friend had any part in what happened. And now she was at it again! In the middle of a perfectly normal conversation with this man recounting an amusing anecdote from his past, she'd flown off the deep end, acting like a nervous, unstable and immature child. All she'd proved was that she was *far* from all right. How could anything be all right if everyone had to walk around on eggshells in case they triggered her?

All she'd succeeded in doing was making this wonderful man feel bad.

Just to spite herself further, tears flowed down Alyson's cheeks: tears of anger at herself, frustration and panic from a tumult of uncontrollable and runaway emotions. 'I'm sorry... You've got nothing to apologise for! I... I didn't mean to make you feel bad. It's pathetic.' She stared at her shaking hands, blurred shapes through the tears. '*I'm* pathetic! No wonder you didn't want dinner with me. *I* don't want to have dinner with me!'

In a rush to extract herself from this mortifying situation and escape from herself, not that it was possible, Alyson pushed her chair away from the table and scrambled up. 'I… I'll tidy this up in the morning. I'm really sorry...'

Tiger remained in his seat as Alyson bolted to the door. Wasn't this what he'd wanted? To be left alone to get his head together, away from distractions?

Yet it wasn't. He'd been enjoying himself. Actually *enjoying* himself. He'd felt different – like *himself.* He'd forgotten the problems, the burdens, the shit he shouldered. If only temporarily, it was a breath of fresh air - one which he couldn't remember ever happening before.

Jumping to his feet, he bolted after Alyson. Catching up

with her in the hallway, he grabbed her arm. 'Don't go. You've done nothing wrong,'

'Yes, I do! I've done *everything* wrong!' Alyson tugged away from Tiger's grasp. 'I've ruined the evening. What happened shouldn't still be affecting me like this.'

'For fuck's sake! Of course it will!' Tiger snarled. 'I want to kill that cunt for what he did to you.'

Alyson blanched at the language, Tiger's raw fury both unnerving and exciting. That a man like him should be so furious at what had happened to her was strange - *empowering*, even. 'It's not your problem, Tiger.'

'Yes, it is,' Tiger said. 'I don't like shit happening to women. It ain't right.'

'There's nothing I can do about it now.' Alyson sighed. 'I must forget it.'

'What that wanker did won't just disappear, Alyson! Some stuff *never* goes away!' Tiger said, the vision of his own mother invading his head. 'I should know…'

Alyson looked up at Tiger, for the first time seeing pain behind his granite features. 'Wh-What do you mean?'

Tiger paused, inwardly berating himself. 'Just a term of phrase.'

How could he be so careless? How could he be so lax to almost mention what he *never* discussed. Lulling himself into a state of familiarity with someone was not something he did. And not something he *should* do. The shutters clanged back into place. 'Marco will be dealt with for what he did to you. As said, I'm sorry if I upset you. I'm thoughtless sometimes. Thanks for the meal. It was very nice. Get yourself to bed now and I'll clear up the kitchen.'

As Tiger strode away, Alyson was tempted to follow. She wanted to tell him that he wasn't thoughtless. Far from it. She also wanted to ask him what he wasn't telling her.

But she didn't.

It was clear he wouldn't be pushed on this one. But she was intrigued. This man intrigued her. They'd got on so well. Before she'd spoiled things, that was. If she hadn't gone down that road, would it be ridiculous to hope there was a chance that she intrigued Tiger as much as he intrigued her?

Did having the thought of what it would be like to kiss him, make her a bad person?

*Hadn't she thought those kinds of things about Marco?*

Feeling suddenly chilled to the bone, Alyson wondered whether thinking of men in this way after all that had happened, meant that perhaps she *should* be kept in one of those hospitals after all.

Confused, she retreated into her bedroom and shut the door behind her.

# FOURTEEN

'SHUT UP, YOU STUPID BITCH!' Marco snarled, hastily pulling out of the redhead he'd been happily ploughing before his mobile rang.

The slut had been enjoying herself all right, thanks to his prowess. Either that or she believed he wanted her wails of pleasure for the money he'd paid. He didn't and, quite frankly, it was getting on his nerves. He didn't want her dulcet tones audible to whoever was on the other end of the line. He hadn't handed over a wedge for someone else to get off. Fuck that.

Besides, it might be Sofia. Although there was an unspoken agreement that whilst she was still allowing Delgado to put his hands on her - even if she'd got out of shagging the greasy twat these past few months, she was still doing *something* with him. She must be.

No red-blooded man in his right mind would withstand complete abstinence from their wife, regardless of the reason. So, whilst Sofia proceeded to wrap her luscious lips around Delgado's cock, Marco wasn't about to starve either.

But the thought of Sofia touching anyone but him fuelled his rage. 'I said shut the fuck up!' he roared, giving the redhead a sharp backhander. 'I'm on the phone!'

The woman's screams of pleasure became muffled sobs as she scrambled up, her frightened eyes darting around for her discarded clothes. Marco watched coldly, waiting for her to disappear before answering the call. It had best not ring off before he answered. Something else this bitch would be responsible for.

His teeth ground impatiently. This was what thinking of Delgado's hands on Sofia - *his* Sofia, did. It put him in a bad fucking mood. And he didn't want to be in a bad fucking mood.

Finally able to take the call, he pressed the mobile to his ear. 'Yes?' Marco's face screwed into a scowl. Since when did Whittaker have the clout to question what took him so long to answer? If he didn't need this jumped-up, pretentious cunt, he'd have had the wanker killed long ago. But it wouldn't be for much longer. 'Yeah, I was just in the middle of something. Yeah… Ha ha! Something like that, yeah.' *I'll pretend you're funny, you slimy piece of …* 'Oh! You have?'

All thoughts of slowly torturing Sam Whittaker to death faded. *For now...* Shoving the phone in his neck to free his hands, Marco shrugged on his shirt and began doing up the buttons. 'Excellent news... When? What? This afternoon?'

His brows knitted. *Bollocks*. That was too soon to get *certain* things in place – namely the vital thing that had to happen to ensure this worked. How could Delgado be unexpectedly gunned down when taking delivery of the car without his gun-for-hire psycho-freak in place?

It wouldn't happen. Nor did he yet know when the next coke delivery was due.

*Fuck!*

'Yeah, yeah, I'm still here,' Marco muttered, his brain trawling through ways to make this work. 'Okay, so here's how it has to go. Take the car to Delgado, agree the price and then arrange for it to be delivered back to him at a later date. Next week, perhaps? I'll let you know.' That would give enough time for things to slot into place.

'What? What do you mean "what if he wants it now"?'

Marco spat. *This bloke was getting on his tits*. 'He can't have it now… What? Yes, I just said so, didn't I? Of course I'm prepared to sell it!'

Marco took a breath, fighting to keep rational. Whittaker was too much of a yellow-bellied cunt not to leg it if he smelt a rat. 'Yeah, it's just that I need to replace the two front tyres. They should have arrived last week, but there's been a hold-up at customs. I had to get them imported from the states. You know what it's like. Yeah, that's right… I can't sell the man something that isn't tip top.'

*If this guy questioned one more fucking thing…*

Willing himself to keep steady, Marco plastered on a smile which he hoped conveyed in his voice. 'Anyway, look on the bright side - doing it this way will give you a further opportunity to meet with him. I know what you're like, Whittaker,' he said, enjoying chucking a sarcastic dig into the mix. 'It'll tick another box in your I-Spy book of celebrities, yeah?' He laughed, pretending to have good-natured banter when it was anything but. *Yeah, I-Spy book for the use of arse-licking, grovelling, fudge packers…*

Marco rolled his eyes. Whittaker was *still* talking. 'Yeah, yeah, that sounds fine…' *Whatever, just get the fuck on with it, you prick!* 'Yes, good stuff. Call me afterwards and let me know how it went. What? No, there's no way he won't want it!'

Sofia would ensure that wasn't an option. What Sofia wanted, Sofia got. And Diego Delgado, despite his big-gun-narcotic-king reputation, was wrapped around her little finger.

*Which made everything so much easier.*

Realising Whittaker was still talking, Marco cut the call. He was bored now. He'd answered all the questions; told him what to do and how to play it, so what else was there to say?

Fastening up his trousers, Marco glared at the creased sheets of his now unmade bed. It was a good job the housekeeper was due shortly. He hated mess.

Pulling up his contact list, he scrolled through it until he found the entry marked 'HH'.

He wasn't about to incriminate himself on the off chance he lost his phone and someone found 'Colt Shoreham' listed within his contacts. If it were discovered that *he'd* been the one to pay that bastard psychologist a veritable fortune to declare Colt fit for release it would be detrimental to his fast-coming ascension to royalty in the criminal underworld. And nothing was jeopardising that.

Putting that looney tunes under 'HH' was a more fitting than 'Colt' anyway.

Marco chuckled to himself at his wit. 'Half-Head' suited Shoreham down to a tee and the nut-nut better be ready for one of the jobs he'd been booked for. If he wasn't, Marco would sling him back inside Broadmoor himself.

• • • •

ZANE PULLED HIS CONCENTRATION away from the text. His fury ignited, he glared at Erin. 'First of all, I find out *after* the event that Leo's paid Pete Mayer more than agreed for the subtle use of his car crusher. The man demanded further payment to sort the disposal of the woman found in our vent. Leo should have told the greedy twat to do one! Now you're going on about *Sofia*?'

Getting up, he paced across to the massive window overlooking the Thames. 'How did I know Sofia was Diego's wife? I had no idea Delgado stepped in when I bowed out!'

'It's not that which bothers me!' Erin said, determined to keep her cool. She didn't want this to turn into an argument. 'There's something not right about that woman.'

'You said that last night. Several times!' Zane snapped. 'If I remember rightly, you did nothing but moan about how rude she was. Christ, Erin! Sofia isn't a threat to you.' He dragged his fingers through his hair. 'I can't believe you're going down this road again!'

'You're not listening.' Erin jutted her chin out indignantly. 'I'm not going down any "road". I'm telling you that Sofia has an agenda and I don't trust her!'

Zane sighed. 'You went through this with Hazel, with Shirley and even with Skye! You were wrong about all of them, apart from Skye...' Just thinking of the girl he'd believed to be his daughter dramatically worsened his mood. 'Diego and Sofia are perfectly happy! They're having a child together and I'm pleased for them. I never wanted to be with Sofia and it's clear she's happy where she is, so why make an issue out of this?'

'Are you *sure* she's happy where she is? Because I'm not!' Erin raised an eyebrow. 'Regardless of what you think *I* think, this isn't about me or my "paranoia". It's not even about *you*! This is about *her*! Sofia is a bitch who doesn't like her husband. She doesn't want a child either. She's a nasty piece of work and doesn't like *me*!'

'Ah!' Zane exclaimed. '*This* is what it's really about, is it? The fact that Sofia doesn't like *you*.' He shook his head in frustration. 'Are you purposefully trying to screw this deal up for me with Diego? Causing bad blood between us all? What's the fucking matter with you?'

'*Me*?' Erin shrieked. 'I'm telling you that Sofia is trouble, Zane. Trouble! She isn't all she seems and if you don't watch her, she could...'

'Could, *what*? I wonder if you'd be so adamant that she hates you, her husband and wants to kill us all if she wasn't the woman who it had been arranged for me to marry? I doubt it!'

'I've already told you that's nothing to do with it.'

'It's *everything* to do with it!' Zane yelled. 'Christ, Erin! I need this deal with Delgado to work and to do that, everyone has to get on! Can you not, just for fucking once, put your jealousy aside? I didn't want to marry Sofia then and I *still* don't. And as for her comments - she's a classic, spoilt Sicilian mafia princess, nothing more!'

Erin got out of the chair and snatched up her handbag. 'Okay, if you say so. I hope you're right. I'm not arguing about it.' She wanted to though, she really did. 'That's the last thing I'll say on the subject.'

But she doubted it would be the last thing she'd say about

it at all. Whether Zane refused to see the wood for the trees or not, call it women's intuition, this was nothing to do with Zane and Sofia's history. It was that under the beautiful exterior of Sofia Delgado, danger lurked. In what way, Erin wasn't sure, yet now it looked like she'd have no choice but to experience that woman's veiled poison on another occasion, or worse - *frequently* if Zane made a habit of becoming friendly with Diego Delgado. If he did, then she'd have no choice but to find a way to grin and bear the constant stream of vicious remarks - not only at her, but everyone.

She pursed her lips. 'I'm off to the Starbright now but before I go, tell me one thing: did you not sense the unrest between Diego and Sofia? Diego wasn't happy with her on several occasions and she resented him being anywhere near her!'

'You read too much into things,' Zane sighed. 'Diego loves Sofia - anyone can see that. They're about to have a child, so leave them to it! And should I remind you that you said you wouldn't say anything else about it…' With a lopsided grin, he then pulled Erin into his arms. 'Now come here because I won't leave things on an argument.'

• • • •

ZANE NODDED TOWARDS the small pane of glass in the wall of the room he used as an office. 'How is he getting on?'

Leo paused in answering. After yesterday he'd fully expected Colt to display further off-the-cuff behaviour and was ready to tell Zane or rather 'strongly suggest', that the man's job offer should be rescinded. But whatever Tiger had said to his brother when he'd eventually showed up triggered Colt to undergo a personality transplant. And Leo was unsure whether he was pleased about that or not.

With the man's oversized leather coat absent for once from his huge frame and instead thrown over a pile of boxes, Leo watched Colt employ his immense strength, making light work out of stacking crates that although, despite his own power putting most men to shame, Leo admitted he'd struggle to lift that weight with as much ease. The guy was a machine! 'He's doing okay,' he mumbled with a touch of resentment. 'He's done everything I've asked and more.' And that was the reason why he'd no choice but to cut the guy some slack and let him leave the canning works last night, rather than remain behind closed doors. If Tiger couldn't be arsed to watch the man like he'd promised, then Leo sure as hell wasn't doing it. Colt Shoreham gave him the fucking creeps.

'You seem surprised Colt's doing okay.' Zane frowned. 'Why is that?'

As Leo reluctantly filled Zane in about the incident involving Jimmy Pinn, his jaw tightened. 'Why didn't you inform me about this before? This is the second time you haven't kept me up to speed - your dealing with Mayer being the other... I received a text from him earlier thanking me for my "understanding" about adding on the extra payment. Why the fuck did you pay the greedy cunt more cash?'

'Because we'd have got the body back else,' Leo said, not liking the way this was going. 'I didn't tell you about that or Jimmy because you've got so much on. When Tiger *finally* got here, he spoke to Colt and against my better judgement, the man's worked like a Trojan since, that's why I haven't pushed for him to lose his job.'

Zane tensed, aggravated. 'Hold on a minute. I gave Colt a chance and I decide when whether he keeps it or not. And what's this shit with Tiger?' He could sense a whiff of bad blood and that he did not like. 'What's the issue? Why the sarcasm?'

Leo bristled. He didn't want to discuss Tiger, but he had little choice now. 'There's been some instances where Tiger's been unreachable. He seems more bothered about that bird at his flat.'

'You mean the one that *you* volunteered him to look after?' Zane folded his arms. 'I promised Alyson Read would be protected, so if Tiger needs to be there, then he needs to be there.' He studied Leo curiously. 'What's the *real* issue here? Why are you suddenly uncomfortable in stepping up to the plate?'

Leo glared at Zane, that comment the equivalent of slapping him around the face. 'Are you saying I'm not pulling my weight?' Tiger had also insinuated that and Leo appreciated that as little as he appreciated *this*. 'I don't like Colt Shoreham. He ain't right in the head and Tiger's not himself either.'

'Just fill in what needs to be done for the time being, Leo, regardless of who "should" be doing what. That's what's needed right now.' Zane glanced back in the direction of the man still busy shifting crates, not having broken a sweat. 'As for Colt, he's Tiger's brother, so give him the benefit of the doubt. 'He's a bit of a loose cannon, but that's handy to have and Tiger's assured me he'll keep his brother in line.'

*Providing he's not AWOL*, Leo thought, but said nothing.

Zane got to his feet. He wasn't having the best of mornings. Erin muddying the waters about Sofia and now Leo playing his face? 'I need to inform the packers to expect runners before schedule today and then I'm going to check on the Starbright. Let me know if there are any more problems. And this time, do it before I need to ask!'

As he went through the door, Zane glanced at his ringing mobile and frowned. 'Hello? Solenzo? Yes, she's... What? When?'

Zane strode past Colt, giving him a small nod of acknowledgment. He'd have stopped to speak to the man but was fully centred on what Mr Solenzo relayed. 'Tiger refused point blank to follow your instructions? Right, well, no... If you thought it best Alyson was sectioned, I don't understand why he thought otherwise.'

Making his way through the canning works, Zane continued to listen to Solenzo's rant, not noticing Colt's attention on him.

# FIFTEEN

SAM CRUNCHED the awkwardly positioned gear stick for the fourth time in as many minutes.

He was used to his brand-new BMW three litre auto. And very nice it was too. His Z3 was hot off the production line because he'd had his name down for one since he'd read about the prestige make's most powerful convertible yet. In Oxford green metallic it didn't just look the business, it had poke like shit off a shovel, whereas this strange contraption was supposed to be supercharged and so fast for its time it was a feat in itself. But how the bloody hell was it supposed to be driven?

Sam stared at the inset dials in the metal plate of the Bentley's dashboard. Some he could work out, like R.P.M. and M.P.H., but as for most of the others, he hadn't got a clue. His beamer did all sorts of things without him even knowing about it. *Including changing gear...*

The steering wheel of this bloody thing was the size of a bus and the suspension felt like square tyres driving over rocks. The only good thing was the leather seat.

Sam glanced up at a particularly ominous cloud in the distance. If it rained, he hadn't a clue how to get the roof cover unfolded from the back, let alone how to put it into position.

Marco would go spare if this thing's interior got soaked. And no doubt so would Delgado, especially as Marco reckoned the man would be prepared to part with at least a couple of million for it.

Sam grinned. An extra two million plus in his pocket wouldn't go amiss. Neither would meeting Delgado.

Reaching the address in Kensington, Sam felt an unfamiliar flutter of nerves. He'd hobnobbed with all sorts of well-known characters and celebrities over the years, so why was he so nervous about meeting Diego Delgado?

He knew why. Because Delgado was dangerous – the equivalent of a world-famous serial killer with a collection of a million other nutters working for him, prepared to kill by a mere click of the man's fingers. He was possibly the most infamous, richest and notorious of the criminal underworld. And this was his house... *One of them, anyway...*

Pulling up outside the imposing property, Sam saw two figures moving down the path. One of them an obviously pregnant woman; the other a huge man, who had to be Delgado.

Sam's pulse thundered in his temples so much he stupidly allowed his concentration to wander. Failing to pay attention to the swinging of the huge steering wheel, he scuffed the green-spoked tyres against the kerb. *Fuck*!

Cringing, he was sure he'd lost three inches in height and prayed neither Delgado or his wife noticed his faux pas.

Fumbling with the ignition key to shut the engine down, Sam then fought with the door handle, desperate to remember how to open the bloody thing.

'Oh darling! Just look at it!' Sofia squealed. 'Isn't it beautiful!'

Sam knew he was gawping as this vision of gorgeousness who'd come within six inches of him to splay her hands over the Bentley's bonnet. He didn't think he'd ever seen such a stunning beauty in his life. Her raven hair tumbled to her waist and even her distended belly didn't distract from the exquisite perfection of her face.

*Jesus. No wonder Delgado had staked his claim on this one.*

Horribly aware that Delgado was standing next to the example of female wonderment, the look on his face not exactly what Sam would class as welcoming, he realised that it may be beneficial to drag his jaw up from the floor and quit ogling the man's wife. Instead, he scrabbled from the car and extended his hand in Diego's direction. 'It takes me a while to work out how to open the door. Ha ha. This motor's a bit different to my BMW. Ha ha ha.'

Diego ignored Sam's outstretched hand and stared coolly at him like he'd just been released from an adult daycare centre. Sam wished he hadn't used wit as his introductory sentence. He had to get a grip and stop acting like a starstruck groupie.

Keeping his well-practiced smile in place, he continued. 'Mr Delgado? Very nice to meet you. She's lovely, isn't she?'

Belatedly realising that his words could be taken the wrong way, Sam laughed again, equally as strained and loud as the last time. 'The Bentley, I mean. She's a lovely motor. A joy to drive!' *No, it wasn't. It was horrible!* 'A fantastic choice of car, sir. You'll enjoy taking to the road in this.'

'I have no wish to drive it,' Diego said, his grey eyes steely. 'It is what my wife wants.'

'Oh! I... Erm…'

'Why do people assume cars are for men?' Sofia eyed Sam with open displeasure. 'The Bentley is for *me*.' She limply held her hand towards Sam as an afterthought. 'Sofia - Sofia Delgado.'

'Very pleased to meet you, madam.' Sam stared at Sofia's hand. *What did he do with it? Shake it or kiss it?* As he went to take it, she moved it back to her side. He wanted to stamp his feet in frustration. He'd never get invited to one of their gatherings at this rate. All of these years he'd waited for this moment, yet he was screwing it up. *Press on and rectify the mess.*

'Erm, so Mr and Mrs Delgado...' He felt his smile slipping. '…what do you think of the car, then? You're more than welcome to take it for a test drive.'

'I should expect so, Mr...?'

'Whittaker. Sam Whittaker,' Sam blathered. 'I own Whittaker Inc on Canary Wharf. You may have heard of me and I...'

'How much do you want for parting with your car, Mr Whittaker?'

'Oh... Erm…' Sam wracked his brain. *Marco said it was worth at least two mill, so what should he add on top?*

'What does it matter what it costs, Diego?' Sofia trilled. 'I want it. I don't need to test drive it. I love it!'

Regaining his confidence, Sam met eyes with Diego. 'Four million,' he said, his mouth moving of its own accord. If Diego's wife was desperate for the car, the man would pay. There was no flinch about the over-inflated price either. Not even a hint.

*This was promising.*

Diego peered into the car. 'The paperwork?'

'It's in the glove box, sir. Everything's in order and I...'

'Yes, yes.' Diego pulled a chequebook from the inside pocket of his immaculate suit jacket.

Sam frowned. *A cheque?*

'Is a cheque a problem, Mr Whittaker?' Diego's eyes drilled into Sam's. 'You surely do not expect cash?'

'No, no! Of course not!' Sam laughed again, inwardly cringing. *What was he doing?* It wasn't like someone like Delgado would write a cheque that bounced. He instead focused on the words, *'Four million pounds only'*, that Diego wrote with a gold fountain pen whilst leaning on the Bentley's bonnet. He also hoped he wasn't salivating when Diego scrawled his signature.

This car alone had pulled back a large part of the original outlay he'd paid Marco for those cars and he still had the rest of the motors to shift yet. *This was good.*

'Keys?'

Remembering Marco's clear instructions, Sam's world

suddenly came crashing down. 'Erm… would delivery next week be suitable? Or the week after, if next week is awkward?' *Marco had said next week, so either would be okay, surely?*

Diego's brows furrowed. 'What are you talking about?' He waved the cheque in Sam's face. 'The car is here now. This is the full payment.'

'It's just that I'm awaiting delivery of two tyres. As soon as they're fitted, I'll bring the car back to you immediately.'

Sofia's heart skipped a beat. *Next week?* Marco's instructions were to ensure Diego bought the car. Next week or worse, the week after? No way! She wasn't waiting that long to be rid of her husband.

She should have got the finer details about what Marco planned. She glanced around, unsure when the 'act' would happen. Maybe this Whittaker person would dispatch Diego? She surreptitiously weighed him up. He didn't look the type, but that meant nothing.

It was irrelevant. Marco said to ensure Diego bought the car and that had to happen. 'I want the car now!' Sofia cried, her red lips pouting. 'I'm *not* waiting until next week!'

'Mrs Delgado.' Sam's voice was sickly smooth. 'I wouldn't expect you to take receipt of this beautiful car without new tyres. They've been specially imported and...'

'I. Want. The. Car!' Sofia's eyes were hard, unmoving. She clutched Diego's arm. 'Darling, tell him you'll arrange for tyres yourself.' She glanced at the Bentley's wheels. 'They look fine to me, anyway.' *Like tyres - round.*

Sam began to sense a problem. He could hardly stand on the pavement arguing, but Marco said... 'I really must insist the tyres are replaced. I'd be doing you a disservice if I allowed y…'

'We're taking the car *today*, Whittaker. Right now!' Diego's expression made it clear there was no room for manoeuvre. He snatched the keys from Sam's fingers and folding the cheque in two, tucked in into Sam's top pocket. Nodding abruptly, he turned on his heels and walked towards his house with Sofia attached to him like a limpet.

Left standing on the pavement, Sam glanced up and down the road, looking for what he had no idea. *Shit*. Marco would not be happy about this. And in all honesty, neither was he. Not a word about invitations or anything. Still, he thought triumphantly, four million for an hour's work wasn't to be sniffed at. And it wasn't difficult to get a taxi.

• • • •

'THE GIRL'S MAD,' Colt said, Lyndon's latest hypocrisy boiling his blood. Pulling the burner phone away from his ear, he stared at it with his one good eye. 'Can you hear me? Yes, I said she's mad. No, that's all I know. Yeah, I heard your brother on the phone to Sollento someone or other.' His massive shoulders shrugged. 'Oh right – Solenzo – yeah, that could have been it. Anyway, apparently he told Lyndon that bird of his needed sectioning, but he fucking refused. Yeah, Tiger… Yeah, I know. Okay.' Colt spat the words so violently, he showered himself with saliva through the gaps of his missing teeth, sure his face would fold in two.

He'd never get used to calling his brother by anything other than his *real* name. This 'Tiger' bullshit was a joke - applied to give the man kudos – hinting that he was a ferocious animal, not to be messed with.

Was it fuck! Lyndon Shoreham was a spineless, lying, bullshitting piece of crap who did everything to make things easier for himself.

His brother's attempt at reinventing himself in no way absolved the bastard from the choices he'd made. Refusing for his own bird to be sent down the same path he'd chosen for their mother didn't relinquish the original crime. For fuck's sake! The only reason Lyndon didn't want his chick banged up in a secure facility was because he wouldn't have a shag on tap, not because of what he'd actioned before.

What Colt had attempted to pin on Lyndon before to get him back may have failed, but not this time.

Realising his hands were shaking and had curled into fists threatening to crush the phone, Colt exhaled slowly, reminding himself he was still connected on the line to the man who had given him an opportunity for retribution. And as much as Colt disliked Marco Morelli, if it hadn't been for *him*, he wouldn't be out at all. 'Yeah, I know,' he muttered, listening to Marco's analysis. 'But as he said, she's leaving shortly, so maybe he changed his mind? Yeah, I'm aiming to do something... When? Tonight? Yeah... Oh, but...'

Colt stared at the phone again. The cheeky cunt had cut him off! What call could Marco have coming in that was more important than speaking to *him*? The fucker had asked him to dig on that Alyson bird – and he had. Albeit this new information had landed at his feet by luck alone, he'd got more dirt on the slag.

Colt sneered. Luck or not, now he knew for definite that Lyndon was *exactly* the same. So, what was the common denominator? That everyone around Lyndon Shoreham got bunged in the loony bin?

What made this Alyson chick so special if the same hadn't happened to her? *Yet...*

But there was a good way to see *exactly* how thin a tightrope this chick was on. And with that, how long Lyndon would stabilise it before it broke and he took the straightforward, less hassle route. Because he would. He always did.

It was a case of *when...*

Colt strode towards the pub, the leather of his coat flapping around his ankles. After a day of lugging shit around, he'd earned a fucking pint. Even Leo watching him like a hawk hadn't fazed him. That knob end had to eat shit and accept he was doing the job.

Okay, so he knew he'd fucked up with the clump he'd given that Jimmy bloke. He'd misjudged it, thinking it would score brownie points to collar a thief, but how was he to know the silly cunt had worked there for years?

No matter. He'd quickly played a different tactic. He'd

gladly done the grunt lifting and he'd done it well. That Leo twat was pleased and was now letting him be, which was what he'd needed.

Colt yanked open the Red Lion's door. Walking to the bar, he ignored the dubious looks of the barman. Maybe this guy would suit? *Perhaps not.* 'Pint of Stella,' he growled, slapping a fiver on the bar.

Waiting for his drink, he glanced around. Having one eye made surveillance trickier these days, but all he needed was to spot a contender who would suffice to remind his brother that he was not untouchable. It didn't matter who it was. If that silly tart of Lyndon's was on the edge, what he had planned would shunt her off the precipice, leaving Lyndon with no alternative but to rethink his decision.

Snatching his pint, Colt necked it in one. He dragged his forearm across his face to remove the froth and centred his focus on a man getting up from a table over the far end.

*Ah, now* that *bloke would do just nicely...*

• • • •

WALKING THROUGH the canning works, Tiger didn't expect to see Leo. 'Everything all right?'

'Yep. Everything's fine.' Leo continued pulling out the last bale of coke ready for the final runner. 'Just one to go now.'

'Oh!' Tiger glanced at his watch. 'I didn't think collections were due until eight? I'd have come in earlier.'

'That's why I'm here,' Leo said. *Because you weren't...* 'The schedule was brought forward.'

Tiger was aware something was needling his friend and comrade but said nothing. There was too much filling his mind to open another can of worms. But he had theories to explain Leo's recent off-hand attitude towards him. It was clear Leo resented that Tiger's mind wasn't fully on the job. *And he'd be right...*

Tiger's distraction came in the shape of Alyson.

Alyson had unearthed memories, as well as glimmering

feelings – both of which he struggled to process. It knocked him off kilter. Leo was spot on. Tiger wasn't himself and he knew it.

But what he *didn't* know was how to reset things and that burden invaded his waking hours. No point mentioning the hours he slept, being as aside from the night of Colt's arrival, his sleep had reverted to being as scant as always. Perhaps worse.

And that was the other thing: his *brother...*

Suddenly realising he hadn't yet seen Colt, dread that there had been further unrest and trouble, bloomed. 'Where's Colt?'

Leo paused, the tightly sealed kilo of cocaine in his hand midway between the shelf and a pizza delivery bag the runners used. He'd wondered how long it would take Tiger to notice the man who he'd promised to watch like a hawk was nowhere to be seen. 'He's gone.'

'Gone?' Tiger's heart lurched. Unable to shake the notion that Colt should not be this side of Broadmoor's fence and that he'd gone AWOL, wasn't something he was willing to uncover just yet. 'Where's he gone?'

Leo shrugged. 'Probably down the pub!'

'I thought he was staying here at all times?'

'Since your talk with him, he hasn't put a foot out of place. Colt finished everything plus more hours ago, so I told him to do what he liked, providing he returned here. It was the same yesterday.'

To say Tiger was uncomfortable about this was an understatement. He preferred knowing exactly where his brother was - especially with him now being in the vicinity. But how could he voice that without revealing details of how dangerous Colt could be? Yet his brother wandering around London free to his own devices underlined that *his* own absence had a knock-on effect. Tiger hadn't honoured his promise to himself of keeping an eye on Colt and had to hope that Leo giving Colt his freedom wouldn't also mean he'd broken his promise to Zane.

'You don't seem too happy?' Leo raised an eyebrow. 'If you'd been here, you could have made the call rather than me.'

Tiger glared at Leo. 'I'm aware I ripped your head off yesterday and I apologise for that, but if you've got something to say, then just fucking say it!'

'As it happens, I have!' Leo folded his arms across his chest. 'As much as I'd lay my life down for you, mate, you're not yourself. I'll ask you again - what the hell is going on?'

Tiger hesitated. He wanted to tell Leo. They went back *years*, but he couldn't. He just *couldn't*. 'It's complicated...' he muttered. 'Nothing to do with anyone else. It's me. But I'm dealing with it.'

*Except he wasn't*. How did he put right something from years ago with no means of achieving it? On top of that, how did he remove the dread that wouldn't shift over Colt's unexpected return? The man was his brother, for God's sake - his blood. Furthermore, how did he prevent the feelings he didn't want for someone who was off limits from continuing?

Right now he felt like a stranger in his own home – an alien of his own making. Purposely avoiding Alyson, he'd kept out of the way all morning by religiously ensuring he was either in his bedroom or bathroom every time he heard her move around. He'd succeeded, short of shouting through her door, saying to call him if she needed to.

There was nothing else to say. He didn't want to see her - *couldn't* see her. She'd only talk about last night, or worse, apologise again for what *he'd* been so thoughtless to say.

He'd let his guard down last night and started opening up. He didn't know how or why he'd done it. It was stupid. All it brought was problems.

So, no - he didn't want to see her. Or look at her. It ran the risk of making him...

He shook his head to jolt the thoughts out of prime position. If Alyson was within reaching distance, it would be harder to keep control. And like last night, without even realising it until it was too late, he'd lost his iron grip on control.

If the same thing happened on *this* one, then he'd kiss her.

Out of all of the things he'd done his life; all of the things he'd faced and the things he still no doubt would *yet* face, that was one thing which scared him.

Kissing Alyson Read would be the beginning of the end on so many levels. None of which he wanted to experience.

Tiger didn't know how to deal with any of this, but he'd have to sort it out and do so quickly. He looked at Leo. 'Yeah, so like I said. I'm dealing with it.'

Leo frowned. 'I hope so, mate. I really do.'

Tiger nodded tersely, then turned away. *So did he...*

# SIXTEEN

KEEPING A DECENT DISTANCE, despite his big size and noticeable features, Colt hadn't lost the ability to remain unnoticed as he followed the man back from the Red Lion.

Apart from stopping to buy chips, the bloke hadn't sidetracked off anywhere else. This was good because Colt had lost count of the hours in the past spent on someone's tail before getting chance to strike and that this dickhead still had his chips wrapped and untouched leaned towards him taking them home.

But if he decided to eat them elsewhere, such as a girlfriend's, Colt could be hanging around for hours. And he didn't have hours. No doubt that fucking Hitler, Leo Holland, would be on his case the moment he was a second later than the set 'curfew' of 10 p.m.

*What was this? Prison?*

Colt chuckled at that thought. There was no curfew where he'd been. Why bother? Locked up all but 24/7 with a bunch of raving psychos there was no need. Still, thanks to Marco and a dimwit psychologist, that was no longer an issue.

Besides, he thought, continuing after the target, it was unlikely this loser had a girlfriend. And as luck would have it, it looked like the guy was heading a stone's throw away from

Lyndon's place. The place where he should already be, rather than the shitpit factory. Still, that would soon change when his dear brother showed his true colours.

Sliding into a shop doorway barely big enough to house his bulk, Colt paused, waiting. *What the bloody hell was this geezer doing?*

With his good eye, he peered around the edge of the inset entrance, seeing the man stop to rummage in his pocket. The guy was so pissed, Colt was surprised he could *find* his pocket, let alone get anything out of it!

His adrenaline thrummed along his veins as the man tugged keys from his jeans along with a dirty tissue.

Almost mirroring the target, Colt patted the deep pocket of his coat and his anticipation grew. *How he'd missed this.*

Unsure how he'd achieve what was needed but confident that he'd do it come what may, Colt slipped from the doorway and closed in on the man who had resumed walking.

One bonus Colt had with speccing out tasks was that he *didn't*. Brazen to the core, no matter day or night, possible repercussions or witnesses - *none* of those factors influenced whether something was feasible or not. He centred solely on what was needed. Working on the fly, he ironed out blips as they appeared. It was the way he'd always done it and it served him well.

With speed that contradicted his size, Colt darted after the target into an alleyway leading to a block of flats. Before the man even got chance to see who wore the heavy boots thundering after him, he was kicked to the floor.

The man's head hit the deck with a sickening crack, the packet of chips flying through the air to explode on the concrete of the gloomy passageway.

'What the fuck?' the man yelled, his head spinning from the impact. He blinked, trying to focus on the lumbering giant looming over him which blocked out most of the dim illumination from the ancient lights spaced along the alley walls. 'Who the hell are you?'

Colt didn't feel the need to answer that with words. Not wishing to give his target the opportunity to squeal and draw attention to anyone passing the alley mouth, he slammed his size twelve down on the man's chest.

Letting out a gasp as the air expelled from his lungs, the man's terrified eyes bulged. 'I don't have nothing! I... What do you want?'

'Nothing,' Colt sneered. 'I want nothing...'

The man blinked, struggling to pull air into his crushed chest and winced as the pain from his head made itself known. 'I ain't done nothing. I ain't...' The words tailed off as Colt pulled out the sword concealed in the specially built pocket in the lining of his long coat. 'NO! You can't do...'

The man's frantic bleating turned into a strange gargling noise as Colt plunged the sword's blade into the man's throat at an angle that drove deep. He smiled, the feel of this something he would never tire off.

He waited, almost in a blissful trance as the blood flowed, deepening in colour and then turning frothy as the target made a final effort to cling onto a life that had fully deserted him.

Now all that was left to do was work out how to shift this random cunt into position without anyone batting an eyelid in the still light of the evening.

• • • •

OPENING THE DOOR, Marco wore a suitably pleased grin. 'Come in, come in!' He strutted up the reception hallway expecting Sam to follow. 'Good idea to come around rather than go into details over the blower. You haven't left the car on the road, have you? Some pricks can't gauge kerbs around here and I don't want it damaged.'

'It's not outside.' Sam stared at the back of Marco's head as he followed him into the drawing room. *He didn't want to talk about kerbs...*

Luckily, Delgado hadn't appeared to have noticed his error when parking, but whether Marco would be okay about the car already being in Delgado hands was different. Surely it wasn't a big deal? Marco said it was imperative Delgado purchased that car so...

'That you're here shows me Delgado bought the Bentley.' Marco swept his arm in the direction of a wingback chair opposite the Chesterfield sofa he sat himself in. 'What date and time next week have you arranged for it to be delivered?'

He tingled with anticipation. Delgado would receive more than the car with the delivery and that time was almost here. A mere matter of days and his life would become everything it should have always been.

Marco clapped his hands together, amused at Sam's flinch but then realised the man hadn't answered his question. He didn't look too comfortable either. 'Delgado does want the car, doesn't he?' *It was unlikely Sofia's influence on her husband had deteriorated, so what the hell was Whittaker's problem?*

'Oh, yes, he wanted the car,' Sam said, knowing he could no longer delay the inevitable. 'It was for his wife and she *really* wanted it.' Remembering Sofia's stunning looks, the colour rose in his cheeks. 'Actually, she was insistent,' he added. 'Although I can understand Diego Delgado wanting to please her. *Any* man would want to please her! She's a fine-looking woman and...'

'Your opinion of Sofia Delgado is irrelevant!' Marco snapped. *No one got to voice opinions about his Sofia.* 'For the second time, what have you arranged regarding delivery?'

'That's the thing,' Sam muttered. 'The woman was most insistent and... well... I mean, it hardly matters, does it? You said Delgado must buy the car and he has.' He smiled brightly. *It was fine.* He'd done what Marco wanted, plus he had a cheque for four million in his pocket, which was a touch. He was about to embellish how pleased Sofia was with the Bentley, when out of nowhere the air flew from his lungs.

'You let Delgado keep hold of the fucking Bentley?' Marco's fingers crushed Sam's neck, embedding him into the chair. 'You left it with him?' *He couldn't believe this.* 'Did I not make myself clear that it had to be next week?'

Sam's hands clawed around the crushing grip of his throat, the pressure in his eyeballs immense. *What the hell was going on?* 'MMMPFH!'

Through his fury, Sam's bulging eyes and rapidly reddening face came into focus, making Marco remember this man wasn't one of his. He wasn't part of a firm – Whittaker was a yuppie prick, not a face and unless he killed the cunt, he'd go to the police. Then things really would be fucked.

Marco's eyes narrowed. He couldn't kill Whittaker. Not yet. But thanks to this imbecile, the plans would now have to change. *Fuck.*

Resentfully releasing his grip, Marco smoothed Sam's suit jacket down. 'Sorry about that. I overreact sometimes,' he said, the urge to stab the useless bastard in the face so strong he could taste it.

Containing his shock, Sam wiped his streaming eyes. 'H-He bought the car like you wanted. He wouldn't entertain me taking it away. I-I had no choice.'

'It's fine.' Marco lied, pulling a tight smile into place. 'I just get stressed over fine details, that's all. I'm thinking of you and don't want Diego Delgado coming back, saying the tyres were bald. That would ruin your reputation.'

*What was Sofia playing at? He'd told her what needed to happen, hadn't he?*

Marco frowned, unable to recall whether he'd informed Sofia of the exact details or not. And if he hadn't...

But now what? He'd already paid Shoreham half the fucking wedge for the next part of his job and at this precise moment, thanks to this bloody idiot here, there was no job to do!

He had to rethink. And quickly. *Bollocks!*

Marco's eyes swivelled back to Sam, the man's unnerved expression underlining there was further arselicking to do if he wanted to avoid this moron running to the boys in blue - after he changed his shitty pants, that was.

'As said...' Marco jerked his head towards Sam's neck, red welts in the shape of fingers bright against the white of the shirt. 'Sorry about your neck. I act without thinking sometimes. You see, people I usually deal with are different and I keep forgetting you're not one of us.'

*Hardly*. Whittaker wouldn't last two minutes in his world, which is why it made it all the more galling having to be nice to the prat. Apologising twice was even more insulting, but this was the *last* time. Once this balls-up was rectified and Delgado out of the picture, Sam Whittaker was fucking well joining the bastard.

'Anyway, no harm done.' Marco's smile was fashioned from concrete. 'Out of interest, how much did you get for the Bentley? I hope Delgado paid you the full two mill?' *Greedy twat that Whittaker was, he'd probably doubled the price.*

Sam decided it was best to forget Marco's lapse in behaviour towards him. 'Yes, Diego Delgado paid up in full,' he smiled. 'I think his wife would have had something to say if he hadn't!' *Paying up in full wasn't a lie. He didn't need to go into details of the exact amount.* 'I still don't understand why you wanted him to buy the car so much.'

Marco pushed the irritation surging back to the surface away. 'That, Whittaker...' He tapped his nose, '...is something you don't need to know. All you need to know is that you'll benefit from the deal if it works.'

And 'if' it worked wasn't an option. It *would* work. But regardless of whether Sofia had spoilt the way he'd planned things to go was neither here nor there. Being as Whittaker hadn't followed his instructions to the 'nth' degree, any benefit the prick had been set to receive was now null and void. Not that there ever had been anything in the bag for this cunt.

Marco smiled slyly. He'd let the twat discover that at his leisure.

# SEVENTEEN

NOT SURE WHAT TO DO with herself, Alyson moved from the lounge into the kitchen and then back again. She'd peered from the window about three hundred times this last hour alone, looking for what, she wasn't sure.

Her lips pursed. *Who was she trying to kid?* She was looking to see if there was any sign of Tiger, even though she knew in her heart of hearts that he wouldn't be back until way past the time she'd gone to bed.

What was she supposed to do? Jump from her bed and rush into the hallway and collar him so that he had no choice but to speak to her and demand to know whether he was purposely ignoring her?

Because since last night it felt Tiger had been avoiding her like the plague.

She frowned. What was the point of asking that when she already knew the answer? Of *course* he was avoiding her. And if she was honest, she was glad because if he'd sought her out or she hadn't remained in her room until she knew for definite he'd left for the day, then she'd have been in the position she'd dreaded. Being in his presence now was too awkward.

Something had shifted between them. Something

substantial and Alyson didn't know what to do about it.

Half the night she'd lain awake with the thoughts of what she would have done if he'd kissed her and what thinking that she'd *wanted* him to kiss her, said about her.

The same rush of loathing she felt for herself over being unable to disassociate her body's reaction to what Marco had done with any similar feeling, returned.

What Marco did was wrong - she knew that. *Everyone* said the same, so in that case, how could experiencing the strange physical effect by even thinking of Tiger be okay?

*Did that not make her a slut? Wanton? Mentally ill? What?*

Alyson sighed. She didn't know and that was the problem. Her sole experience amounted to Marco which didn't give adequate knowledge or a healthy viewpoint on anything. How could she differentiate between what was good and what was wrong? What was *normal*?

For the first time in her life, Alyson regretted her unwavering attitude in refuting contact with the opposite sex. All virginial chastity had brought was a warped viewpoint, leaving her with nothing to compare and contrast.

The only experience she'd had, as everyone kept saying, was abuse, so how could she tell the difference?

And what did that say about her that she couldn't?

The burn of frustrated tears grew which Alyson angrily pushed away. Feeling physical pleasure from a man abusing her must signify she was twisted.

Dread pooled. Perhaps that was why Tiger was giving her a wide berth, rather than the possibility of feeling something for her. What would she know? She knew nothing of men and could be reading how Tiger looked at her last night completely wrong.

He was probably aghast: looking at her with pity, horror and revulsion. *The crazy girl who'd turned into a slut.*

Shaking her head, Alyson traipsed back into the lounge. She was ridiculous. She didn't know anything one way or the other, so the only way she'd ever get answers was if she grew a backbone and asked Tiger herself.

She jutted her chin out. *She'd do it.* She'd wait up until he got back, however late and ask him. She had nothing to lose.

Alyson swallowed her crawling humiliation. Tiger already knew she was as unexperienced as it got. He also had a good idea what Marco had done during her time spent drugged up in his bed. He knew it *all* so there was little left to be embarrassed about, short of spelling out this humiliation to the man she found so fascinating. But at least she might end up getting more of an idea what was right or wrong.

*But when would Tiger be back?*

Alyson glanced at the clock on the wall. *Just after nine. It would be hours yet.*

She then jumped with a sudden noise from the hall. *Was that the doorbell?* She hadn't heard it ring before, so didn't know what it sounded like, but it must be the doorbell.

She edged from the seat. *Should she answer it?* What if it was the postman? Tiger could have ordered something and it wouldn't be good if a delivery was missed. It might be important.

Alyson chewed her lip.

Wasn't she supposed to remain out of sight? She wasn't stupid enough not to realise that Zane and his men were concerned Marco would retaliate if he knew her whereabouts.

She shuddered. But she couldn't hide away forever either and besides, no one would be crazy enough to come to *Tiger's* door. That's why she'd been placed here and not in a hotel.

Edging towards the hallway, Alyson peered around the doorjamb to see if Tiger's keys were on the hook. If he'd left them behind by accident it could be *him* at the door.

She peered up the hallway, not seeing a figure through the small panel of frosted glass.

She sighed loudly. It must have been the postman. He'd left a parcel on the doorstep and, not wishing to cast aspersions or anything, this flat wasn't in the best of neighbourhoods. The front door was on a long walkway to many other flats, giving an opportunist wandering past chance to steal it.

She'd better fetch it in.

*It wouldn't be risky to quickly open the door and grab it, surely?*

Having made her decision, Alyson strode determinedly to the front door and turned the Yale knob. Giving the stiff door a tug, it opened.

*No one there, as suspected.*

Her eyes tracked to the step. *What on earth was that?*

A huge bag with handles - the sort she'd seen used for garden waste, sat a couple of feet away. *What had Tiger ordered which would come in that? Maybe it was a mistake?*

Gingerly stepping through the doorway onto the walkway in her fluffy pink slippers, Alyson glanced inside the bag and frowned. *There was something in there, but it was covered with... with what?*

Reaching forward, she eyed the bin bag tucked neatly around the contents inside. Whatever it was, it was bulky. It must weigh a ton!

Worrying if she'd manage dragging this huge thing inside, Alyson pulled aside the black bin liner. If it was something that wouldn't get ruined if it rained, she'd leave it for Tiger to do when he got b…

Screaming, Alyson let the bin bag fall from her fingers and stumbled back against the doorjamb. Vomit surged up her throat, her hand flying to her mouth. 'Oh my God!'

Sucking in air, little specks of dancing lights flashed behind her eyes.

Daring to glance around, she willed her legs to move. Should whoever left this be still around here she wouldn't chance her luck by looking too hard. Crashing back inside the flat, she slammed the door, her fumbling fingers scrabbling to pull the deadlock into place.

Sweat poured down her forehead, her nausea stronger than ever and on jelly legs, she staggered into the lounge to look for the phone Tiger had left her.

He'd said to call if she needed him and Alyson needed him

now like never before.

• • • •

DIEGO WATCHED SOFIA recline in her usual position on the sofa whilst flicking through a copy of *Vogue* magazine. 'Are you not taking that car for a drive?'

'Not just yet.' Sofia didn't glance up. She wanted Diego to go away. Her mobile had just vibrated against her skin in its hiding place and she needed to see what the message said.

It had to be from Marco. She hadn't had chance to text to let him know she'd succeeded and the Bentley was now safely outside their house. He must know though because that man who delivered the car would give Marco an update. It was likely that guy was in the know about everything, wasn't it?

Regardless, she had to know one way or the other, yet Diego was hanging around like the proverbial bad smell and had been ever since buying that crummy car. And no, she wasn't driving it. She wouldn't be seen dead in such an unfashionable claptrap of a thing. Who did Diego think she was?

'Being as you were so insistent on having that Bentley, I'd have thought you'd be desperate to drive it.' Diego eyed his wife curiously. 'I hope you haven't changed your mind. I've just paid four million for it.'

Sofia finally looked up. 'To be honest, I'm not sure how enamoured I am with the colour. I didn't realise it was *green*. I would have preferred pink. Even red, at a push.' She struggled to shift her ungainly shape from the sofa, resenting every further second this thing was strapped to her. When would Marco rid her of this man? She done above and beyond her duty.

Diego rushed to help his wife up, but Sofia batted his hand away. 'Leave it, I'm fine! As for the car, has it not crossed your mind that because of *this…*' she pointed to her belly, 'I'd struggle to fit behind the wheel? Think about that before giving me a hard time about spending money!'

Utter rubbish, but it would shut him up. Any mention of the

'baby' and Diego folded like a pack of cards. She glared at him again for good measure. 'I'm going for a lie down. I'm tired.'

Flouncing from the room, Sofia barely cleared the doorway before shoving her hand down her top to retrieve her mobile. Slipping into another reception room and glanced behind to make sure the coast was clear before bringing the screen to life.

*She was right - a text from Marco.*

What are you playing at? I said next week to accept the car. You've screwed everything up.

Sofia stumbled against the door. *Screwed everything up? He said to ensure Diego bought it!*

The burn of tears stirred as she stared at the screen, unable to take her focus from it. The only person in this whole life with the power to crush her was Marco. He was *everything*. What anyone else thought, said or did meant nothing - only Marco. It had only ever been *him*.

And that he was angry with her or disappointed, ripped her heart clean out.

With shaking fingers, Sofia tapped out a response.

I don't understand. You said he must buy it.

Sofia dabbed the wetness in her eyes away. *If Marco left her...*

He wouldn't, would he? He *couldn't*. He'd promised she'd be free from Diego.

But she was still here. And so was *Diego*.

Staring at the mobile, Sofia opened the incoming text before it had chance to vibrate its arrival.

I said NEXT WEEK. Not today. No choice but plans have to change now.

Sofia's heart lurched. *What did he mean by 'plans'? Killing*

*Diego or being with her?*

Almost at the point of hyperventilating, she sank into a chair, the phone still in her hand. Life with Diego in it but not Marco, was pointless.

• • • •

'SORRY FOR DESCENDING unannounced.' Diego strutted into Erin's office at the Starbright. 'I was told I'd find Zane here, so...'

Erin smiled. This time, Diego's presence was nowhere near as unnerving as it was at dinner last night. She gestured to a chair. 'Zane's here, but he's in a meeting with the head guard. I'll call and tell him you're here.'

As Erin reached for the phone, Diego placed his hand on hers. 'I have no wish to interrupt him. I'm happy to wait if that won't disturb you?'

'Not at all.' Erin nodded to the small selection of spirits on the side. 'Can I get you a drink?'

'I'm fine, thank you. Don't trouble yourself.' Diego looked around the office and nodded in approval. 'I'm impressed with the setup you have here. It was good of Zane to do this. Offering hope to the less fortunate isn't something I'd have thought to do.' He smiled wryly. 'I guess that doesn't say much for me!

'I don't think many people would invest in this unless they had a personal reason,' Erin said. 'Zane had that. We all did.' She hesitated, unsure whether she was being too liberal. Zane might not want the issue about Marco and Hazel being discussed.

Almost reading her mind, Diego smiled. 'By that, I presume you refer to how that piece of shit treated his wife? Zane did mention it.'

Erin blinked, surprised with the venom behind Diego's reference to Marco. 'It seems you hate Marco almost as much as we do!'

The base fury in Diego's grey eyes faded. Leaning back in his chair, he rested one ankle over his knee and studied Erin with interest. 'I like you. You say it how it is. Many don't.'

Erin laughed. 'Some say it's a bad trait of mine, but it's just the way I am.' She studied Diego equally. Something was needling him and her first instinct was to ask if he was all right, but she refrained. She hardly knew the man and infringing on his personal life by asking questions was not something that would help Zane. She'd stick to safe subjects. Or rather what 'should' be safe. 'How is Sofia? She was feeling unwell last night? I hope she's recovered now.'

A dark flash passed across Diego's face. 'Sofia's fine. She usually is...' And after seeing her with that phone earlier for the second time, he believed she might be *more* than fine – with someone else… Remembering himself, he then smiled widely. 'Actually, that's why I'm here. Sofia was upset that she had to cut the dinner short and insisted I come to invite you both over again tonight.'

Erin hoped her horror was hidden well. The last thing she wanted was to spend another evening with that woman. 'That's very kind, but Sofia doesn't need to feel bad. I'm not sure whether we have plans for tonight so...'

'Dinner sounds good to me!' Striding into the office, Zane shook Diego's hand. 'We have no plans so we'd love to come, wouldn't we, Erin?'

Erin avoided giving Zane a death stare. 'Yes, of course. That would be wonderful.'

'Although shouldn't you come to *ours* this time?' Zane suggested.

Erin almost choked. *Could this get any worse?*

'No, come to ours. Sofia enjoys bossing caterers around.' Diego stood up. 'I'll see you both later. Shall we say six?'

Arranging another dinner at such short notice would pull Sofia off centre. That way, he'd have chance to study her in more detail.

Last night, she'd let her usually well-kept guard down on more than one occasion with her snide comments. He needed to know what the spoilt bitch was up to and what was going on in that plastic head of hers. She was becoming slack and that was unfortunate for *her* because he'd find out *exactly* what her game was before long.

As he left the Starbright Centre, Diego's face slipped into a furious scowl. That phone he'd seen her using twice now wasn't one he'd bought her. There was usually only one reason why someone had a second phone – especially one kept hidden…

She was texting someone, he'd seen that much. If the bitch was conducting an affair behind his back, then he'd rip the man she was messing with to pieces. The minute the child was born, Sofia would be leaving. Diego had already decided that would happen a long time ago and now it was guaranteed.

Diego strutted towards his brand-new Maserati Spyder, a horrible thought occurring. If Sofia was having an affair, was the child even *his*? That thought terrified him to the point of feeling physically ill.

He'd find out. If that child wasn't his heir, then Sofia would die too.

# EIGHTEEN

TIGER RETURNED TO HIS FLAT as quickly as he could, convinced Alyson was mistaken. Loping up the stairs to the first floor, he moved along the walkway, seeing the bag on his doorstep was indeed big enough to hold a body and realised she wasn't exaggerating. *Jesus Christ!*

Without a second thought, he glanced over his shoulder, then hefted the heavy bag into his hallway out of sight of prying eyes.

'Oh my God!' Alyson shrieked. 'You brought it in here?'

Tiger saw Alyson's fear; her face so pale she resembled a ghost. He tugged at the bin bag, revealing the corpse of a man with a deep wound in his throat - the obvious cause of death.

'Tiger! Alyson screamed hysterically. 'Who is it? What does it mean?'

'I don't know,' Tiger muttered. *And he didn't*. He searched his memory for a hint of having seen the man before, linking him to a particular person, place or time, but there was nothing. This guy, whoever he was, was a complete stranger.

Shaking, Alyson pressed herself face-first against the wall with her forearm over her eyes. 'I can't... I can't look at it. Oh God, he's dead. Dead!'

'Keep your voice down,' Tiger growled, then softened his tone. 'I know it's upsetting for you, but...'

'Who left him here?' Alyson wailed. 'Who would do such a thing?'

'I don't know,' Tiger repeated. But realistically, *plenty* of people would do such a thing. It wasn't commonplace but not entirely rare either in his world. Still, he didn't have the answers to Alyson's questions.

'W-What will you do? I was going to call the police, but I called you first,' Alyson said. 'I'll get the phone now so you can call them. I can't face it. I...'

'NO!' Tiger barked. 'No police. I'll deal with it.'

Alyson flinched at the urgency of Tiger's tone. *He'd done this kind of thing before, hadn't he?*

Daring to turn slightly from the wall, Alyson inched her forearm away from her eyes only to see Tiger moving the body around in the bag. All thoughts of the conversation she'd planned to have with him evaporating. Vomit threatened once more.

She watched as Tiger hunched over the body, his wide back thankfully blocking out the sight of that... that *thing* inside. Even after a million years she didn't think she'd rid her mind of the image of the gaping mouth, staring eyes and the slash in his throat... The blood...

Standing up, Tiger moved up the hallway and stood under the light to read the contents of the note in his hand.

'Is that a *message*?' Alyson screamed. 'A note was in with the body? What does it...?' She stopped abruptly from the look Tiger shot at her and waited. He'd tell her what it said, wouldn't he? But did she want to know?

Tiger squinted at the note. It was crumpled and smeared with blood, but just about readable. There was no question this hadn't accompanied the body. The small pocketknife pinning it to the flesh of the corpse's back underlined that as non-negotiable.

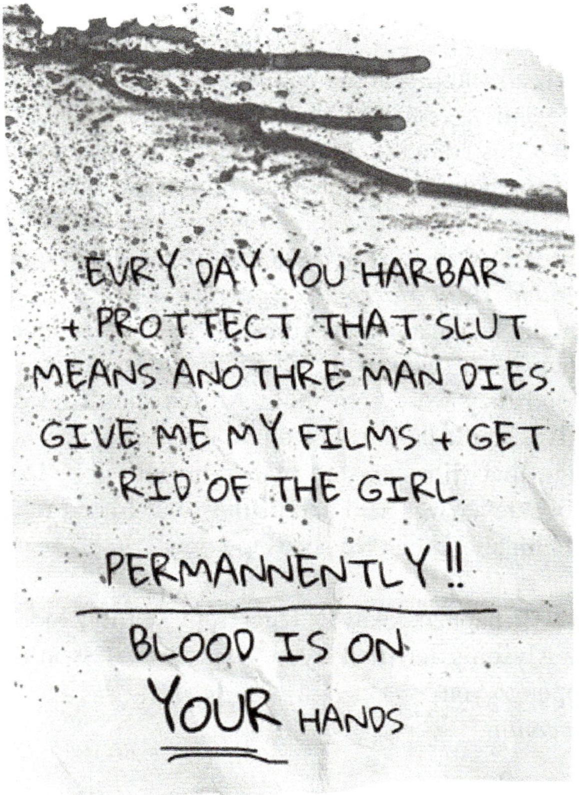


*What the actual fuck? How had his address been discovered? He guarded that knowledge closely.* Tiger's face morphed into a ferocious grimace.

Alyson edged closer and peered around Tiger to read the note. Her face paled further. 'Is... is that about *me*? A slut?' Suddenly the penny dropped. Her legs began to shake. 'It's Marco, isn't it? He knows I'm here and... Oh my God! This poor man died because of me! Marco wants me dead, doesn't he!'

Tiger caught Alyson as her legs gave way, the note

fluttering to the floor. He held her trembling body tightly to his chest.

'Tell me! It *is* Marco, isn't it? And what he said...' Alyson burst into tears.

'It's Marco all right, yeah,' Tiger snarled, knowing it was the only viable option, even though he'd always been so careful over concealing this address. 'And he still can't fucking spell! But don't take any notice about what that note says.' Putting his finger under Alyson's chin, he forced her to look up at him. 'You're no slut, do you hear me? It's just words. He wants to scare you.' *And he'd kill Marco twice over for it.*

'But what did he mean about "films"?' Alyson hiccupped.

Tiger knew very well what films that dirty cunt was referring to and they were something Alyson didn't need to know about. If he could help it, he wouldn't make her deal with the knowledge that films existed of her having sex. 'Don't worry about whatever was said about films, but I need to call Zane and tell him about this. He needs to know.'

'But...'

Nothing will happen, okay?' Tiger said sternly, looking straight into Alyson's terrified eyes. 'I promise I won't let anything happen to you.'

*And he meant it.*

• • • •

TRYING HIS BEST to ignore the furious glares Erin was still sending him for agreeing to a second dinner at Diego's, Zane grabbed his ringing mobile. *Ah, Tiger - he had a bone to pick with him.*

'I'm glad you've called,' Zane said. 'Why have I received a call from Solenzo this morning, telling me you refused to act on his instructions to have the girl staying at your place sectioned?' He frowned, sick of not being kept in the loop. 'No, you listen to *me*! If Solenzo advised she should be sent to a proper unit, then that's what should happen. It's not up to you to make decisions like that. Since when are you a qualified psychia… You *what*?'

On instinct, Zane's eyes flipped to Erin. He bristled with rage. He'd hoped for more breathing space before Erin had to go back into lockdown for her own and his child's safety, but it seemed the time had come. 'I'll come now. No, no. I'll sort it.'

Erin listened to the exchange and saw the concern on Zane's face. All annoyance about another evening in the company of Sofia Delgado evaporated. Getting up from her desk, she quickly moved to his side. 'What's happened? What's this about Alyson being sectioned? Why didn't Tiger mention this or…'

'That's the least of our concerns,' Zane frowned. 'A body's been dumped on his doorstep.'

'*What*?' Erin cried, the way Zane looked at her, she knew exactly what this meant. 'You think it's Marco?'

'I *know* it's Marco.' Zane sighed. 'A note was attached to the body - embedded in the back with a fucking knife!'

Erin's hand flew to her mouth, her other hand instinctively falling to her belly. 'It's started then?'

Zane nodded, his eyes fierce as he grabbed his phone. 'I need to up the protection.'

'I'm not being locked behind closed doors again. I've only just got back to normal!' Erin folded her arms defensively. 'I'm not doing it, Zane.'

'You'll do whatever it takes to keep you safe.' Zane's eyes dropped to Erin's stomach. 'Both of you.' He then enveloped her in his arms. 'But this time, I'll assign someone to you 24/7, rather than keeping you behind closed doors. Marco could get to you anywhere it seems, so this is the best way.'

Erin pressed against Zane's chest, relieved she wouldn't need to be a prisoner again, but she was still concerned. 'How did Marco get Tiger's address? He keeps that under wraps, like we all do.'

'It's easy enough if someone is determined.'

'Who... who was the body?'

'I don't know but I'm finding out and you're coming with

me.' Zane brought his mobile to life. 'First though, I'm bringing someone in to remain with Alyson. I need Tiger on duty, not in his flat.' He dialled Leo to send Colt. He could guard Alyson from now on. He'd given the man this job on the notion that his psycho tendencies would work well in dealing with Marco. Being as Marco had made a beeline for Alyson as Target Number One rather than anyone else, there stood a good chance he'd attempt something again. But now Colt would be waiting.

A smile flickered on Zane's lips. He knew Colt would come in useful - just perhaps not quite so quickly.

Breaking from Zane's embrace to put her shoes on, Erin felt a twinge of guilt at her relief both for not being put under house arrest, but also that the upcoming dinner at the Delgados would have to be postponed.

• • • •

DOING A LINE OF COKE on the table, Marco couldn't be in a better mood. Okay, he was still pissed off that between them, Whittaker and Sofia had forced him to rethink how to off Delgado, but in Sofia's case, some of that might be on *him*...

He'd accepted that he hadn't specified to Sofia that the car couldn't be delivered until next week - not that he'd admit it. It never hurt to keep women on their toes. But as for Whittaker - he knew *exactly* what he was supposed to do, yet he'd done the opposite like the pointless bastard he was.

However, Marco's foul mood was placated somewhat by the hurried phone call he'd just received from Colt. That bloke definitely wasn't as brain dead as his misshapen head led people to believe.

Putting the wind up Zane and his band of merry idiots by making out a dumped body was courtesy of *him* was classic. That Zane had taken the bait like a good little boy and brought Colt in to guard Tiger's flat and that cunt bitch, Alyson, was better than Marco could have foreseen. It would take Colt seconds to despatch the silly tart and with her, everything she knew and might stupidly choose to use against him at some point. It was now merely a question of working out how to do that whilst remaining in situ, plus being available to remove Mr Diego Delgado.

Licking his finger, Marco dabbed the few remaining specks of cocaine off the table and rubbed them on his gums. *Waste not, want not.*

He shouldn't have been quite so hard on Sofia on that text. He'd send another message later after getting a few more quid's worth out of the hooker he'd booked to pass a bit of time.

Gazing salaciously at the naked blonde on the bed, Marco grabbed one of her shapely ankles and pulled her towards him. He was readying himself for round two when the doorbell sounded. 'For fuck's sake,' he muttered, deciding he should invest in a full-time housekeeper, a butler or someone. *He* shouldn't be answering the bloody door. Especially not now Zane was undoubtedly further primed to kill him.

Snatching a pistol from the bedside table, Marco ignored the blonde's look of horror and made his way to the video intercom. 'Oh, you've got to be kidding,' he hissed, seeing the unmistakable figure of Sofia Delgado on the doorstep. *Was she fucking insane?* He'd told her last time she'd risked everything coming here not to do it again, yet here she was.

Leaving the room, Marco then doubled back and jerked his head at the blonde. 'Fuck off out of here and make it pronto. Someone's turned up that I don't want seeing you.' It wasn't so much that Sofia could give him grief over this bird - he wasn't starving himself in the bedroom department, but he couldn't risk the blonde tart playing her face about seeing *Sofia*. That could really screw things up.

# NINETEEN

'I HAD TO COME.' Sofia pushed past Marco into his Mayfair hallway. 'I won't let you desert me.'

'You shouldn't be here.' Marco gave the street outside a quick glance over before shutting the door. As usual, his first thoughts were for himself. *Had Delgado found out? If so, she'd led him straight here!* 'What if you've been followed or...'

'Diego arranged another dinner for your brother and his bitch girlfriend, but Zane just called with an unexpected issue and has cancelled, thank God, so Diego's busy with other stuff.

At this, Marco forgot Sofia had just arrived unannounced and a smile inched onto his face. It sounded like Colt's 'present' had been found and Zane was running around like a cunt trying to organise his men, giving Colt the opportunity to rid the world of that stupid Alyson bitch. The sooner than happened, meant one less thing delaying Marco's rise to the top of the pile. Things were good. Things were *perfect.*

'Is something amusing?' Sofia shrieked. 'I'm here and upset because you want to call things off between us, yet all you can do is grin?' She pummelled Marco's bare chest. 'How could you do this to me? I believed you! Believed everything you said! I thought we were the same, you and me.'

Sofia's tear-stained face suddenly registered in Marco's brain. 'Erm, what's happened?'

'I won't let you leave me!' Sofia splayed her hands against Marco's chest. 'You said it was me and you against the world! You gave me your promise we'd be together, but you've...'

'Hey, no! What's this about?' Marco pulled Sofia against him, the fake pregnancy that he'd seen for the first time, a turn-on. Soon it would be a real baby in there - *his*. 'We *will* be together! Why would you think otherwise?' *There was nothing Marco wanted more, unless Delgado's empire counted?*

'You said plans had changed,' Sofia snivelled, her glossy lips pouting. 'What else can that mean? And being as you're so clearly bothered - no one followed me here, so you're safe!'

'I don't care about that,' Marco lied. Of *course* he cared about that. Nothing could risk his ascension to full power. *Nothing*. 'When I said plans, I meant how Diego will be removed now that…'

'But I thought he was being killed today!' Sofia cried. 'Why didn't it happen? You should have told me if…' Tailing off, the other things Marco said seeped into her frantic mind and her panic subsided. 'You… you're not leaving me? Our promise still stands?'

'Of course it does.' Marco stroked Sofia's hair, coming to the conclusion that he quite liked this vulnerable side of her. It made him feel important. 'You and me, babe, yeah?'

Sofia physically sagged, her relief stronger than she believed possible. 'Then when will you...' Suddenly her smooth forehead twitched. 'Who the hell is that?'

With a sinking feeling, Marco followed Sofia's icy glare over his shoulder to the other end of the hallway and realised the blonde hadn't quite left. *Shit!*

Sofia's face hardened, finally noticing Marco's semi-naked form. 'You... You've been screwing a hooker?'

'Hey!' The blonde stepped forward. 'I'm no hooker! Hookers are cheap, I'm not! I'm an escort and a fucking expensive one, I'll have you know.' Her eyes narrowed. 'Wait a minute… Aren't you that drug baron's wife?' She looked Sofia up and down, focusing on her belly. 'I've seen you in photos from fashion shows.' Her lips curled into a sneer. 'Well, well, well… I wonder if your husband knows you're here? Now, what's his name again? Let me think…'

Marco flinched at the veiled threat. Making a mental note not to book this particular whore again, he prepared himself to fork out a hefty wedge to keep the slut quiet when Sofia suddenly lurched forward catching him unawares.

In a weird slow motion, he watched her grab a vase from a pedestal in the hallway and bring it down on the blonde's head with an almighty crash.

'WHOA!' Marco stared in dismay at the smashed pieces of china on the floor. *Shit the bed!* That was a fucking Ming vase. *And it wasn't his*. He'd get sued by the Arab he rented this bloody place off if he wasn't careful. The blackmail against that bastard only stretched so far. 'Sofia! What the fuck are you doing?'

He was too late to stop Sofia from jumping astride the blonde on the marble floor as she snatched up a piece of smashed porcelain and drove it into the woman's face.

'You bitch!' Sofia screamed, her strap-on pregnancy skewing to one side in the scuffle. 'You slept with my man. I'll kill you! Marco is *mine*!' She slashed repeatedly at the woman's face leaving the skin hanging in strips.

As the blonde woman shrieked with enough volume to drown out a rave, Sofia panted as she about removing every trace of anything Marco might find attractive from this creature. No one would come between her and the man she loved. *No one!* 'Did you hear me? Marco is MINE!' she repeated, a fake nail snapping as she wedged it into the woman's eyeball.

Snapping from his trance, Marco hoisted Sofia off the unconscious woman. 'Jesus, Sof, you've made a right mess of her!' But it was such a turn-on. Sofia was crazy for him - that was now proven in more ways than one. He eyed the ruined face of the blonde on the floor with disinterest. She was alive, but out for the count.

He sighed. For fuck's sake! It wasn't as simple as paying her off now.

Gripping Sofia's shoulders as she flailed like a wildcat, still determined to continue slashing at the woman, Marco knew he had to finish it. 'STAY STILL!'

Something in Marco's tone made Sofia freeze like the pause button had been pressed. Gasping, she stared at the woman on the floor, her ample chest heaving with the prior exertion.

Marco rolled up his sleeves, then pulled out the gun he'd taken from the bedside table. He knelt down next to the trashed face of the woman and glanced up at Sofia, his erection growing. Grateful for the silencer attached to the pistol, he delivered a single bullet to the smashed-up woman's temple.

Sofia flinched with the muffled shot but said nothing. She then calmly stepped her Louboutins out of the path of the rapidly spreading pool of blood blooming around the woman's head turning the white marble floor into a ruby puddle.

Tossing the gun onto an occasional table, a lazy smile spread over Marco's face. He'd have to arrange to get this shit cleaned up. He might even have to do it himself for once, God forbid. But right now, there was only one thing that could take precedence.

Stepping over the growing puddle, he yanked open the buttons of Sofia's shirt dress, then ripped off the pregnancy prothesis. Pushing her onto the sweeping staircase, he pulled his engorged cock from his lounge pants and pushed into her. 'I love jealous women,' he growled. 'And because it's you, I love it even more.'

Sofia mewled with pleasure, her hips bucking to meet each of Marco's thrusts. They were made for each other and nothing could stop that. This man loved her as much as she loved him, and that was all that ever had or would, matter.

• • • •

FROM HER BEDROOM, Alyson peered through the crack in

the door, her panic growing. 'Oh, my God!' She turned to Erin. 'Who is *that*?'

Erin smiled weakly. 'I'm not sure.' She'd promised to calm Alyson down whilst the men dealt with the unknown body. She hadn't expected it to be easy - far from it. Alyson was beside herself and the man Zane had brought in to replace Tiger was what most would politely put as 'unnerving', which wasn't helping. It would have been useful if she'd been filled in with exactly who he was beforehand. She knew most of Zane's men, if only by face, but she definitely hadn't seen *this* guy before. Being unable to give Alyson a reasonable answer about the bloke wasn't making the girl feel any more at ease.

She placed her hand reassuringly on Alyson's arm and attempted to steer her away from the door. 'All I know that he's one of Zane's men. It's been arranged to have someone here with you all the time now for safety.'

Alyson's eyes widened. 'But Tiger? What about Tiger? I don't want anyone else here. I...'

'Ah! Alyson!' As the cleanup team finished their work, Zane spotted Alyson peeping through the crack of her bedroom door and beckoned her out.

Alyson looked to Erin, her hands clinging to the door jamb. 'I-I don't want to go out there. Th-that man… he...'

'It will be fine,' Erin coaxed. 'I'll be with you.'

'But...'

Before Alyson could procrastinate further, Zane strode over and pushed the door open. 'Alyson, meet Colt. He's here to look after you from now on.'

Alyson stared at the grotesque and terrifying looking man standing in the hallway. 'No… I…'

'You could have got someone a bit less scary! Who the hell is he?' Erin hissed under her breath into Zane's ear. 'And what's with the coat?'

Alyson's eyes darted from Colt to Tiger. 'I thought Tiger was... Where is Tiger going?'

'I ain't going nowhere,' Tiger growled, his anger palpable.

Erin frowned. *What was going on here? Tiger looked furious.*

'Don't worry, Tiger will still be around. It's his flat after all,' Zane said. 'But what with the threat now so blatant, constant protection must be in place.' He smiled reassuringly at Alyson, then glanced at Erin, knowing she'd demand an explanation for what he was about to say next. What with everything going on he hadn't got around to mentioning that he'd employed a man fresh out of Broadmoor, nor who he was. 'As I was saying, Colt here will be guarding you, Alyson, okay?'

Alyson remained clinging to Erin, her eyes searching for Tiger's attention, but he was locked in a silent world of his own making. 'Well... I... I was kind of used to Tiger and...'

Zane placed his hand on Alyson's shoulder, dismayed as she flinched and moved away. 'Tiger's one of my most experienced men regarding the current crisis. Colt has had no dealings with Marco, that's why I need Tiger on duty at the firm, rather than here. Things are especially frantic as an important delivery is coming ahead of schedule, but your safety is paramount, Alyson, as is everyone's, but I need the right people in the right places, as I'm sure you understand. Colt is excellent at what he does and I'm confident he'll guard you as fiercely as his brother has.'

'*Brother*?' Erin knew she should have stopped her mouth from falling open at this revelation, but it did nonetheless. Her gaze shifted to Tiger, whose face was so stone-like it looked like it may shatter. She then turned to the man with the strange face and even stranger head. 'You're...'

'Lyndon's brother, yes.' Colt moved forward to shake Erin's hand, but promptly backtracked with the warning look from Zane.

'Lyndon is Tiger's real name,' Zane explained, watching a nerve ticking in Tiger's jaw, knowing he was discussing the man like he wasn't here.

'Sorry, sorry!' Colt grinned bashfully, exposing the

remains of his teeth whilst mentally pigeonholing the reference to the early 'important' delivery. Marco would be interested to know of that, but he'd keep up the act. 'I keep forgetting you lot call him "Tiger".' *The animal his brother was not. Oh, this was such fun.* He swivelled his huge head around to look at Alyson, further pleased to see her shrink in front of him. 'Ah, I get it. This shit with Marco that everyone's been going on about - it's you, ain't it? You're the one in those films that Leo mentioned and...'

'F-Films?' Alyson stuttered. *That was the second reference to films.*

'A quick word?' Zane pulled Colt into what he presumed was Tiger's bedroom. 'I've already told you that nothing about any of that is to be mentioned to the girl!' he hissed.

'Shit! Sorry!' Colt blurted, trying his best to look contrite. 'I forgot. I thought... Look, it won't happen again.'

*Oh, yes it would.* Things like this would happen a *lot* and judging by what he'd seen in this simpering jelly-like bird that Marco somehow classed as a threat, it wouldn't take long to inch her over the edge of her own mind. This part of his immense payout would be a piece of piss. And getting one – no, *several* things over his lying twat of a brother was the icing on the fucking cake!

He raised his head, adopting a patriotic, unbreakable military look. 'I won't let you down.'

'I hope not,' Zane muttered. It was awkward enough having to arrange the removal of an unknown body and shelve Delgado's dinner invitation, but Colt dropping things in the shit and Tiger acting like the taste had been slapped out of his mouth was something he could do without. And his misery didn't stop there because now he faced a round of fucks from Erin for keeping her in the dark.

Jesus, he'd be glad when this day was over.

# TWENTY

ZANE SWIRLED REMNANTS of whisky around the cheap cup, then tipped into his mouth. He'd put away a fair few during the long hours of the night spent back at the canning works, they all had, but there was no risk of the spirit dulling their minds or reactions. Everyone was far too wired. Him, especially.

More to the point, he was exhausted to the extent that the ability to sleep had passed the point of no return and it would be impossible, even if there was a chance.

*Which there wasn't...*

He dragged his hand over the stubble on his jaw in frustration. No matter how many times he, Leo and Tiger had been over who the mystery man in the bag on Tiger's doorstep was, no one could make the connection why this particular person was chosen. No one recognised the guy - and very rarely, if ever, was a face forgotten.

It was confusing. Even though it was obvious who the message came from, without that all-important link they were getting nowhere in deciphering the full meaning.

Zane shook his head in irritation. That man must signify something. Why the fuck else would he be used? It was a question which had been asked many times during the night, but one which still evaded delivering a useful answer.

Leo folded his arms and leant against the rickety table, partly to keep himself upright such was his level of fatigue. 'Perhaps there is no meaning – just a base threat? It could be that simple. We might be looking for something that doesn't exist.' He looked from Zane to Tiger, not missing Tiger's lack of contribution. He'd added little, if anything, to the night's discussion. 'Marco could be playing with us - making us presume there's a link to something important, when there isn't. None of us know that man, we've deduced that much, right?'

Seeing Zane nod, Leo waited for Tiger's response but received none. 'Tiger? You don't know him?' The slight shake of Tiger's head was the most interaction he'd offered so far. 'So, let's take it the bloke is a random,' Leo continued. 'It's feasible.'

'It's unlike Marco, though,' Zane frowned. 'All of his messages, whatever form they come in, have hidden links. There's always a connection somewhere. It's how he works, so there *must* be something - we just haven't found it. And amongst other things, that's what's worrying me.'

Leo mirrored Zane's frown. It *was* unlike Marco's usual way of doing things, but that didn't mean it wasn't feasible the wanker was leading them up the garden path to waste time. But Leo also realised Zane's additional concerns weren't helping his concentration. His thick fingers knitted together. 'Look, I know I didn't think much of Colt at first.' He shot a cursory glance at Tiger. 'No offence, mate, but I didn't. But now I believe that Erin and Alyson are safe with him stationed here at the flat.'

Zane agreed with Leo. Colt was more than capable. Despite this, he'd hated leaving without Erin safely in his sights, however it was riskier moving the women here, even if Alyson was at the top of Marco's hit list.

He sighed heavily. It was a toss-up where the target would be next – Tiger's, here, or even the penthouse. Any of those places could be in Marco's sights. Nowhere was safe for his woman and unborn child. But with Tiger's psycho of a brother in situ, even minus Zane's presence, Erin and Alyson were safer there than anywhere else. That was all he could trust on and hoped to fuck he was right.

When push came to shove, Marco was fuelled by greed, so if Tiger's flat wasn't targeted again, the next most likely place would be here at the canning works. It presently housed millions of pounds worth of gear and would soon be a lot more than that, plus earlier than expected, thanks to the message he'd just received, hence them holding the fort. But then, with the out-of-character nobody delivered to the doorstep, Marco had thrown a curveball which was bothersome.

'How did my address become common knowledge?' Tiger's voice after his prolonged silence took everyone by surprise.

'You must have been followed.' Zane lit up a further cigarette. He'd got through loads during the night. 'We don't know who else Marco has on board and let's face it, we expected him to resurface.' But for that resurfacing to be aimed for Tiger, rather than him was admittedly strange. It was *all* strange.

'Yeah, Marco's had you followed or followed you himself. He may have gone to ground, but none of us believed *completely*, or, like Zane says, permanently.' Leo pointed to Tiger's jacket. 'That note. Let's have another look at it. I reckon I'm right! We've been making it more complex than necessary.'

Tiger dutifully fished the note accompanying the body from his pocket and chucked it on the table, along with the cheap pocketknife it had been attached with.

Picking up the scrap of paper, Zane's tired eyes focused on the scrawled writing. 'It looks like Marco's writing, just messier.'

'Probably pissed and coked up,' Leo sniped.

'But why Tiger?' Zane frowned. 'Listen, it says, "Every day you harbour and protect sluts means another man dies". Every day "*you*"… - that's the bit I don't get.'

'It's not Tiger though, is it?' Leo pressed. 'Think about it. In this note, Marco's rattling on about his films. He's losing money on those whilst they're not in his possession. You notice the note says "another man"... Like I said, the victim was a random. I reckon a random bloke would have been delivered to *wherever* Alyson was being sheltered. I don't take it as being aimed personally at Tiger.' He shrugged. 'If Alyson was at mine, I'd have received the stiff. Likewise, if she'd been at yours, Zane, a stiff would have turned up there.'

Continuing, Leo shook his head in disgust. 'Marco wants Alyson dead because as long as she breathes, she can dish the dirt on him and he knows it. He wants her gone and his films back in order to make a few quid, the sad fuck.'

Zane nodded. 'Jesus Christ, he really is desperate, ain't he?'

'Of course he is!' Leo laughed acidly. 'The cunt is boracic, with no workforce, no shag all! He wants to make money from his sick-as-fuck films because it's all he's bloody got left.'

'Well, he ain't having them,' Tiger snarled. Snatching up the note and knife, he handed them to Leo to be locked in a cabinet for future reference if required. 'He ain't having those films and neither is he killing Alyson.'

Zane and Leo exchanged glances. 'We weren't suggesting he'd succeed with either of his demands!' Zane eyed Tiger with unease. 'Okay, so look – if our deductions are correct, then we have a decision to make. If Marco's threats are to be believed, we have to expect that while Alyson remains at Tiger's flat, it's likely another victim will show up. Do we let that run, using Alyson's presence as bait and hope Marco runs straight into a waiting Colt or do we move her elsewhere as a safety precaution?' *Because whatever happened, Erin wouldn't be staying there any longer.*

Zane then frowned. But where could Erin go where she would be as protected right now?

'One thing I don't get is the line, "Blood is on your hands". Or am I looking too hard and it's coming across as blood being on Tiger's hands because as far as Marco is concerned, Alyson is in Tiger's flat and under his protection?' Leo mused.

'It's just a reference to where the girl is.' Zane shrugged. 'Tiger, what's your take? Should we leave Alyson at yours as bait so Colt can do the job when the next delivery comes or what?'

'Why ask me?' Tiger snapped. 'I'm no longer even in my own fucking flat, so it makes no odds. Bludgeon Marco to death on my living room carpet if you wish, I don't give a fuck!'

Leo turned to Zane at Tiger's unexpected bitter response, but Zane didn't appear fazed.

'Right, that's settled!' Zane said. 'We'll wait and see if Marco delivers a second body.'

Glad to have finally got to the bottom of the body dumping and what their next move would be was a relief. Now he'd arrange further protection for Erin and decide how the incoming shipment of coke due from Paraguay earlier than scheduled would be overseen. Because that had to be in place in time, otherwise Diego would go tits!

Talking of which, he also needed to give a proper explanation and apologize for his and Erin's last-minute cancellation for dinner last night – something he should have already done.

• • • •

'ARE YOU LADIES all right in there?' Colt's booming voice vibrated through the bedroom door.

'We're fine, thank you,' Erin replied. She waited until she heard the clumping footsteps of Colt's massive boots retreat down the hallway before she turned to Alyson crushed up into the far corner of the bed. If it were possible for her to bury herself into the wall to extend the distance between herself and the door, then she would have done so.

Alyson was a nervous wreck and the long conversation Erin found herself in during the night about Skye had been uncomfortable and painful for them both. Erin was reluctant to tell Alyson exactly what her alleged 'friend' had *really* been like, but remaining devastated over Skye's death, unaware of the true depth of her deception would have been detrimental in the long run. Alyson had the right to know the truth of what Skye was *really* like in order to fully heal. And now she did.

At least the poor girl could no longer cling to the disbelief surrounding that vindictive little bitch's actions. But despite the uncomfortable conversation and the added stress Colt Shoreham's presence inflicted, Erin had to admit that during the hours he'd spent here, the man had done nothing to put her on alert.

Leaving them in peace, he'd kept a dignified distance down the opposite end of the hallway, only occasionally venturing along to gently tap on the bedroom door to make sure they were all right.

Maybe an occasional reminder not to judge a book by its cover was fitting?

'I know he looks scary,' Erin whispered, 'but Colt seems okay and doing what he's supposed to be.'

Alyson nodded. She knew this was correct, but it didn't stop dread invading her veins with a freezing liquid that travelled slowly but consistently along every pathway of her body, spreading as far as the ends of each hair on my head and had done so since first laying eyes on the man.

This persistent feeling, no matter how much she'd tried to convince herself it was unjustified, showed no signs of abating.

'Besides, he's Tiger's brother,' Erin continued, that fact still sending shockwaves through her system. 'And on that basis alone he must be okay.' She eyed Alyson curiously. 'But let's be honest - you'd prefer Tiger here with you, wouldn't you?'

'Definitely!' Alyson blurted. 'Tiger's nice. He's been lovely to me and...' Stopping abruptly, she blushed and turned away from Erin's inquisitive gaze. 'What I mean is that I'd got used to him and... well, yes, I suppose I'd feel better with him still being here.'

'I can understand that.' Erin smiled, for the first time wondering whether Alyson might have fashioned some kind of crush on Tiger. It seemed an unlikely pairing, but then so were her and Zane. Not to mention the strange dynamics between Diego and Sofia Delgado...

She quickly pushed how that woman made her feel, away. That she'd been able to get out of the dinner last night was a godsend, albeit at an unfortunate cost. But in the weird life she resided in, bonuses came in odd shapes and sizes.

Concentrating back on Alyson, Erin decided not to push further about Tiger. It was none of her business. Besides, the girl had been through enough, without being interrogated over something so futile. At least all of this helped to keep her mind off the lurking and obvious fact that Marco had resurfaced. Or what it meant going forward... Still, she'd known the future road would be the opposite of smooth.

Erin studied Alyson, the girl's eyes wide and her countenance like that of a startled deer. She really was terrified, but then, how could she not be? Yet now she seemed more agitated than ever. 'What's up?'

'I...' Alyson squirmed in the tiny corner of the bed she'd shoehorned herself into. 'I just really need the loo.'

Erin couldn't help but laugh. 'Off you go then!'

Alyson's eyes darted to the door. 'But... but *he's* out there...'

'And?' Erin chuckled. 'Colt's here to protect us, remember? And let's face it, one sight of him would scare even the most terrifying intruder!' *Even Marco...*

Injecting a touch of humour into the situation was the best thing to do. 'Look, the toilet's only down the corridor, but I'll come with you if you like?'

Alyson shook her head. 'No, you're right - I'm being daft.' As she made her way to the door, her legs felt like jelly. She spoke like her fear was under control, but in reality, it was getting worse and however much she wanted to shake off the irrational feeling of panic, its claws remained embedded too deep to shift.

Taking a deep breath, she turned the doorknob, stepped out

into the dark hallway and skittered along the carpet in the direction of the bathroom.

# Twenty One

COLT REMAINED STATIONARY within the dark shadows in the kitchen listening to Alyson Read use the toilet next door. He knew it was her, rather than Erin because the second he'd heard the bedroom door open, he'd waited just the right amount of time before sticking his head around the doorjamb so his one good eye succeeded in clocking the back of the pathetic bitch rushing into the bathroom.

But by Christ, how long was she going to be? The dirty bitch must have stored up her piss for *days* to warrant it going on this fucking long!

But what did time matter when it brought him closer to destroying something so important to his piece of shit brother?

And regardless of Lyndon's denial of this mealy-mouthed little cow being a big part of his life, Colt reckoned he'd hit the nail on the head. Alyson was his brother's piece of fluff. She *had* to be because he'd seen the rage in Lyndon's face when Big-Boss-Zane instructed him to go to the canning works.

A wide smile cracked Colt's ravaged face. What a fitting irony – Lyndon taking up residence in the line of duty at that crummy shithole factory, whilst *he* moved into the flat where he'd planned on being stationed all along. And, with the unexpected bonus of being left to look after Lyndon's bird – the bird he would slowly destroy.

Colt had to physically hold his breath not to laugh. It would ruin his cover for taking the slag by surprise the second she got her arse off the shitter. And that wouldn't do because he had to break that little girl and send Lyndon-'Tiger'-Shoreham into a tailspin.

How Colt would have loved to witness his brother's face when he'd found the body he'd left. And the note... That's if he had found it yet?

Maybe the note was still undiscovered on the body and the fun of that part was still to come?

By the time he'd finished, Lyndon would be a gibbering mess, questioning his own fucking sanity, let alone anyone else's.

But Marco believing Colt had optioned to get into this fucking flat with the sole purpose of acting as his braindead mole, showed the cunt was utterly clueless. Marco could instruct him to kill Alyson Read being as she was such a 'threat' all he liked. He could demand what the fuck he wanted for his money, but all in good time.

Yeah, Colt would kill the slag, but not before attaining *his* objective.

Finally hearing the toilet flush and the water running in the sink, Colt edged into place at the right of the bathroom. Being as this thick bint was stupid enough to shut the bedroom door whilst she came to the bog, the only illumination in the otherwise dark hallway was a faint wisp of light seeping in from the grubby glass panel over the front door.

There was less light than a spluttering candle, but enough to witness the horror on the little tramp's face now he'd started his plan. He glanced towards the living room, seeing the television. *This would be glorious.*

• • • •

SITTING IN THE DARK and overriding the pain of having a

back as stiff as a park bench, Diego remained unmoving in the leather office chair. His gaze fixed on the crack of the door he'd purposely left ajar half an inch, affording him a reflection, courtesy of the polished frontage of his drinks cabinet, of the front door.

*Along with who came through it.*

There was only one person who could come through that door. And every further second which passed before that happened riled him further.

Not that he would give his location away even when it happened because regardless of his burning desire to slam his fist into the beautiful mouth of his lying wife, he would not lay a finger on her. He wouldn't harm a woman. He wasn't raised that way.

Especially not with his child growing inside her.

That's if it was his, which judging by how things were unfolding, seemed more unlikely every day.

That it had reached 6 AM and Sofia still had not returned home showed she believed Diego to be out on unexpected business. After telling her exactly that last night, it was obvious she thought he hadn't a clue about her lies and the shit she was pulling. And that assumption was incredibly silly.

Hearing the sound of the key in the lock, the telltale trembling of adrenaline buzzed along Diego's forearms down to the tips of his fingers. It took an immense amount of control not to jump from his seat, yank the door open to pull Sofia into the reception hallway and push his unborn child from her body. That way, he wouldn't have the irritation of waiting a further three months before throwing the lying whore out of his home, his will and his fucking life.

But he wouldn't. He *couldn't*. The child was the sole reason Sofia continued sharing the same air as him on this earthly plane.

But as for not hurting a woman, he would exercise his right to change his mind about that if the DNA test scheduled to run the second the child was born showed that baby contained anything other than *his* genes.

Diego's jaw tightened as Sofia slipped soundlessly through the large front door, taking the effort to close it behind her equally as quietly. Holding his breath, he eyed her tangled hair - the opposite of the styled-to-perfection look his wife usually exhibited.

He gritted his teeth. 'Wife' being a loose term...

A bit like Sofia herself...

*And was the front of her dress torn?*

Diego refrained from bursting out of his office to inspect the state of Sofia in more detail and instead turned away, his temples pounding from the heightening rage swirling in his head. No guesses what she'd been doing, the dirty, two-faced, vindictive, fucking whore.

But he'd wait.

His eyes tracked to Sofia's bump. He'd have to wait. But that some other man - some cunt had been sticking his cock into something that belonged to *him*, inches away from his child growing inside that treacherous bitch's womb, made Diego sick to the core.

Leaving Sofia to tiptoe up the staircase, no doubt to creep into bed pretending she'd been there all night, Diego fumed with impotent rage. Yes, he'd wait to deal with his errant cow of a wife, but there were no time constraints as to when he could kill whoever she was screwing.

But until he knew exactly who that person was, there were other things to deal with. And now Sofia was back, he'd get on with them.

Snatching his jacket off the hook, Diego stormed from his home office and out of the front door, not bothering with the silence his wife had delivered. Let her sweat with the possibility he'd witnessed her snake-like return to the marital home. He didn't give a fuck.

But what Diego *did* give a fuck about was being taken for a mug. Zane Morelli not showing up for dinner with a pathetic, vague voicemail was bad enough but finding out he'd failed to pass on the news that the Paraguay shipment dates had changed was worse. And Diego was in just the mood to take his anger out on someone. If his ability to judge characters had become skewed and Zane was yet another in the list of people thinking they could treat him like a cunt, then…

Firing the throaty engine of his Maserati, Diego screeched up the drive, blood thundering in his ears.

• • • •

FEELING SLIGHTLY CALMER, Alyson came to the conclusion that Erin was right. She had nothing to be frightened about - well, not exactly true - she had *plenty* to be frightened about. *Terrified about, actually.*

That she'd seen with her own eyes a written threat from the man who had removed the chance of her ever having a normal life put the fear of God into her. It scared her to the core of her marrow. Knowing that Marco - even thinking of his name freaked her out - wanted to kill her, chilled her to the bone.

Alyson guessed from what she'd seen, and with how Zane, Erin and Tiger reacted, that Marco was an extremely dangerous person and being guarded 24/7 only underlined that. Marco saw her as a threat - believing she would speak out against him for... for what he'd done. She realised that now. But she wouldn't. She wouldn't say a word. Not only was she too scared, but it wouldn't give her back what he'd taken, would it?

But she was lucky in a way. She had to remember that Zane and his men were protecting her. Imagine if they hadn't stepped in and taken her from that penthouse?

Alyson shuddered. If they hadn't, she'd already be dead…

Giving a slight shake of her head to shift the snowballing terror, Alyson took a deep breath. *Remember what they taught you in the clinic*, she told herself. *Accept, deal and heal. It was the only way forward.*

Now she knew the truth about Skye, albeit something which hurt terribly and she still struggled to comprehend, Alyson was grateful to Erin for levelling with her.

It would be okay. These people really did seem to care about her and for that, she should be thankful and keep her head.

Stopping being silly over Colt's presence was a start.

She'd never wanted to be the sort to judge on appearance. It was wrong, wasn't it? But how she wished it was Tiger here, instead of his brother.

A timid smile played on Alyson's lips as she opened the bathroom door. Even thinking of Tiger made her feel fuzzy inside. Was it so wrong, so implausible to hope that maybe one day - even sometime soon she might find there could be something more between them?

She'd got a glimpse the other night that there was perhaps something between them.

Alyson stepped into the dark hallway, wishing she'd put the light on. Her nerves jangled but she quickly pushed the feeling away. Maybe when this present situation calmed down, she and Tiger might...

'Get in here!'

Alyson didn't have chance to scream before a huge hand clapped over her mouth and her feet left the floor. Frozen with terror, she was lifted like a rag doll, her reeling senses scrambling to make sense of what was happening. She stared wide-eyed at who the arms propelling her into the living room belonged to, although she already knew.

*Colt.*

Instinct finally overtook Alyson's paralysed reactions and she kicked out. One foot made a connection, but it had no effect on the man spiriting her away into another room. Before she could make sense of the flashing images in the darkness, her feet were back on the floor and her body shoved up against the wall.

Gasping as the air rushed from her lungs, she cowered at the terrifying face of Colt inches from hers.

*Was he going to do what Marco did? Or worse? Oh God. No, please, no.*

Colt's hand remained over Alyson's mouth and she could

barely breathe. She willed Erin to pick up on her thoughts and come out of the bedroom to save her.

But what would Erin do against this monster of a man?

Tiger could though. If Tiger came back, then he'd make sure that...

Listen to me, you scanky cunt whore,' Colt hissed. 'You need to sort your crazy head out and accept that you will soon die. Do you realise that? Do you understand?'

Colt's voice was low and barely audible, but Alyson heard every word like it was screamed through a loudhailer. Petrified, yet unable to speak, she wanted to move her eyes away from his, but she couldn't. The one crazed normal eye contrasted sharply with the dead blank fake one. It was horrible.

Vomit surged. *Oh God, God, God.*

Suddenly, as quickly as she'd been held against the wall, Alyson found her feet leaving the floor once more. Flailing in the air, she was turned around and held from behind by Colt's huge shovel-like hands.

*He was holding her rigid. What would he...?*

It was then the flickering images on the television focused in Alyson's brain.

She blinked and sucked in a horrified breath, not processing that Colt's hand was no longer over her mouth. She could scream and shout for help, but instead, all she could see was the vivid and undeniable moving images of herself on the screen.

*She was naked, with Marco on top of her...*

The film then changed to a close-up of Marco's penis slamming into her most intimate regions, leaving blood to trickle onto the white sheet beneath. The camera angle moved once again to travel slowly up Alyson's body, revealing the lips of a blonde woman hungrily sucking Alyson's nipples. The camera finally moved again - this time to Alyson's face, her expression that of ecstasy.

Alyson's legs buckled underneath her, but Colt had hold of her shoulders. Unable to help it, she let out a loud, anguished moan.

'Bad, ain't it?' Colt growled in Alyson's ear. 'And you loved it, you fucking whore!'

'No...' Alyson whimpered, realisation dawning. *These* were the films referred to beforehand - the films with *her* as the unknowing star. 'NO, NO, NO!'

The room started to spin and somewhere she heard muffled laughter, along with something about being a 'dead fucking whore cunt'.

Rushing into the room, Erin flicked the lounge light on. 'I heard shouti…' Her eyes immediately moved to the television screen. 'What the hell is this?'

'You tell me?' Colt turned to Erin. 'I was in the kitchen getting a drink. You girls were okay the last time I checked, so I thought... Then I heard a noise...' He glanced at Alyson and pulled on an anguished face. 'She was in here and... and this filth was on the screen.'

'No, no,' Alyson whimpered. 'You...'

'Christ! I can't believe my brother's got these. I saw videos on the side earlier, but I didn't think they were.... I had no idea they were *those* videos. I'd have moved them. I...'

'NO!' Alyson waved her arms, pressing herself further against the wall. 'It wasn't... You didn't d...'

'Calm yourself down, sweetheart, please.' Colt pretended to struggle to keep hold of Alyson's shoulders and turned to Erin, his eyes beseeching. 'I've been trying to calm her down but it's difficult, the poor bitch. Jesus, if I'd have known they were in here… And worse, already in the video recorder! God, has my brother no respect?'

Erin watched Alyson flail under Colt's grasp, a strange squeaking noise coming from between her lips.

'I'm so sorry, sweetheart,' Colt said, gently patting Alyson's shoulder. 'I ain't happy with my brother. You shouldn't have had to see that shit. I can't believe he's been watching these!'

Erin stared in horror once again at the film documenting Alyson's graphic ruination and she darted over to pull the plug from the video recorder.

'I'd have done that, but I didn't get chance. I was too late,' Colt added, lowering his head to hiss the words, 'Dead bitch,' into Alyson's ear that only she could hear.

Erin was just about to say something - *anything* to try and make this even a tiny percentage better for Alyson, when the girl suddenly snapped and flew into full bore screaming hysteria.

# Twenty Two

SAM WHITTAKER SAT BACK, sipped at his Perrier water and gazed out across the perfect view over the river. It was a top idea calling a business lunch away from the city. A leisurely drive out to this golf club in Richmond was a welcome distraction from what he'd soon be doing.

It was disappointing that the chance to become better acquainted with Diego Delgado yesterday amounted to so little - like *zero*, but ever resourceful, Sam now had the perfect excuse to get himself back in front of the man.

He patted his blue linen jacket containing the receipt for the Bentley within its envelope. Providing a receipt was good practice, but in his rush to take ownership of the car, Delgado had not received one. What sort of a businessman would that make Sam if he didn't provide an adequate record for the man's accounts? That was presuming Delgado ran accounts for a company doing what *he* dealt in?

Sam shrugged. It made little difference to him, but delivering a receipt to Delgado was a good excuse to go there again. Plus, it was the only thing he could think of.

As his crudité platter with a spring pea and goat's cheese dip was brought to the table by a collection of uniformed waiters, along with the rest of the food, Sam smiled. 'Ah, this looks nice.' He patted his stomach appreciatively. 'I could do with topping up the old tank as I expect it will be a late one tonight.' *Wait for it - this lot would be sure to ask.*

Sam's anticipation heightened. This was the part he loved - seeing the impressed looks on his staff's faces was what it was all about.

Miranda, a trainee in her early twenties pouted. 'Are you not returning with us to London? Are you staying here for the regatta? That's on around now, isn't it?'

'The Regatta happened over a month ago!' Sam rolled his eyes and then paused an acceptable amount of time before responding further in order to heighten the interest. It was a shame this girl wasn't his tasty secretary, but he could hardly justify inviting a *secretary* to a business dinner.

'I take it that we're not invited to wherever you're going?' Rufus raised an eyebrow along with a hint of a smile.

Sam grinned. Rufus was Eton alumni and a similar age to himself. The man was a decent entrepreneur. Obviously, not in the same league as *him*, otherwise Rufus would be running his own firm rather than taking a salary - albeit a good one, from Whittaker Inc.

Sam scraped out the last bit of the dip and finished chewing the last heritage carrot on his platter. 'I've a further appointment with the man I sold the Bentley Blower to. He's asked for my advice on business investments.' He paused to check the interest level around the table. 'What with being foreign, he needs insider knowledge.'

Rufus rolled his eyes. 'Another Arab? They're so bloody demanding!'

Sam joined in the laughter. 'No, he's South American. From Bogotá. That's in Columbia in case you weren't aware…'

'I don't think I know of anyone wealthy from Columbia,' Miranda wittered, inspecting her nails.

'I'd be surprised if you hadn't heard of *this* Columbian!' Seeing the piqued interest in his companion's eyes, Sam leant over the table and lowered his voice. 'It's Diego Delgado. He bought the Bentley for his wife, who, I should add, is simply stunning!'

'Delgado!' Rufus exclaimed. 'You mean, *the* Diego Delgado? The international drug lord?'

'What?' Miranda shrieked. 'Seriously? And you're talking about his wife, Sofia, aren't you? Oh my God! There was an article about her fashion choices in *Tatler* a few months ago. She's soooo amazing!'

Sam puffed his chest out. 'The very same.'

'You're winding us up. Why would Delgado ask *you* for business advice?'

'Connections, Rufus, connections...' Sam tapped the side of his head like it contained a world of secrets. 'This proves that when I say networking is important, it is. And...' He knew he shouldn't add this bit - in fact, he probably shouldn't have said anything at all, but it wasn't like these two would bump into anyone of note. 'Delgado wants my advice because it was suggested by another in my circle...'

'Who?'

'Marco Morelli. I take it you've heard of *him*?' Seeing the amazed nods, Sam continued, his self-importance at an all-time high. 'Delgado and Morelli have a close relationship and want advice on investors for their upcoming new venture.'

'Wow! That's brilliant!' Rufus gushed. 'But aren't they involved in... you know... illegal things? You can't encourage investors on Whittaker Inc's books to buy into that!'

'Do you think I don't know that? It is my company, after all! Anyway, their new venture is nothing like that!' Sam scoffed. 'And before you ask, I can't say what it's about because it's top secret.' *And also because he didn't know himself...*

Which was a good point. If Marco and Diego wanted him to line up investors, the very least he should know was what line of business was involved otherwise how could he select relevant people? He'd ask Diego himself tonight if Marco hadn't made such a song and dance about not mentioning his name. And, Sam thought, getting a sharp reminder of Marco's quick temper, he didn't want to rub anyone up the wrong way. 'Anyway,' he smiled, suddenly eager to get off the subject. 'That's enough about where I'm at. Tell me more about what you two are working on at the moment.'

• • • •

STEPPING OUT OF THE huge shower enclosure of the en-suite bathroom onto marble tiles, Marco wrapped a thick white towel around his waist and admired his physique in the mirror.

For added effect, he flexed his muscles, proudly acknowledging the fine build that most men would give their right arm for, before chuckling at his analogy. If a man gave his right arm, their body wouldn't look anywhere near as bloody good, would it?

Marco raked his fingers through his towel-dried hair and contemplated having another shave. But then again when she'd left during the small hours, Sofia hadn't complained his overnight growth had chafed when his head was between her legs, therefore he'd leave it be for now.

Besides, he'd already done plenty of exercise because on top of the marathon workout with Sofia, he'd dealt with the cleanup alone.

Marco searched his face for new wrinkles as he grimaced over the disposal of that stupid hooker this morning, adamant he'd avoid booking any further sluts from that outfit from now on.

'High class, my arse,' he muttered. Top class birds didn't dish out threats to clients or their client's acquaintances. And now, because of the gob on that stupid tart, she'd be uttering fuck all ever again. It was her own fault.

Marco shrugged his huge shoulders. Still, with Sofia shortly due to be with him full time, he was doubtful whether he'd bother with hookers. That was a concept he'd never thought feasible, but then Sofia was all he'd ever wanted so it was a possibility that she alone would be enough.

*But it never hurt to keep your options open, did it?*

Slicking on deodorant and a dab of aftershave, Marco let his towel fall to the floor. Kicking it to one side, he strutted back into the master bedroom to put on his clothes. The housekeeper would be here shortly and she could sort this mess out.

Downstairs was a different story. The place was now so clean he could eat his fucking tea off the floor!

Yeah, he could have done without the job of ditching the body. Or the mess. But it wasn't like he could call in any cleanup crews he'd used in the past. Too many of those wankers had jumped ship to Zane. And those who hadn't, Marco didn't trust not to.

The only person who could have done the job, other than him, was Colt. Half-Head taking the slack would have been preferable, but the man couldn't exactly leave the place he'd finally got himself in. Being in Tiger's flat was where Colt needed to be.

Marco's face cracked into a smile. He owned Colt Shoreham. How many other people could secure someone's release from Broadmoor?

No one.

*And Colt knew it.*

Grunting, Marco reached to cut a line of cocaine before the old boot housekeeper showed up. Yeah, Colt owed him and owed him plenty. Plus, Colt was fully invested in the cause, therefore the perfect mole. And Marco couldn't be more pleased about that.

Colt was correct - he wasn't stupid and would succeed in removing that possible thorn in his side - Alyson. Colt would devise a way to dispatch her without relinquishing his place too. Being on the inside: both at Tiger's residence and within earshot of Zane's inner circle at the canning works, was perfect.

Doing up the last button on his shirt, Marco snorted the line of coke, enjoying the immediate buzz. Feeling refreshed, rejuvenated and with a spring in his step for the approaching future his life would soon offer, Marco scrolled through his mobile.

Time to give that prick, Whittaker, a call and see how he was doing. After slightly losing his rag at the bloke yesterday, it served well to pretend he gave a toss.

And Sam Whittaker may yet prove useful for one last thing…

• • • •

'I DON'T GIVE A SHIT about excuses, Morelli,' Diego raged, pacing around Zane's small office. 'Are you taking liberties or what's the fucking crack?' Stopping to lean on the desk, he lowered closer, his eyes blazing. 'More like your brother than I believed, yes?'

'Now, wait right there!' Zane bellowed. He'd swallowed Diego bursting into his office with no warning. He'd kept his cool about the man's offhand attitude in front of Tiger and Leo. He even accepted he was out of order for giving Diego vague reasons why he and Erin were unable to make it last night.

However, there was a limit.

'I'll be fucked if I'm sitting here to be accused of being anything like Marco, by you or any fucker, Delgado!' Zane then jerked his head in Leo and Tiger's direction, giving them the nod to leave the room. He waited until the door shut behind them before continuing. 'I appreciate I should have done better than a rushed voicemail about dinner and I also should have informed you that the next delivery schedule had changed, but things happen quickly in this game, as you yourself know,' he seethed. 'So, if your opinion of me has changed, then take your coke, our arrangement and sling your fucking hook out of my goddamn building!'

Diego seethed with rage, his fists balled. 'Maybe I should do just that. You seem more trouble than you're worth and I don't deal with dishonesty.'

'Nor the fuck do I!' Zane countered, standing to square up to Diego. 'But when a body turns up at my man's doorstep with a note attached from my fucking brother, I have to react accordingly and for that, I will not apologise.'

This knowledge made a nerve in Diego's jaw tic but did little to calm his ire. 'Your brother's reappearance was expected and offers no excuse for lack of manners or the risk of losing your concentration.'

'You're right about the lack of manners, but my concentration is not at risk,' Zane spat. 'This is the second time you've questioned my ability, so it's clear you don't trust me. In addition, you're likening me to the piece of shit who shares my name?' He shook his head, his eyes ice cold. 'I thought we'd moved past this stage, but if the friendship I thought we were developing counts for nothing, then it's better to knock things on the head right now and divert the shipment that's due at my factory in two days' time.'

Losing this deal with Delgado was a disaster but reputation could not be thrown away. He'd somehow start afresh elsewhere.

'I don't appreciate not being kept informed,' Diego snapped. 'I expected you at six and...'

'Your insults and anger are centred on me not showing up for a fucking meal? Oh dear! Have I offended Sofia!' Zane barked sarcastically. It was then that he clocked a slight flinch on Diego's face that coincided with the mention of his wife. He shook his head in disbelief at what filtered into his head. 'Jesus Christ. Is the reason for you coming here barking shit and insinuating worse is because, despite what you said, you *do* have an issue with mine and Sofia's past?' Erin's paranoia and jealousy was bad enough, but he wasn't dealing with the same kind of crap from someone he was doing business with. *No fucking way!* 'I told you before and I meant it. I was never interested in Sofia and that still stands.'

Suddenly it was like all the rage leaked from Diego's pores, appearing to lose him inches in height, as well as width. 'I have no issue with your past, aside from that I only wish *you'd* married Sofia. She is no wife to me!'

Zane struggled to comment on that. It was the *last* thing he expected to hear. Instead, he found himself opening the metal filing cabinet and fishing out the whisky bottle, along with two plastic cups.

# Twenty Three

LEO STARED AT Tiger's stony expression and wanted to scream. Not so long ago they'd have been busy discussing what to do about Diego appearing out of the blue and ranting at Zane. Not to mention what it meant. But recently, it felt he was on his own on all sides.

Since Skye's accusations, Alyson coming onto the scene and the arrival of Colt, Tiger had been nothing like his former self and Leo was sick of it. Everyone was preoccupied and acting out of sorts, so where the fuck did that leave him?

'For fuck's sake, mate,' Leo growled. 'Don't you have an opinion? What do you make of Delgado and what he said? If things are going tits up with a huge new shipment about to drop, we kind of need to know about it!' Because the way this was going, he'd be dealing with the fallout on his tod, as well as juggling everything else. Marco's latest ploy with throwing in more complications made it even worse. 'I can't deal with everything, so snap out of whatever's in your head.'

Tiger looked up slowly, his face twisted with anger. 'And what is it in my head that you're so obsessed with referring to?'

'I don't know because you won't tell me!' Leo threw his hands in the air. 'You won't say fuck all, despite it affecting the crew. Just tell me what the hell it is that's happened? It used to be me and you on everything, but now it's...'

'Maybe I just decided it's better to keep shit to myself rather than you lot closing ranks and believing a lying little bitch over me!' Tiger barked.

'Don't start that! We've been through this before!' Leo cried in exasperation. 'You know it wasn't like that and if you felt that way about us all, you wouldn't have agreed to return to the firm.' He gave Tiger a look. 'It's just an excuse. A total, fucking excuse. What's the *real* deal?'

Tiger glowered but said nothing. Leo was right. Blaming Skye *was* an excuse. How could he explain what was *really* needling him? How could he put into words what was driving him to distraction and diverting his mind from? How could he speak of what was causing his turmoil when he didn't quite know himself?

Was it being shoehorned from his own flat and back at the canning works whilst Colt took his place? Or was it by not being there meant he couldn't be near Alyson? Was it because Alyson was causing feelings within him which he wasn't sure how to decipher? That's if there *was* anything to decipher? Was his turmoil down to Colt's reappearance because he had an instinct something was far from right instead or was it that his brother's sudden and unexpected release from Broadmoor dredged up memories that Tiger would rather leave buried? *Needed* to leave buried?

Could it be guilt over decades-old decisions he'd made and, along with this, letting his friends and comrades down? Or was it the remnants of the gnawing injustice over Skye's lies and his subsequent treatment which lingered within the fibres of his body to blame after all?

Was it one of these or a combination? Perhaps *none* of those things?

Maybe he was just done with this whole bloody lark. Maybe everything had finally caught up with him and it was time to step down and disappear? Perhaps he'd never had true sight of himself at all, but covered that with a smokescreen which had now drifted away to expose him and all of his faults, wrongdoings and weaknesses?

Leo reached the point where the silence mocked his sanity. 'You need to level with me and let me know what the fuck is going on becau… Oh, for Christ's sake!' Snatching his ringing mobile from his pocket, his blood vessels strained with frustration. 'Yes? What is it? Oh, Erin! Everything all right?'

Leo glanced in Tiger's direction, finding him mirroring his stance of high alert. 'It was a good idea to call me. Yeah, Zane couldn't have heard his phone... Delgado's shown up and the shit's hit the fan... I don't know yet... but what's up? Everything okay at the flat?' His brows furrowed as he listened. 'Fuck! Okay, yeah... I'll do that now. Yeah, I understand... Okay.'

Ending the call, Leo placed the mobile down. What he'd just been told would do nothing to help Tiger's unexplained state of mind or get *him* any closer to reaching the bottom of it. But if what Erin said turned out to be right then things really didn't look good for Tiger. Either way, it needed sorting.

'What the hell was that about?' Tiger's gruff voice failed to conceal the hint of wariness in his eyes.

'There's a problem at your flat.' Leo took no pleasure in delivering this one. 'Alyson's found the stack of films Marco shot. She's hysterical and saying all sorts of stuff.'

Tiger stood up, his heart sinking. 'I know we're both supposed to remain here, but I've got to go and deal with this.'

Leo nodded. 'I'll let Zane know if he's done in there with Delgado before you get back.'

He watched Tiger rush from the office, refraining from asking the question that popped unwanted into his mind: *Why were those films of Marco's lying around Tiger's flat and furthermore, why were they in his video player in the first place?*

• • • •

ERIN COULD BARELY UNDERSTAND Alyson's words she

was so hysterical, her voice hiccupping and scratchy, peppered with staccato sobbing. She kept her hands firmly on Alyson's shoulders to quell the violent shaking coursing through the young woman's body.

Glancing over her shoulder down the hallway, Erin checked Colt remained in the living room like she'd asked. Trying to get any sense out of Alyson in the hallway wasn't ideal, but it was the furthest she'd got before the girl lost it again.

'You... you... you're not listening,' Alyson spluttered, her fingers clawing for a grip against the wall. 'He... he...'

'Please calm down,' Erin repeated. 'I'm trying my best, but I can barely understand what you're saying.' She moved so that Alyson had no choice but to meet her eyes. 'Look at me. Look at me, Alyson. Right. Now, take deep breaths.'

Alyson swallowed and closed her eyes before doing as instructed. She breathed in slowly, held it and then relaxed - just like the clinic taught her. *She must calm down. She had to make them understand.*

Keeping hold of Alyson's shoulders, Erin waited patiently as the girl composed herself. *Was Tiger coming or not?* She'd asked Leo to tell him to come immediately, so how long would he be? She *had* to talk to him.

Hearing things had kicked off with Diego was not what she'd expected either. Or wanted. It could ruin everything, if that was the case, but being as Zane was tied up with whatever was going on, it left her no choice but to deal with *this*.

It seemed improbable for Tiger to leave those videos readily accessible for Alyson to stumble across, and even less believable that he'd been watching them himself. But there were few other explanations.

'He grabbed me!' Alyson said suddenly. 'He grabbed me when I came out of the bathroom! I didn't put those films on or press play! I...'

'Colt grabbed you?' Erin cried, sure she'd misheard.

Alyson nodded. 'He shoved me up against the wall. Those films...' She sobbed loudly, flapping her hands to rein her reigniting panic in. 'They were already playing. He *wanted* me to see them. Called me all sorts of names. He...'

'Where did he grab you?' Erin asked, frowning as Alyson gestured firstly to her neck, then her shoulders and then began pointing randomly around. There was no bruising or even a hint of redness on Alyson's neck or shoulders.

'He told me I was dead and other awful things,' Alyson cried, her voice getting louder and more hysterical. 'I told you he was strange! I *told* you! He called me a dead bitch while you were standing here. You must have heard!'

'Okay, so let's just calm back down,' Erin soothed. She hadn't heard Colt say that or anything like it. Surely she would have? She didn't want to disbelieve Alyson - didn't want to contemplate not taking her word, but... but none of this made sense. Alyson had been terrified of Colt from the start and she was far from stable – jumpy and nervy. Colt had done nothing, said nothing and not acted in any way to flag him up as pulling a stunt like this. Sure, he looked terrifying, but the behaviour Erin had witnessed from him was exemplary. On top of that, he was Tiger's *brother* and Zane had personally deemed him suitable to be placed here.

Christ, this was difficult.

The memory of what had happened with Skye and the accusations about Tiger flashed through Erin's mind. A difficult scenario for sure but look at what had happened from believing that devious little cow instead. However, Alyson was Skye's friend, so was it possible she was as devious? Had they got Alyson wrong or was she telling the truth and Colt *had* behaved in this appalling manner?

But what benefit would he get by putting those films on and forcing Alyson to see them?

*None.*

Erin pursed her lips. It seemed more likely that Alyson had gone into one of her 'removed from reality' periods. She'd already had several - trying to throw out herself out of cars; screaming at Tiger; refusing to accept Skye's death...

It was hardly surprising she wasn't quite the ticket after what Marco had plied her with and what he'd done, but that didn't mean she had a grip on reality.

Erin wasn't sure, but the most likely scenario was that Alyson was confused. One thing she *did* need to know and had to ask, was why Tiger had those videos here in the first place? And furthermore, why he'd been watching them or left them lying around for anyone to stumble across them - including Alyson.

And that would be bloody awkward…

• • • •

INSPECTING HER PERFECT POUT in the mirror for the umpteenth time meant Sofia could bypass the gnawing sensation lurking within her. But that relief didn't last long before it made itself known again.

At least she looked fantastic. The tell-tale soreness between her legs confirmed that Marco was still in her life. The thought that he might leave her after all their plans and joint promises was a feeling she never wanted to experience again. But now she knew that would never happen. He was in it for the long haul, the same as her.

That blonde escort Marco had previously bedded when she'd arrived last night inched into Sofia's mind and she promptly elbowed it out. It wasn't *her* problem the trappy slag had got herself killed. If the bitch hadn't chucked in hints of telling Diego, then she'd most likely be back in her flea-infested council flat or wherever she parked her sorry backside. Admittedly, even though Marco had needs, Sofia resented anyone else being in his bed, but in a matter of days, *she'd* be meeting those needs so there would be no need for him to go elsewhere.

But that feeling - the uncomfortable nagging in the base of her gut continued.

Sofia picked up the burner phone from the dressing table. There was no need to hide it as Diego was still not back.

*And that was the problem...*

'Babe? Yeah, it's me.' Just hearing Marco's voice down the line soothed Sofia's soul, wrapping it in a protective cocoon where nothing could touch her. 'I'm fine, but I'm not sure whether something's happened.'

She frowned. And she wasn't sure because there was nothing she could explain for definite, but... but regardless, there was *something...*

'I don't know exactly. I think he was here when I got back this morning. No, I didn't actually see him, but I thought I heard the d… Yes, it could have been... What? No, he's still not back.' Sofia relaxed further at Marco's words. He was right. All of that business believing he was calling things off between them yesterday had put the wind up her - that's all it was.

'Diego *did* say something had come up last night.' Sofia's lips curled with a sneer. 'Probably something to do with Zane and why the dinner was cancelled. That or something to do with an early shipment delivery I heard him mention. Talking of which, shall I arrange another dinner for Zane and that bitch? Did you... What? I don't know! He just said something about an early shipment!'

Sofia bristled at Marco's change in tone. 'You know Diego doesn't discuss business with me! Yes, of course! I always do. Okay... Yes, all right then. I lo…'

Before she could utter the words she planned to say, the call disconnected. Disappointed, she stared at the blank screen before placing the phone back on the side.

Why Marco was so bothered about Diego's shipments confused her. Now he had nothing to do with that side of things, he shouldn't concern himself with it. He'd always said being binned off from the arrangement wasn't a problem, so why should he care? It wasn't either of them would need the money that brought in a couple of days because it would all be hers and Marco's anyway.

Sofia's face transformed back into the serene, well-practised expression of contented perfection. Soon, she and

Marco would be in possession of *everything.*

# TWENTY FOUR

ZANE REFILLED BOTH WHISKY GLASSES for the fifth time and lit another cigarette. What started out as a potential disaster for his business and would force him to remain in the thick of less salubrious and dangerous dealings that he'd hoped to gradually distance himself from now he had a growing family to protect, had turned into a strange and unexpected heart-to-heart with a man he barely knew.

Discussing personal information was unnatural for Zane, but somehow this conversation happened because the driving force between these two men, feared by most, was their children.

But Diego's feeling over Sofia were gobsmacking. *And there were more.*

'You understand yourself how vital it is to keep the name going and for a heir to be provided. It's what families are built to do in our industry.' Diego's face was hard and unmoving. 'You also understand that wives are arrangements – ones that are predetermined.' He raised an eyebrow. 'Apart from you... You're the only man with the position you hold who has not followed that rule.'

Zane nodded. That was true - all of it. And from what Diego

had said about Sofia, he was glad he'd stuck to his guns despite his father's disappointment.

His skin bristled at the memory of Guiseppe and what he now knew about him. 'You're correct, but leaving your wife the moment your heir is born will not be taken as good conduct within the ranks.' That was a no-go in his world - in Sicily especially and undoubtedly the same in Columbia and the rest of South America. 'People will not wish to work with you.'

Women - a wife - should be treated like queens. It was the unspoken rule.

'That is a risk I will take,' Diego snarled. 'Even though Sofia reciprocates little, I have given her everything and I will not sit here and allow her to cheat on me. Therefore as soon as my son is born, Sofia will lose everything!'

Zane saw the pain behind the anger in Diego's face. 'Cheating? Sofia is *cheating*?' he spluttered. 'With who? How?'

'I do not know.' Diego turned the cheap plastic cup of whisky in a circle on the desk. 'But I will find out.' He raised his eyes. 'And I will find out because she is becoming slack. She has a, how do you say it, a "burner" phone. I've caught her twice now, but she doesn't realise. She disappears and then sneaks back into the house too. Sofia is allowing another man to stick his cock near my baby and I will kill him!'

He banged his fists on the desk, sending droplets of whisky to jump from his glass. 'She is betraying me. I will not put up with betrayal on any fucking level!'

'Are you sure?' Zane asked, still in shock from these suspicions. 'Could there not be an explanation?'

'There is no plausible explanation,' Diego raged. 'Sofia will have the child and then I cut her from my life.' He swished his hand through the air like a blade.

'You'll kill her?'

'I do not plan to kill her.' Diego's words spat through his clenched teeth. 'But I will if a test proves that child is not mine. Would you not do the same? It's a matter of honour and principle.'

Zane rested his chin in his hands. *Fuck, this was hard.* Could Sofia really be so stupid to cheat on Diego? Being Sicilian and from a mafia family, she of all people knew what that meant. What Diego said didn't sound good and his life with Erin, despite its ups and downs, came into perspective. He was bloody lucky! But would he kill her if she cheated?

Zane flinched at the thought. Even thinking that being a prospect - both Erin cheating and killing her out of honour, turned his blood to ice.

But there was one major difference between him and Diego's situations. 'I think the answer to your question will be answered by this,' he continued. 'Do you love her?'

Diego snorted with sarcastic mirth. 'Of course not. I tried to like her and she's beautiful, yes, but love? I wouldn't know what that was!'

'Nor did I until Erin,' Zane admitted. 'So, in answer to your question - my head would need to kill her, but my heart would not allow it.' His expression hardened. 'But I *would* leave her and take the child.'

Diego nodded, somewhat comforted by this. 'I could have loved her, I think... Had she let me...' Suddenly remembering himself, he hardened once again. 'I need to find out if I am right.' He crossed his arms over his chest. 'But in the interim, it is business as usual. That's why I wanted you and Erin to come to dinner – see if Sofia talks or drops hints, woman to woman - you know what women are like.'

Zane couldn't help but smile. 'Trouble is, Erin isn't like most women. Plus, she thinks Sofia is a wrong 'un.'

'Then she is very astute.' Diego nodded. 'I suspected she would be. You will help me, yes? Help get to the bottom of this?'

'Of course.' Zane's eyes darkened. 'After what my father and brother did, I'm well aware of the damage betrayal causes.'

• • • •

SAM WAS ALMOST GRATEFUL for his mobile interrupting having to listen to Miranda blather about how fantastically well she was progressing with a client at one of London's leading model agencies. That was until he saw the contact on the screen as to who was on the other end of the line. And with that, the reminder that his mouth might have overstepped the invisible line about what he should and should not have divulged earlier to the two members of his staff he was presently sitting with, prodded again in his mind.

But that was paranoia, wasn't it? Neither Miranda nor Rufus would say a word about Marco and Diego Delgado. And they certainly hadn't said anything to anyone yet because they were both still here with him, so Marco wasn't calling about that.

Sam's fingers involuntarily moved to the still sore area of his neck - a sharp nudge to what he perhaps should have recalled before the desire to impress took over.

Pulling up his usual unflappable indifference, he glanced at his two companions. 'Excuse me, I need to take this call.'

Quickly getting to his feet, he moved away from the table. 'Hello?' Sam pressed the mobile to his ear, holding it in place with the aid of a shoulder pad of his blue linen jacket. 'No, no I'm not busy. I just couldn't get to my phone as quickly as normal, I... Oh no, it's fine now... yes, yes... Not a problem. I understand.'

Sam concealed the irritation filtering into his head. If Marco was so bothered about how his neck was after yesterday, then perhaps the man should have thought about that before going crazy over a few minor details. 'No, honestly, it's fine,' he simpered. 'Like I said yesterday, it's all forgotten... I... yes... I... Pardon? Okay, well, I was actually planning to take a receipt over to him later on and...'

'Sam, do you want another drink?' Miranda appeared from nowhere, making Sam swing around like a red-hot poker had been pressed between his shoulder blades. *Why the fuck had she snuck up on him like that? She could see he was on the bloody phone!*

Flapping Miranda away, Sam turned back to his mobile. 'Sorry about that, I... Oh, I'm just having lunch with a couple of my staff. I... No, God, no! Of course I haven't! I know better to discuss anything like that!'

Sam's heart thumped treacherously within his rib cage, a lone bead of sweat trickling down his forehead and threatening to drip onto his collar. 'No, no one can hear. I moved away from the table the minute you pho… No, she was just asking if I wanted another dri… Yes, I know! I wouldn't... I assure you, I...'

Stopping, Sam frowned as Marco's rant down the line suddenly changed direction back to normality. Disappointment bloomed at the words. 'So, you *don't* want me to take over a receipt tonight?'

Damn. He'd set his heart on making himself known to Diego Delgado once more and this time making a better bloody job of ingratiating himself. There was no way he was passing up the chance of getting in that particular man's orbit, yet he was being instructed not to take the receipt to the man? 'I really should give him a receipt. I think that... Oh, oh, okay... No, that's fine.'

Sam's chest inflated with self-importance as his hope in the future was immediately restored. 'Absolutely! That's a great idea! I'll wait to hear from you, then. The next couple of days, you say? Wonderful! I'll make sure I'm available and...'

Sam blinked, unsure at first whether the call had definitely been cut off. He stared at his mobile and toyed whether he should call Marco back. In any other circumstance, he would when a mobile signal dropped, but in this particular instance, he knew that the mobile signal from either end had not dropped. Marco had hung up.

Rolling his shoulders to loosen up the stuck tension, Sam casually slipped his mobile back into his pocket. He wouldn't take the abrupt dismissal personally. That was just Marco Morelli's way. Those sorts of people had etiquette at the opposite end of the scale to well-bred people such as himself – a point he had to consistently remind himself of.

Forget worrying that Marco had put the kybosh on his plan for a repeat visit to Diego Delgado because arranging for them all to meet up to discuss the venture and how he, Sam Whittaker and Whittaker Inc, could help find the right investors was better than his receipt idea tenfold. In fact, this was fantastic! He would actually be sitting down with Diego Delgado so there was no option of not being invited to soirees and parties after that. It was just a case of when this in-person meeting would happen and where, but Marco said he'd arrange everything.

Clasping his hands together, Sam strutted back over to the table.

'Was that one of your special clients?' Miranda cried loudly, her eyes bright. 'Was it Delgado or Morelli? Don't keep us in suspense!'

'Keep your fucking voice down, for Christ's sake!' Sam hissed, irritation about the damage Miranda could have done by interrupting his call, growing. Now she'd done *this*? He glanced around, relieved that no one was in earshot. 'Never interrupt me on a call again! Furthermore, you know mentioning clients' names in public is a no-no.'

It was irrelevant that he'd done exactly that. He was the boss of Whittaker Inc and could do what he damn well liked.

Seeing Miranda's crestfallen expression at his outburst, Sam took the opportunity to further relinquish his own part in what could have been a disastrous faux pas. Thankfully, it had turned out the opposite but that wasn't the point. 'I'm very disappointed in the unprofessionalism I've seen today, Miranda. I think I need to consider exactly what future you have with Whittaker Inc.'

With that comment, Sam turned on his heels and stalked away from the picturesque riverside table and back to his car.

• • • •

THE SHOCK OF discovering Marco's films had found their

way into the living room and worse - been played on his video recorder for Alyson to see overtook Tiger's initial indignation over the question. Had the question come from anyone but Erin, he was unsure whether even the shock of the unexpected situation would have been enough to calm the unsavoury insinuation.

'I kept them here rather than storing them at the canning works for obvious reasons,' he said calmly. 'I wanted them to be somewhere I knew they'd remain untouched. But...' Tiger stepped into the hallway and pointed in the direction of his bedroom. 'They were in there, in a box under my bed, *not* next to the television!'

'They were already in the video recorder, not next to the TV like Alyson said!' Colt chipped in. 'She couldn't have started watching them if they weren't. Sorry, bro, but I'm really disappointed that you'd do this. Watching those filthy fucking tapes of that poor girl?' He shook his head in disbelief. 'It's so unlike you.'

Tiger flinched, his fury igniting. 'I did not watch those films,' he roared. 'What the fuck do you take me for?'

Colt shrugged. 'The only other possibility is that Alyson put the tapes in the player herself and is confused with what she remembers, but you shouldn't have left them lying around for her to find. Christ, bro. What's got into you?'

'I did *not* leave them lying around and I did *not* fucking watch them! How many more times?' His eyes blazing with rage, Tiger lurched towards Colt.

'Okay, that's enough!' Throwing herself between the two men, Erin held her hands up in exasperation. 'Colt, could you give us a minute, please?'

Tiger glared at his brother, sure he'd just seen the hint of a sneer on that smashed up mouth of his. He waited as Colt dutifully exited the room, leaving him and Erin alone. Tiger then turned to her. 'Another instance of everyone being unsure whether I've done something underhand or endangered or hurt a young woman?'

Erin looked down awkwardly. There was no real way of asking the question without it insinuating wrongdoing. 'I'm sorry, but I had to ask, Tiger. You understand that,' she said quietly. 'If you haven't been watching them or...'

'I have not watched one fucking second of that shit, Erin,' Tiger seethed.

'Okay, okay!'' Erin nodded, accepting that as the truth. After all, no one got this angry if they were guilty. 'So, you weren't watching them and Alyson must have found them, but if you didn't leave the videos there and...'

'I didn't leave them *anywhere*! They were in a box under my bed, like I've already said!' Tiger repeated, the words hissing through his teeth like sparks. 'And I doubt whether Alyson would snoop around my bedroom.' He'd seen how she'd reacted over the paperwork that had fallen from the top of the fridge.

Erin frowned. 'Then who did?'

'I have my ideas…'

'Colt?' Erin exclaimed in surprise. 'What would he gain from that?'

'I don't know but it's got to be him,' Tiger said, struggling to control his rage. 'I'm going to kill him.'

'No, you won't. That won't help,' Erin said, scrambling around her brain for what else to say. There were few choices and as she believed Tiger was telling the truth, that left only one other person, if not Colt. 'Regardless of you saying otherwise, it *could* be Alyson who found them. She doesn't exactly behave normally and has been lurching from one crisis and hysteria since we've known her.'

'Alyson wouldn't go through my stuff,' Tiger repeated. 'Anyway, you've been with her all night.'

Erin nodded. 'Yes, but she might have *previously* found the videos. She kept going on about the films she's heard mentioned. And,' she glanced over Tiger's shoulder, 'it could be an excuse to get Colt out from here. She made no secret of that he freaks her out and wants you here. She's already accused

Colt of attacking her and...'

'Attacking her?' Tiger's fists clenched and he started towards the hallway. *If Colt had laid a finger on Alyson, then he'd...*

'Tiger!' Erin raced to grab Tiger's arm. 'I don't want to disbelieve anyone, but there were no marks on her. If what Alyson described is true, then there would surely be some form of redness or bruise and there was nothing!' She looked up into Tiger's furious face sadly. 'I think it *is* possible Alyson tried to get rid of Colt and that backfired because the finger's ended up being pointed at you.'

Tiger shook his head, rage mixed with confusion. 'Where is she, anyway? I need to see how she is.'

'In her bedroom,' Erin said, keeping her grip of Tiger's arm. 'But before you see her, I need to ask... Don't take this the wrong way, but you're quite defensive about Alyson. Is... is there something going on between the two of you?'

Tiger paused - only for a split second but long enough to be noticeable. 'No, there is not. I was instructed by Zane to protect her and that is what I've been doing. How the hell can I do that if I'm not allowed to give a shit about what she's doing or where she is? Tell me that!'

Clocking Erin's surprise at his outburst, Tiger shook his head. 'I don't mean to bark at you. I know you're only asking what's necessary and that you're lumbered with it because Zane is with Delgado, but no, there's nothing going on with me and Alyson.'

And that was something Tiger would have to ensure happened, despite the confusing thoughts hounding him of late. But what did he do about this current situation?

He couldn't afford to be suspected of any wrongdoing like this again and furthermore and perhaps more worryingly, if it were possible that Alyson went to these sorts of lengths to keep him in the flat, then she wasn't who he thought she was. And, more to the point, maybe she was more unstable than he'd believed.

# TWENTY FIVE

'IT'S NOT DIFFICULT, SOFIA,' Diego sneered. 'You don't usually have an issue with demanding things, barking orders or playing the role of "Little Miss Important", so what's the problem with calling the caterers?'

Sofia's nervousness from this morning about whether Diego had discovered her indiscretions with Marco evaporated as his contemptuous tone and sneering insults overtook her previous worry. 'A bit of notice is usually required,' she snapped, her eyes narrowing. 'Even people like *caterers* probably need more than two hours' warning to prepare and cook a meal. A decent one, anyway!'

'Well, let's think...' Diego leant against the doorjamb of the bedroom, a cold smile playing on his face. 'You could always cook it *yourself*! How about that for an idea?'

Sofia felt like she'd been physically slapped. 'Me? Don't be ridiculous! How am I supposed to deal with an oven and all of that with *this* in the way?' She glared at the bump jutting out in front of her.

'Millions of other women somehow manage it, Sofia.'

Sofia blinked, disturbed the reference to her 'pregnancy' hadn't immediately removed the sneering look on Diego's face.

Studying her husband more closely, she stalked towards him. She jutted her chin up and sniffed. 'Are you... drunk?'

Diego rolled his eyes. 'Drunk? Of course not!' Admittedly, he and Zane had put away a fair bit of whisky during the unexpected conversation they'd found themselves in earlier, but he wasn't drunk. If anything, it was the opposite. But what *had* occurred during the time he'd spent discussing what he'd never breathed a word of to anyone, was a strange kind of release.

Offloading the constant build-up of pressure enraging him to a cellular level to someone on the same pegging as him, both on the ways their world worked and the nuances and arrangements that families such as theirs ran by had helped. Someone who actually *understood* how it all worked, and furthermore, who was on board with helping him with this delicate issue had made things clearer. All considered, it was the equivalent of knocking the vent off a pressure cooker.

But when Zane opened up too - disclosing things that Diego had not realised, especially the shocking truth about Guiseppe Morelli, which he still couldn't quite comprehend, he realised he wasn't the only one with a mountain on his back, albeit for different reasons. Though the outcome was the same and the ensuing result a heightened sense of consciousness akin to being high or perhaps drunk. But intoxicated he was not. That level of relaxation was not something Diego would allow to be employed within his own body, *ever*.

But the conversation with Zane had supplied the resolve Diego needed and for that, he was grateful. And in return, he would see if he could shed any light over the revelations surrounding Zane's father.

Although Diego had never dealt with the man, something about what Zane had unearthed didn't ring true. Something which remained as a wisp at the back of Diego's mind. And if he could get hold of the right man back home, they might be able to find out more, one way or the other. But that would have to be instigated later.

He stared at Sofia's beautiful face, seeing only the epitome of lies and fake platitudes, along with a thick layer of manipulative tendencies. His urge to wring her neck grew but he couldn't do that until the child was born and he knew for sure of her unfaithfulness. 'Did you not hear? I told you, I am not drunk!'

'You smell like a brewery!' Sofia sniped, still pointedly sniffing around Diego. 'Is it not bad enough that you come in acting like this and reeking of booze without expecting me to drop everything to arrange another dinner with your sad little friend and his thick bitch of a girlfriend?'

Her eyes shone with malice as she inspected her long manicured nails. Putting up with Diego was fast becoming unbearable. She shouldn't even be here - she should be with Marco - the man she *wanted* to be with - the man she should *always* have been with. Not playing this charade of Diego Delgado's trophy wife and walking around like a fucking whale in the process. She'd had enough. It had gone on too long.

Raising her head, she resumed her glare at the husband she'd never wanted. 'I'm not doing it! I don't want dinner with those people. I don't want to talk niceties to them either, so I'm not arranging a thing! Why should I jump to your beck and call? Why should I, when I...'

'Because you're my fucking wife, that's why!' Diego roared. His controlled temper fracturing, he grabbed Sofia around the throat and pressed her up against the door jamb. 'Remember, Sofia, you're married to *me*! I've had enough of you acting like you're not and it stops *now*!'

Sofia's aggressive countenance and cockiness vanished to be replaced with pure fear. Realising her resentment towards her unwanted marriage had made her lose sight of who she was actually wed to, her panic reached an all-time high. She'd been tied to this man for a long time. *Too long*. Long enough to lend the mistaken belief that she was exempt from who he actually was and what he was capable of.

Her status as Diego's wife had granted her the unique accolade of pushing him to places no one else would dare. It was true she'd never wanted for anything and the 'baby' had granted her even more manoeuvrability.

*Or it had...*

She'd always been exempt from his rage. *Always*. But something had changed.

Through her panic, Sofia looked beseechingly into Diego's eyes. That always worked. But today it didn't. All she found was dark orbs flashing with vitriol.

She started to tremble, her back pinioned up against the wall beginning to ache. 'Diego… The baby...'

'No, Sofia!' Diego kept his grip on his wife. 'I will not put up with your shit anymore. You *will* arrange this meal tonight and act the perfect hostess!' His scowl deepened. 'No catty remarks. No rudeness. No fucking nothing! You're done with messing me about and embarrassing me with your lack of manners. Recently you have underlined *and* whilst in company, that our marriage is a bag of shit!' He poked his finger into Sofia's shoulder. 'Act the part for once in your goddamn life. Be gracious and pleasant. Make the effort with our guests - get to know Zane Morelli's intended instead of bitching and moaning. *They* have a good relationship, so you might learn something!'

Sofia was close to blurting out that she already had a good relationship with the man she *wanted* to be with, which wasn't him, but quickly realised that would be the nail in her coffin, so kept her thoughts to herself.

'Remember, Sofia,' Diego added. 'This... is your saving grace.'

Sofia flinched as Diego's hand dropped to rest on the silicone mound pressed between their two bodies and prayed he didn't dislodge it. Not expecting him back so suddenly, she couldn't be certain she'd fully secured the strapping or even whether the disgusting thing was in a realistic position.

Perspiration gathered in the nape of her neck under the mass of extortionately expensive hair extensions. *Don't move*, she begged silently inside her own head. 'I'm sorry,' she squeaked.

'I don't mean to upset you.'

But as he'd referenced the non-existent baby again, so she'd play on that. It wasn't difficult to make her bottom lip quiver, although this time it wasn't for the reason she'd make out. 'I know I've been difficult recently. It's... it's just I'm finding this pregnancy hard. I'm exhausted all the time and it's sent my hormones haywire.' Her hand caressed Diego's swarthy face like she always did when she wanted something. 'I'll make everything up to you and of course I'll arrange the dinner. I... I just feel so ugly and frumpy at the moment.'

Hanging her head, she waited for Diego's usual compliments and assurances to spill from his mouth, but there was nothing. Her brewing worry upped a further notch. *This couldn't mess up now she was so close.*

Sofia suddenly realised Diego no longer had hold of her and instead he'd took a step back to eye her with the same level of coldness as before. 'Diego...?'

'I'll leave you to arrange dinner and freshen up. Expect our guests at seven.' Diego turned to walk out of the bedroom but then stopped to look over his shoulder. 'I want you back in my bed tonight,' he growled. 'There are other things aside from intercourse that you can do as a wife.'

Giving her a long look, he left the bedroom leaving Sofia to sag against the wall in a mixture of relief and renewed panic.

*What was she going to do?* She didn't know what had changed but something definitely had. She couldn't go to bed with Diego under any circumstances. Not having sex was one thing, but he'd *touch* her. Laying his hands in the wrong place would blow everything out of the water.

Shutting the bedroom door, Sofia rummaged down her top to extract her hidden phone. She had to get hold of Marco. It had to be tonight. Marco had to kill Diego tonight.

*Somehow.*

She didn't care how he did it as long as he did. If he didn't, she'd be dead and everything would be ruined.

• • • •

HEARING A LOUD KNOCK on the bedroom door, Alyson remained frozen. That was until she heard Tiger's voice. Relief flooding through her, she yanked the door open. 'Thank God you're back!' she cried, throwing herself against his chest.

Tiger awkwardly extracted Alyson from against him and shut the door. He didn't know what to think about what he'd been summoned here for. Was it the anger of being accused again or what *felt* like more accusations over something he had no part of, coupled with the fury over whether there was truth behind Colt attacking Alyson? All these things clashed with the overpowering urge to comfort the young woman in front of him.

Tiger's tumult of conflicting emotions did nothing but lend him an expression and mannerisms which sent Alyson into a tailspin, her initial relief on his return dissolving into dust.

'What exactly has been happening?' Tiger asked, his tone gruff and expressionless.

Unaware that this was Tiger's natural defence mechanism, the words Alyson had overheard spoken between him, Colt and Erin slammed back into her mind and suspicion overtook all else. 'Just tell me - did you watch those films? How many copies of them are there?'

She almost choked saying the word 'films'. Just the thought of those tapes containing her at her most vulnerable; behaving like the wanton slut everyone knew she must be, was something she couldn't unsee. The images were burnt onto her retinas for eternity.

Tiger's heavy brow furrowed, the flash of anger clear. His mouth moved but before he could speak, Alyson continued. 'That you haven't denied it, speaks volumes,' she yelled. 'How could you?'

Before she could stop herself, she slammed her balled fists into Tiger's chest. Pummelling his muscular frame did nothing but it mattered little. 'You watched me... doing... doing those... those things... You didn't even tell me about the films! Something else you've hidden from me when I asked! First Skye and now this! You... you...'

'Be careful what you say,' Tiger bellowed, grabbing Alyson's wrist. 'You're talking shit, girl! You're accusing me of things you shouldn't be!'

Alyson stared at Tiger's hand on her wrist. Her eyes tracked to his, seeing them flashing with hurt and rage and she sagged, her arms dropping to her sides realising yet again she'd launched at the wrong person.

Tiger glared at Alyson's visibly shrinking figure, the conflicting emotions within him still battling for control. 'Since when am I beholden to inform you about anything?' he yelled, the hurt of yet another accusation and from *this* particular person, triggering his own defensive stance. 'You were foisted onto me, remember? Unless I'm mistaken, I wasn't aware I'm liable to run anything past you! You're part of my job, that's all. But no, I did *not* watch those films!'

He folded his arms over his wide chest, not reacting to the tears now flowing freely down Alyson's cheeks. Inside, he wanted to pull her into his arms and explain that he had been trying to protect her by not mentioning the films - trying to save her dignity. But the hurt that she'd had to ask if he'd watched the fucking things overrode. 'Which is it then, Alyson? Who's the guilty party? Me or Colt? I heard that you'd said *he'd* forced you to watch the films and that he'd attacked you as well, but now it's *my* fault?'

'No, no, it's not you!' Alyson sobbed. 'I shouldn't have said... I'm confused... I...'

Tiger's face screwed into an even fiercer scowl. 'I'm surprised you haven't accused me of attacking you yet!'

'NO!' Alyson yelped. 'I'd never say that!'

'You're happy to accuse me of watching that stuff that filthy bastard filmed to degrade you instead though?' Tiger shook his head. The anger at himself for keeping on at Alyson was now almost as strong as the rage he felt about what had been done to her in the first place. 'What about you? Did *you* put those videos in the player?'

Alyson's mouth dropped open. 'Me? Why would I do that?'

As much as Tiger didn't like admitting it, he had to accept that for all of Colt's faults, he'd never known his brother to mistreat or hurt a woman. And now, thinking rationally, Colt was angry at *him*, believing *he'd* left the films lying around or watching them. Colt wouldn't have been so furious if he'd been behind it himself.

And this brought Erin's other unwelcome theory back to the fore.

Tiger stared at Alyson. If he allowed it to be visible, the confusion and hurt in her eyes mirrored his own. 'Those films were under my bed out of harm's way. It's only *you* who has been here when I haven't.'

Alyson was horrified. 'I haven't been in your room! I told you, it was...'

'Level with me. Did you do this to get rid of Colt because you wanted me here, not him?'

Unable to get her words out, Alyson's mouth silently flapped up and down. She knew her reaction appeared like Tiger was correct. But he wasn't.

'I'll ask you again. Did Colt attack you?' Tiger pressed.

Alyson's tears flowed harder. *Tiger didn't believe her*. They *all* thought she was making this up. She shook her head in frustration. 'I...'

'So, he *didn't* attack you?' Tiger barked.

'No! I mean, yes!' Alyson sobbed. 'He did. He grabbed me. Called me a dead whore bitch and said he'd...'

'Fuck's sake,' Tiger shouted. Those words coming from Alyson's mouth made him cringe. 'I was ready to kill Colt but it's all shit. What's the matter with girls like you?'

'But Colt did grab and threaten me! Why won't you believe me?' Alyson overrode her misery and clutched Tiger's arm. 'What do you mean, "girls like me"? Like sluts? Like easy whores? Is that what you meant?' Her voice rose to fever pitch and further scalding tears rushed down her inflamed cheeks.

'No, I did *not* mean that! I meant that young women say things without realising the implications. Like... like Skye.'

Tiger pulled his arm from Alyson's grip. 'Okay, so if Colt grabbed you, where's the fucking marks?'

As much as he didn't want his brother here or anywhere near him, he didn't want to kill the man either. And that's exactly what would happen if Colt had laid a finger on this beautiful, sweet, yet damaged young woman.

Alyson glanced at her arms, unable to remember exactly where Colt had grabbed her. 'I... I don't know.' Terror had reduced everything to a blurred mess. She gulped in air, unable to breathe, her lungs slowly suffocating her. Why was panic and terror confusing her? She wasn't imagining things, she knew she wasn't. Why wouldn't anyone believe that? Why didn't *Tiger* believe that? She thought he was different. Thought he was...

'You need to calm down!' Tiger held Alyson's shoulders whilst making another quick appraisal of her skin. *Erin was right - there wasn't a single mark.* 'You're getting hysterical.'

And that only served to wonder whether Erin was right about Alyson doing this because she didn't want Colt here. As Erin reminded him: Alyson was hardly stable with the way she'd acted on several occasions since leaving Solenzo's. Even Colt suggested Alyson might have put the tapes in herself being as she seemed so 'confused'.

For the first time, Tiger wondered whether he'd made the right call by going against Mr Solenzo's advice, but his train of thought was cut short by the bedroom door bursting open; the door slamming hard against the inside wall with a loud crash.

Zane appeared in the doorway, his face like thunder. 'I don't know what the fuck's going on in here, but it stops *now*!'

• • • •

MUMBLING TO HIMSELF, Marco swiped the aggravated scowl off his face as fluidly as a top chef smoothed royal icing over the top of a cake. Christ knows he'd had enough years of putting on faces depending on situations and if he hadn't mastered it by now, that didn't say a lot for him.

Obviously, as far as he was concerned, he'd perfected *everything* to give away no hint of what was really going on inside his head. This was convenient, considering most of the time he didn't actually know.

But he *did* know that today had been a shit one.

Marco looked up the steps of the Burgundy Cellar and strutted past the area where people patiently waited for a seat, thankful that *he* didn't need to bother with that kind of crap.

Ensuring his usual booth offering privacy as well as comfort, situated at the back of the room was left vacant for the occasions he decided to turn up, he was momentarily placated to find his instructions had been obeyed.

Making his way over, he snapped his fingers in the direction of a random waiter. He said nothing else. If these people didn't know by now what he drank and exactly how he liked it, they didn't deserve his custom.

Settling into the booth, Marco grunted his approval at the fast delivery of his wine and after checking there were no smudges on the glass, pulled his mobile out.

*No calls or text yet. Good.*

Getting out his Marlboros, Marco then remembered himself and fished in his other pocket for the white menthol fags. He lit one, dismayed to notice the slight trembling of his fingers. For God's sake, the day hadn't started out too badly, despite weighing out a wedge to a new disposal firm to rid him of the slapper who'd paid the ultimate price for trying to pull a fast one, things had only started going really pear-shaped after he'd phoned that jumped-up prick, Whittaker, and then getting a call from Sofia, who'd sounded more stressed than he'd ever heard her. But Sofia's demands that the job on Diego had to be done *tonight* had seriously pissed him off.

Marco frowned. At first, he'd thought she was trying to move forward the agreed time slot of the job being done within two weeks. He'd needed that leeway to get Colt in place and things just right for everything to play out as required. But that was until he heard *why* Sofia needed Diego removing tonight.

Marco's blood silently bubbled within his veins.

The Dago worm had turned. Insisting Sofia act the wife in his bed again, was he? Well, he'd see about that! If that greasy arsehole cunt thought he'd sit back and allow that to happen and accept such things could be demanded from *his* Sofia, then Diego was more stupid than ever. If that wasn't insulting enough, once Marco had got her to calm down enough so that he could understand a word she was fucking banging on about, Sofia had pointed out that if Diego discovered the 'baby' wasn't a baby, then she would exist no longer.

There was a click as Marco's grinding teeth scraped together just that little bit far. Wincing, he took a sip of wine. It tasted like shit, but right now he had more important things to worry about.

Just the thought of Sofia being killed by her bastard husband, who should never have been granted her in the first place, was enough to send Marco psychotic. His palms were sweating and he knew his heart was ramping up to cardiac arrest level ten. Losing Sofia would be bad enough, but there was also the major problem that if that happened, he'd no longer be eligible for either the Buscemi money or Delgado's empire.

If that bastard wasn't dead, but Sofia was, that cunt would get the lot. And that was not something Marco would risk.

Marco sighed. He'd tried to calm Sofia down. He'd told her over and over that he'd sort it. And sort it he would. He just didn't know exactly how yet. But the first thing to do was to put Colt on standby to do what was necessary tonight, on guard in that poxy flat or not.

Bringing his mobile to life, Marco scrolled through for the contact listed as Half-Head, stopping as the unnaturally loud screeching voice of a woman in the next booth seeped into his brain. He'd been aware of the grating drone since sitting down, but what with everything else racing around his mind he'd successfully zoned it out.

But hearing his own name mentioned by whoever owned the cackling voice, he tuned into the conversation, his finger stuck hovering over Half-Head's number.

'I'm telling you that's what he said,' the voice screeched. 'If I play my cards right, I could get to meet those two famous gangsters myself! It's not like I'm taking his threat seriously about thinking about firing me!' The woman laughed loudly, clearly finding the concept amusing. 'He gets like that when he's stressed and he's stressed at the moment dealing with these high-profile clients. Nope - no way will Sam risk losing me. After all, he can't do *everything* on his own!'

Marco's knuckles turned white as he gripped the edge of his table. *Sam?* Who else could that be but Sam-fucking-Whittaker? Who else would be so retarded to spout off? It had to be Whittaker because how otherwise could this screeching tart, whoever she was, know about a 'new venture' between 'Morelli and Delgado'?

Sam Whittaker was the only person Marco had given the spiel about a non-existent new venture to.

Forcing himself to remain in his own booth rather than jump over the top of the glass partition and wrench the girl's scalp clean off her head, Marco concentrated on the woman whose voice was becoming overshadowed by a donkey-like laugh of a man from another booth.

'I might even get chance to meet the wife. You know, that one who was in Tatler? If I could connect with *her*, it would help me with my model agency client!'

Marco's teeth began grinding again, the noise sounding like broken glass. *Fuck, fuck, fuck!*

'No, I don't know what the venture is,' the screechy voice continued. 'Sam wouldn't say. Apparently, it's all hush-hush. I tried to listen when he was on the phone to one of them earlier. That's what I got balled out for interrupting his conversation. But he's meeting up with both of them soon and I intend to tag along.'

Marco's brain raced at ten to the dozen. *So now what?* He could not let this slide.

He might have known Whittaker, the pointless jumped-up

piece of shit, couldn't resist bigging himself up to someone. And, he thought, with a sudden flash of recognition, this voice was the same one he'd heard when on the phone to the prick earlier. One of the dickhead's staff, was she, this woman?

Marco stubbed his cigarette out in the ashtray, his mouth fixed in a thin line. This wasn't something he could pass over - the bitch had a gob like the Dartford Tunnel. He'd have to do something and do it *now*. Being as Whittaker didn't have the balls to fire this slag, he'd do it instead. Except she would be in no need of a P-45...

For fuck's sake, this was just what he fucking needed when he'd still got to call Colt and get Diego killed.

Straightening down his suit, Marco stood up and began to walk past the booth containing the two women. He casually glanced over at them. Shame really, although no oil paintings, they weren't mingers. Still, life was a bitch sometimes.

'Good evening, ladies.' Marco pretended he would keep on walking, secretly smiling as he clocked the recognition and surprise on the women's faces.

'Mr Morelli, isn't it?' the blonde stuttered.

Stopping, Marco gave the women one of his best lopsided smiles and leant on their table with both hands. 'It is indeed. And…' he grinned, 'No disrespect, but I couldn't help overhearing your conversation just now...'

'Oh God! I...' The blonde blushed furiously. 'I... erm...'

'I tell you what,' Marco winked, quite enjoying himself. 'If you like, I could give you a quick interview. I might even give you a hint as to my new "venture". How does that sound? Despite what some people think of me, I'm all for helping beautiful women's careers in this man-led world.'

Miranda almost squealed with excitement, her bright pink lips forming an 'O'. 'Oh my God! Really? Would you? When? Here?'

'No, not here!' Marco laughed. 'There's far too many undeserving ears. Why don't you two come to my office. I have one just down the road from here.' He then made a big deal of looking at his watch. 'I can only spare you ten minutes, I'm afraid, but if you have the time now, then so do I.'

'Definitely!' Miranda stumbled in her haste to grab her handbag and leave the booth. She clutched her friend's arm, barely able to believe her luck. 'See?' she whispered. 'There's no way Sam can afford to piss me about!' She'd get a whole host of kudos for this, plus she might even have a chance of getting Mr Morelli to swing an interview with Sofia Delgado for her too.

Marco couldn't help but smile as the two women tailed him out of the Burgundy Cellar. He didn't have an office around here at all. Neither did he have ten minutes.

But he wouldn't need either.

His hand brushed against the pistol secured in the inside pocket of his suit jacket. There was a convenient alleyway not far away. He'd say it was the back entrance to his office that he used to avoid hangers on. Then he'd quickly and quietly offload these two.

In all fairness, this unexpected incident wasn't an unwelcome break from the turmoil today had brought. Whatever happened, he couldn't let either of them live to continue spouting off. After he'd sorted this, he'd call Colt and brief him with the *important* business of the evening.

And last but not least, when everything else was done, he'd decide exactly how Sam Whittaker would die for going against instructions for the second fucking time.

# Twenty Six

'I DON'T THINK WE SHOULD be doing this tonight.' Erin eyed Zane in the back seat of the taxi next to her. 'Insisting Tiger returned to the canning works after what happened, well, I'm not comfortable with it.'

Zane didn't break his gaze from the window as the streets gradually changed into the opulence of Kensington. 'Tiger's needed at the factory. He hasn't time to babysit Alyson Read. She's being guarded, like I promised, so that's my decision.'

Erin swallowed. 'But... Colt... What if he...'

'Look!' Zane swung away from the window. 'Colt's doing what I asked of him. He's Tiger's brother, Leo's initial dislike of him has turned around and even *you* said his behaviour has been exemplary!'

'Yes, but...'

'Can't you just let me get on with things the way they need to happen?' Zane massaged his aching head. 'I did what you and Tiger wanted. Against my better judgement, I called over yet another guard to join Colt, even though I can barely afford to lose any cover at the factory. I only agreed to it so Tiger would fuck off back to where he should be and you'd get off my back! Not that I should have had to. For fuck's sake! What else does everyone expect? I've got to keep all bases covered but instead I find myself pandering to some little bitch who should have been sectioned in the bloody first place!'

Erin frowned, concerned by Zane's attitude. Her gaze flicked to the taxi driver, clocking him avert his eyes from his rearview mirror. It would have been difficult for the man to have missed her and Zane's exchange - Zane was roaring, stressed and not himself.

*And Erin did not know why.*

Leaving the silence to hang for a few more seconds, Erin eventually broke the stalemate and touched Zane's arm. Leaning closer, she lowered her voice. 'Has something happened that you're not telling me? I know something kicked with you and Diego earlier, that's why I took it upon myself to try and sort out the mess at Tiger's flat.' She watched Zane stare into the footwell with his head in his hands. 'Is there a problem between you or the arrangement? Is that why we're going to his place again tonight? Not that we're dressed for it, but somehow I feel that's the least of the issue.'

Beneath his hand, Zane's mouth remained set in a thin line as he battled his crashing mind. He knew he was being spiky with Erin. He didn't mean to - it was just his brain was fried. Since the earlier conversation with Diego, he'd berated himself for divulging things about Marco, and worse, the truth over what he'd uncovered about his father. Zane spoke of what Guiseppe had done to no one. He hadn't even revisited it with Erin, Leo or Tiger, even though they'd all witnessed when the truth of his father's betrayal was uncovered.

What that man had done by ordering the despicable actions against Shirley Wilson in order to free Zane up for Sofia was the worst. That his own father had sanctioned and then covered for it and removed comeback on Marco by banishing the Wilson family from London, whilst continuing his hypocrisy of having standards to his eldest son and trusted workforce, was something Zane found impossible to discuss with anyone. Even *himself.*

It was better all round, namely to ensure he remained sane, to bury the devastating truth somewhere in the annals of his mind. Yeah, all that had happened, so why make it worse by analysing it? There was nothing that could be done to change it now so there was no point. Get on with things - that was Zane's mantra. Doing anything else would place him in an unwanted position. There was too much riding on the future to squander on sentimentality and what should not have happened in the first place.

So why the fuck had he spoken to Diego Delgado about it? Someone he barely knew and someone he needed to remain in business with for his future family's sake?

Sweat bloomed underneath Zane's T-shirt and leather jacket. He didn't know why he'd told Diego his deepest darkest secrets, apart from that it felt natural to do so. It was like they were both in a place where a creature slowly and surely gnawed away the very essence of what made both men who they were. But out of the womb of the shoebox office at the canning works, Zane now felt like he'd sold out and exposed a weak part of himself. He'd given away points he never wanted to discuss – especially not with a man who could use them to break him.

That Diego had put himself in an equally open position with what he'd disclosed about his marriage, suspicions and plans, was different somehow.

*Because Diego was not Zane.*

'Zane?'

The slight increase of pressure on his arm reminded Zane that he'd said nothing in response to Erin's question. He was being a twat to her and that would be rectified. Apart from anything else, the conversation with Diego reminded Zane that, aside from a shit brother and the worst hypocrite of a father, he had a *real* relationship with this woman. It brought home, not for the first time, just how lucky he was to have Erin in his life. And shortly, the child they would have together.

Moving his hand from his face, he took Erin's hand in his. 'Sorry. I'm sorry, yeah? Things were strange with Diego today but all of that's now rectified.' He'd tell her what he'd divulged and admit he was not the best company when wandering out of his mental protection zone when they got home, but first there was something else he needed to say. And he'd have to be quick about it because they'd almost reached Diego's.

He smiled as Erin studied him inquisitively. 'By the way, it seems like I was wrong and you were right...'

'No change there, then!' Erin grinned, attempting to inject humour into the previously terse taxi journey.

'No, seriously.' Zane said earnestly. 'I think you were right about Sofia and I need you to do some digging. I need you to get her to dish the dirt on what she's up to That's the main reason why we're going there tonight – to find out more.'

Erin blinked, unsure she had correctly grasped what Zane was asking. 'What? You want me to do, *what*?'

Zane peered out of the window as the taxi slowed ready to pull up outside Diego's large townhouse and pulled some money out of his leather jacket to pay the fare. 'I'll tell you more before we ring the doorbell. Don't worry, it'll be fine, but Diego's counting on you.'

As Zane grabbed Erin's hand and pulled her out of the taxi, she realised the previous importance of their unsuitable clothes paled into insignificance.

• • • •

ALYSON STAYED IN EXACTLY the same place and position that she'd been in since Zane burst into the room. The look on his face had been enough to render her motionless - he'd been furious. And more to the point, furious with her *and* Tiger.

That someone who had shown such kindness to her, offered her shelter and gone above and beyond to protect her, even though she was unknown to him, despite the fearsome reputation which preceded him and the look on Zane Morelli's face deleted all prior interactions with him in one fail swoop.

Alyson's back and legs were so stiff from not having moved

a muscle for so long, but even this burning, aching pain wasn't enough to push her into changing position or reminding anyone of her existence. The more invisible she was, the better.

Despite her statue-like stance, the tears continued rolling down her cheeks. She was surprised there were any left.

Oh, she'd heard Zane's words. She'd heard what he'd said to Tiger: that she was *'fucking insane'* and *'shouldn't be here'*. She'd heard Tiger being told he was *'wrong to go against Solenzo's advice'*, that *'the girl should have been sectioned'*, and *'your job is not to babysit'*.

Alyson swallowed, the act scratching her dry throat.

She'd then heard both Erin and Tiger from the other side of the door as they attempted to reason with Zane, explaining she shouldn't be left like this, but Zane was having none of it. Tiger was to immediately return to his post at the canning works and that was that.

But, Alyson thought, choking back a sob, it wasn't like Tiger believed anything she'd said. *None* of them did. And that resulted in her being left here with Colt who terrified her to the marrow.

Regardless of what anyone thought, she knew she hadn't imagined things. She hadn't been snooping around Tiger's bedroom. She hadn't found those films and then put them in the video and pressed 'play'. She hadn't manufactured a story about Colt grabbing her and forcing her to watch what was playing on the screen, nor had she dreamt up him threatening her. She definitely hadn't engineered this mess to keep Tiger here instead of his brother.

Not that it made any difference because she'd been left with Colt regardless.

Alyson suddenly jolted from a noise somewhere else in the flat. It wasn't outside the bedroom - it was further down the hallway - possibly the kitchen, but she had no wish to find out. Any slight noise, creak or sense of movement only underlined that she was not alone and *that man* was also somewhere within the same four walls.

Chewing her lip, barely able to breathe and with her nerves in tatters, she glanced at the bedroom door. *Was it opening?*

Squinting, Alyson concentrated through the endless roundabout of questions and spiralling panic.

The door wasn't opening but it would. It would be Colt with more threats.

Even though it had fallen on deaf ears, he was hardly likely to let it go that she'd told Erin and Tiger what he'd done.

Alyson risked turning to look around the room. Did she have a bag to put her few meagre bits in? Where were her shoes? Was the only footwear she possessed the slippers Tiger had bought for her?

She stared at the pink slippers abandoned in the centre of the room. What had seemed a lovely gesture now felt tainted.

Why had she accused Tiger of watching those films? She knew he wouldn't do that.

Alyson frowned.

But *did* she? It wasn't like she knew him - not even slightly. Her instinct about Tiger and the unfathomable pull she experienced towards him; the sexual desire she'd begun to harbour, might be madness or another side effect of what she'd recently endured.

What did it matter? Tiger didn't believe her. Well, that was certainly the way it seemed.

The only saving grace was Tiger and Erin insisting another guard be brought over to the flat in addition to Colt. Colt couldn't touch or threaten her with someone else here, could he?

Alyson felt the familiar tendrils of panic curl around the base of her spine. Just because someone else was here didn't mean anything. They could all be in on it together. It could be the start of something worse…

Bringing her knees up to her chest, she clasped her arms around them and rocked back and forth. Not knowing whether she was right or wrong, who to trust or what to do was taking its toll.

Perhaps she *was* crazy? Maybe she was utterly mad and everything was in her head?

The questions were pointless. She just had to get out of here.

Returning to her parents and explaining the sordid truth was better than this. Her degradation captured on celluloid for eternity was no longer the primary focus because whilst no one she'd thought to be on her side believed a word she said she was in more danger than ever.

She had to get away.

*But how?*

There was also one other small issue that Alyson had momentarily forgotten in her desperate bid to think of how to escape the psychopath in this flat…

The whole reason Colt was here was because there was a bounty on her head.

Unable to prevent the whole-body trembling coursing through her once again, Alyson now knew without a doubt that Marco would succeed in killing her the second he had the chance. Escaping here to venture out alone would open the door for him to achieve just that. In fact, being as the note attached to that poor, dead man showed Marco knew she was staying here, he could be lurking outside somewhere, watching and waiting for that moment she stepped outside alone.

*She'd be walking headfirst into her own death.*

Worse than that, she couldn't risk running back to her parents either now. While she was a threat to Marco, he would follow. He'd find her wherever she went.

He could follow her to her parents and kill them too!

Another sob escaped from between Alyson's lips and her hand flew to her mouth to muffle it. *She had to be quiet.*

The sad truth was, Alyson knew that as long as she continued to draw breath, she was a threat to Marco Morelli, therefore there were two choices: be killed and risk dragging others with her or remain the prisoner of a madman who *also* wanted to kill her.

But the one thing Alyson did not understand was why Colt hated her so?

She didn't know him and had done nothing to the man, so why? What possible reason was there. Unless he was something to do with Marco?

But that was a stupid thing to think because Colt was Tiger's brother!

• • • •

ERIN SMILED WARMLY at Diego and Sofia across the table as she placed her dessert spoon down on the plate holding the now empty dish of Crystal Macaroons. 'That was lovely.'

'It certainly was,' Zane added.

'I wish I could say dinner was *my* culinary genius, but I have to hand that accolade to our caterers,' Sofia said brightly, resting her manicured hand on her bump. 'I asked them to do something extra special as a means of apologising for cutting short our evening the other night. I know I haven't given you the best first impression of me, Erin.' The words stuck in her throat, but she'd play any game necessary to ensure her plans came to fruition. Or worse, being killed by her own husband. 'The rigours of pregnancy have got me down a little of late, but I hope we can start again. I'd very much like it if we could be friends.'

'Of course.' Erin smiled, not believing the platitudes spewing from Sofia's cerise-lipped mouth. 'I'm sure I'll experience these pregnancy rigours myself in a month or so.' *Except she doubted it.* Thankfully, she was nothing like Sofia. For a start, she *wanted* to be with the man who had fathered the child growing inside her. And she wanted her child – more than anything.

'I'm lucky to have such a supportive husband. I'm sometimes not the easiest person,' Sofia gushed, her fingers stroking Diego's suit sleeve just like a good wife would do and ignored the look Diego shot her.

Was she overdoing the niceness? What did he want? He

said, 'make the effort', so she was making the fucking effort. She'd rather err on the side of caution and be overnice in order for this to work than the opposite. By now, Marco would have his man in place to do what was needed. Or he'd better. He'd promised her it would be tonight and would act the minute she gave him the nod.

'Anyway,' Sofia purred, still stroking Diego's arm. 'I hope Zane is as good to you as Diego is to me.'

'Zane has been very supportive.' Erin attempted to reciprocate Sofia's saccharine smile, but the tinkling laughter following Sofia's comment which sounded as fake as anything, almost turned Erin's painstakingly difficult smile into a grimace.

She avoided looking at Zane, knowing without meeting his eyes that he was also unconvinced by Sofia's turnaround towards her and that the pleasant attitude towards Diego was as plastic as the woman herself. Erin instead found her gaze flitting to Diego, whose expression remained unaffected. But the flash of something she couldn't quite put her name to behind those grey eyes of his sent the unspoken message to go along with everything that was happening.

Regardless of how difficult, infuriating and obnoxiously irritating the new 'Oh-So-Nice' Sofia was being with her forced niceties, Erin would follow through with what had been asked.

As they'd approached the Delgado's front door, learning what Diego confided in Zane earlier was a shock, to say the least. Erin had already guessed something was far from right in the Delgado camp - especially from Sofia's side, but what she'd learnt since was worse than she'd foreseen.

Diego's suspicions that Sofia was having an affair and the possibility of the child not being his was one hell of a double whammy.

Although reticent to be involved in others' personal business, Erin was between a rock and a hard place. No matter how much she didn't want to, she had little choice but to do what was asked. Whilst hers, Zane's and their child's future depended on the association with Diego continuing, it was vital there were no extraneous issues muddying the waters, especially major ones.

Yes, Sofia came across as having short shrift for her husband, but an *affair*?

Erin sighed inwardly. She'd do her best to find out more. Befriending Sofia and encouraging the woman to confide in her seemed unsurmountable, but seeing how overfriendly Sofia was now being towards her, it may not be quite as difficult as she'd initially thought.

It was still something she did not want to do. The thought of spending more time than necessary with Sofa left a sour taste in Erin's mouth but she'd just have to get on with it.

'Sofia, why not take Erin shopping tomorrow?' Diego suggested, his smile towards his wife, although wide, failed to reach his eyes. 'Have some quality time together. Harrods, perhaps? You can take one of the chauffeured cars and a minder, so you'll both be safe.'

Erin glanced at Zane, hoping she'd concealed the revulsion at this unexpected suggestion better than Sofia had. The unrivalled flash of abject horror on the woman's face would have been funny if Erin was not equally aghast over the unpalatable prospect.

'Fabulous idea, darling! Sofia simpered. 'What do you think, Erin? Are you available tomorrow for shopping at Harrods? Perhaps a treatment at a spa too? I know I'd love it!'

'That sounds amazing! I'd love to,' Erin lied, quietly grinding her heel into the toe of Zane's boot. 'I meant to ask you - has your Bentley arrived yet?'

'Oh, yes!' Sofia squealed, her hands flying to her face in such a blatantly over-dramatized manoeuvre that Erin was forced to disguise her giggle as a cough.

'Now we've finished eating, you must both come outside and take a look. I can't believe you didn't notice it when you got here!'

As Diego rolled his eyes, Zane got up from the table and

Erin followed, hopeful that by being outside and looking at a car would dilute the chances of being lumbered with any further horrendous arrangements with Sofia Delgado.

Sofia waddled from the table towards the front door, the saccharine smile plastered over her face dropping. If she could get them interested enough in this stupid old banger, it might give her chance to slope off and text or call Marco to give him the go-ahead that things were good for the hit.

All she needed to know was where and when she needed to position her husband so he could meet his death.

# Twenty Seven

'YOU DON'T NEED TO KNOW why I sound out of breath, Shoreham,' Marco snarled as he headed back down the street as fast as he could without coming across as dodgy. His feet were fucking killing, but he couldn't risk taking a cab. He glanced at his leather shoes, confident they were free from blood splatters. He didn't need to worry about the rest of him. He was far too precise by now to avoid splashback on clothes.

Marco frowned as Colt muttered away down the other end of the mobile. 'I don't give a fuck whether you're at the flat or not! When you get the nod, find an excuse to leave... Yeah, you'll think of something...'

He flicked his cigarette butt into the gutter and continued his pace. It shouldn't take much longer to get back to the house and by the time anyone found the bodies of those two trampy whores in the alley he'd be long gone. 'Yeah, yeah,' he continued. 'I get that, but like I said, I need you on standby. Remember, as and when you get the signal from me, the job needs doing straightaway, so be ready to move on it. I'll let you know if there's a change of pl…'

Marco paused, one eyebrow raising towards his hairline. 'Important delivery, eh? And when did he say this was due?'

A grin broke out on his face. *So, the next shipment was coming early? Thought they could change the course of events by trying to fool him with the drop coming before schedule, did they? Well, think again, dear brother.*

But this also ballsed things up somewhat, Marco thought, quickly calculating the plans he'd already changed once now couldn't run in parallel. He'd be lifting that coke when it arrived and the perfect way to do that to ensure everything ran smoothly, giving no lead time for any of the proceeds to go to anyone else's pocket but *his*, was for Diego to die just as the delivery arrived at Zane's dump of a factory.

But how the fuck was that supposed to happen if the shipment wouldn't be here for another day or so and Diego had to die tonight? *Bollocks!*

Oh, well, one thing at a time. Perhaps the universe would provide a way - it usually did.

Remembering Colt was still on the other end of the line annoyed Marco. Did the overgrown, deformed bastard enjoy listening to him breathe or something? 'What the fuck are you still on the phone for?' he barked. 'Get on with whatever you're doing and, like I said, be on standby if needed.'

In the interim, he'd wait to hear from Sofia and wrack his brains how to pull the warehouse job off afterwards.

• • • •

WHEN THE CALL WITH MARCO abruptly ended, Colt stared at his mobile for a few seconds before shoving it back in his pocket.

The rude bastard! Still, putting up with Marco and his bullshit what's a means to an end in pulling in what he needed.

Colt grinned. The project to fuck Lyndon up was nicely underway.

He headed back towards the kitchen where he'd left the 'spare' guard. The plan on what to do with this unexpected extra so he could get on with terrifying that stupid bitch barricaded in the bedroom was doubly required now.

Colt's thick brows furrowed. The quicker he got on with this, the better - especially if he was shortly instructed to go out and do the deed on that foreign bloke.

Shrugging, he made a concerted effort to remove the annoyance off his face as he entered the kitchen.

'Are you sure about this?' Art Wilson drank the fresh drink Colt had previously poured for him.

'Yeah, it's fine, mate,' Colt said, his one working eye glaring at the back of Art's head as the man sat at the kitchen table. Topping his own rum up, he then proceeded to refill Art's glass for the umpteenth time. 'My brother rarely drinks this stuff and won't notice that we have. I won't tell if you don't!'

Relaxing, Art grinned and reached for his topped-up drink. 'Just gotta hope Zane doesn't come back, then. We'll be pissed as farts at this rate!'

'Nah, he won't. And as for anything else, that little girl in the bedroom isn't likely to pull a stunt, regardless of whether we're paralytic or not! She's as meek as a mouse!' Colt pretended to take another swig of his rum, letting the spirit in his mouth carefully flow back into the glass through his smashed teeth. He'd bung the rest in that Yucca plant in the corner like he'd done with the last three drinks. There was no chance he was getting pissed, but this cunt would. And by the look of him, he was halfway there.

Colt glanced up the hallway towards the bedroom containing Alyson. This prat best get a move on with getting hammered because there were things to do.

'I tell you, mate, you're onto a good one here,' Art slurred. 'Cushy number or what! But what I don't understand, is why this girl needs a guard in the first place, let alone a double guard. Surely you tasked to watch her is enough?'

Colt shrugged his huge shoulders. This cock was a nosy fucker but at least it proved that no one else had knowledge of what was *really* going on. Not surprising - Zane Morelli wouldn't want it disclosed that his brother was on the warpath in areas other than expected ones. He grinned. *He* wouldn't be saying a thing to contradict that either.

Fucking insulting it was though that his prick of a brother insisted on another guard being brought over in addition. Lyndon and that airhead bitch, Erin, must believe that little whore to some extent and this change of events could have fucked things up. It was just lucky he was so resourceful.

Saying *this* wouldn't do any harm either...

'It is kind of weird that she needs two of us, but I guess it's for our own protection.'

'*Our* protection?' Art spluttered on his rum at the prospect. He'd glimpsed Alyson Read when he'd first arrived and she looked no more than seven stone wet through!

Colt sparked up a cigarette and slowly exhaled the smoke through his missing teeth. 'I agree it sounds bizarre, but…' He leant over Art and lowered his voice. 'I probably shouldn't be telling you this, but she's a bit doolally.' Putting his glass down, he tapped the side of his head. 'A mental case.'

'Really?' Art raised his eyebrows and then grinned as Colt gestured to the rum offering him yet another top-up.

'Yeah, she's supposed to be in a mental hospital, but Zane felt sorry for her being as she was the friend of his dead daughter - or rather the girl he *thought* was his daughter...' *That part was no secret*. 'The trouble is,' Colt continued, filling Art's glass up higher than before. 'Alyson has a habit of accusing men of stuff. You know...'

'Fuck!' Art gasped. 'I don't want no one saying that sort of shit about me!'

'Me neither,' Colt grimaced. 'Hence why there's safety in numbers. Luckily, she rarely leaves her room.'

'I guess it makes sense now,' Art slurred, unsteadily getting to his feet. 'I'm just going for a slash and then shall we have a game of cards?'

'Sure, why not!' Colt watched Art waver towards the bathroom. Grinning, he replaced the inch of rum Art had just slurped from the latest refill, then plonked himself down in the opposite chair.

It wouldn't be long now. He'd give this tosser fifteen minutes before passing out and then he'd be clear to get on with what he had to do to Alyson before a signal from Marco came in. He might even take the opportunity to win a few quid off this pissed-up loser whilst he was waiting.

• • • •

SOFIA RAN HER HAND over the Bentley Blower's bonnet and fawned with fake delight. *If any rust flicked off and went under her French manicure, she'd go tits*. 'What with it getting towards twilight I know it's not the best time to fully appreciate the gleaming paintwork, but...' She strutted around to the driver's side and leaned over the open cab. Resisting the urge to shove the annoying distended belly to one side so she could gloat a bit more about her latest extortionately expensive gift, she made do with pointing at the antiquated dashboard. 'Look at all the darling little dials. Aren't they just wonderfully vintage?'

Erin feigned interest. Cars weren't her thing, although the same couldn't be said for Zane. As expected, he was taking an intense interest in the old car.

'Isn't it special?' Sofia gushed, secretly pleased at the look on Zane's face. *Bet he wished he had one of these!* But why Marco deemed it so important that Diego bought this particular one still flummoxed her. Wouldn't it make more sense to get a Lamborghini? Now *that* would be fitting.

She inwardly shrugged. Marco clearly had a reason behind wanting Diego to buy it, but she hadn't been interested enough to ask what it was. All she cared about was getting out of her marriage and being with Marco.

Whilst everyone else was distracted with the 'allure' of the vintage car, Sofia took the opportunity to glance around, hoping to spy the barrel of a gun in the close vicinity from a sniper on a roof, the sights aimed between her husband's eyes.

But she hadn't given the nod yet, had she? *Damn!* Coming outside was the perfect opportunity for Marco's hitman, whoever he was, to take Diego out. Why the hell hadn't she made an excuse to nip to the toilet and send a text before they came out here? It could have all been done by now if...

'Are you all right?' Erin placed her hand on Sofia's arm.

'*What*?' Sofia snarled, then remembering she had a part to play, giggled coquettishly. 'Sorry, sorry! You made me jump! My mind keeps wandering off. "Baby brain", they call it. It's just...' She leaned into Erin conspiringly. 'I have an appointment with the midwife on Monday. I haven't felt the baby move recently and I want it checked out.'

Erin's hand instinctively moved to her own belly, the thought that something might be wrong with Sofia's baby not something she would wish on anyone - *even Sofia*. 'You think something's wrong?'

'I don't know but I hope not,' Sofia whispered. 'I haven't told Diego. He'll be frantic and I'm stressed enough as it is, so please don't mention anything.'

Feeling an unexpected pang of sympathy for this woman, Erin quickly reminded herself that this could be part of Sofia's plan. It was awful thinking that, but it *was* possible Sofia was making this up as an excuse to nip off and see this lover of hers. That's if what Diego suspected was true?

'I thought so!' Zane cried. 'What the fuck?'

Erin span around, surprised. 'What is it?' *Please don't say something else had happened back at the flat with Colt and Alyson. She knew they should have stayed there rather than come here.* 'What's happened?'

'This!' Zane looked up, his eyes wild. 'This is my father's - my father's Bentley!'

'What?' Erin couldn't believe it. The Bentley that was taken by Marco, along with all of Zane's other cars in the penthouse underground car park? 'It *can't* be the same one.'

'I'm telling you it is.' Zane pointed to the dashboard where a small scratch was indented in the metal. 'See that, there? That was me. As kids, my father let us sit in here sometimes and the buckle on my shoe scratched it as I clambered in. He was not happy with me!'

Sofia looked from Zane and then at Diego who seemed as confused as everyone else. 'This is silly! The car is old. I expect loads of old cars have random marks on them.' She laughed, but Zane wasn't laughing.

'I know my cars and this is a rare model. There aren't many, if any of these around anymore,' Zane snapped, vaulting himself with ease over the car door into the open cab. 'And I'll prove it.'

'Hey, stop!' Sofia squawked. 'You'll damage something and...'

'My father insisted on having lap belts installed in the back for me and my brother and I bet you that...' Zane leant over the front seats to the back and shoved his hand down the back of the real leather seat. 'Yep! Here's one.'

Erin stared in amazement at the old lap belt Zane pulled from under the seam of the seat.

'The other one got broken.' Zane rummaged further down the opposite end of the back seat. 'In exactly the same place as *this...*' He looked from Sofia to Diego. 'Without a doubt, this *is* my father's car. Where did you buy it?' There was only one person who had taken his cars and therefore only one person who could have sold it. *Marco*.

Diego laughed. 'What are the chances of me buying your father's car?'

'I'm deadly serious, Diego,' Zane growled. 'You don't understand! Just tell me who sold it to you.'

'It was an advert in the paper,' Sofia interrupted, her heart racing. She couldn't make sense of this. If what Zane said was true, then why would Marco insist on her husband buying a car that belonged to their father? One which Zane might recognise? It *couldn't* be the same car. Marco wouldn't risk Zane tying this back to him. What would it achieve? *Unless...* 'You must be wrong about it being the same car.'

'Nope! It's the very same one.'

Erin watched the proceedings with a mixture of disbelief

and concern, her mind racing. She'd seen the flash of panic flit across Sofia's face but pretended not to notice.

'Diego, who sold you the fucking car?' Zane repeated as he clambered out of the old Bentley.

'Some jumped-up cretin.' Diego frowned as he fought to recall the irritating little man's name. 'Whittaker. That's him! Sam Whittaker. A fucking blathering idiot!'

Zane scouted his memory for links to a man named Sam Whittaker but found nothing. Either way, he had to act on this.

Grabbing Diego's arm, he pulled him out of earshot of the women. 'This car was one of many taken from my collection by Marco.' He gave Diego a look. 'Don't react, just listen. This Sam Whittaker, whoever he is, might be selling the Bentley for Marco or could have bought the motor himself and now selling it on, therefore he was merely next n the chain and nothing to do with anything.'

Diego's eyes narrowed, scarcely able to believe what he was hearing. 'But there's a possibility this is something to do with Marco? A setup? Against me?'

Zane shrugged. 'I don't know, but what I *do* know is that we need to rule this Whittaker person out.'

Diego nodded and walked back over to the car. 'Me and Zane need to pop out.' He smiled like he hadn't a care in the world. 'We shouldn't be long, so you ladies chat and relax in our absence.'

'What's going on, Diego?' Sofia whined. 'What are you...'

'Work, Sofia,' Diego said, his voice stiffening, the tone underlining there would be no more questions on the subject.

Erin looked to Zane, not needing to ask a thing. They were off to find Sam Whittaker and discover where the trail led. And it was clear by the looks on both men's faces they had reached the same question ricocheting around her own head: Was Marco behind putting the advert for this Bentley in the paper? And it so, had they considered why Sofia was so desperate for this *particular* Bentley in the first place?

• • • •

LEO RAN HIS EYES ALONG the mass of empty shelves and racks in the warehouse cleared in readiness. Half of the gear from the previous shipment had already been moved on and with another load going out from the other end of the place throughout the course of the night, the remaining cocaine had been shifted into another area. 'I think we can safely say that everything's in place for the next load due to drop!'

He smiled proudly to himself. It was a tall order getting everything to tie up in the way it had. Especially with things so fraught and all over the place the way it had been lately. There were plenty of times when he'd doubted anything would be ready being as the dates for the drop had been unexpectedly brought forward, but everything was done.

Leo turned around, his jubilance deflating at Tiger's expression. It was like he'd been talking to himself this past ten minutes. He wasn't surprised that Tiger had returned from the flat. When Zane had arrived at the canning works, he hadn't been in the best of moods and uncharacteristically subdued. This only turned into worry on realising he'd missed calls from Erin and Leo found himself with little choice but to explain what had happened with the grief at Tiger's flat otherwise Zane would have gone off on one worrying about Erin and the baby.

But Tiger returning with a face resembling a slapped arse did not correlate with the snippets Leo had winkled out about what had caused the ruckus between his brother and that girl, Alyson.

'Look, mate,' Leo said, checking no one else was in earshot. 'I know it can't have been easy but at least you know that none of us think it was you.' *But*, he thought shamefaced, the question had crossed his mind whether Tiger *was* behind those films appearing in his video player. Not that he would admit that - the man already looked like he had the weight of the world and then some on his shoulders. But getting no response, his irritation tingled. 'Are you listening to anything I say? I said tha…'

'I heard what you said,' Tiger growled. 'Am I supposed to

be grateful you've decided not to accuse me for once? That's if I believed that to be the case!'

'What? I...'

'Erin's already asked if I was responsible. Even Alyson accused me. Colt did the same too, so I can't imagine it hasn't gone through your fucking mind!' Tiger went from stone-like statue to rabid in five seconds flat. 'Then I get sent back here!'

Gritting his teeth, Leo leant against one of the empty worksurfaces. 'Nothing's ever right as far as you're concerned, is it? Surely you understand that questions have to be asked? The point is that you're believed.' He folded his arms, knowing Tiger would not like this one bit, but it had to be said. 'You need to move past this shit, mate. I've told you before - your mind isn't on the job. Everyone knows it and you won't tell anyone why. Even me!'

Tiger's face flushed with both embarrassment and anger. Leo was right of course, but even that wasn't the main focus of what was needling him. What was prodding in the deep recesses of his brain was, in many ways, worse than the insult of being told he was letting his comrades down.

Bypassing Leo's last comment, Tiger was unable to stop the words form and before he knew it, they'd left his mouth. 'It not being me is all very well, but as it *wasn't* me, that only leaves two people.' *And he didn't want it to be either option.*

Leo rubbed his rough fingers across his mouth. He'd been half waiting for this awkward question. 'I know, what with Colt being your brother and all that, I totally get you don't want it to be him. But as much as it surprises me to admit it, there's no way it was him. It's that dopy bitch Alyson!' He shook his head with guilt. 'I feel kind of responsible for half of this latest crap. What started out as a wind-up getting you lumbered with putting her up in your flat hasn't turned out the way I thought. I'm sorry for that, I really am.'

*And it hadn't.* Instead of removing Tiger's hangups acquired thanks to Skye, all dumping Alyson Read on him had achieved was getting him accused of more things, deflecting half of the firm's workforce and losing his brother-in-arms in the process. Since Colt appeared on the scene in addition to Alyson, Tiger hadn't been the same and Leo couldn't help but feel partly responsible.

'She needs to go, mate. Alyson is fucked in the head. Forget Marco fucking her body, he fucked her good and proper up here and all!' Leo got as far as tapping the side of his own head before he found himself pressed by the throat against the work surface. 'What the fuck are you doing?' he spluttered, his big hands pulling against Tiger's equally huge ones in this unexpected assault.

'Don't speak about Alyson like that!' Tiger roared, spittle spraying from his mouth. All the conflicting emotions mixed with rage poured from him, fuelling his onslaught. 'I should kill you for what you just fucking said! I should kill you, like I should've killed that cunt, Marco, being as Zane let the bastard walk!'

As quickly as his rage exploded, the opposing side of the argument jostled for position in Tiger's head. *Was it really about that?*

Yes, but it was also about the nagging dread that wouldn't leave him be. The same conclusion that, by the sounds of it, everyone else had already reached: Alyson *was* acting unstably. She always had and this could be another facet of it. It *was* feasible she'd found the videos and planted them to make it all fall on Colt's shoulders.

Tiger's admission to himself allowed Leo to get the upper hand and he pulled the grip from his throat. Wild-eyed, he jumped to a standing position, the fury for his once trusted friend afire. 'You've just about pushed me to the fucking limit!' he barked, his throat sore. He rubbed at his neck, his eyes not moving his glare off Tiger.

He brushed the dust off his T-shirt, only barely holding together the urge to lay into his comrade with his fists. 'Okay, I was out of turn by saying that about Alyson and for that I'm sorry, but the rest...? Fuck me, Tiger! What the hell's happened?

You're down my throat all the time and your head ain't on the job. Even your fucking loon of brother is more trustworthy and hardworking than you!' He began pacing the room. 'We've had a shit load on here and still have, but you've left the lion's share to me because you're off with the fucking fairies all that bloody time! I ain't having it anymore!'

Tiger opened his mouth to retaliate and justify his actions and why he'd been the way he had, but he couldn't. He just *couldn't*.

And through all of it, there was one thing which overtook everything, including anything Leo or *anyone* could possibly say. 'I shouldn't have left Alyson with Colt, no matter what Zane ordered,' Tiger muttered, now also pacing around the room. 'I should have refused.'

Leo stared in amazement. 'You're doing it again! What the fuck is the matter with you? Do what you should have done in the first place and get that bitch sectioned! Everyone, including me, knows that's what is really necessary here, so stop messing everyone around. You're becoming a liability!'

'Liability?' Tigers anger reignited but then so had Leo's. 'I won't presume Alyson is crazy just because you and the others say so!'

'Why the fuck not?' Leo spat. 'What does it matter?'

'Because I had my own mother sectioned, that's why!' Tiger screamed, the veins in his temples looking ready to pop. 'I had her put away because I was told it was the "right" thing to do. It wasn't! She ended up dead because of me!'

The retort Leo had been ready to throw melted back into his tongue. 'I'm really sorry to hear that,' he mumbled. 'But it doesn't mean that in this instance th…'

Tiger turned to deflect the burn of hot tears threatening to overspill. 'You're not to mention what I just said about...'

'No, fine. I won't... I...'

'Whatever anyone says, I'm not doing the same to Alyson.'

'Even on this occasion when it's the right thing to do?' Leo pushed, knowing he was treading on thin ice. 'Whether you like it or not, mate, that chick ain't right in the head. She'll get someone killed. Not to mention the damage she's already done to this firm by various means.'

'Yeah, even on this occasion I'm not doing it,' Tiger snarled, pulling on his jacket. But if Alyson *was* genuinely cracked, like everyone thought and he too had begun to suspect, whose interest was he acting on by not getting her the help she might need? Things weren't like they had been in his mother's time, so was he doing the right thing by digging his heels in or was it purely for himself?

Leo watched Tiger, his stomach slowly sinking. 'Where are you going now?'

Tiger looked up, his eyes cold. 'Back to the flat. I should never have left there in the first place, so if you or Zane have a problem with that, then bin me off from the firm.'

Turning on his heels, he stormed from the canning works, the instinct that Alyson wasn't safe too strong to ignore. If he was wrong - wrong about *everything*, and she was off her trolley, then he'd know soon enough.

And if that was the case, then he'd just have to deal with that and what it brought, if and when it happened.

# Twenty Eight

'PLEASE LEAVE ME ALONE,' Alyson cried, only loosely controlling the urge not to slip into hysteria. She kept her gaze fixed on the floor – Colt's boots a better alternative than looking at his face which terrified her. Her eyes then darted to the bedroom door which had splintered around the jamb. Her effort to barricade it with the bedside table had proved pointless because now even that lay on its side on the deck.

'Hmm,' Colt sneered, his finger running underneath Alyson's jawbone to tilt her face up to his. 'What if I don't want to?'

Alyson's panic slammed into first gear. 'Oh no! Don't... please don't do...'

'Don't flatter yourself, girly,' Colt chuckled. 'Not all of us find you irresistible. I prefer my women to have substance, both in the flesh and in the head.' His free hand poked Alyson's temple and then dropped to squeeze her breast.

Yelping in disgust and fright, Alyson was silenced with a hand over her mouth. 'Don't make a fucking scene, you silly bitch!' Colt hissed. 'Considering what *you've* been up to, you shouldn't be so uptight.'

Nausea brewing in Alyson's belly, her eyes darted back to

the door. *Where was the other guard? She'd seen another man arrive as Tiger left, so where was he? And why, oh why wasn't Tiger here?*

With a sudden flash of resolve, she stared into Colt's gruesome face. 'When Tiger comes back and finds the door broken, he'll know what you've done. He'll...'

'Ah! Didn't take long for the bitch's claws to come out, did it?' Colt jibed. 'Attempting to set me up with your lies again? It's a shame no one believes you.'

'They'll have no choice but to believe *that*!' Alyson pressed on, her courage remaining in place. 'No one can dispute a smashed-up door.'

Colt smiled, exposing the smashed gaps of his teeth. 'I didn't have much choice about that though, did I? I mean, what else was I supposed to do when I thought you were doing something stupid?'

'Wh…?' Alyson's question cut off as Colt pulled out a pocketknife.

'You see, when silly, mentally unstable chicks attempt suicide, others have no choice but to intervene.' Colt grabbed Alyson's slender wrist and sliced a shallow cut across it.

Alyson squealed, her eyes widening as blood seeped to the surface of her wrist.

'Luckily for everyone, little girls playing attention-seeking games don't do any *real* damage to themselves.' Flicking the knife shut, Colt ran his finger along Alyson's bleeding wrist and slowly sucked the blood from it. 'Everyone knows that kind of behaviour is a play on people's emotions and a mode of manipulation. Even so, no one would put a damaged doorframe above checking on someone's well-being, would they sweetheart? However undeserved…'

Eyes narrowing, he gripped her wrist and twisted it behind her back. 'So, start telling me what the fuck you thought you were doing by speaking shit about me to Erin and my brother.' Colt leant close to Alyson, his rancid breath hot on her face. 'Actually, I think I've changed my mind about you. Although I don't make a habit of bedding mental patients, I might make you the exception being as you clearly enjoy certain things so much.'

Alyson staggered forward, the thought of this beast of a man knocking her off balance, but she had nowhere to move - his bulk blocked any chance of her falling, apart from into him.

'Now, now, don't pull the old shrinking violet trick.' Colt's tongue ran along his lower lip, the prospect of getting his hands on the little slip of a bitch who had successfully captivated his brother's attention, a massive incentive.

He trailed a finger between Alyson's breasts then moved down to her stomach but stopped just below her belly button. 'Before we have some well-earned fun, I want to know what you saw at Marco's?'

He'd get the info Marco wanted out of this little whore before doing anything else. As another goalpost had changed with having to offload some foreign geezer tonight, his time here was short, but there should be enough to tick a few things off the list and keep everyone sweet.

Alyson's revulsion over where Colt's hand was travelling to was promptly replaced with a surge of additional fear. *Marco?* Just that man's name was enough to make her dizzy with fright and loathing. *But if this monster was asking about Marco, did that mean...?* 'I wondered if you were involved with him!' she cried, forgetting the position she was in. Even the stinging of her sliced wrist took a back seat to this. 'You *are*, aren't you?'

'So what if I am?' Colt sneered, thoroughly enjoying his game. 'Tell who you like! Tell my brother if you wish! He won't believe you because he thinks you're a mad cow too, just like everyone does! If he has anything to do with it, you'll be banged up where you belong because that's what he does to people.'

'*You*, you mean?' Alyson spat, finding a new spurt of defiance. 'You're clearly insane therefore he was right to do it to you!' Tiger didn't think she was mad. He'd have agreed with

Mr Solenzo if that was the case. *And he hadn't.*

'You really think you have his protection?' Colt swung Alyson against the broken door, her head whacking against the wood. 'Well, think again! My brother will have you gone, mark my words. And you want to hope he achieves that and fast, otherwise you'll be dead.'

Alyson's surge of courage slipped away as it sunk in what was being said. *This man was here to kill her on Marco's orders?* Her hands started shaking even though she didn't want them to. Tiger, who she hoped might one day love her, thought her crazy and *this* man was here to kill her. But the question about Marco sparked another memory of a time she'd tried so desperately to delete. That woman she'd seen on the film doing... doing those things to her…

Little visual snippets flooded her mind about the haze of that drug-filled night. Alyson dragged air into her lungs in ragged gasps. If she didn't, she'd suffocate or forget how to breathe.

Marco *had* done something to that woman. Flashes of him hitting the blonde with something nagged in Alyson's mind's eye; small subliminal clips of that woman's body being dragged along the floor wrapped in a bag or something...

Alyson's brain hurt trying to remember whilst at the same time blocking things out. This could all be a figment of her imagination. How could she be sure? How could she...

'Ah-ha! You know something, don't you, you treacherous cunt!' Colt gripped Alyson's jaw and squeezed, smiling as her eyes bulged. 'I knew it! What do you remember?'

'N-Nothing!' Alyson spluttered, unable to properly form words through her squashed mouth. 'I...'

'Now, listen and try to understand. Personally, I don't give a toss.' Colt released his grip. 'You'll be dead soon, but I've been instructed to find out what you know, so you might as well tell me.'

On the verge of being powerless to refrain from falling into a spiral of hysteria, Alyson glanced up the hallway and in a final attempt of saving herself she started screaming. *Surely the other guard would rush in to save her?*

Colt's hand clamped back over Alyson's mouth. 'Shut it, you stupid slag! He won't hear you - I've made sure of that.' His eyes glistened with malice. 'It's just me and you, babe.' *He was enjoying this.* He'd be the very last person to stick his cock in this tramp and as his parting shot, would make sure Lyndon knew all about that before he killed this little cunt.

But first, he'd watch his twat of a brother unravel when he was forced to do what he did to every fucker and get this little whore chucked in the loony bin. This vacuous little slut had so far been exempt from that bonus but not for much longer...

Oh, he'd been so completely and utterly clever with this whole thing. He'd made sure he had an answer to explain away every last little thing that anyone could think to question.

Once he'd clocked this silly bitch was the subject of these films that everyone, including Marco, rattled on about, it was easy to know where to find them. Colt suspected that his brother wouldn't have changed *that* much. When they'd been kids the first and only place Lyndon ever hid anything was under his bed. There was a loose floorboard and anything and everything he hadn't wanted their mother to see had gone under it.

Colt grinned. And this time was no different. Even though there was no loose floorboard, the principle remained the same.

It had been a gamble to look there – the films being a 'nice-to-have' addition to the ammunition to use against Alyson and his sad, predictable brother, but there they were. Locating them had taken all of one minute, of which he'd managed to wrap up and complete in the blink of an eye.

*Easy fucking peasy.*

And the subject of those films had worked out better than good in chucking a spanner in the works here.

'There's nowhere to run, darlin',' Colt said, his hand slipping inside Alyson's top. 'No one wants you - even mummy and daddy when they see your films.'

The clanging in Alyson's head silenced. *The films? Her*

*parents had those films?* Her eyes darted to Colt's horrible beady eyes.

'Oh, yeah, you think I'd miss a trick like that when I got the chance? Shame you're not believable enough when you said it was me who arranged those tapes.' He laughed loudly. 'I ain't stupid, see. Far fucking from it, girly. I've made several copies and one's already gone to your parents, so by this time tomorrow, they'll have washed their hands of you. Posh folk lot don't accept sluts for daughters.'

Not that he'd actually made copies at all. Admittedly, he would have done if he'd had time. He still might at some point, but it didn't matter anyway because this thick pointless little whore believed there were copies – many of them. One of which was buy winging it's way to her dearest parents. It was freaking her out and that alone was almost as enjoyable as getting to properly watch those films himself. And to top it off, Marco believed he was here doing *his* bidding, when the coked-up cunt couldn't be more wrong.

Marco securing his release from Broadmoor in exchange for pretending to be grateful about doing a poxy piece of piss job was fine to get the perfect opportunity to do what *he* needed. And Colt was achieving everything he wanted just perfectly.

Putting his finger to his mouth, Colt looked to the ceiling in mock thought. 'All in all, you're not doing too well, are you? My dear brother thinks you're a sad case who he never wanted to be lumbered with in the first place. No one believes a word you say, Marco Morelli wants you dead and oh… I nearly forgot… your parents will know you're a prostitute, which means for the time you have left remaining, you're stuck with me.'

Hearing screaming - very loud screaming, Alyson concentrated on that, rather than anything else. She was now nowhere near the right state of mind to realise it was coming from her.

• • • •

'I HAVE A CONTACT who can get his home address.' Moving away from the huge office building of One Canada Square, Zane flicked through his mobile and located the number of a detective on his payroll.

Diego glanced back up at the immense building. *The supercilious twat, Whittaker, had his firm based here?* It hadn't been difficult to find where the company was located, but the man's home address was different.

It wasn't like the security guard had said 'home' was where Whittaker presently was, but Diego suspected by the fear in the uniformed man's eyes as they strode into the lobby, then forced their way into the lift to the floor housing Whittaker Inc, that guard would have gladly given them the address if he knew it.

Diego watched Zane speak quietly on the mobile. Whoever this contact in the force was, Diego hoped he'd come good and hand over Whittaker's home address. If they didn't have that, there was nowhere else to look right now and if this connection meant his life was on the line, there was no time to wait until the sap wandered back into his office.

At least leaving Sofia and Erin at the house was safe. The place was secured up to the hilt. Diego had not taken any chances with that, but being outside was a different story.

It was tempting to glance around for signs he was being watched or sights trained on him, but he refused to lower himself to the point of acting scared. Marco did not scare him and behaving like he did was not an option. Instead, he remained focused on Zane, his mind ticking over silently but rapidly.

Adrenaline throbbed along Diego's veins at the thought that the pompous prick who'd sold him the Bentley could be involved with Marco Morelli. That Morelli wouldn't take being removed from their cocaine arrangement and replaced by his despised brother was no surprise, but Diego admitted he hadn't expected *this*. It could be a bizarre coincidence that he should just 'happen' to buy a car previously been in Marco's possession. But then again, it might not.

He frowned. Although furious and on edge, it seemed more likely that posh boy Whittaker was nothing to do with this. After all, Marco couldn't know whether he was interested in a Bentley in the first place to make it a viable setup. Furthermore, he *wasn't* interested in Bentleys - never had been. It was *Sofia* who'd been obsessed with having that particular car, not him and...

Freezing, Diego's jaw clenched. Why indeed had Sofia been so desperate for that car? And that one in particular? It couldn't be possible that she was somehow involved with...

*No! Pull yourself together*, Diego thought. Going down absurd tangents was not a good use of brain power or time. Luckily, before he could analyse anything further, Zane jerking his head towards the street snapped Zane from his thoughts.

'I've got Whittaker's home address. Let's go!'

Nodding, Diego matched Zane's stride as they made their way back to the Maserati.

• • • •

BACK INSIDE THE Kensington townhouse waiting for word from Zane, Erin remained alert. Her mind raced with the prospect of what it meant if the sale of the Bentley was one of Marco's setups. If it was, was the vendetta aimed at Diego for severing their lucrative cocaine deal or was it to do with Zane?

In addition to replacing him on the cocaine arrangement, was Marco aware of the burgeoning friendship between Zane and Diego?

*Probably*. Either one would needle Marco to fuck and everyone knew the sad bastard wouldn't rest until he destroyed anyone and everyone who had ever slighted him. In Marco's world, that was just about everyone. But Zane's list of slights, as far as Marco believed, would be longer than everyone else's put together.

*Or was it something more?*

Erin frowned. There was something jabbing away in the back of her mind - something she was missing but couldn't put her finger on.

She glanced up at the ceiling, hearing Sofia moving around above. As expected, the 'nice' act had dropped the second the men left the house and Sofia disappeared, leaving Erin alone downstairs.

That was fine by her - the less time she spent in that woman's company the more palatable things were. But Sofia had been gone *ages* and Erin couldn't forget what she'd been asked to do before things got sidetracked. Sofia must confide in her - or at the very least, slip up, let her guard down and reveal something, like she had before. But how could she do that if the woman was nowhere to be seen?

Getting to her feet, Erin headed to the large wooden door of the immaculate reception room she'd been left in, then stopped. With her hand on the doorknob, she listened.

Holding her breath so the sound of air passing through her lungs didn't interfere with any sound from above, Erin concentrated hard. *Yes, Sofia was still definitely upstairs.*

Slowly turning the knob, Erin moved into the hall, now glad that she wore gear unsuitable for a formal dinner. In this instance, her favourite flat leather boots rather than the stilettos she'd normally wear for an invitation such as this, were a godsend.

Zane and the others always laughed at her insistence in refusing to part with this particular pair of boots, well past their best. She'd had them for *years*. The sole was loose and the leather scuffed, but she loved them. The embossed gold star on the sides was the best and most favourite part and she wasn't getting rid of them for anybody!

And tonight, they gave the ultimate advantage by being silent against the tiled floor of the large reception hallway.

Now she'd go upstairs and see if she could garner any clues to help Diego suspicions.

She began creeping up the stairs as quietly as possible. She had to be careful how she approached Sofia. Now the men had gone it was clear that Sofia wanted nothing to do with her and this task had reverted back to its original difficulty level.

Her mind flicked once again to Zane. Aside from wondering how they were progressing with locating this Whittaker person, his recent state of mind was bothering her. She knew that despite Zane trying to shield her and pretending otherwise, he was overloaded. The mental anguish over Skye's death, on top of the devastating hurt the girl wasn't his daughter after all was something he'd refused to discuss. He pretended he was okay with it, but how could he be? Then the unexpected revelation over Guiseppe's part in Shirley's rape and the cover up surrounding Marco was something Erin believed Zane would never recover from.

Guiseppe Morelli had always been Zane's idol - the father he missed dreadfully and whom he based his whole way of working, morals and *everything* on. Guiseppe was the man Zane wished to make proud, but if what was said was true, now it was the opposite. And, despite saying little about it, Erin knew the horrific discovery was eating the man she loved away from the inside out.

She'd truly believed Zane was close to desecrating his father's grave at one point. Thankfully, he hadn't, but with the additional responsibility of Alyson, Marco's latest threats and resurgence, the body in the air con vents, as well as Tiger and Leo being at each other's throats half the time seemed to be threatening to push him over the edge.

And Marco... Deep down Zane didn't want to kill his own brother. He'd never admitted that to her or anyone, but Erin knew. He'd have done it by now, otherwise. But time was running out and he'd shortly have no choice but to break his own rule of not killing family.

Erin sighed, wishing she could do more to help. Some things couldn't be changed, but she could do *something*.

She didn't yet know what had kicked off between Zane and Diego earlier, but suspected it was adding to Zane's stress. Making sure she delivered on her promise regarding Sofia could only help in keeping Diego and Zane on track and therefore the arrangement - another thing which bothered Zane.

Finally reaching the top of the stairs, Erin glanced around the maze of landings and numerous doors leading off to places unknown. *Sofia was up here somewhere, but where?* She was dreading locating the woman and cajoling her into a chat, but if it helped Zane in the long run, she'd do anything.

Suddenly, Erin heard a noise. Stiffening, she waited and weighed up the sound. Yes, it was. It was a voice.

*Sofia's voice.*

Heart thumping, Erin edged along the landing to pinpoint the muffled noise. *Was Sofia on the phone?*

Diego had told Zane he'd clocked Sofia sending texts via a phone that he hadn't bought and suspected it could be texts to a lover. *Was Sofia on the phone right now to that lover? That's if there was one?*

With a renewed sense of determination, Erin located the room Sofia was in. And not only could she hear her clearly, she could also see through the gap in the door. She prayed Sofia didn't spot her lurking outside, but the risk was worth the gamble as it might shed light on Diego's questions.

# TWENTY NINE

HUMMING ALONG TO RADIO 2, Sam continued along the A4. The traffic was heavy and only stood to get worse, but it didn't faze him.

After things had taken on that rather unpalatable turn during his working lunch in Richmond, he'd made the decision to take a detour and destress for a while at his parents' house. This had turned out to be a good call. It had been a while since he'd seen his folks and a few hours being the centre of the avid attention his doting parents always gave him and eating his mother's scrumptious apple turnovers which she never failed in winning first prize at the yearly village fête, was a tonic to his nerves just as he knew it would.

His parents had only ever shown genuine interest and admiration for their son's high-flying career. Sam's most faithful supporters, he'd even go as far as handing them the accolade of instilling him with the confidence required to achieve the success he'd attained.

Obviously, Sam thought with a smug grin, they were especially impressed with the news that he was working with two of the world's most influential and wealthy men - men who had come to *him* for advice.

He grinned. His mother had all but swooned with pride at the height of 'her little Sammy's' success.

Just thinking of his mother's pet name for him made Sam all fuzzy inside. It went without saying that he'd omitted the parts about Delgado and Morelli being drug lords. His parents didn't know about that bit. Besides, it wasn't relevant. Nothing *he* was working with them on would be illegal or anything like that.

His father was so impressed hearing about the Bentley Blower, there was a small part of Sam that wished he'd given the car to his dad rather than sell it. But then, four million was a lot to lose on sentiment.

Anyway, the visit had done him the world of good with resetting his stress levels. In fact, he was in such a good mood, he'd text Miranda when he got home. He'd been a bit hard on her, but she shouldn't interrupt important conversations. She wouldn't make that mistake again, Sam thought, pleased with himself. But thanks to his newly-formed good mood, he'd smooth things over with her tonight, rather than make her sweat it out until tomorrow like he normally would under such circumstances.

Sam weaved in and out of the traffic. All that was left to do now was wait for Marco to tell him when the joint meeting with Diego would be and then things would get even better. He was just about to turn the radio up louder when his mobile rang. Glancing at the phone in the built-in holder of the BMW's dashboard, Sam frowned. *The office?*

He pressed the button to answer the call. 'Sam Whittaker speaking.'

The voice of one of the building's many security guards boomed through the car speakers. 'Sorry to bother you, sir, but I thought you should know that... erm... that two men entered the building tonight looking for you.'

Sam frowned. 'For *me*? Who were they? Everyone knows the office is closed in the evening. Are you sure they were there for me?'

'Oh yes, sir,' the voice crackled deafeningly. 'They made that very clear both to me and to the guard outside your office.'

'They went upstairs to *my* floor?' Sam gasped. 'What in God's name?'

'The men... how can I put it... They were... well… unsavoury-looking, if you get my drift? Not in the "rough tramp" kind of way though.'

Sam's happy bubble popped and sweat trickled under his collar. 'Wh-What did these men look like?'

'Difficult to say... Foreign, perhaps? One of them was well-dressed, the other looked more like a motorbike person. They wanted your home address and were very insistent about that. I made it clear I didn't know it.'

Sam's mind raced. *It wasn't Marco. Marco wouldn't come to his office.* 'Okay, thanks for letting me know. I'll get to the bottom of it in the morning.'

Ending the call, he grimaced. What he'd just learned angered him, rather than worrying him. For a minute there, he'd thought it might have been Marco, still narked about the interrupted phone call this afternoon, or perhaps it was to let him know a date for the meeting with Diego?

But Marco would phone rather than come to the office. He wouldn't ask for his home address either.

Shaking his head with irritation, Sam realised he knew *exactly* who these two men were. The guard said 'foreign', so it was that bloody Arab Prince and his son. The elder man had been most put out last week when Sam broke the news they weren't a good fit as investors for a particular scheme they had enquired about and the pair took a personal affront to this.

'Pffst!' he snorted in derision. Arabs were too used to getting their own way. Well, he wasn't lining up investors who weren't a good fit. He had a business and a reputation to protect. Plus, only arabs would think it acceptable to demand a home address and turn up uninvited.

Sam might have taken a different approach had he realised he was wrong with his identification, however he was too busy turning the radio back up to lend any more time to that irrelevant occurrence.

*He liked this tune too.*

Sam was just about to sing along when the station was interrupted by breaking news:

*"...the bodies of two young women have been found in an alleyway..."*

Sam rolled his eyes as the newsflash continued.

*"...The women died at the scene from bullet wounds delivered at point blank range, thought to bear the hallmarks of an execution-style killing. The victims are yet to be formally identified and traffic remains busier than usual around the area as police have sealed the..."*

'For God's sake!' Sam muttered, slapping the radio mode to CD. He wasn't listening to that. Now it would take even bloody longer to get home! London was getting worse, it really was. Where had all the law and order gone? First of all, foreigners thinking they had the right to demand personal addresses and the non-existent policing on the streets was obvious if people got gunned down just like that?

Okay, so those two women had made themselves targets by choosing to be prostitutes or whatever they were. Why else would they be in an alleyway? But to be shot like animals with no one seeing or hearing a thing showed exactly what this place was becoming.

Sam continued driving, glad he was as far removed as possible from the scourge of society where this kind of thing happened as a matter of course and instead allowed the Rachmaninov CD to soothe his ears from this latest unsavoury offence.

• • • •

JUST HEARING MARCO'S VOICE made Sofia feel a hundred times better. Although she'd love for her husband to exit the planet tonight, that couldn't happen if he wasn't here and with Diego's unexpected and sudden need to leave on 'work business', it was unlikely he'd be back tonight.

'Seriously babe, you can stand your man down,' she said, taking the opportunity to scrutinise her reflection in the mirror. What she saw, she smiled at, giving the whiteness of her teeth a quick appraisal. Even though Marco was on the other end of the phone and couldn't see her, it was important to look her best. She always looked her best for Marco and always would. She'd prove that every single day once they were free to be together, like they should always have been.

'No. From the gist I got, it's unlikely he'll be back tonight. Yeah... but even *he* isn't the sort to accost a woman whilst asleep. What? Don't be ridiculous! You know I don't want him in my bed. He *can't* be in my bed, you know that!' Her eyes hardened. 'Do it tomorrow instead - that's if he's back... Oh… right, okay...'

Sofia wasn't in the mood for jokes. Anything about Diego discovering the 'pregnancy' being fake was bad taste and not something she found amusing - even from Marco. 'What? No... I don't know exactly what it's about. They got a bee in their bonnet about the car, so I reckon they went off looking for the prat who sold it. What? I don't know! I didn't hear that!'

Sofia's bottom lip trembled. *Was Marco shouting at her?* 'I'm trying my best, babe... No... I don't know... Zane was convinced it was his dad's car, but I said it couldn't be. It's not, is it? Why would he... No... no, *she's* still here... No, she's downstairs… I'm supposed to take her shopping tomorrow.' She laughed sarcastically. 'Yeah, I wish, but I've got to go through the motions. Oh, okay... Yes, let me know.'

Sofia stared at the phone long after Marco hung up, resisting the temptation to throw it through the mirror in front of her. Smashing the glass to smithereens summed up how her life felt, but instead, she dutifully crammed the mobile back between her breasts and underneath the prosthesis.

Why did Diego have to disappear? His death could have happened tonight and she'd finally be free. It was almost like Zane had purposely made a song and dance about that bloody stupid car on purpose!

Her plucked brows moved slightly despite the vast amounts of botox.

Why was Marco so bothered about where Diego and Zane were going anyway? What the fuck did it matter if they scoured London for that slimy piece of crap who owned the Bentley before? Honestly, Marco was such a hothead. But then again, that was part of the reason why she wanted to wrap her legs around his neck every waking minute.

Thankfully, that would soon be normality because the time had almost come – and, she thought with a mischievous smirk, so would she - *multiple* times, when she had Marco all to herself with no more sneaking around.

*She couldn't wait.*

Taking a deep breath, Sofia adjusted the uncomfortable prothesis and strutted out of the bedroom. She'd better force a pointless conversation with that brainless tramp downstairs. She'd left Erin alone for ages and she didn't want the bitch whining to Zane that she'd been left by herself all night. He was bound to repeat that to Diego - that's if there was the time before her husband found himself lying face down with a bullet through his heart.

As she neared the top of the stairs, Sofia pulled her concentration away from her latest set of false nails and finding Erin in front of her, almost tumbled down the wide steps in shock.

'Are you okay?' Erin asked, a look of concern on her face. 'I was coming to see if I could find you. You've been gone so long and with what you said earlier about the baby, I wanted to make sure you were all right.'

Sofia frowned as much as her face allowed. What thing about the baby? What the hell was the stupid cow going on about? Most likely she was snooping around, so it was a good job she'd already finished on the phone.

Suddenly remembering the rubbish she'd spouted about seeing the midwife, Sofia rapidly replaced her scowl with a grateful smile. Personally, it felt like a shit-eating grin, but she'd practised this one to perfection and it looked the part: the perfect combination of benign thankfulness and warm friendliness. 'That's *so* nice of you to check on me. I just felt a bit sick but I'm okay now. I'm sorry I left you alone for so long.'

Suddenly a horrible thought entered her head. 'H-Have you heard from Zane? Are they coming back?' Because if they were, then she'd totally messed up by calling the hit off. Could she set it back up if needed? *No*. She'd told Marco to stand his man down. *Shit, shit, shit!*

'Don't worry, nothing's happened,' Erin soothed, gently taking Sofia's arm to steady her down the stairs. 'I haven't heard anything but I'm sure they'll be back soon. Let's go and have a nice glass of cold water. You look a bit pale.'

*Pale?* Sofia thought. This bitch had nearly given her a heart attack. And it wasn't water she needed - it was a jug of wine. 'That would be great. Shall we plan our trip for tomorrow and take our minds off things?'

'Yes, let's do that,' Erin smiled, knowing she'd have to go along with it. After what she'd just heard it was imperative she found out who Sofia was talking to and hoped Zane and Diego got back soon because she had to tell them what she'd heard.

One thing was for sure though: Diego was correct. Sofia was involved with someone else. And that someone was due to kill Diego.

• • • •

SENDING A TEXT to Colt with the code words meaning the job was off and to stand down, Marco paced around one of the many beautifully furnished rooms in his house, finding everything in it grotesque.

Hearing what Sofia said, his fury with Sam Whittaker

exceeded the top of the Richter scale where it had already been hovering for some time. Not only had that cunt been flapping his trap to that stupid mouthy cow, which he'd had to remove, along with the dim-witted friend of hers, hadn't helped his irritation levels. But now it seemed Zane and Diego had linked him with Whittaker. Or *might* have done. Either way, even if that hadn't happened, it would soon.

But it wouldn't have happened *at all* if it hadn't been for that private school cock.

Marco clenched his fists and stared at his reflection in the gilt-framed mirror over the mantle. If Whittaker had followed the clear and simple instructions that under no circumstances was Delgado to retain hold of the Bentley until a later date, then it wouldn't have been there for Zane to recognise it as being the very same fucking one their father had taken such pride in.

Marching over to a drawer in the carved walnut sideboard, Marco pulled out his silver case and cut a line of cocaine on the sideboard's polished top.

*What a fucking utter wanker Whittaker was.*

Oh, it was a definite that Zane would have eventually recognised the car, but not before Diego was dead and gone. Then it would have served the carefully planned insult of rubbing his brother's face in things a little further.

Snorting the line, Marco sniffed hard, his mind racing. How come Zane was at Diego's again tonight anyway? Surely they weren't *that* pally?

He dragged his hand under his nose and sniffed again for good measure. Not that it particularly mattered if Diego and Zane were best buddies. But it *did* matter that they'd gone off in search of Whittaker.

That spineless greasy piece of shit would sing like a bird about his part in everything and confirm the link with *him* to that Dago wanker and cunt of a brother. After that happened, if they hadn't already known, they'd immediately realise it was a setup and that Diego would be ready for the hit that they'd so cleverly and painstakingly arranged. *Not to mention costly...*

Marco seethed with rage. He'd already given Colt half the payment for the job but there wouldn't be a job at all if Diego and Zane got their hands on Whittaker. And he was fucked if that was going to happen because aside from the obvious reasons, *he* was the one who would be responsible for taking that stupid bastard, Whittaker, out, not *them.*

Marco snatched up his mobile, his head buzzing as the cocaine fuelled his brain. It was a tall order refraining from killing that slimy bastard immediately or swallowing the injustice of providing protection for him, but it had to be done. Whittaker could not be removed tonight by *anyone.*

It would happen tomorrow and Diego would be taken out at the same time. *Decision made!*

Bringing his phone to life, Marco stabbed in Sam Whittaker's digits, his teeth grinding as he waited for the call to be answered.

'Ah, Whittaker,' Marco drawled, his tone jovial. *He could hear engine noise which was a good sign.* 'Not at home? Where are you then? Oh! That's nice…'

*What a prick! Gone to see mummy and daddy, the sad twat?*

Oh well, Marco thought, a glint in his eye, no one could say he wasn't a fair man. Allowing someone a final visit to their dear parents before departing this mortal coil was most altruistic. 'No, don't bother going home. Come round here for a drink. I have news. Yeah, my house. It's on your way back if you're coming from Richmond way.'

Marco rapidly concocted a plan. 'Oh, you're almost at Mayfair? Well, that's good timing. Actually, fuck it! Why not stay here for the night? It's not like I don't have the room! That way you can have a few drinks. Yeah, yeah, of course it's fine. Oh, and I meant to say - I've set the date for our meeting with Diego, so it's time I filled you in with the details of this venture. Yeah... I'll tell you all about it when you're here. Okay, see you shortly.'

Smirking, Marco placed his mobile down. He could almost sense Whittaker about to come in his pants with the news. *Not that any of it was true.*

He carefully set up another generous line of cocaine. That prat would be here within minutes, so he'd have to get suitably wired so not to lose sight of himself and wring the fucker's neck the second he arrived.

It would be difficult to constrain himself, but he'd do it because this was the only way forward.

Unbeknown to Whittaker, the prick had just been assigned an important new role.

Marco smiled at his resourcefulness. Diego and Zane's search for Sam Whittaker tonight would prove pointless. And as for coming for him - they wouldn't attempt that until they could 100% confirm the link between him and Whittaker. That's what Zane's 'fair' morals did for him – made him lose out time and time again.

Tomorrow everything would come together and anything those pair of losers had planned would be irrelevant.

*Along with Diego and Whittaker...*

Marco clapped his hands together, then leant over the line of cocaine, silver straw in hand. By this time tomorrow, he would be richer than anyone, plus he'd have Sofia in his bed.

# THIRTY

HEARING FOOTSTEPS COMING along the external walkway over Alyson's never-ending screaming was impossible to decipher without the heightened level of hearing Colt now possessed. It was instances such as this where he was grateful to be missing an eye. 'I'm glad you're back,' he gasped, rushed out into the hallway. 'She's gone absolutely nuts this time and I didn't know what else to do.'

'*Tiger*!' Alyson screamed, clattering out of the bedroom. 'Get him away from me!'

Tiger stared at Alyson in horror. She looked wilder and more unkempt than he'd ever seen her - even at Marco's or when he'd brought her back from Solenzo's. She looked... looked possessed!

His eyes then darted to the splintered upright of the bedroom door. 'What the fuck's going on?'

Alyson clutched Tiger's shirt. 'He... he was about to... He threatened to... He touched me... He said he'd...'

Tiger swung towards Colt, his eyes ablaze. 'You did what?'

'Oh, for fuck's sake!' Colt threw his large hands up in frustration. 'The chick's crazy! She's been in there crying and wailing. She even fucking barricaded herself in!'

'That's not true! He...'

'I did kick the door in,' Colt admitted. 'I had to, bro. She was trying to fucking well top herself!'

A wave of cold dread flooded Tiger as he turned to Alyson. 'You were trying to do *what*? You...'

'Look!' Marching across, Colt reached for Alyson's arm, but she thrashed around like a dervish, screaming so loudly it hurt everyone's ears. 'Fucking hell!' he hissed, retreating. 'See what I mean? I was trying to show you her wrist, but you can look for yourself!'

Restraining Alyson, Tiger held her steady. 'Calm the fuck down. Calm down!' he yelled, horrified by this unravelling chain of events. *What the hell was going on?*

Tiger's bellowing voice had the effect of subduing Alyson. Not for long, but long enough for him to clock the hairline cut across her wrist that looked more like a bad paper cut than a suicide attempt.

Sensing Tiger's thoughts, Colt took full advantage of the opportunity offered and silently congratulated himself on how well he'd set this up down to the very last detail. 'As you can see, it was a clear play for attention, but I wasn't to know that, hence...' He nodded to the broken door. 'I had to ensure she was okay, bro, but I'll pay for the damage.'

'No! He did it! Your brother! He cut my wrist, not me!' Alyson shrieked. 'He smashed my head against the door as well. And he touched… touched my breasts!'

Colt stood to one side shaking his head. 'I'm making things worse by standing here,' he mumbled. 'I tried my best, mate, I really did. Maybe the poor disturbed cow will tell you the truth if I'm not around.'

Tiger nodded, grim faced. 'Don't leave but wait in the kitchen, would you?'

'He's lying,' Alyson spluttered, her eyes puffy from crying. 'Why don't you believe me? He admitted putting those tapes in the player. *He* found them. He said he knew you had a special hiding place. He's also sent copies to my parents.' Reminding herself of that nightmarish point, she broke down in loud wracking sobs. 'What am I going to do? No one believes me! *You* don't believe me! Why won't you fucking believe me?'

Tiger's jaw tightened. He didn't like hearing Alyson swear. He was about to reason with her and ask exactly how Colt had chance to locate those tapes, let alone get copies of them. This was the first time he'd been in the flat and had never been alone.

The stuff Alyson was coming out with was ludicrous! Jesus Christ – there was no point whatsoever in attempting to reason with her. The way Alyson was behaving she wouldn't take any notice.

'*He* cut my wrist!' Alyson hiccupped. 'He said he'd make it look like it was me. He broke the door down on purpose. I wasn't screaming – I wasn't doing anything! I did barricade it with that though.' She pointed to the broken bedside table. 'He just kicked everything in and... Oh God! What will I do? I've got to get away from here... from him!'

Dropping her grip of Tiger's shirt, Alyson darted around the bedroom, snatching up her few meagre possessions. 'Did I have any shoes? Do you remember? Oh, what does it matter!'

Stopping still for a moment, she stared miserably at Tiger. 'I wanted you to like me. I thought maybe... that…' Her face crumbling, she shook her head and resumed dashing around the room.

Tiger frowned. Had Alyson been about to say she felt something for him? Once, that might have helped work out how he felt about her, but now... Watching her lurch around the room in a state of panic, he remained rooted to the spot. His heart wanted to believe her. He wanted to believe her about *everything*, but how could he take what she said seriously when she was acting like this? This erratic behaviour - this... this *madness*. It was crazy.

Alyson stopped in the centre of the room again as another piece of what happened tonight slammed back into her brain. 'I can't go anywhere! I'll be killed. He said you'll have me locked up - that you have *everyone* locked up.' Her eyes widened. 'He also said if I don't get locked up, he'd kill me. Tiger, you've got to listen. I... I think he's something to do with Marco.'

'*Marco*?' Tiger stared at Alison incredulously, now finding it impossible to justify why he hadn't adhered to Solenzo's instructions.

'No! NO!' Alyson's hands flapped like she was surrounded by swarms of flies as the vision of Marco killing that woman elbowed its way back into her consciousness. This time in vivid detail. 'Tiger! He killed the woman! That woman at the penthouse. Colt asked me what I remembered about it, so Marco must think I'll go to the police. Marco's ordered Colt to kill me. He told me that himself. You must believe me!' she squawked. 'You don't though, do you? Oh God, God!'

'Jesus Christ,' Tiger muttered under his breath, unsure of what to do or say. Leo was right. Erin was right and Zane was right. Even *Colt* was right. Alyson had lost it. The girl needed help and as much as he despised the concept of specialist hospitals more than anything else, he didn't have the know how himself to give her the help she needed.

Her being here wasn't good for anyone.

• • • •

'I'M REALLY SORRY, BRO,' Colt said, crestfallen. 'I know you want to fight Alyson's corner.' He subtly glanced around the kitchen double checking he'd removed any incriminating evidence that Art Wilson might have left. Finding nothing, he shrugged his huge shoulders. 'I know you and her had... or have something going on.'

'No, we didn't. And we don't!' Tiger snapped. Suddenly feeling drained, he sank into the kitchen chair that Art had only very recently been dragged from. For once, he felt unable to put up his usual defence. It was like his force had been syphoned out via an invisible tube and there was nothing left. 'But,' he continued, looking at Colt, 'I thought perhaps that maybe... maybe there *could* have been something. Perhaps in another lifetime...'

Colt rested his meaty hand on his brother's shoulder. 'Either way, it's clear you have feelings for the girl, so it will be difficult to accept, but sometimes things aren't meant to be.' *Like you! His brother shouldn't still be walking the earth after what he'd done.*

Colt accepted he'd been slightly off in his judgement if nothing was actually going on with that little slag and his brother. But for Lyndon to have feelings for her amounted to the same thing. Maybe even better because now there would never be the chance. 'Bro, you've got to accept that the girl's unhinged,' he said, emboldened by the waver behind his brother's stone-like mask that slipped just enough to afford him a chunk of what was underneath.

It had been a long time since Colt had witnessed even a *glimpse* of what lay behind his brother's front and now was the perfect time to see it. His plan was working. Lyndon was hurting over this Alyson chick - hurting *bad.* And he'd ensure it got a lot worse.

It was disappointing to miss the chance of fucking the silly bitch because Lyndon going against Zane Morelli's orders only underlined how much this bird meant to him.

*Shame...*

'I know you don't want to do this and I also understand why,' Colt continued, his voice uncharacteristically reassuring. And there it was - the reference to his bastard brother getting their Ma sectioned. 'The past can't be changed but there's no point avoiding what's needed now because of what happened before.' *No, we can't change the past, but if you think I'll ever let you get away with it...*

Ignoring the pain on Tiger's face at their shared nightmarish past, Colt knitted his big fingers together and sighed. 'There's no easy way to say this, bro, but in Broadmoor I saw lots of people reacting similar to how Alyson does, so the sooner you accept it and do what's needed, then...'

'Where's the other guard?' In all the craziness, Tiger hadn't clocked that Art Wilson was nowhere to be seen. Plus, anything was better than concentrating on the subject Colt was talking about.

Colt smiled sadly. 'I know it wasn't my place to do so, but when I went to the kitchen to give you and the girl some space, I sent Art away. No point in three of us being here, was there?' He shrugged. 'I also didn't think you'd want it going around the canning works about...' He nodded towards the bedroom. 'I wasn't sure what else she was going to say. Obviously, Art heard and saw some stuff, but... Ah, that's a thought – if Alyson denies what happened, you could ask him. Art heard her screaming and knew why I had to break the door down. It freaked him out a bit as I think an ex of his killed herself some years back.'

Art Wilson would agree to whatever Colt told him to say because when he'd slapped him about enough to sober him up, there was no time wasted in telling the prick to sling his hook. It was easy enough to convince the man it was for his own good. Neither of them expected anyone else to turn up and Art would get the sack if he was found to be pissed on the job. *Yeah, I'll cover for you - no problem, mate...*

Tiger didn't consider checking with Art. The things Alyson had said were too crazy to warrant. *Colt working for Marco? Making copies of the tapes? A hit out on Alyson with Colt doing the job?*

It was insane and looked certain that Solenzo and everyone were right.

'What are you going to do with her?'

'I don't know.' But Tiger wished he did. He continued looking at the floor, Colt's size twelve boots taking up most of his field of vision. He stared blankly at the shiny toecaps for what seemed like ages before noticing the dried-on blood splatters. He fleetingly wondered who Colt had been fighting with this time but came to the conclusion that was the least of his problems right now.

• • • •

DESPITE SEVERAL EFFORTS to calm Alyson down, whatever Tiger tried didn't work. What she'd really wanted to know, he was unable to answer and equally unable to lie about it, so he'd said nothing. But at some point around the time dawn broke, Alyson eventually exhausted herself and fell into a restless sleep.

Sitting on the end of the bed, Tiger remained still, not wanting to move a muscle for fear of rousing her and risking the questions he couldn't answer starting again. If he'd been in a quandary not knowing which way to turn this last week, his position was now doubly worse.

He pulled his hands over his face and sighed with agitation. He was trapped on a treadmill within his head – an endless roundabout that revolved in circles, making no traction in either direction.

Going against what he'd instructed himself never to do, Tiger found his gaze moving from the spot near the skirting board to Alyson tossing and turning in a fitful sleep, her mind troubled. Fixated on her eyelids fluttering, the long eyelashes set in clumps from now dry tears twitching occasionally, he watched them cast spidery shadows onto her cheeks. *Cheeks he wanted to touch.*

The weight of what he should do where Alyson was concerned pressed down onto Tiger, making his head heavy and his shoulders stiff. He didn't want this woman committed.

Whatever the history with his mother, there was something else - another reason why he was looking for all and any excuses in the book. What if everything Alyson said was right, however far-fetched? What if the unexpected closeness he'd experienced with Colt tonight was unwarranted? What if the way Colt handled the accusations thrown at him in a much better manner than Tiger himself had handled the ones thrown at *him* was a smokescreen?

For the first time in decades, Colt had behaved like a *proper* brother - kind and understanding. Even though the subject of their mother and what had happened was touched upon, it had for once, been done without malice or questions. So why was there still that niggling seed of doubt; the pressing sense of urgency that something wasn't as it should be? Was it past history? Or was it because it was easier to accept Colt was at fault rather than Alyson?

Carefully getting up from the edge of the bed, Tiger inched towards the door. Successfully slipping from the room without waking her, he moved stealthily along the landing, seeing Colt slumped on the sofa half-asleep.

He moved into the kitchen. *He needed a fucking drink.*

Opening the fridge, Tiger cracked a can of lager open and necked it, the blood he'd seen on Colt's boots pushing back into his mind. That was it! Colt had punched that bloke in the canning works not long ago and had never been one to clean his shoes, so it would be from that.

Fuck, his head was mashed with the endless turmoil of questions and to-ing and fro-ing.

Tiger returned to the fridge, frowning to see no more beer left and made his way over to the pantry instead. He'd just have a warm one. It didn't matter.

Pulling open the door, he scowled at Colt's leather trench coat hanging on the back of the door. *Why the hell did he put that bloody thing in here?*

Fighting through the immense bulk to reach the four-pack of lager on a back shelf of the meagrely stocked cupboard, Tiger found himself struggling to push past the mass of leather. There was something hard in it – like a rod...

Getting irritated, he grabbed the middle of the coat and stopped when his hands felt the shape of something very distinct. Knowing exactly what it was, with a surge of dread, Tiger turned the coat inside out, spotting the telltale handle of a sword sticking out from the oversized pocket specially sewn into the lining.

*Why the fuck was Colt still carrying that thing? He thought all of that was done now.*

*Unless...*

Letting go of his brother's coat like it was poisoned, Tiger snatched the beers and shut the pantry door. At an utter loss, he sat down at the table to stop himself from going into a tailspin.

That sword had jogged his memory about something.

*And that something was not good.*

Without opening a can, Tiger got to his feet. He might have had no sleep, was completely exhausted and didn't know which way to turn, but he had to put this thing to bed once and for all. It was the only thing - the *final* piece left of anything deemed an excuse why not to do what was right and act on the evidence, what he'd seen with his own eyes and get Alyson sectioned to receive proper help.

He didn't need anyone to tell him that he was starting to suspect his brother of everything, even knowing deep down that wasn't the case. And, Tiger thought with a jolt of confusion and equally dreaded fear, it was because he *had* developed feelings for Alyson. *And big ones...*

He didn't want to have Alyson sectioned because he was falling in love with her.

*And he couldn't.*

Not only did he not go down that road *ever*, but it wouldn't make her better. It certainly didn't justify saying that what Colt had been accused of was true. Despite all of his faults, Colt was his brother.

Tiger hastily pulled on his jacket. He was being ridiculous and shouldn't be here. Leo was right. He was a liability. He had to get out of here - away from Alyson and where she couldn't influence his decisions.

Alyson was better off being guarded by Colt. Despite his past and his faults, Colt would never hurt a woman or his family. More than what could be said for *him...*

Tiger quietly let himself out of the flat, leaving Colt half-asleep. He'd wake up if there were any problems. He'd already reacted accordingly when Alyson slit her wrist. And as for him being something to do with Marco...

*Stupid!*

Jumping into his van, Tiger sped off in the direction of the canning works. There was just one last thing which would dispel any suspicions of his brother being involved in any of this and he knew exactly what that was and how to prove it to himself.

He grimaced, his tired eyes struggling to focus on the road ahead, realising with the state of his head lately, it was feasible he'd completely imagined what he was now going to check for.

# Thirty One

GRITTING HIS TEETH, Marco handed Sam Whittaker a coffee from the Faema Jubilé machine. That the Arab prat who owned this gaff had money to waste by spending thousands on a coffee machine was irritating enough, but not as irritating as serving this useless bastard like he was a goddamn waiter.

Marco glanced at his Rolex. The night had been long - drawn out further by snorting so much coke there was little chance of any kip even after this twat had overindulged the Rémy Martin and passed out.

He was completely knackered and counting the seconds before he could get the show on the road. Still, time ticked on. It was a new day - and today was *the* day.

Marco glared at the back of Sam's head as he lounged on the sofa, half-watching the news on a massive flat screen TV mounted on the far wall. The sound grated on Marco's wick, the nasally voice of the newsreader ricocheting around the room through state-of-the-art surround sound speakers.

The set up was nowhere near as good as the cinematic equipment he'd had installed in the penthouse, which no doubt Zane was now enjoying, however the acoustics of this one was still pretty good. Not helpful with the squeaky voice of the newsreader.

Marco managed a slight grin. In a couple of hours from now he'd never have to put up with Whittaker again. Better still, Diego would also be gone.

The bullshit Marco had fed Sam last night as he'd got steadily drunker soaked into the man's overinflated brain. The prick could barely contain himself as he'd calculated the percentage he'd pull in from the new 'venture' he was now part of.

Marco sneered to himself. He'd been clear to state that a lot hinged on things working out, which of course also depended on the quality of investors that *Sam* brought to the table. But in that jumped up little scrote's mind, there was no possibility of it failing.

The prick wouldn't be quite so cocksure had he known that every single thing he'd been told regarding this joint venture with Delgado was a figment of Marco's imagination. Christ, it sounded utter tosh even to him, but he was a dab hand at concocting stuff up at last knockings with the added bonus of making it sound believable. It was also helpful that Whittaker was a gullible, greedy wanker and saw little past pound signs.

'I heard something about this on the radio on the way over here last night,' Sam said suddenly, his bleary eyes focusing on the television. Reaching for the remote, he muted the volume to nothing. 'I don't want to listen to it all again. It bloody irritates me!' Neither was it helping the sore head he sported this morning.

Marco glanced up at the screen. 'Oh yeah?' he muttered uninterestedly. 'What's that about then?' *Like he didn't know...* The footage of the alleyway where those two birds had been dispatched last night was instantly recognisable. Yeah, exactly as he remembered, except now with the addition of police tape. Someone had stumbled across those pair quickly which was a bit of a shit, but no one was on his case about it so therefore it was irrelevant.

'Two more people murdered. It just shows the tax we pay

doesn't get spent on policing the streets!' Sam moaned. 'London's crawling with nutters. It's terrible.'

'Yeah, mad people everywhere,' Marco agreed, rolling his eyes. He hadn't paid tax in years and had no intention of starting now. As for as the police went – they could remain absent for as long as they wanted.

'It doesn't look like they've identified the women yet either!' Sam snorted in derision. 'The police probably can't work the computer database. Still, these women choose to become prostitutes and are aware of the risks when they put themselves in a situ...'

Bored with Whittaker's rant, Marco was glad that something had shut him up. He glanced back up at the screen where side-by-side photographs of the same two women from the wine bar last night were displayed.

'I don't believe it!' Sam yelped, scrabbling around for the remote. 'Fuck! I can't find what I've done with the controls.' His eyes remained fixed to the screen.

'I didn't think you wanted to listen to it,' Marco said, trying not to allow sarcasm to creep into his voice. He was wondering how long it would take before Whittaker realised one of his staff was no more, then grimaced, hoping this cunt wasn't knobbing the blonde chick otherwise he might get maudlin and that couldn't happen when he had to get his arse over to Delgado's.

Not forgetting getting himself killed too...

'The one on the right is someone I employ at Whittaker Inc. Her name's Miranda. Oh, this is dreadful!' Sam's fingers clenched the creased material of his trousers.

'*You* employ her? Marco walked around the sofa. *What a surprise...* 'You just said they were hookers!'

'Miranda isn't a hooker!' Sam snapped indignantly. 'I don't know the other one, but Miranda wouldn't associate with someone like that! Dear God – I can't believe it! Miranda was an excellent worker.'

Guilt prodded Sam. He hadn't got around to texting Miranda last night either. She was murdered thinking she might have lost her job. He quickly pushed away theories she'd gone out with a friend and got drunk because of what he'd said, made a bad decision and...

*No*, he admonished himself, she'd made the choice. Besides, he'd every right to pick her up about the unprofessional way she'd interrupted his telephone conversation.

Turning away before he rabbit-punched Whittaker in the head for the pathetic expression on his face, Marco pulled out his phone and quickly composed a text to Colt.

`Be in place waiting at DD's by midday. Will have better idea of his return time soon`

Pressing send, Marco grinned. Sofia was correct about Delgado not returning last night. A nice, wasted night for his brother and Delgado looking for a man who was right here and had been all night. That alone was worth sitting on his own fucking hands and allowing this prick to continue breathing just that little bit longer.

Sofia would text the second Diego showed his knackered hairy face back at their house and then it was time for the off. Meanwhile, she'd be safely out of the way with Zane's bitch doing a bit of retail therapy. Diego would be dead and so would Whittaker... And then that just left Zane.

Maybe he should offload Zane too? Marco raised an eyebrow. He wasn't sure, but even if he decided to let his arse of a brother walk away, he'd pull *something* out of the bag to make sure the man wished he didn't exist.

All he had to do now was gauge it so that this dickhead arrived at Delgado's at the right time. It would be tricky, but not impossible.

Glancing at Whittaker still staring at the newsreader's mouth moving with words no one could hear, Marco leaned over and snatched up the remote and clicked off the television. Whittaker must be blind as fuck not to have noticed it right next to his arse. 'Come on! No point in dwelling on things you can't change. Go and grab a shower. We'll need to make tracks soon if we're to be at Diego's on time.'

Sam sat bolt upright. *Shit! The meeting with Delgado!* He scrambled to his feet. A shower was just what he needed to wash away this hangover. He couldn't be anything but on the ball and make the best impression for this meeting. It was a shame about Miranda - of course it was, but as long as he got someone else lined up to take over her clients by the end of the week, he shouldn't lose any deals. 'Okay, I'll go and get a shower now. Sam smiled. 'I take it we're going to Diego's together?'

'Yes, I...' Marco then frowned pretending to remember something of vast importance. 'Actually, no... You take a cab and I'll meet you there. I've just remembered I need to drop a letter off with my solicitor – things concerning the venture our meeting with Diego is about.' His eyes twinkled with excitement. 'But don't worry, I'll be there. Besides, if one of us gets stuck in traffic at least the other will be there to get the meeting started.'

Sam felt a little deflated. He'd hoped to have the additional kudos of travelling with Marco being as his initial meet with Diego hadn't gone well, but what Marco said made sense. 'Okay,' he said, walking to the door. 'I won't be long.'

Marco waited until Sam left the room before sending an update to Sofia.

• • • •

'OH! I DIDN'T REALISE you'd come back.' Leo entered the office at the canning works and warily eyed a stony-faced Tiger.

'There was something I had to check,' Tiger muttered, motioning for Leo to sit down. He'd been sat here himself for far too long wondering what the hell to do about what he'd proved. His hand inadvertently tightened around the knife accompanying the note in his pocket from the body dumped on his doorstep – the body sent as a message from Marco.

The atmosphere in the room was cloying, the uncomfortable confrontation between these two men from yesterday, thick and unresolved, but there was no time to discuss that now. He needed Leo's take on this and needed it *immediately*.

He wasn't sure how he kept a neutral expression in place. His face felt like it had melted from the inside and his head was so crammed with spinning thoughts and questions there was no room for manoeuvre, yet at the same time it felt numb and empty.

The answer had been there all along. At least he *thought* it had, but his molten mass of a brain was sure of nothing anymore.

Tiger hadn't clocked these particular details the night the body was dumped. He'd been too concerned with Alyson and the immediate issues to deal with and subtler details had faded into oblivion. But tonight, in the harsh light of the mess in his head he'd remembered something he hadn't previously processed.

It was something he couldn't pass off as anything else. He now knew exactly what that particular line in the note, *'Blood is on your hands'*, meant.

Leo and Zane's previous opinion about it was wrong because that line *had* been aimed at him. Blatantly so and Tiger couldn't quite believe he'd missed it in the first place. But by fuck, he wished he had.

It couldn't be right. It just *couldn't.*

*Yet it was…*

His fingers brushed the outline of the pocketknife, his fingertips reluctant to trace the all too familiar shape.

A pocketknife was a pocketknife, right? Those sorts of knives were ten-a-penny, all similar looking and this one was no different. Yet the mere touch of the metal seared the skin on his calloused fingers.

The knife was old. Even the blade was slightly chipped. He'd spotted that when extracting it from the flesh of the unfortunate recipient. That alone wasn't an anomaly - many old knives had chipped or damaged blades. But this fault now had major significance.

At the time, Tiger remembered Leo's comment about what a shit state of a knife to use. There had even been a dig or two about Marco being on the bones of his arse if that crappy blade was all he could lay his hands on. From what Tiger recalled, Zane had laughed. Perhaps even *he'd* managed a chuckle or sneer himself. His fried brain couldn't remember, but the sole focus was now only disbelief and shock at what was staring him in the face.

Tiger slowly raised his eyes as Leo sat down, disappointed but not surprised to see the mistrust in his eyes. He couldn't blame Leo for it and could only hope their long history prevailed. He pulled out the knife and note and with slightly shaking fingers, placed them on the desk. 'I need you to look at this.'

'I've already seen them, don't you remember?' Leo frowned. 'They were in that locked cabinet so wh…'

'I got them out because I needed to look at something,' Tiger interrupted. 'I needed to see if what jolted into my head was real or imagination.' He stared at the knife. 'And I *didn't* imagine a thing. This knife shows that the body - despite what everyone thought, was a message to me and me alone.'

'What the fuck are you talking about?' Leo gasped. 'We've been through this. We know it was a message from Marco. We still don't know who the victim was but that barely matters. What matters is that no more bodies have turned up like we expected.'

'And they won't,' Tiger muttered. 'As I said, the note and warning were for *me*.'

'Christ! What is the matter with you? You went off on one last night and now you're back being weird again.' Leo jabbed at the knife. 'What the hell has this got to do with anything? It's hardly the holy fucking grail! We all had knives like this back in the day, so how is it aimed at you? You're paranoid!'

Tiger nodded. Yeah, the knife was very much like the one he'd had as a youngster too. It was one like many lads in the 70s and 80s got as standard.

The difference was that this knife was *his*.

He locked eyes with Leo. 'This blade is mine. Or *was*...' One he hadn't seen for years and one he hadn't thought of - *tried* not to think of since he'd last set eyes on it, knowing what it had been used for.

Leo laughed and then promptly stopped, realising this was not a windup. 'What are you talking about, man? *Your* knife? How?'

Tiger shuddered, a wave of nausea and hopelessness crashing over him. There was no way around this - he had to speak of what was now abundantly clear. He nudged the knife closer to Leo over the table, unwilling to touch it longer than he had to. 'There's no doubt this is my knife. I was about fifteen, Colt around fourteen. We'd been given identical blades by our Uncle John.' He shrugged miserably. 'We argued over whose was whose, as brothers do, so to avoid the squabbles, Uncle John scored our initials on the blades.'

And still to this day, after all this time and with all the history this knife had seen and caused, those initials were still there - glowing like a beacon in the glare of the overhead strip light.

Picking the knife up, Leo turned it over in his hands and stared at the worn but visible initials:

***LS***

'Lyndon Shoreham.' The sound of his proper name coming from his own mouth only made Tiger feel sicker, but saying it made it real and it needed to be real because Leo had to believe this. Everything depended on it.

Leo remained staring at the blade, his forehead creasing into folds. 'You're saying you did over a nameless bloke and dumped him on your own doorstep? Have you lost the plot?

Why would I believe that shite? Jesus wept, mate, this has gone past any...'

'It's *my* fucking knife,' Tiger snarled. 'But no, I wasn't the one stabbing notes into the backs of people on my doorstep!'

'Then... then what *are* you saying?'

'Nothing I want to acknowledge.'

Leo listened grim-faced as Tiger reluctantly explained that this knife - this very same one, had been one of the things to help his mother end her life. How she'd got her hands on it and squirreled it into the secure hospital, Tiger never knew and probably never would.

But she had and she'd *used* it.

Tiger clenched and unclenched his fists to stop his blood congealing.

Leo shook his head. *This was fucking bad.* 'Okay, but if that *is* the case, then how did the knife appear again from a hospital's scene of death after all this time?'

'I don't know, except...' Tiger swallowed with difficulty... 'It... it has to be Colt.'

'*Colt*?' Leo's eyebrows shot into his hairline. 'But...'

'Unbeknown to me, Colt must have received what there was of our mother's worldly goods after her death.' Tiger couldn't meet Leo's eyes, expecting they held either disbelief and accusations, or worse - pity. 'I... I wasn't in a good place at the time and left Colt the only contact for her things to go to.'

'But it doesn't make sense!' Leo blurted. 'Why wouldn't he have said? Why wouldn't he mention...'

'Why *would* he mention anything to me about it? He fucking hates me!

It took all of Leo's power not to shake his head clean off his neck. *It couldn't be Colt. Colt was Tiger's brother.* 'What are you saying?' he asked, already dreading the answer.

'Colt killed that unknown man using my knife and left him on my doorstep. Look at the fucking message!' Tiger jabbed at the crumpled blood-splattered note. 'How much clearer can it be? It *has* to be him behind this. I clocked blood splatters on his boots, which I put down to a fight. But… but then I saw the sword in a specially extended pocket in that fucking stupid coat of his.'

'And a sword matching the fatal wound on that man…' Leo stared at Tiger and paused, deep in thought. 'Okay, but it being Colt doesn't tie up with the references to the films and Alyson,' Leo cried. 'That's *Marco*. We know that's him. It can't be anyone else.'

Tiger looked up, his face twisted with rage. 'All of these years I'm well aware my brother blames me for what happened to our mother. I was the one to section her, remember? And it was my knife she slashed her own wrists with to free her from the decisions *I* made. *"Blood is on your hands"* is a reference to that. But to confuse matters and make everyone jump to the wrong assumption, he's made it look like it came from Marco.'

Leo turned a strange shade of green as things slowly dropped into place. 'Fuck!'

Tiger nodded slowly, his stomach lurching. 'There's only one conclusion to come out of this: Colt - my brother, is linked with or working for Marco. Alyson said this last night but I didn't believe her. She told me Colt *admitted* working for Marco and that Marco wants her dead. Colt's been trying to convince me Alyson's mad – like you all have… And I… I fell for it.'

Leo dragged his hand over his mouth, shaking with an uncharacteristic lack of control that he passed off as a cough. *Could there be a rational explanation? No. Not in a million years*. His chair scraped loudly as he shot out of the seat. 'We've got to stop this. We must tell Zane he's got a traitor in the ring.'

'And one that's...' Pausing, Tiger turned ghostly white. Alyson was telling the truth about *everything*. Colt slitting her wrist was yet another message – like his mother all over again. *And he was still sitting here doing nothing?*

He snatched out his phone and rang the mobile he'd left for Alyson. *Please answer it, please*. He'd sat here for *ages*, his thoughts going around in circles. What the fuck was he doing? All the time he'd wasted when he should have reacted. Should have protected her, yet the enemy was right there with her. *Fuck!*

As the phone continued to ring out, he turned to Leo, fear burning. 'I have to warn Alyson but she's not answering! I must get back to the flat. Fuck! I've left her being guarded by a fucking lunatic.' *And a lunatic that was in with the enemy.*

'I'll get hold of Zane in the interim,' Leo added gravely.

It was at this point, much to Tiger's short-lived relief that the phone connected.

# THIRTY TWO

DIEGO RAN HIS HAND over the stubbly overnight growth on his face. His beard was always meticulous, making sure the shaved parts of his cheeks were tended daily. He did not appreciate having to deviate from his impeccable grooming routine - especially on the account of a bastard like Sam Whittaker. 'What a waste of bloody time that was!' he muttered.

'I know what you mean,' Zane said, equally annoyed. Spending the entire night outside Whittaker's house with no sign of the man was aggravating to say the least. Not to mention disastrous. If Whittaker *was* part of something untoward with Marco, then this turn of events could end up fatal for Diego or *all* of them.

Visions of Erin floated into his head, but Zane quickly pushed them away. He didn't need to worry. She was safe at Diego's house, plus she'd be off shopping with one of Diego's minders in tow this morning. It just left the rest to stress over... 'Any other day and I'd have waited until the cunt showed up, but sod's law has it this is the one day I can't.'

'Doing final checks that everything's ready for tonight's drop is more important in the grand scheme of things,' Diego agreed. 'Besides, it's more likely Whittaker is way back in the chain regarding the Bentley and has nothing to do with Marco.' But he still couldn't shake the nagging feeling that the man was connected *somewhere*. It was just how... He glanced at his watch. 'I'll join you at the canning works for the checks, if that's okay?'

'Yeah, sure.'

'I just want to pop home first and make sure everything's fine there, although I suspect Sofia and Erin have already left by now,' Diego said. But if they hadn't, he'd ask Sofia why she had such interest in that particular car. It was about time she answered some questions.

'Drop me off on the way and I'll grab my bike,' Zane said.

• • • •

COLT HEARD THE PHONE, he'd heard it loud and clear, yet it took a moment to register. He scrambled from the sofa, anger with himself belting through his veins. 'Stupid fucker!' he hissed as he lumbered to the door to pinpoint where the ringing originated.

It wasn't his phone – it was the wrong ringtone. Good job too because if he'd missed Marco's signal to offload the bloke that had 'dead' stamped on his head, he'd be throwing away the other half of that massive wedge with *his* name on it.

It was unlike him to fall asleep. What the hell was he thinking by allowing tiredness to make him relaxed enough to switch off? Sure, that he was confident he'd finally convinced Lyndon to lock up that scrawny bitch was great and gave ample room for further games, but even so... *Slack, Colt, that was slack*, he thought.

It must be Lyndon's phone ringing, so the silly fuck must have dropped off as well. Ready to play the newly acquired act of 'concerned brother', Colt entered the kitchen. 'Hey, I think someone's trying to call y…' He stopped in the doorway, his massive bullhead turning to scan the room. *Shit! Where the fuck was Lyndon?*

Eyes narrowing, he hastened towards the bedroom. He'd be

in there with that dozy cow. Yep, he could hear talking. *Okay, so how should he play this?*

Unable to quite believe he'd wasted valuable time to scheme how to further screw up the chick his brother was sweet on, Colt was about to enter the bedroom but paused outside the door.

*What was this?*

Leaning closer to the splintered frame temporarily placed back in situ, he frowned. The only voice he could hear was Alyson's.

'So, you believe me? I... What?' Alyson's voice was high-pitched and changed from relieved to frantic within a split second.

Colt snarled, his hand on the doorknob. Lyndon wasn't here, he was on the other end of the bloody phone! The bastard must have snuck out when he'd stupidly dropped off. Oh well, maybe he'd now have the chance to shag this whore like he'd originally planned and...

'I was right? He's in with Marco? What knife? Oh my God, that one? It was *him*? He dumped that on... What? How am I supposed to do that? I don't... I don't know... There isn't anything to block the door with now.'

Colt remained motionless, his temples thumping. He refrained from breaking the door down for the second time and stayed where he was. *They knew*. He had to think. *Think!*

'But what about *him*? He's still here somewhere!' Alyson shrieked. 'Sorry, sorry, I'll be quieter. No, I don't know whereabouts he is... Okay, but how long will you be?'

With Alyson's voice now confined to a whisper, it took all of Colt's effort to piece together what she was saying down the phone line. But one thing was crystal clear - he'd been rumbled.

*Fuck!*

*And it was too soon.*

Unusually for him, Colt stood like a statue, unsure of what to do. The only thing he *did* know was that he had to get out of here. Lyndon was on his way back to rescue his fucking damsel in distress and he'd be fucked if he was waiting to be taken out by his bastard brother. *No fucking way!*

As for Marco, he could do one. Getting away unscathed was what needed to happen.

Colt's ugly face twisted with hate at the sound of something heavy being slowly dragged from within the room. For fuck's sake! After all of these years he'd finally got the opportunity to even the score – he'd pulled this all together like a genius, yet now because of his own stupidness of taking a nap, he'd lost that window.

He gritted his teeth. The way he'd planned for this to go was wrecked, but that didn't mean that he couldn't still damage his wanker of a brother by leaving a parting reminder. And then on his way out of town, he'd blast that other cunt to pieces.

He'd have to lay low for a while after all of this because every fucker would be on his case, but he'd be back. And Lyndon would still be here…

With a renewed gleam in his eyes, Colt pulled his pistol from his waistband and turned the doorknob.

• • • •

STARING AT HIS MOBILE, Marco grinned.

We have gone shopping so the stage is all yours.

Until later

S

xxx

Taming the wide grin spreading across his face, Marco closed the text from Sofia and then scrolled to Half-Head on his contacts. Hearing Sam Whittaker approaching the lounge, he hastily tapped out a message:

It's on. Go and wait at the address I gave you.

Do job whenever opportunity arises.

BOTH jobs as discussed.

Sending the message, Marco glanced at his watch. Colt was ready for the off, he'd made sure of that. All the man had to do was wait until Delgado arrived back at the house. And if he got a move on, it would be timed just right to blast the wanker, plus that scrote, Whittaker, into smithereens, opening the door to his and Sofia's new life that was sitting ready and waiting for them to jump into.

'You look pleased with yourself!'

'And you look and smell much better for having a shower!' Marco controlled the snarl itching to replace his smile at Whittaker's comment. This fucker thought he was oh-so witty, didn't he? But there would soon be sod all for the cunt to comment on. Sooner than he thought. The bastard wouldn't even see it coming. *Ha fucking ha!*

He stared at Whittaker's blue linen suit. What an utter cock! And why did he look so pleased with himself? The prat had best not have had one off the wrist in his shower, the dirty bastard. And on that note, it was time to send this prick on his merry way. 'Are you ready to go?'

'What now?' Sam frowned, glancing at his watch. 'We'll be there too early, won't we? I thought you said we'd arranged to meet Mr Delgado at...'

'We must take the traffic into consideration. There's still holdups around the area of that double murder yesterday,' Marco said, his palms itching - a sure sign that if he didn't get this turd out of his hair, his house and his fucking life soon then he'd kill the fucker himself. And that would not be a promising start to his new life with Sofia. Three murders in two days was pushing the boundaries, even by *his* standards.

And no, he didn't know if the traffic still had problems or whether roads were still closed. He didn't give a flying fuck what was right, wrong or indifferent, providing Sam-fucking-Whittaker buggered off straight into the path of Colt's waiting bullet.

'I'll just grab my phone.' Sam reached past Marco to take

his mobile from the table.

Marco's eyes narrowed. *Had the cheeky bastard helped himself to his best aftershave?*

Refusing to let anything distract him, Marco kept his neutral expression, when in reality it was difficult to contain his enthusiasm. Just think - in a few hours from now, he and Sofia would be together, safely ensconced in his bed where no one or nothing could interfere.

*And that, he could not wait for.*

Marco grabbed his suit jacket from the arm of the sofa and shrugged it onto his muscular shoulders. 'Ready?'

'Yes.' Sam smoothed his already tidy hair. 'I know you said you needed to drop by your solicitor on the way, but being as we're leaving early, why don't I give you a lift? I'm sure we could go there first and still get to Mr Delgado's in plenty of time.'

Marco bristled. This twat really couldn't leave him alone, could he? 'No, it's fine,' he said, his jaw getting stiffer by the second. 'You make your own way there like we agreed earlier. As I said, going separately rules out problems if there's traffic delays.'

'And you're sure I shouldn't take a receipt for the Bentley?' Sam pressed. It might be an ice breaker, especially if he arrived before Marco.

'No need.' Marco headed towards the door, at risk of losing his rag. *I. Already. Told. You. There. Is. No. Fucking. Need. For. A. Receipt.* There was no need of anything where either Whittaker or Delgado were going.

'I wonder if the Sofia will be there?' Sam surmised, trailing Marco down the hallway to the front door, excited at the prospect of laying his eyes on that gorgeous bird again.

Marco's nails dug into his palms. That this cunt had deemed to even think of Sofia made the urge to kill him even stronger. *Control, Marco. Control...* 'Diego mentioned his wife was off shopping with a friend this morning, so it's unlikely she'll be there.'

And she'd better not be because he didn't want his beautiful Sofia witnessing anything that would shortly happen. The further away from this she was, the easier it was to prove she was nothing whatsoever to do with it. The same applied to *him*.

Waiting while Sam got into his BMW, Marco waved him off, the grin returning to his face as he got into his own car. Now to make the short trip to the solicitor and keep the old codger talking for as long as required until he received a signal from Colt that the job had been done.

That way he'd have an alibi in the unlikely event anyone asked questions. Then all he had to do was wait until the coast was clear before meeting up with the one and only love of his life.

# THIRTY THREE

ERIN PRETENDED TO BE interested in everything Sofia said, the same way as she had the whole bloody night. It was hard work. *More* than hard.

She glanced out of the window, hoping the movement deflected from her stabbing the PIN code into her phone at the side of her left thigh. There was plenty of space in the back of this chauffeur-driven car, but Sofia was still close enough to spot the mobile if Erin wasn't careful.

A shopping trip was the last thing Erin wanted but she had to keep up the act of being unaware that Sofia was planning to have Diego killed today. So far she'd failed to warn either Zane or Diego of what she'd heard. Sofia had only left her alone long enough once to make a call or text and there had been no further opportunity to call or text anyone and now Erin was frantic. She had to warn Diego as the hit Sofia had arranged could be anytime.

*It might have already happened...*

Jittery at the prospect, Erin fumbled to enter her PIN code into her phone.

'You seem nervous this morning,' Sofia said, grabbing Erin's arm.

Hoping she hadn't flinched, Erin readjusted herself, blocking Sofia's line of sight of the phone. 'It sounds ridiculous but the thought of going to Harrods intimidates me.'

Sofia laughed. 'Are you telling me you've never been?' *Oh, how pathetic!* This horrible bitch should stick with what she was used to, like Primark or Matalan. But the countdown was on and soon she'd never have to sully herself with associating with skanky trolls ever again. 'I can't say I've been shopping with a Harrods virgin before, but don't worry - all of the best boutiques in there know me personally, so I'll make sure they look after you.'

'That's a relief,' Erin lied, successfully inputting the PIN code. 'I'm glad you who know how to deal with all this.' *Yeah, right.*

Sofia launched into epic details of the countless occasions she'd been to this or that designer and Erin nodded in all the right places, doing a sterling job of looking suitably impressed. *That's right, keep talking, Sofia. We all know your ego requires constant stroking.*

Her fingers moved deftly over the phone buttons with only the occasional glance required. Who gave a toss if there were typos as long as she got the message to Zane?

On way shopping. D in danger. He was rite about S. There is hit on him 2day. Don't know wen

Hitting send, Erin didn't dare glance down and push her luck to check the message had sent. Not that she had chance to anyway because Sofia started squealing in that horrible high-pitched spoilt little girl voice.

'Look! Here we are!' Sofia's eyes gleamed with the prospect of racking up more debt on the myriad of Diego's debit cards she had in her handbag. Soon, every single penny would be hers to do exactly as she liked with.

She slapped her manicured talons on the back of the chauffeur's headrest. 'Anywhere here will do,' she squawked, revelling in the towering façade of the Harrods store on her right. And Stiller - make sure to keep up with us today, do you understand? Otherwise my husband will not be amused!'

The minder in the passenger seat nodded, leaving Erin to swallow her smirk at the man's gritted teeth in the reflection of the wing mirror. Quickly sending a second text to Zane, she reminded herself that this wasn't exactly a bed of roses for her either and prepared to get out of the car.

• • • •

ROARING UP THE ROAD on his Yamaha, Zane's mind flitted between doing checks at the canning works for tonight's big drop, to this latest spanner in the works in the guise of his brother. The wasted night searching for that man, Whittaker, had not aided a decent frame of mind and the heavy load of items still requiring sorting all vied for attention.

The only thing running on target was the cocaine shipment. The word he'd received from his contact at the docks not long ago underlined that. The container due to make its way here during the night had passed customs with no issues, which was a blessed relief. So, with any luck, the handover due to commence would run equally as smoothly.

If only all the outstanding items ran the same, he'd be in a much better place.

Zane pulled his bike over at the side of the road, the urge for a cigarette taking centre stage. Kicking his side stand out, he removed his crash helmet and lit a cigarette. Inhaling deeply, he savoured the calming effect of the smoke in his lungs.

Frowning at where he'd chosen to stop, Zane wondered whether this was his subconscious telling him to deal with the outstanding rage for his father because the road he'd stopped on led to the cemetery where the man lay cold in the ground.

He hadn't set foot in that place since uncovering the facts about the man he'd always idolised. Despite previously promising the granite headstone that he'd visit more often now he was free to do so, he hadn't been able to stomach it since finding out the truth.

Zane's lips pinched tightly around the filter of his cigarette and took a hard drag. The only urge he'd had to visit his father's resting place since was to smash the fucking thing up.

Spilling his guts in the uncharacteristic manner to Delgado only exacerbated just how much Zane buried his rage over the betrayal. And instead of making things better by voicing it to someone, it had achieved the unpleasant opposite effect of accentuating just how much the whole thing bothered him. But the thought of whether going to the graveside might negate a percentage of the pain about what he'd unearthed flitted constantly into his mind.

There was time to go there. Erin was in safe hands with one of Diego's minders and the canning works would be checked by both him and Diego soon. There was nothing he could do about Whittaker for the time being and Marco springing out from under a rock could happen at any time. Zane was fucked if he was tiptoeing around on eggshells for the foreseeable and where Marco was concerned, what would be, would be. Yet another situation that would become inevitable at some point.

Zane chucked his cigarette butt onto the floor and was about to replace his crash helmet to ride into the graveyard when he stopped. Who was he trying to kid? Short of them not existing, nothing would make the lies his father had told any better. And they *did* exist, so there was no point pretending otherwise.

He pulled out his mobile from one of his many zipped pockets. He'd quickly text Erin and check to see how she was.

[ Erin: 2 messages ]

[ Leo: 6 missed calls ]

Zane's heart hammered as he read the text from Erin. *A hit on Diego from Sofia? What the fuck? Erin was with Sofia, so was she safe?*

His fumbling fingers opened the second message from the woman he loved and relief washed over him.

BTW - I'm fine & acting normal.

No need 4 u 2 intervene here

xx

Yes, Erin was okay, but that was more than could be said for Diego. He *had* to warn him.

Quickly dialling Diego's number, Zane clenched his jaw as the call rang out. *Come on, Diego. Where the fuck are you?*

Maybe he'd gone for a shower when he'd got back to the house? Zane knew *he* could do with one after sweating like a pig from sitting in the car all bloody night, but he had to get word to Diego because there was no hint of when this hit would be.

His eyes narrowed. *That bitch Sofia! Erin was right all along. As was Diego.*

Cutting off the unanswered call, Zane dialled Leo. All he needed now was to learn the cocaine drop had been cancelled or the canning factory had been raided!

'Leo!' Zane cried, relieved that at least one of his calls had got through. 'I need to pull Colt off guard duty at the flat. I want him at the canning works - we have a problem… Sofia has a fucking hit out on Diego and I must warn him. Full alert at the canning works and... What?'

Fury bubbled along Zane's veins. *Colt? Colt was a traitor? He'd killed the man dumped at the flat? How the actual...?* 'Wait! How do you kn…?'

His face fell further hearing Leo garble snippets of his and Tiger's conversation, but not as much as hearing that Colt was or had been working for Marco.

Suddenly, things clicked into place.

'Fuck!' Zane yelped, kick-starting his bike. 'Colt has to be the one doing the hit!' Fuck the canning works. That could wait. Leo could deal with it there. Tiger was already on his way to the flat to intercept Colt, but *he* had to reach Diego in time. If Colt was Marco's hitman, then Zane knew his brother – and if

Tiger succeeded in apprehending Colt, then Marco would do the job himself.

Hanging up the call, Zane shoved his crash helmet on and roared up the road with a heavy heart. The time had come. He had to kill his brother and do it as soon as possible.

He only hoped he could end this before Diego took a hit. If Marco wasn't there, then he'd have to find him. Without knowing where his brother lived it would be difficult, but family law or not, there could be no more chances.

• • • •

TIGER COULD BARELY BREATHE by the time he'd raced up the steps and along the walkway to his flat. Not because he was out of breath and unfit - that was not a possibility. It was that his very own brother had set him up and planned to destroy him by any means necessary was what forced the air from his lungs.

Tiger knew this stemmed from Colt's base hatred of him over what had happened to their mother but was there more to it than that?

His own knife getting in the hands of his mother whilst in a secure hospital didn't seem feasible. Not unless someone gave it to her... And the thought that Colt had taken their mother *his* knife, knowing she might use it to harm herself, and at the same time perhaps hoping to frame him for the deed, was something Tiger couldn't bear to give time of day to.

But that thought remained nevertheless and wouldn't go away.

Reaching his own front door, he fumbled with the key. He could knock, but once Colt saw his face he'd know the game was up and Tiger wanted to take him by surprise.

For fuck's sake! He'd had reservations about Colt being on the scene in the first place! He'd even felt guilty about not wanting Zane to give him a job. He hadn't liked it when Leo started singing Colt's praises either and despised things even further when Zane ordered Colt to guard Alyson rather than *him*

- all but throwing him out of his own fucking flat to be a gopher at the canning works.

Tiger had put his resentment down to the feelings he'd unexpectedly developed for Alyson, but it wasn't about that - he knew that now. It was because his senses had been screaming out to listen: *'Your brother is a danger and should not be here!'*

Worst of all, Tiger had almost fallen for the web of lies Colt had schemed whilst doing Marco's dirty business.

He turned the key in the lock It made perfect sense now how Colt had been released from Broadmoor. *No one* got released from Broadmoor unless they had oodles of money, a fantastic brief and masses of connections in the right places.

Now it was obvious how Colt had ticked those boxes...

*Marco.*

Marco had hired Colt to do his bidding and get into Zane's inner circle. He'd relied on the one golden ticket Colt possessed: Tiger had always stupidly promised him help and work if he ever needed it.

And because of that, Tiger had put everyone he cared about at risk.

*None more so than Alyson.*

But Colt wouldn't be doing this work purely for Marco, no matter how much the guy paid him. Tiger knew how Colt worked – or *had* – and it seemed nothing had changed. Colt had his own agenda and always had: to ruin Tiger's life. And he'd all but managed it.

*But not quite.*

Bursting through the front door, Tiger resembled a man possessed. If he'd sported a dent in his head and smashed-up teeth, he'd look more like his brother than anyone.

Primed to tackle his brother to the floor, beat the fuck out of him and keep him where he could do no further damage until he'd decided when and where he'd kill the cunt, Tiger bolted up the hallway. Brother or no brother - Colt was dead for this.

Colt hadn't won this one. Because this time, Tiger would tell Alyson what he *really* thought - he was falling in love with her and providing she forgave him for his ridiculous behaviour and for starting to believe Colt over her, then perhaps they had a future or...

Tiger suddenly stopped to listen. Something was wrong. *Very* wrong.

*It was too quiet...*

Storming into the kitchen, Tiger hissed with frustration, fury spewing through his teeth. The bastard had done a runner. Colt must have heard the conversation between him and Alyson.

*Alyson!*

Turning on his heels, Tiger raced towards the bedroom. She'd better have done what he'd told her to and barricaded herself in. Or had Colt snatched Alyson and taken her?

Fear bubbled.

*No.* Once Colt knew he'd been rumbled, he'd be centred only on getting away. Everyone would be gunning for him, so...

The bedroom door opened under a mere touch of his finger. It wasn't barricaded, neither further smashed in...

Tiger froze, his blood turning to ice.

*No, no... Colt hadn't...? He wouldn't...*

Tiger didn't want to step into the bedroom. He hadn't seen inside yet, but as the door creaked open, the blood splatter on the far wall told him only one thing: gunshots.

Christ knows he'd seen and been behind enough himself to know the fallout they caused.

*But it wasn't... it couldn't be...*

Feeling fear on a scale he'd never before experienced, Tiger sucked air into his lungs and stepped into the room.

The sight of the young woman he hoped a future with might now be possible, lay in pieces, along with the shot off parts of the back of her head. Her beautiful face, the velvet cheeks, the long eyelashes which filled his dreams, were replaced by a bloody gaping mess.

There was no point checking for signs of life. There was none.

Without realising he'd even done it, Tiger sank to his knees and with an animal-like roar, pulled the remains of Alyson's body into his arms and sobbed.

# Thirty Four

BLOWING LIKE A STEAM TRAIN, Colt raced from the taxi he'd flagged down at the bottom of his brother's road and clumped along the pavement, each lumbering step jarring his knees.

He hadn't bothered paying the driver. That cunt hadn't the minerals to report him or think about following him to demand the fare. Aside from it being most likely the man was an illegal immigrant who had to stay under the radar, it didn't take rocket science for the fucker to tell just by looking in his rearview mirror during the journey not to mess and he had things on his mind.

*Plenty of things.*

And the journey to Delgado's house had been spent running over and over what he would do about them.

Colt dragged the dripping snot from under his nose using the back of his leather coat's sleeve. The fucking coat was getting hot. *He* was hot, but that didn't matter. All that mattered was offloading this pent-up stress from his system before his head went bang.

Nothing had gone to plan, apart from despatching that wailing bitch.

A slight smile cracked over Colt's face as he pounded the pavement, the grin quickly dislodged by his jiggling jowls.

In a perfect world, he'd have dragged the whore's death out, taking the time to arrange her in a position befitting her shitty status for his cunt of a brother to stumble across. Something along the lines of legs akimbo, underwear pulled off, a tell-tale pool of semen dripping out to bring to Lyndon's attention that *he'd* been the last one in. And the final bauble - his knife with the initials 'CS' shoved up the miserable tart's cunt.

That would have been *perfect.*

Then he'd have hung around just out of sight, to witness Lyndon's pain first hand.

But none of that had happened and that pissed Colt off big time. It took the shine from what should have been a gratifying and wholly deserved moment for his shit-fuck of a brother. However, self-preservation was the key and so he must be patient and wait to finish his dear brother's complete demise.

Rounding the corner to the address Marco had given for Delgado, Colt took up position behind a parked car, not giving a flying fuck it was broad daylight or if anyone saw him. *No one could touch him because he was invincible.*

He leant against the immaculate paintwork of a brand-new Jaguar and caught his breath, his beady eyes focused on the Kensington townhouse.

There was no sign of either of the targets at present, but he could wait. He'd wait as long as necessary.

Colt might ask himself why he was still hanging around being as shortly, if not already, everybody would be gunning for his blood. Why wasn't he already away on his heels?

It wasn't like he was duty bound to complete anything for Marco Morelli. Marco might *think* he called the shots, but *he* was the one who decided whether things would happen or not.

Colt didn't give a rat's arse about Marco's orders. It wasn't even the outstanding money pressing him to do this. What he'd already been paid would see him right until he could return. No, although the rest of the brass wouldn't go amiss, it wasn't that.

A sick sneer spread across Colt's smashed mouth. His reasoning was simple: killing that bitch hadn't fully scratched the itch festering inside and until it was scratched, he couldn't fire on all cylinders. By killing the Delgado cunt and a nameless yuppie prick - watching their two-in-one death, would offset the gnawing disappointment for failing to capitalise and feast on Lyndon's ruination.

Yeah, these killings would soothe his annoyance enough to cope with being forced off radar for a while.

Pulling his gun out, he checked it was loaded. *Tick.*

Two bullets were all that was required for this. It was simple. It had been more important using the rest on that dumb-arsed whore.

Colt's amplified hearing then detected the sound of an approaching engine. *This could be one of them now...*

The question was, did he wait for both targets to be in his sights or just take the first out and hope the second was stupid enough to follow?

• • • •

SOFIA'S RESENTMENT of showing her face in her favourite Harrods boutiques whilst resembling a beached whale threatened to throw her carefully tended persona out of the window.

Luckily, she was saved from diluting her manufactured niceness towards Erin by spotting a new dress. 'Oh my God!' she gasped. Forgetting she despised the woman accompanying her, Sofia grabbed Erin's arm. 'Look! It's the latest Balenciaga!'

Erin stared in the direction Sofia dragged her and found herself in front of a rail of what looked like identical dresses. It seemed like years of putting up with Sofia fawning over dresses had passed already and this was only the second place within Harrods they'd been. *It would be a long day.*

She surreptitiously checked her mobile phone, seeing the messages she'd sent Zane had been read. Thank God. He must be dealing with Sofia's plan and with it, hopefully got to the bottom of who was undertaking the hit, not to mention who she was playing around with. Erin hoped so because despite her carefully put questions she'd got no further on that score.

'Look at the additions Balenciaga has made to this!' Sofia's fingers trailed over the exquisite fabric. 'This has to be the very latest this season!' *And she had to have it.* She'd wear it when her and Marco made their first public appearance as a couple.

'Mrs Delgado!' A slender woman glided over from what appeared to be from inside the rack of dresses. 'How lovely to see you! I was beginning to think you'd deserted us as we haven't seen you for months and... Oh!' The woman's eyes trailed to Sofia's huge belly. 'I see congratulations are in order!'

Sofia burnt with rage and humiliation. She'd avoided going anywhere decent whilst wearing these steadily increasing in size ghastly prostheses. How could she possibly be seen in public looking like this? Yet now, because of Erin, the riffy scanky cow, she'd been forced to break her cardinal rule. *Deep breaths, Sofia*, she told herself, forcing an icy smile. *It's almost over*. 'Never mind that. I'm more interested in this dress. The new season, yes?' She'd buy several of these. The dress was too nice to only have in her London location.

'Yes, it's the brand-new version,' the assistant gushed. 'Divine, isn't it? Absolutely beautiful!'

Leaning across and almost pushing the assistant off balance, Sofia snatched the dress from the rail. She checked the label and smiled. 'Size six! Perfect! I'll try it on.'

Erin glanced at the assistant at the same time the woman looked at her with slight confusion that she professionally concealed within a split second.

'She'll try one too,' Sofia added, nodding to Erin. And as an afterthought, added, 'this is Erin, my... erm... my friend.' *God, that stuck in her throat like a fishbone*. But if it kept the stupid bitch busy and out of out her hair while she tried this lovely dress on, she couldn't care less.

The assistant fidgeted awkwardly. 'Would you not rather

wait a month or so for baby to arrive and…'

'No, I would not!' Sofia snapped, her eyes shooting daggers. 'I'm trying it on *now*. Next month will be too late!' Remembering herself, she then smiled sweetly. 'Obviously, I can't try it on *properly*.' She laughed loudly. 'I'll just hold it up against me to check the length and neckline, but I'm definitely buying it today.'

The assistant moved backwards with a strange acquiescent bow. 'And you Madam? I'd say you're a...' Her eyes ran over Erin's still svelte figure. The only sign of her pregnancy a slight rounding of her previously flat stomach. '…size eight, yes?'

'Yes, that's right,' Erin nodded, not wanting to try the dress on at all. It was beautiful for sure, but that it didn't possess a price tag scared her. However, if going through the motions wasted more time and kept Sofia happy, she'd gladly do it.

Taking the dress, Erin followed the assistant to the changing rooms which were almost as exquisite as Sofia and Diego's house.

'I'll be in this one,' Sofia trilled, pushing the door of the cubicle shut in Erin's face. *Size eight, the cow? And Erin really was pregnant too, the fucking bitch!*

Catching sight of the stunning dress hanging on the gilt hook, Sofia's attention moved to that. She was trying it one on and *properly*!

Glancing in the mirror at her distended figure, Sofia snarled, then unzipped her dress and set about releasing the straps of the despised prosthesis. She'd played this charade for far too long and deserved a break. She was trying this dress on for real and in the confines of this cubical no one would be any the bloody wiser.

• • • •

STEPPING OUT OF THE BATHROOM, Diego got dressed quickly and picked up his mobile, when something outside caught his eye.

He moved to the window, seeing a BMW pulled up next to

that damned Bentley Blower and watched in disbelief as out of it stepped the prick he and Zane had been looking for all night.

He growled in frustration. *This gimp had the gall to show up here now?*

Slapping his mobile back down, Diego shrugged on his jacket and darted down the stairs. He'd find out if this man had anything to do with Marco and he'd be doing that right here and right *now*.

Had Diego known what was about to unfold, he would sorely wish his urge to collar Whittaker and find out what involvement, if any, the man had with Marco Morelli wasn't so intense to prioritise that before checking his phone.

If he had done that, he might have seen the numerous missed calls and text messages Zane had sent whilst Diego was busy washing the fruitless events of the night before down the shower's plughole.

# THIRTY FIVE

ARRANGING HIS GUN into a suitable position to ensure a good shot, Colt made sure he kept out of sight. He stared at the figure of a man getting out of a Z3.

*What the fuck was this cunt supposed to be? Who wore blue linen suits?*

This was one of the targets?

Colt swallowed the snort of mirth gathering in his throat.

For fuck's sake! It was insulting wasting a good bullet on this piece of piss. The guy looked about twelve and like a gust of fucking wind could finish him off. Still, he thought, shrugging, his good eye peering through the gun's sights to line up the coming shot on the back of Whittaker's head. Killing was killing and he'd enjoy the buzz regardless.

Besides, sometimes it was extra gratifying bumping off a rich, privileged fuckhead.

It was just a shame the other target wasn't in the car with this dickhead because then things would have been easy peasy and...

*Hang on...*

Colt moved his gaze from the gun's sights to squint at a man bolting through the opening door of the fancy townhouse and a wide smile twisted his features.

*Now, this was more like it!*

He hadn't recognised the photo of the other man Marco wanted offloaded when he briefed him about this job. The name rang a bell but now everything dropped into place.

*Oh, cracking - it's that Colombian cartel bloke.*

Trembling with glee, Colt swapped the gun into his other hand and wiped the sweat from his palm down the leg of his jeans.

*This was excellent*, he thought, taking proper hold of the gun once again. He knew Marco had been involved with some narc stuff, but this was a great tally to chalk off on his list of kills. It more than justified taking out that yuppie twat. In fact, he'd put that one down as a freebie - thrown in as complementary for getting the kudos of *this* hit.

And the drug lord did not look happy with his face twisted in rage like that. And the rage seemed to be directed at the yuppie…

Applying pressure to the trigger, Colt remained motionless, his thigh muscles screaming from his crouched position. It would be interesting to watch and see how this played out first, he mused, before reminding himself he had a job to do.

Resuming his precision focus, he moved his gun slightly to the right. All he needed was for the drug lord to come a little closer, move to the right a bit more and... *That's it...*

Colt's excitement reached fever pitch.

There was a chance he could get both these fuckers with the same bullet.

• • • •

'MR DELGADO!' Sam exclaimed, taken by surprise seeing the man he was so eager to impress rushing down the path towards him. He hadn't expected such an enthusiastic welcome. Then seeing the savage look on Diego Delgado's face, he felt the first stab of uncomfortableness. *Was he late?*

The wide smile slid from his face. 'I hope I haven't kept

you waiting? I...'

'What the hell are you doing here?' Diego roared, the urge to pound this man into the pavement threatening to overtake the fact that he required information. 'We've been looking for you!'

'I… I'm not late, am I?' Sam spluttered, his heart sinking. *This wasn't going well.* He'd wanted to put right that dreadful first meeting he'd had with Diego Delgado, but this was not encouraging. 'Marco said our meeting was arranged for midday and...' He glanced at his watch. '...I thought I was punctual. Has Marco already arrived or...'

'So, you *are* to do with Morelli, you fucking little shit! That man would not dare step within a mile of me!' Diego lurched towards Sam at top speed. 'You! The car was a fucking set up!'

'What?' Sam shrieked just before a hand clasped around his throat. What did he mean Marco wouldn't dare come here? What was going on? 'The meeting… I'm here for our meeting Marco arranged. He's supposed to be here too so we can discuss your joint venture. I...' His words faded as the pressure increased on his throat. *Why was Delgado acting like this?* The man had specifically asked for his input, so what was this about a set up? What had the car got to do with it either?

Before he could ponder over any further analysis, Sam was dragged towards the house, his feet fighting for traction along the path.

'Get in the house and fucking explain exactly what you know and what my wife has to do with it!' Diego growled, his voice loaded with the power of an erupting volcano.

Sam lurched from one possible scenario to another and came up with nothing. 'This has to be a mistake,' he wheezed, his throat on fire. 'I don't unders...'

The crack that resounded through the air, shattering Sam Whittaker's head and spraying Diego with brain matter, caused both men to drop to the ground.

• • • •

COLT WATCHED as his targets hit the deck in slow motion, fragments of skull and blood splattering in an arc like a pretty firework. 'Bingo!' he murmured, mesmerised as both men crumpled to the ground.

He could do with putting an extra shot into the kingpin to guarantee he was kaput but...

*What the fuck?*

In the split second between the men hitting the ground and the image processing in Colt's brain, Diego jumped up and threw himself behind the Bentley Blower.

Colt stared in horror at the vintage car he hadn't noticed beforehand. Not exactly in a position to wonder what the hell it was, he seethed with rage. *He'd missed the bastard?* He'd got one of them for sure, but this one – the *important* one, had cover behind that claptrap. Plus, the man was armed…

This was made clear by the barrel of a gun appearing over a part of the old car. Colt wasn't sure what part of the car it classed as, but he didn't have time to worry about that. He readied his gun. He only had one bullet left and it must hit home.

Moving his burning legs out of the position they'd been stuck in for the last however long, Colt edged along the side of the Jaguar and paused before making the short, exposed leap over to the next parked car.

The crack that accompanied his movement showed Delgado's weapon was functioning perfectly well.

Colt glanced around for blood. He didn't feel pain as a rule, so unless he was dead, he couldn't be sure he hadn't been hit, but it looked promising the cunt had missed.

His Neanderthal-shaped forehead creased. But with one shot left and that fucker well concealed behind that Thunderbird car, how the hell would he do this?

Another shot rang out in Colt's direction, the sharp noise stinging his sensitive hearing.

There was little choice. He'd have to go for it - distract the fucker, take him off guard and then shoot him. *If he got this spot on, then...*

Holding his breath and keeping his head tucked out of view, Colt froze.

*Fuck!*

*He could hear them.*

*Fucking sirens.*

*Bollocks!*

He glanced both ways up the exclusive road, snarling at how fast the cops responded to calls about disturbances in posh areas. He might have known some nosy cunt in one of these obscenely expensive houses had put a 999 call in the second a shot was fired. Where *he* came from, it was weird if there *wasn't* the sound of gunfire. But this was Kensington and gunfire wasn't likely to be commonplace.

Colt took the gamble of popping his head over the boot of the car only for a bullet to skim the side of his ear.

*Delgado was still there then?*

And the sirens were getting closer...

*Shit.* He couldn't risk a tug for this. They'd bung him straight back in Broadmoor.

Colt looked around again and even though they were still a fair way off, the sirens now all he could hear.

*There was no choice but to abandon the job.*

Without spending any further time contemplating the situation, he broke into a weird bent-over scuttle along the side of parked cars, two further shots ringing out as he went.

His one leg hurt like fuck, but that might be because he'd got cramp, rather than copping a bullet. *Whatever. Keep going...*

Nearing the corner of the road, Colt disappeared around it and glanced behind to see if Delgado was on his tail.

*He wasn't - he was clear.*

Delgado would have enough sense to drag that yuppy's body into the cellar and put his gun away before the police arrived, so in the meantime he'd get the fuck out of here.

Straightening up, Colt shoved his gun back into his waistband and took up a leisurely pace in the opposite direction of Diego's house. He glared at an old woman busy staring at him from the other side of the street. Normally, in cases like that, he'd blast the face off the old goat in case she'd seen his gun or anything, but he couldn't. He might need the one remaining bullet and couldn't use it until he'd sourced a refill.

Instead, he pulled out his phone and dialled Marco. 'All right? Yeah, it's me. Yeah... well, I could only do one of them. Yeah, one. The police are on their way so... What? Yeah, the yuppie cunt copped it. You what?' Colt laughed menacingly. 'With the rozzers on their way I won't be going back at all, Marco! Fuck that!'

Besides, he'd just seen the police – three cars, but every single one had sailed past, sirens blaring - going nowhere near the Delgado's road. Looks like he'd overreacted about the cops being inbound, but Marco didn't need to know those finer points. Besides, it wasn't just that which dictated he didn't have the luxury of time to hang around. 'By the way, Morelli, it seems I've been rumbled by my brother, so I need to lay low for a while. Yeah… that's about the size of it… No, it was fuck all to do with me. I don't know if they've worked out about my link to you. It's not like I can ask, is it? Anyhow, if you still want that geezer done, he'll be back in his house by now, so you'll have to do the job yourself. Laters.'

Not giving Marco chance to continue his rant and endless questions, Colt hung up and continued his pace towards the nearest tube station. He was done with Morelli and his fucking orders. The bloke could weigh him in with the remaining cash he owed later.'

# Thirty Six

UNDER DURESS from Sofia to try the Balenciaga dress on, Erin had little choice but to go through with doing so, otherwise Sofia would kick up a stink. The trouble was the security tag blocked the zip running the length of the back of the dress. Unwilling to set off an alarm and come across that she was attempting to remove the tag, she reluctantly decided she'd have to ask Sofia how to get around the problem.

Leaving her cubicle, she reached the one down the corridor containing Sofia, the door which had not long since been shut in her face. About to lightly knock on the slightly ajar door, Erin stopped, unable to believe what she was seeing.

It wasn't her intention to spy on Sofia, but Erin couldn't bring herself to look away. There, clear as day, was Sofia stepping into the size six Balenciaga dress.

Her eyes widened. There was no question the dress wouldn't fit because Sofia's pregnancy had miraculously disappeared to reveal a tanned and perfectly flat, toned stomach.

*There was no baby…*

But *how*?

Erin's gaze moved to the pile of straps and mound of silicone discarded on the changing room floor and she swallowed dryly. *Dear God.* The woman had orchestrated this to the 'nth' degree. It would be genius if it wasn't so abhorrent.

Her breath caught in her throat and her hand reached for the wall to steady herself. In all her doubts and suspicions about Sofia, she hadn't expected *this*.

Erin's thoughts flew to Diego. That poor man. For all his harshness and less than palatable career choice, that baby was his prime importance. That was clear to everyone. His worst fear was that his child would turn out not to be his was now irrelevant. Because there wasn't a child.

*Christ!*

Sofia's plan to kill Diego not being enough, she'd been humiliating and using him this entire time to ensure her plan worked.

Perspiration gathered on Erin's brow, all thoughts of the dress waiting for her to try on slipping into oblivion. She inched away from the cubicle door, her hand reaching into her pocket for her mobile. She must pretend everything was normal to Sofia, but she had to let Zane know about this. He'd have to break it to Diego. *If the man was still alive...*

Suddenly hearing the shrill ring of a mobile, Erin froze exactly where she was and listened.

'Hey, babe,' Sofia purred. 'Yes, I'm in Harrods. Guess what? I've got on the most *gorgeous* Balenciaga dress. I'm buying it, courtesy of Diego!' She giggled loudly. 'Yeah, you wait until you see me in this, you'll... *What*?'

Erin didn't dare move, not wanting to give her presence away. Whoever Sofia was on the phone to, it wasn't Diego.

'What do you mean it's gone wrong? How can it have gone wrong? *How*?' Sofia's voice reached screaming pitch. 'No, I won't keep my voice down! There's no one here! How could he have fucked it up? You said he was the business! For God's sake, Marco! You *promised* me this guy would sort it. I'm not doing this anymore! No! I don't care!'

Erin's skin paled to a strange translucent shade. *Oh no. No, it couldn't be...*

*Marco?*

Sofia's lover was *Marco*?

She found herself leaning harder against the wall, light-headedness washing over her.

*Fuck!*

*Marco? Sofia was in with Marco and Marco had a hit out on Diego? Oh God!*

'I don't care! I'm telling you, I don't! You'll just have to... *What*?' Sofia's tone changed from angry to terrified. 'What do you mean, they're "onto" us? You don't mean...? You know that for definite?'

Erin heard Sofia choke back a sob. 'What do I do? What do I do, then, Marco? For God's sake! Diego will kill me - no ifs or buts. What? I *am* calm! Yes... yes, okay, I'm listening, I'm listening! What? All right, I will, but promise me you'll sort this? Okay, okay, bye.'

Darting away, Erin rushed back into her own cubicle and leant up against the door. Closing her eyes, she took a deep breath to steady her spinning head. Slowly and carefully, she dialled Zane, only praying this time it didn't go to voicemail.

• • • •

ZANE WAS WAITING at some traffic lights when the insistent buzzing of his mobile inside his jacket forced him to make a quick decision. Although he was in dire need to reach Diego's he had to answer this. Perhaps Tiger had been too late and Colt had already succeeded in carrying out the hit?

He felt sick with apprehension. Diego might already be dead and Colt could still be on the loose. Erin was out there and could be in danger.

Her being with Sofia made things worse. Even though it was almost impossible to think Sofia was involved with Colt, it didn't mean she *wasn't*. It had been unthinkable to suspect Sofia could put a hit out on her own husband, yet she'd arranged it. But who with? Her lover?

*That wasn't Colt, surely?*

The second the lights changed, Zane deviated off course. He pulled back the throttle and took a left into a side street. Bringing his bike to a stop he unzipped his leather to retrieve the ringing mobile. 'Come on!' he roared, hurrying to turn the mobile the right way round. *If anyone had harmed Erin or his child, he'd kill every last person in the fucking world!*

'Oh, thank Christ!' he gasped, the relief of hearing Erin's voice like nectar to his fractured nerves. 'I still haven't got through to Diego. I'm heading there n…' Stopping, Zane listened in abject disbelief to Erin's garble down the line.

*Sofia and Marco?*

*And the pregnancy was fake?*

Zane's teeth clenched so hard he was surprised they didn't snap. This would finish Diego. It would rip his soul clean through his chest. 'Shit!' he finally hissed through his teeth. This had stepped across the line of no return. 'I'm coming to get you. You can't spend one more second with that woman.'

In the Harrods cubicle, Erin kept her phone pressed tightly against her ear, her whispers urgent. 'No! You mustn't. It will give everything away. I'll carry on as normal and pretend I know nothing. Do what you've planned. I'll be fine.'

'No fucking way!' Zane barked. 'This could be a trap. That woman... Marco might be waiting and…' His voice trailed off as unwanted images of his brother taking Erin hostage slammed into his mind. He shook the vile images away. He'd go insane if he didn't.

'Sofia can't hang around now, knowing what she knows,' Erin whispered. 'She's going into hiding. I don't know where but go and get Diego. You must! Find Marco and stop this. The hit's already been attempted and failed, but he'll come for Diego again.'

'What?' Zane barked. *So, it had already happened? How much worse could this get?* 'And Colt? Where is he?'

'I don't know that either,' Erin hissed. 'But you have to track Marco down. You must stop him once and for all.'

'I want you to stay where you are,' Zane instructed. 'Let

her leave, but you stay put. No one can get to you in a place like Harrods and I'll come for you as soon as everything's sorted, okay?'

'Okay, but I'll be fine. Sofia doesn't know that I know. I'll see you later, okay.'

In a quandary, Zane stared at the phone as the call disconnected. His instincts were telling him to go to Erin right now – barge into Harrods and get her away from that poisonous bitch. But she was right. If he did that, Sofia would know they were onto her and Marco which would make things even worse. If that bitch was capable of faking a pregnancy, putting a hit on her own husband, as well as sleeping with Marco, there was nothing she wouldn't do.

Zane fired his engine, his stress levels mounting. If only he'd listened to Erin in the first place, they wouldn't be in this pile of shit right now.

But why he had received no update from Leo or Tiger? They must know by now that Colt had not been intercepted, so why had no one told him?

Zane quickly fired off a text to Leo and then sped off to Diego's house.

• • • •

'DID YOU TRY THE DRESS ON?' Sofia asked, not sure how she formed the words so meticulously in her spiralling panic.

Spinning around, Erin smiled at Sofia at the changing cubicle door. At least she hoped it was a smile, rather than the look of horror she keenly felt. She desperately tried not to look at Sofia's belly which had reappeared back in place perfectly. 'I couldn't open the zip. The security tag was in the way.' Hastily shoving her phone back into her pocket, she moved to the dress on the hook and pointed. 'Look, can you see the...'

'You've been in here all this time wondering how to get that tag off?' Sofia tittered, not bothering to mask her sneer. *The lying cow. She hadn't been in here at all. From what she'd just heard, the bitch had listened to everything and for that, she would pay. But time was limited.*

Sofia moved forward. 'All you have to do is move the tag to one side. Like this...' Leaning towards the dress, she diverted at the last moment and snatched up a handful of Erin's blonde hair and smashed her face into the cubicle wall. 'Think you're so clever, don't you, you nasty little whore! You've had it in me for me since the start, but you're too fucking late!'

Erin yelped in shock, the smash to her nose making her eyes stream. Despite the pain, her normal reaction would be to fight. But that was *normally*. She couldn't risk anything happening to her baby.

Raising her hands to defend further blows, she saw the rage in Sofia's eyes. The woman hated her - that was no surprise, but now Sofia was cornered and that made things different. It was obvious her conversation had just been overheard, the same way she'd overheard Sofia and Marco's. Sofia knew she'd been rumbled and now, like a cornered animal, she was more dangerous than ever. 'I don't understand. I...'

'Don't play innocent,' Sofia snarled, her talons winding tighter in Erin's hair. Yanking harder, she forced Erin's head down.

'Please!' Erin cried. 'Please don't do this!'

'Don't do *what*?' Eyes dripping with malice, Sofia's free hand dropped to Erin's belly, feeling the first telltale swelling hinting the pregnancy would soon be visible to all. 'You're not worried I'll hurt you, are you?' She traced her hand over the rounded shape. 'Scared I'll hurt the little Zane growing in there?'

She laughed loudly, unsure why she was laughing. *None* of this was funny. If Marco didn't sort this then they were screwed and her plans had been for nothing. Sofia's eyes narrowed. That could not happen because she was a Buscemi - yes, Buscemi, not a Delgado. And unlike the Delgado's, the Buscemi's *never* lost.

'Fear not,' Sofia trilled, moving her hand to dig into Erin's pocket. 'But you really should learn that it's rude to eavesdrop.

It causes more harm than good...'

Despite her head being twisted at a painful angle, a broken nose and being terrified, Erin was unable to stop her stubborn streak surfacing. 'You're finished!' she spat. 'Diego will divorce you, Marco will be killed and you'll have *nothing*!'

'Is that so...?' Sofia pulled Erin's phone from her pocket. Marco *would* sort this. He'd sort everything and then things would continue as planned.

Chucking Erin's phone on the floor, she ground her stiletto heel through the screen. Stamping on it for good measure, she sneered as the plastic casing split, the whole thing rendered unusable. 'You won't need that.' Letting go of Erin's hair, Sofia then yanked up her own dress to rip off the prosthesis. 'And I don't need this any longer either!'

Erin knew this was her chance to take Sofia down. She had a cracking right hook, but she could not fight *anyone* with her precious cargo in situ.

As Sofia's prothesis fell to the floor for the second time, Erin's hand dropped to her own belly. 'Why Marco though? He's...'

Snapped from the trance she found herself in, Sofia slammed Erin back up against the wall – this time by her throat. 'Shut the fuck up. Do not utter his name. You know nothing about my life! Just because your boyfriend lost his chance with me doesn't give you right to an opinion.' Her white teeth sparkled in the changing room spotlights. 'Now I'm going and you're not stopping me.'

Erin pulled against the fake nails cutting into her throat. 'I won't stop you, but Zane will. Diego will too. They'll stop *both* of you because…'

'Are you deaf? They'll be too fucking late!' Sofia beamed savagely. 'A word of advice, Erin. Learn when to keep your big mouth shut!' Dropping her hand from Erin's throat, she bolted from the cubicle, then doubled back and brought her knee up hard into Erin's stomach.

Retching, Erin dropped to the ground, instinctively rolling

into a ball to protect the life inside her from the kicks Sofia began delivering.

# Thirty Seven

LEO STARED AT his mobile and frowned.

[Zane:]
Shit has gone down at Diego's.
Why was Colt not intercepted?
What's the score?

That was the first Leo had heard of it too. His big fingers clumsily tapped out a reply:

I don't know anything but will find out.

Tiger had left for the flat ages ago. *Shit*, Colt must have got away before he arrived. But why hadn't Tiger said? If he'd needed backup or help, then...

Leo quickly fired off a message to Tiger:

Where are u?
Colt reached Delgado!

And, Leo thought with a grimace, he didn't know whether Delgado was dead or alive because he was *here*, when Zane or Tiger clearly needed his help.

He glanced around the warehouse. All the guards were on high alert with one on every doorway and window. Marco hadn't shown up here, but now Colt was on the loose - or *could* be and the treacherous fuck was working for Marco, an attack was more likely now than ever.

But this place was heavily guarded so surely he could leave?

Gritting his teeth, Leo shook his enormous head, not knowing what to do. Having received no response back from Zane or Tiger, he stared at his phone. Zane must be on route or already at Delgado's, but Tiger's whereabouts were unknown and that was a problem.

Dialling Tiger, Leo listened to the call ring out. About to throw his phone down in frustration, he was surprised to suddenly hear a voice.

It didn't sound like Tiger's, but it *was*.

'Where are you?' Leo cried. 'What the hell's going on? It's all gone off and I haven't a clue what the score is. You... She's what? Dead? She's *dead*?'

Leo's heart thumped. *Fuck*. 'Okay, mate, okay. Stay where you are. I'll come to you.'

Hanging up, Leo grabbed his jacket. There was no other option but to leave this lot to defend the canning works and go. If Marco did turn up and brought an army with him, then no number of guards, himself included, would succeed in stopping the fucker.

Whether that was on the cards, Leo didn't know. But what he *did* know was that regardless of the growing breakdown in his and Tiger's relationship and the strangeness, mistrust and one-sided behaviour of late, Tiger was still his oldest friend and comrade - his brother-in-arms. That was hard, if not impossible to break and overtook any issues between them.

Moving to one of the locked arsenal cabinets, Leo restocked

his gun and after giving orders to the guards, raced out of the canning works. He darted across the concrete expanse of the car park to his van.

Tiger hadn't asked him to come. He didn't have to. The sound of the man's broken voice said enough to make that the only viable option.

His whole body shaking with rage, Leo fired the Transit's engine and slammed his foot on the accelerator. That bastard had killed Alyson purely to spite his own brother. Because for all Leo's teasing and later, annoyance, Tiger had developed feelings for the girl – the one *he'd* pushed into the man's life to wind him up.

Because of that; because of *him*, the girl was dead and Tiger wrecked.

And Leo couldn't feel more shit about that if he tried.

But he *could* ensure the fucking traitor in league with Marco didn't return to satiate his all-encompassing need to finish Tiger off. Whilst no one knew where the fucker was, anything was feasible and Leo wasn't standing around waiting for any of his theories to be proved right.

• • • •

'WE'LL DEAL WITH THIS LATER,' Zane said, breathing heavily with the stress and exertion from carting Sam Whittaker's body down very narrow and steep, dark steps into one of Diego's many cellars. 'We just need him out of the way for now.'

Diego wiped the sweat from his face with the back of his hand. 'I don't know whether I shot the fucker who did this. I thought I had, but he still managed to escape,' he spat, furious at the rare occurrence of his failing to take a target down. 'Then I had to get this body off the street.'

Zane nodded. 'Yeah, I get that. Listen, Diego, I...'

'We now have the answer to our question,' Diego interrupted. 'Your brother is gunning for me. And you know what that means?'

'Yes, I do.' For a split second, Zane wondered why Diego thought it might bother him that Marco had to die. It was on the cards all along. Zane knew it, Diego knew it, Erin knew it - *everyone* knew it.

Zane also knew that despite his previous efforts to remove his bastard brother off the face of the earth, nothing had succeeded. It had almost reached a point in his mind where he'd considered whether the universe was telling him something and that Marco's death wasn't meant to be. Plus, for a very short time when Marco had gone off radar, there was a microscopic part that hoped, despite the unmendable history between them, that Marco backing off meant there was a remote possibility things wouldn't come to this.

He sighed. Deep down, somewhere in the recesses of life's memories, there remained a handful of images bouncing around of two little boys who always had each other's backs.

But that was before Marco turned his *own* back on family, honour and everything that mattered. With a heart that became heavier with every minute, the 0.001% remaining in Zane's soul that didn't want to kill his own blood, meant he knew with startlingly sour clarity that the time could be nothing but *now.*

Dying himself as a by-product of this was one thing, but Zane couldn't extend that to all the people who had become more than family, including Erin and his soon-to-be-born child.

*No. It was time.*

Zane's eyes met Diego's cold grey ones. 'It will be done. Marco will die.'

Diego laid his hand on Zane's shoulder. 'You will not be alone in your quest.'

Feeling unexpectedly grateful at Diego's show of unity, Zane faltered. Before anything else there was something else he had to say.

'Let's get going.' Diego banged his hands together. 'I need that fucker dead befo…'

'Wait! There's something else,' Zane said, dreading this. How could anyone take this well? Selfish or not, he needed

Diego on form to help him take out the one person in the universe he would struggle to snuff out alone, but this revelation would knock him for six. 'It's about Sofia...'

• • • •

OUT OF CHOICE, Marco seldom drove these days. Living in Mayfair, it was easier to take a cab. But for *this* job, being in command of a motor was necessary, especially afterwards. Determined to start his new life with Sofia with the style, grandeur and insurmountable wealth that would be theirs for evermore, he'd chosen to use the one motor he'd retained from Zane's collection for this exact occasion.

*Sofia would get a Lamborghini after all.*

The car's throaty engine roared underneath him as he navigated the traffic towards Kensington. With the vibration of the V12 engine fuelling his inner power, Marco chuckled at the envious looks he collected from other drivers. Considering what he was about to embark on, a less glamorous and stand-out car than a red Diablo might have been a better choice, but why should he?

'I am Marco Morelli,' he shouted, his voice bouncing off the low roof of the car. 'I can do what the fuck I want!'

And he *was* doing what he wanted. *Everything* he'd fucking dreamt of was now coming to pass.

Confident there was no need to conceal it, he reached over and touched the sawn-off shotgun on the passenger seat. Feeling the bulky steel of the barrel, Marco's grin widened. His pistol would have sufficed, but to even the score of the years being without what should have been rightfully his, *this* was a better choice of weapon.

And, he thought, with a wry smile, it brought back the hands-on period of his younger years. Getting his hands dirty had been enjoyable times. Perhaps it was the subject matter that made him feel like he missed those years? Or maybe it was that when push came to shove, he enjoyed the rush that nothing else came close to from extinguishing someone's life.

*And never was the prospect of extinguishing a life as sweet as the one he would shortly undertake.*

A strange mixture of relaxation, combined with the wired buzz of cocaine and excitement flowed through Marco's body. He prodded his phone in the dashboard holder to bring it to life.

'Marco?' Sofia's voice screeched through the car speakers. 'Don't tell me something else has gone wrong!'

Marco laughed. *Why would anything be wrong?* The only thing that had gone wrong was involving anyone else in this. He didn't know why he hadn't taken the reins in the first place rather than getting that dickhead, Shoreham, to do the job. He should be angry at the fucker for only completing half of it, but surprisingly he wasn't. In all actuality, the twat had done him a favour.

Whether the coke rampaging around his brain brought Marco to that conclusion or whether it was down to madness was difficult to deduce, but he cared not a bit. Shoreham had removed Whittaker and now he was stepping in to undertake the *proper* and most enjoyable job of all.

'Marco?' Sofia squawked. 'Are you there? Can you hear me? What's happening?'

'Everything's fine, babe,' Marco drawled. 'Don't stress. I'm only ringing because I wanted to make sure you'd done what I asked.'

'Yes, I'm at your house now. I've only just got here because I had to give Erin a kicking before leaving Harrods.'

'Excellent!' Marco couldn't help but smile hearing Sofia chuckle, her stress dissolving to allow the standard, world-class bitch that he loved so much to reappear.

If Sofia had done a good enough job, the kid Zane had planted inside Erin would leave the building and after *he'd* finished, there would be not one drop of that side of the traitorous bloodline left to walk the fucking earth. 'Remain at my house,' he continued. 'No one knows where I live. That, I know. They'll be wasting time discussing where to look, so just make sure you stay there.'

‘Okay, but where are you now?’ Sofia asked.

‘Never you mind about the details. Your husband will die today and then it’s just me and you, babe.’ Marco felt his erection growing. *Yeah, him and Sofia, plus all that coke. All that money...*

Diego would be pacing around his house this very moment, phoning everyone he could think of to try and work out where to search. With any luck, Zane would be there too, making this a 2-for-1 deal. But if Zane wasn’t with Diego, then he’d track the bastard down afterwards.

*It was time for the big one and nothing could stop him.*

‘You... you are sure it will happen?’ Sofia’s tinny voice through the speakers reverted to holding a hint of insecurity.

‘Aside from you, I’ve never been surer of anything in my life!’ Marco’s free hand kneaded the aching bulge in his trousers. ‘Now remember - stay where you are. I might be some time, but I’ll let you know when things are completed.’

# THIRTY EIGHT

AS IF PHYSICALLY WINDED, Diego lent on the sideboard in his favourite reception room, the urge to vomit stronger than his need to breathe.

He'd expected to receive confirmation of Sofia's unfaithfulness. He'd suspected it for some time, but what he *hadn't* expected was for that unfaithfulness to involve Marco Morelli.

Neither had he expected Sofia to be behind the hit on him which had very nearly just succeeded.

But the worst, absolute *worst* thing of all was...

Diego dragged air into his ragged lungs.

'I'm really sorry, mate,' Zane said. 'I wish I hadn't had to bring this news. If it's any consolation, I'm shocked too.'

'No, it's of no consolation!' Diego snarled, his head snapping up. 'How can *anything* be a consolation to what that fucking bitch has done?' The veins on his neck protruded like he'd been lifting weights. Hatred and anger burned brightly, blinding any who should lay eyes on it.

All this time - all the years he'd put up with that spoilt bitch. All the money he'd allowed her to spend to make her happy. All the snarky comments… When they'd shared a bed, she'd made him feel like he was taking something that others would class as taboo. Even *that* had stopped.

And now he knew why…

Coming to the conclusion that Sofia had exhausted his patience, as well as their marriage several months ago, Diego had been ready to take the flak from his culture and family. His marriage was a business arrangement which could never be reneged upon, yet he'd been about to do exactly that. But he'd had to rethink because Sofia had dropped the bombshell that she was finally pregnant.

The heir growing inside Sofia's body - his child - was the only thing keeping Diego sane these past long months. For sure, once the child was born his marriage was over, but with a heir, the years he'd spent with the spiteful, ungrateful cow would not have been in vain.

Yet *everything* had been for nothing.

Even the recent fear that the baby was not his didn't come close to this!

But, Diego thought grimly, it wasn't Zane's fault. Zane and Erin were the only people to help him to act on his suspicions. They'd found out the truth. Now *he* knew it too and it was a lot worse than he'd expected to be possible. 'You were right to tell me and I thank you for that.'

Zane shrugged, the guilt of bearing the news heavy.

'But...' Diego took a deep breath and straightened his shoulders. 'I'll deal with that lying, treacherous whore later. What matters now is finding your brother.'

Zane nodded. Yes, it was, and although Diego had additional reasons for wanting Marco dead, there were ones that *all* of them shared. 'I suggest we track him to his house and do so fast before he comes for you.'

Diego snatched up his jacket. From what Zane had recounted of the conversation heard between his wife and Marco, Sofia had agreed to go into hiding somewhere - a place unknown. And he suspected, like Zane did, that place was Marco's house - a place no one knew the location of.

But, Diego thought with a sly smile, he might have the answer to that… Retrieving a phone from his pocket once belonging to Sam Whittaker, he looked at Zane. 'If anyone's got Marco's address, it will be on this fucking phone in a message.' Bringing the phone to life, he snorted in contempt that Whittaker was so self-assured he hadn't the sense to protect it with a PIN.

Being so obvious to name Marco 'MM' in his address book also narrowed the search down.

He scrolled through the messages. 'This one looks likely.' Diego handed the phone to Zane. His fire had now reignited to burn in the right direction. *He was ready.* 'Let's go!'

• • • •

LEO WAS FAR TOO USED TO wrapping up and getting rid of bodies, but this one, knowing the effect it had on Tiger, was difficult. As was getting the man to snap out of his silent pain.

Anyone else; everybody in the 'real world', leading 'normal' lives, weren't expected to shrug and immediately carry on after losing someone they cared about. Sometimes it took *years* for people to function properly again.

Or so he'd been told...

In *his* world, the average recovery time allowed was an hour, tops. Preferably it should be under ten minutes, but in most cases, there was no choice for any reaction or grief and it got buried quicker than the corpse itself. People like *them* couldn't react at all without risking being the next fatality.

This was no different, aside from that it was Tiger - the man who, in all Leo's years of knowing him, possessed no emotion. *Until now.*

But he needed Tiger to revert back to the 'normal' Tiger - not this mess!

Leo's eyes remained focused on the bowed head of his friend. Tiger's huge shoulders sagged, his muscular body shrunken with grief. His face remained stone-like, but with the difference of eyes filled with grief rooted in the direction of where Alyson's body lay. The tarpaulin Leo had personally wrapped her in would unfortunately have to remain where it was for the time being.

He'd also finally got through to Zane to let him know the update. And as horrifying as Alyson's death was, she was dead and as it stood, no one else was. *Yet.*

Zane needed them - both him *and* Tiger to help with stopping Marco once and for all. Tiger had to be on form, so how the fuck did he get this man to come back to life before anyone else lost theirs? 'I'm really sorry this happened, mate,' Leo said. 'I know you were in love with her.' Seeing the slight twitch on Tiger's face, the first movement yet, he continued. 'And I'm guessing feeling like you do about her was a first for you?'

Still receiving no response, Leo soldiered on undeterred. This could go either way. It may even result in him getting a punch in the face and push Tiger further in on himself, but if he freed this man back into the here and now, then so be it.

'Think logically. How do you reckon it would have worked out between you two?' Leo asked, sparking a cigarette up like this was a normal conversation; a normal situation between two blokes down the boozer. 'She was a nice girl, yeah? Brought up differently to us, mind. And with that comes a different set of rules. Sure, you *might* have made it work, but do you really think she would have coped long term with our lifestyle and what we do? Would that have been fair on either of you?'

God, that sounded shit and meant little in the grand scheme of things. Didn't people say if things were meant to be they somehow found a way to work?

Leo shrugged. What would he know about that sort of stuff? 'Would you give this up, then? For her?'

'I'd have given anything up for Alyson.'

Leo hadn't expected Tiger to speak, but he had. And he hadn't got a whack either, so riding the wave, he pushed on. 'Right, so you'd have given up the life you've always known and not be resentful? You'd be happy taking a normal job and living for the rest of time worrying how the fuck to provide for her and the kids?'

'She wouldn't have asked me to give things up,' Tiger muttered, his voice hollow. *Alyson was the first person who'd seen him for who he really was.*

'Okay, so say you didn't give it up. Then what? You tiptoe around waiting for her past and what that cunt put her through, to catch up with her? Like it did today? Be grateful it happened now before you both got serious, or kids were on the scene.'

Snarling, Tiger jumped to his feet. 'You're telling me you're *glad* this happened, you cunt? I should have been here! I should have protected her, rather than guarding bags of fucking Class A at the canning works!'

'It would only delay the inevitable?' Leo felt a glimmer of hope. *There was the anger*. Anger was better than hollowness. Even if he got a punch or several, it would be worth it to get Tiger's fight back. There was plenty of time for reflection and now was not it.

He held his hands up. 'All I'm saying, mate, is that what happened today would have happened at some point. Marco would not have allowed Alyson to live. She'd have spent her whole life living in fear – as would you, for *her* sake.'

'If Marco was dead, he couldn't have done anything! He should have already been taken out!' Tiger's eyes flicked back in the direction of the bedroom where Alyson lay.

'Is that so? You see, the thing is, because of *you* - because I'm sitting *here* babysitting you like a kid, that bastard's got every chance of winning. For all I know, he already has!'

'What the fuck are you saying?'

'What I'm saying is, that whilst we're sitting here, Zane and Diego have gone to take Marco out. He's gunning for Diego. After Colt killed her...' Leo's head jerked in the direction of the bedroom, 'he killed another bloke, then tried to kill Diego. Colt failed on that one and did a bunk. To where, no one knows. He could be waiting in the wings for one of us to move, but meanwhile, Marco's free to pick up the slack and right now there's only certain things on his list. To top it all, Diego's wife has been having it off with Marco. She's not even really pregnant! They've got to kill that bastard before any of it happens.'

Tiger stared in horror at Leo. 'And where's Erin?'

'With Sofia. Zane's told her to wait for him to come to Harrods when this is over. The whole thing's a mess.'

'Then we'd better go, hadn't we!'

Grabbing his jacket, Leo closed his eyes in relief. Tiger's fighting head was back on, thank fuck. The man could sort out how he felt about Alyson's death later, but for now, they had to do what was needed.

• • • •

IN A TAXI SPEEDING the short distance to Diego's house, Erin concentrated only on breathing steadily, determined not to let terror over whether Sofia had harmed the baby inside her overtake. Keeping her head down lessened the chance of unwanted conversations with the cabbie, but it happened regardless.

'Blimey, love! What you done?'

Erin self-consciously touched her nose and winced. 'Oh, I fell down the stairs in a shop.' She was unsure whether her nose was broken, but that her eyes had already blackened, her face hurt like hell and the cab driver acted like she'd been ten rounds with Mike Tyson, made it likely that it was.

'Bloody hell!' the cabbie exclaimed. 'You should sue the shop! That's health and safety stuff, ain't it? Go to hospital. They'll log it and then you'll have proof when you take the shop to court.'

'Yeah, maybe,' Erin muttered, wishing the man would shut up. By rights she *should* go to hospital, but it wouldn't be for her nose. She didn't care about that. All she cared about was whether her baby was safe. But what would going to hospital achieve? If she was going to lose the baby as a result of Sofia's punches and kicks, then hospital or not, it would happen.

Biting back the sting of tears, Erin laid her bruised, swollen and agonisingly painful hand over her belly, hoping that taking the brunt of the force of Sofia's pointed shoe with her knuckles had spared the precious life inside her. From what she could tell, there were no cramps or bleeding which was a good sign, wasn't it?

She had to cling on to that because it was the only shred of hope. And with no phone, no knowledge of where Zane was, short of after his brother's blood, she had no way of getting hold of him. Despite her fear about the baby, she had to press on. While Sofia, Colt and Marco were on the loose, *no one* was safe.

Erin clasped her shaking hands together. By doing this she was going against Zane's instructions, but she couldn't just sit in a changing room and wait. With the state of her face, it was only so long before staff asked questions.

Freaking Zane out about the baby would not help either, so she'd do whatever she could to cut down the work. And removing the need for others having to fight their way through London to get her was one of them.

'So, love,' the cabby piped up again. 'Am I taking you to the hospital or what?'

'No!' Erin said, perhaps a little too sharply. 'Somewhere down here's fine. I'll tell you where exactly in a moment.'

The cab was nearing Diego's house and that was where she was heading. Erin had heard Sofia agreeing to go 'somewhere' and bet that 'somewhere' was Marco's house, unaware that Diego and Zane would be locating where Marco lived and taking him out before he had chance to move.

Zane should be at Diego's house by now working out a plan, so Diego's house was the best place to go. Even Marco wasn't insane enough to go there so quickly and make another attempt on the man's life now he knew he'd been rumbled.

Erin frowned, her mind ticking over at record speed. That was it! Marco had told Sofia to go to his house thinking Diego and Zane would not pinpoint his location. Marco thought he'd got time to plan another strike, but he'd be too late. Diego and Zane would source Marco's address even if they had to threaten every fucker in the city to do so. And then this nightmare would end.

# Thirty Nine

SOFIA PACED UP AND DOWN the grand room and for a second was distracted by a painting of a horse on the wall. Was that an original Stubbs? Running her finger lightly over the canvas she raised an eyebrow, suitably impressed.

It was real, all right and worth a fortune. Marco rented this place so there was nothing to stop them taking this picture when they left, was there?

But then again, why bother? When she got her hands on the Delgado fortune, plus the Buscemi money which was hers, but controlled by Diego like how it worked in families such as theirs, she could buy the Mona Lisa if she so desired.

Which she didn't, but that wasn't the point.

Moving away from the painting, Sofia edged towards the huge bay window and peered out into the street. That painting might have distracted her from the worry of the position she found herself in for a second, but not long enough to stop her heart from thundering in a way she was certain would kill her.

From the side of the heavy velvet curtains, her eyes darted up and down the road.

There was nobody around, which was good.

Her pulse rate gradually returned to a normal level.

*It was fine*, she told herself. Everything was running to plan, Marco had said so. There was no need to be jittery. Very shortly, if not already, Diego would be dead and she would be free. Finally, her and Marco could live how they'd always planned. But what that little tramp, Erin had said, rattled her nerves. It was that bitch's fault she was lurching between paranoia and terror.

Why the hell was she allowing a pathetic cow who not only was pregnant by a man who would never marry her and *couldn't* - because Zane would soon be no more, get to her?

Sofia snorted in derision for allowing Erin's words to get under her skin. *She was Sofia Buscemi not Miss Timid!*

She mentally pushed the words clinging inside her mind down and out through the end of her toes, smiling as the last one was removed. 'See, Erin?' she muttered, her glossy lip curling into a sneer. 'You can't screw with *my* head!'

She was *not* finished. Diego would *not* divorce her because he would be dead and Marco certainly would *not* be killed. He was far too clever for that. As was she.

A tinkling giggle escaped from Sofia's mouth as she settled herself back into a proper state of mind.

*What a day to be widowed.*

*And she couldn't wait.*

Sofia's giggle turned into a raucous laugh remembering the sight of Erin curled into a ball and sobbing on the changing room floor. *That was most enjoyable.*

She'd have loved to have given the bitch a longer beating, but getting out of there to be with her *real* man was more important than that blonde scrubber. However, she'd done enough to fuck the tramp up. Zane's kid would most likely have slithered out by now to lie on the floor next to the loser he'd impregnated in the first place.

Gratified with the thought, Sofia glanced down at her flat stomach, overjoyed to finally be rid of the revolting strap-on monstrosity. *Hallelujah! Back to normal and not a minute too soon.*

She took another peep out of the window and satisfied nothing had changed, strutted across the room, wondering where she and Marco would go first once this was done? On a cruise to bide their time in luxury whilst the solicitors sorted out Diego's estate, perhaps?

It was just a shame she hadn't time to buy that gorgeous Balenciaga dress today. It was perfect for a cruise and...

Sofia suddenly went cold. All of her dresses and shoes - *everything*, was still at her house. There were some amazing pieces there which she'd never be able to source again. And what about her handbags and jewellery?

Clammy at the prospect of going on a cruise with only a small selection of off-the-shelf designer clothes grabbed from duty free, Sofia's eyes narrowed. What if another woman had the same dress on at dinner or something?

She glanced at her diamond encrusted Rolex. There was time. Diego wouldn't be at the house - no one would. Even that old cow of a housekeeper would have left for the day by now, the lazy bitch.

Beaming with delight, she snatched up her handbag. Yeah, Marco said to remain here, but he was a worrywart about some things. Being protective was nice, but there was no need. If Diego still walked this earth, then he'd be busy looking for Marco, not *her*. Even if Diego now knew everything about her, Marco and the non-baby, where would be the *last* place he'd expect her to run to?

'My own house!' Sofia exclaimed loudly. 'Diego won't think I'd go there!'

But she *would* go and she'd go there *now*. Marco would soon understand why it was imperative to pick up her things. It wouldn't take long. God knows she'd already forfeited enough in the long, dull years she'd been stuck with Diego and was damned if she was leaving her best couture clothes and Louboutin collection behind.

*Christ knows she'd earned them.*

Sofia left Marco's house and jumped into a taxi. When she

reached the house, she'd go in the back door, grab her stuff and be out again. *Easy.*

• • • •

PULLING UP OUTSIDE Diego Delgado's house, Marco glared at the car once belonging to his father. The plan to hook Diego in by using it and making him a sitting duck had worked, but thanks to that cock Whittaker, it hadn't quite gone the way he'd planned. But that was about to be rectified.

Satisfied Sofia was safely at his own house in Mayfair, Marco glanced up and down the road. A couple of people were knocking about, but this lot around here were too up their own arses to take any notice of fuck all. Priding themselves on their anonymity, they wouldn't have the first clue who lived where or who should or shouldn't be there. It wasn't the East End, thank God, otherwise things would be difficult, but these arrogant fools suited his requirements perfectly.

He picked up his shotgun. If Delgado happened to try and escape the hell hole he'd shortly find himself in, *this* would stop him in his tracks.

Things were good.

Making one last check in his rearview mirror, Marco blinked in surprise.

*Hold on a fucking minute... Was that...?*

Forever resentful his eyesight had not weathered as well as his physique, he squinted at the figure getting out of a black cab further down the road.

*It was! It was that bitch who belonged to his brother. What was this? A fucking family reunion?*

Deciding to wait to see what Erin did, Marco watched her go up the path to the front door of the townhouse and ring the bell.

*Safety in numbers, eh?*

Deciding on a different tack from his latest plan, Marco pressed the button for the electric window and waited as it silently opened. Lifting the shotgun, he took aim at the front door. Would the range reach? He hoped so because he'd blow Delgado's head off the second he opened it. *Surprise!*

The door opened and Marco's smile of anticipation slid off his face and dropped into the footwell as he watched Erin exchange pleasantries with a middle-aged woman and then enter the house.

Had it slipped Sofia's mind to mention that her ponce of a husband employed a housekeeper or what?

But then, conversations like that weren't commonplace whilst fucking each other's brains out. Plus, had he mentioned that he was coming here to kill Diego now?

Marco shrugged. Whatever! Another body to add to the pile was fine. And, he thought with a sly grin, Erin being in there too was an unexpected bonus.

Readying himself for the job, Marco got out of the car, momentarily flustered as the front door opened again.

*It was the housekeeper or whoever she was and it looked like she was leaving for the day... Excellent!*

Looking every inch the respectable businessmen, Marco walked around the car to open the small boot. He pretended to rummage around inside whilst keeping a close eye on the woman making her way down the path towards the pavement. *Come on! If you're going, hurry the fuck up!*

Still playing for time, he pulled the prepped holdall to the front of the boot. *Go on, fuck off*, he willed, mentally hurrying the woman along.

*So now what?* Diego was in the house – he had to be if Erin had gone in. And that *she* had gone in, meant it likely that Zane was also present…

Marco's frustration changed to delight. This was better than he'd hoped. All three of the fuckers in one place, the stupid bastards.

He knew he'd get them, but this was easier than he'd foreseen.

However, there was still a chance Zane *wasn't* there. He glanced around, unable to spot the motorbike he'd heard his brother rode. The Yamaha FJ1200 was a step down from the Ducati Zane had once took pride in, but shit happened and if the clown hadn't got himself banged up he wouldn't have eventually come out to find the world had moved on and most of the stuff once belonging to him had found better things to do.

But the bike's presence or lack of it didn't mean carte blanche that Zane wasn't here, so should he wait a while to see if the brother he hated arrived or not?

Marco frowned. If he waited, what if Diego, Erin or *anyone* spotted him hanging around? That would never do.

Safe in the knowledge that the housekeeper had gone and he was good to go, Marco glanced back down at the holdall. It always paid to have several options and *this* was his first.

He sparked up a cigarette, possibly not the most intelligent thing to do considering what the holdall contained, but he'd made sure the jerry cans inside were sealed tightly. It wasn't likely he would use the fucking things as ashtrays, was it? They'd be put to much better use than that, so there was no need to flap over such irrelevance.

Marco smiled. The way this day was panning out wasn't how he'd imagined, but variety made the world go round. Plus, he'd enjoy this, so it was time to get this show on the road.

On a new high and with a spring in his step, Marco sauntered back towards the house, holdall in hand.

• • • •

'THERE'S STILL NO ANSWER.' Zane's worry mounted. 'Why the fuck hasn't she answered the phone?' This was the *fourth* time he'd tried to get through to Erin and not once had she picked up. The prickle of unease inside him grew stronger.

'Perhaps my dear wife is still there?' Diego spat, finding it impossible to keep the raw hatred from his voice.

'But Erin said Sofia knew her cover was blown.' Zane attempted another redial to no avail.

'Erin's a sensible and clever woman,' Diego said. 'Sofia will have disappeared by now as expected and Erin will be keeping her head down at Harrods like you asked her to. Besides, for all we know, her battery could have run out. I'm sure she's fine.'

Zane nodded. *Diego was right.* He was panicking and he shouldn't. Out of everyone, Erin was the one to keep things together. He'd reach her as soon as he could.

When his phone bleeped, his eyes lit up. He stabbed at the text message. 'This might be her... Oh... It's Leo... He and Tiger are on the way and he's asking where to come.'

Diego pulled the car over at the side of the road. 'Then give him this address because we're here.'

Quickly forwarding Marco's address, Zane then stared at the row of Georgian townhouses, his heart sinking a little lower. *Here it was - Marco's house. It was time to kill his own brother.*

Sensing Zane's inner turmoil, Diego switched the engine off and turned to him. 'I can be the one to do it.'

Zane shook his head. 'No, it will have to be me. What Marco has done to everybody is because of his hatred for me, therefore it will have to be me who takes him out.' But the tiny part within him wishing it hadn't come to this still remained. He'd do it. Of course he'd do it. He just wished... wished that Marco wasn't, well - *Marco...*

Marco had betrayed him, let him down and been his worst enemy for years, but Zane had always hoped that eventually his brother would turn a corner and stop destroying everything and everyone around him. But with how their father had turned out, perhaps it was a built-in gene - a rogue trait the Morellis possessed? One that perhaps he *also* possessed but one which hadn't fully made itself known yet which was a horrible prospect.

With numb resignation, Zane wondered if the dormant gene inside him would activate the moment he took his brother's life. If it did, he'd need to make a concerted effort 100% of the time to keep on top of it and ensure he didn't follow the family trait of destroying people he'd vowed to protect.

# FORTY

ERIN WOULDN'T NORMALLY go upstairs uninvited in someone else's house, but queasy with the stress of what had happened with Sofia, along with the worry plaguing her over her unborn baby, made her nervous. That uncharacteristic nervousness brought with it the urge to put as much distance as possible between herself and any point of entry to the house.

Locking herself in the bathroom, she took a breather. Sitting down on the closed lid of the toilet, she fought the urge to check her knickers for signs she was losing her much wanted child.

*It was then that she heard it...*

Tensing, Erin froze, sure she'd just heard a noise from downstairs. It wouldn't surprise her if her mind was playing tricks on her but...

*There it was again!*

Getting up, relieved that Diego and Zane had returned, she rushed to the bathroom door, then stopped in her tracks. Her hand paused on the gold doorknob. That sound was a door shutting downstairs, but a door in the direction below her. This bathroom was on the first floor at the *back* of the house. Diego wouldn't enter his own house from the back because she clearly remembered him saying once over dinner about how pointless it was having a back door when the only way out was right down the bottom of the 500-foot garden through a gate leading to a back street. It was a route he never used.

Frowning, Erin tried to make logical sense of this. Sound travelled strangely, especially in old houses, so maybe the noise 'appeared' to be coming from elsewhere, when in actuality it...

The doorknob grew slippery in her hand as her palm became slick with sweat.

*Footsteps...*

Footsteps that were coming rapidly up the stairs. And those footsteps didn't belong to the large feet of Zane or Diego. They belonged to a woman...

*Sofia...*

With a surge of nausea, Erin turned her back and pressed up against the door in the glib hope that if Sofia found her, she couldn't get in. But it was fruitless. Was Sofia alone or did she have Marco with her? If they were coming for her, they would get to her whatever she did.

Erin's hand dropped protectively to her belly, not doubting that if that happened her torment would not stop until every shred of life was kicked from her.

Anger mixed with fear snowballed. If Sofia was alone perhaps she stood a chance? If she trapped the woman somewhere until Zane and Diego returned, then...

*But how could she stop Sofia?*

Erin looked down at the swollen mess of her hand. Even if she wanted to punch Sofia to the ground, she wouldn't do much damage with a hand that she suspected, like her nose, was fractured or broken.

Holding her breath as the footsteps reached the landing, Erin exhaled shakily as the clattering continued past the bathroom to stop further along.

There was one set of footsteps - *heeled* footsteps.

The bedroom door slammed; a wardrobe opened; something was dragged from a cupboard. Then a faint tune wafted from the same direction in a shrill, out of tune voice.

*It was Sofia and she was alone.*

This was Erin's one and only chance to get out of here and she must take it.

Hating herself for not doing what she would do in any other space, time or universe and confront Sofia, for the sake of her baby there was no other option but to flee. She could not risk fighting Sofia and take more blows to her belly. It might already be too late - the damage already done, but if it wasn't, she was leaving nothing to chance.

Opening the bedroom door an inch, praying it didn't creak, Erin peeped through the gap into the long landing down to the other end where it sounded like Sofia was. Luckily for Erin, this was the opposite end to the staircase.

*It was now or never.*

As silently as she could muster, Erin slipped from the bathroom and down the stairs. Her heart lurched into her throat when her foot skidded on the carpet runner and she grabbed the solid oak banister for dear life. Wincing as her shoulder took the brunt of the weight, she righted herself and carried on.

Reaching the bottom of the stairs, Erin stopped to listen.

*No one was following.*

Now just to find the back door that Sofia had come through. She'd go through the garden and out that way.

• • • •

TAKING A GLANCE over his shoulder, satisfied the conveniently planted Hornbeam hedge fringing the property concealed him from anyone passing, Marco set to work.

Should anyone in one of the top floors of the other houses spot him, then ho-hum - tough titties. Too late for anyone to stop this even if they wanted to. Plus, the people round here weren't interested in anything but themselves, so it was unlikely anyone would get involved.

Pulling the leather gloves just over the cuffs of his jacket, Marco smiled. It seemed a shame to trash these Italian calf leather driving gloves, but he was fucked if he was lowering himself to donning something unsavoury like plastic or latex gloves. *No fucking way!*

Sofia would be horrified if he made such a blatant fashion faux pas, but aside from that, this was a special occasion – one like no other and therefore one demanding suitable attire.

Marco was fit to bursting with excitement and gracefully accepted the slight tremor of his hands as an accolade to the significance of what he was about to do. Unzipping the holdall, he took out the first jerry can and unclipping the tube, removed the end. His gloved fingers prised open the flap of the gold letterbox where he tucked the tube in. Tilting the can up, he grinned at the spatter of the petrol hitting the tiled floor.

Hyper, Marco jigged around from foot to foot, his brain hitting the point of overstimulation. Inhaling deeply, he relished the sting of petrol fumes in his lungs. *This was beautiful.*

'Goodnight, Diego, you piece of shit,' he muttered. Tipping the can up full tilt, he then carefully reseated the stopper and tube and placed the empty can back in his holdall. *Did he need the second?*

Marco's excitement mounted. *Probably not, but then again, why not?*

He yanked out the second can and fed the tube through the letter box. If Zane was here too, which he dearly hoped his suspicions on that were correct, then *this* one was for him. Erin could share the effects of half of each can.

Chuckling to himself, he continued pouring the strong-smelling liquid into the Delgado house. 'You're welcome. Don't mention it,' he muttered, his imaginary conversation with the despised people in this house fuelling his drive, as well as his sense of power.

'Touch of her skin, feeling silky smooth, colour of café au lait…' Marco sang, his head bobbing to the tune only he could hear. 'Made the savage beast inside roar until he cried, more, more, MORE!'

Controlling himself to keep his voice at a non-deafening level, Marco emptied the second can whilst *Lady Marmalade* continued loudly in his head.

He peered through the letterbox, checking that petrol covered a good portion of the hall floor. Seeing that it did, he stooped down to place the can back in the holdall and moved it off the doorstep. 'Gitchi, gitchie, ya-ya, da-da… Gitchie, gitchie, ya-ya… Mocha chocolate, ya-ya… Creole Lady Marmalade...'

Stepping forward, Marco grinned, his eyes shining maniacally. 'Here it is! TIME TO FUCKING BURN!'

He fishing a lighter from his pocket, wondering whether he and Sofia should go to Paris whilst waiting for the shit following this to play out? He could take her to the Moulin Rouge. She could *dance* at the Moulin Rouge. Sofia was gorgeous enough to do *anything*!'

Sparking the lighter, Marco lit the long taper in his hand and hastily pushed it through the gilt-flapped letterbox. 'Voulez-vous coucher avec moi, ce soir? Voulez-vous coucher avec moi? Voulez-vous coucher avec moi, ce soir?'

Stepping back, he raised his hands over his head theatrically. 'Creole Lady MARMALAAAAAADE,' he cried, turning a small spin on his heels with the telltale 'boomf' sound of the petrol igniting.

Picking up his bag, Marco retreated down the path, the song in his head on repeat. He glanced over his shoulder before turning from the end of the path onto the pavement, gladdened to see the hint of a glow of flames beginning to rage behind the small, frosted panel in the top centre half of the front door.

Now all he had to do was wait. The fire would take hold and destroy rapidly and he wasn't missing Diego Delgado, that bitch Erin, and hopefully his cunt of a brother, burn to death!

But, Marco thought, picking up a fast pace as he walked away from the house. He wasn't hanging around outside the front.

The flames would be too strong for any fucker to cross in order to escape from that entrance, but fear not – he'd done his homework. These houses had gates from the road behind and that's where he'd head now. He knew how many houses to count to work out which gate belonged to Delgado, so he'd go in there and watch the fucking place get razed.

*A ringside seat for the finale.*

It was done. Sofia was now *his*. The empire was *his*. The money was *his*.

*Wonderful.*

• • • •

ERIN MADE HER WAY from the back door across the paved terrace into the lawned area and stared in horror at the length of the garden. In the distance, she could just about make out what looked to be a back gate, but if Sofia glanced out of a back window, she'd be spotted straightaway.

Her eyes darted along the manicured lawn to the thick beds either side. They were heavily stocked with a variety of beautiful bushes and flowers, as well as tall shrubs and a handful of well-established trees - most of which looked to have been planted when the house was built. In any other situation, Erin would thoroughly appreciate the beauty of this garden but at this present time, it presented only as a hindrance - a minefield to cross. She'd be venturing into No-Man's-Land, but if she stuck to the edges, the plants and foliage were thick enough to offer protection and conceal her presence.

Without waiting a moment more, Erin raced to the nearest bush and barged into the undergrowth, scurrying as close back to the fence as possible. Yelping as twigs scratched her face and her ankle tipped over at a worrying angle, she crouched down. Getting her breath, she could see the house clearly. It was only a few yards away, but she was hidden better than attempting to run down the centre of the lawn.

To her left was a tangled mass of thick bushes and branches. If she carefully planned a feasible route, she might escape undetected.

Closing her eyes, she took a deep breath. Calmness was the key and...

What could only be classed as an explosion from the direction of the house took Erin's breath away and with a racing heart, her first instinct was to keep leap out from her hiding place to see what was behind the noise.

*Was it a gun? Had Sofia spotted her and was firing at her? Oh God!*

Ducking lower within the jungle of spiny twigs and branches, Erin twisted around, desperate to change direction and get a better view of the house, but her foot was caught in a mess of trailing vines. Panting, she fought to untangle her ankle from the mess, the searing pain in her damaged hand making it difficult. Gritting her teeth, she continued and finally freeing herself, shuffled around in the bush.

Looking up at the towering house, Erin's eyes widened at the distinct glow radiating from behind the Georgian windows of the ground floor. It wasn't coming from within those rooms but somewhere further away in the house - possibly the front. *It looked like... like...*

Another explosion came from within the building - this one slightly muffled. Erin instinctively tensed, then caught sight of something through a window which made the explanation of what was going on inside painfully clear. The bright curling orange tendrils lapping at the door frame at the back of that room meant only one thing…

*Fire.*

The house was on fire and Sofia was in there.

Or *had* been…

Despite what the woman had done, Erin's first thought was horror, but then quickly realised this was all part of that bitch's plan. Sofia had torched the house and legged it. *That* was what she'd returned for!

Erin's jaw tightened. The bitch had done this to destroy the house as her parting insult to Diego before Marco killed him.

Dread surged. By Sofia doing this, did it mean she'd received word that Marco had succeeded in killing Diego and therefore Zane…

*After everything, had Marco won? If so, she'd never see Zane again and...*

Vomit surged up Erin's throat, but she kept it contained and her spiralling panic was abruptly halted by a noise close by. Her skin prickled.

*Laughter?*

Ducking down even further into the undergrowth, Erin craned her neck, the taut sinews screaming as she forced her head in the opposite direction. Her mouth fell open in shock as she looked down the garden.

*Marco!*

She stared in horror as Marco bounded along the lawn closer to where she was concealed. His face was a picture of rapture, the strange laughter coming from him sounded unearthly and possessed.

Goosebumps broke out over Erin's body as Marco pirouetted around the garden, dancing with an invisible partner.

'Burn, you fucker!' Marco screamed. 'Ha fucking HA! Delgado, Zane, Erin! I know you're in there!'

Shaking with revulsion, fear and rage, Erin continued to watch as Marco span past her hiding place. He was so close his overpowering aftershave overtook the smell of burning wood, plastic and fabric which now spilt into the air.

Closer to the house but still on the lawn, Marco plonked himself down to sit cross-legged on the grass like a child in assembly. He stared with beatific wonder at the blaze in front of him. 'No way of escaping now, you fuckers!' he screamed, oblivious to everything around him.

Erin's hatred for Marco emanated from her every pore. They'd planned to burn Diego, Zane *and* her to death. They believed they'd succeeded too. But Marco and Sofia were wrong. No one was in that house.

Except, she *had* been only a few minutes ago. She'd been locked in that bathroom and if she hadn't acted when she did, then...

Erin shuddered, this thought sending her reeling.

But one thing she didn't understand was being as Sofia and Marco had planned this, why had Sofia come back to the house alone in the first place? Unless Marco had been inside too but downstairs when Erin escaped?

However, if that was the case, then Marco wouldn't be coming through the garden from the rear or...

Another explosion sounded, this time an extremely loud one. Erin twisted her head back in the direction of the house to see the ground floor windows had blown and the fire now well-seated on the first floor.

*Oh, this was awful! All of Diego's beautiful antiques that he'd collected were lost forever.*

'WHOOO!' Marco cried, lost in a fixation of enjoyment.

Erin's eyes narrowed. *Was he staying here until the house burned to the ground? Where the fuck was the fire brigade?*

It was then that she saw it: the unmistakable figure of Sofia banging on the glass of a window on the third floor.

# Forty One

CHOKING FROM THE acrid black smoke curling up the staircase, Sofia clawed at the heavy brass knobs of the sash window. She'd never liked this old, original window furniture and had nagged and nagged Diego to replace all the horrid wooden windows in the house with proper up-to-date PVC ones sporting easy to open smooth catches. But of course, he hadn't. He'd left them exactly as they'd been when this place was built back in the dark ages.

Now it obvious he'd left the old ones in place with *this* in mind, knowing she'd never easily open them - not without breaking her nails. And these windows on the little used third floor were opened less than any others.

Using all of her force, Sofia stuck her fingers between the wood of the two overlapping panels and heaved with all her might. She cried out in pain and desperation when all she achieved was snapping off her long acrylic nails along with her real ones underneath, including the attached nerve beds. With blood flowing down her fingers onto her wrists, she pummelled at the thin glass of the old windowpane.

*Why wasn't it breaking? Why wouldn't it smash? If she could just get some air...*

Dissolving into a fit of coughing and spluttering, Sofia leant against the frame, sweating with exhaustion and fear. The crackling of the fire below was now louder than it had been. If only she'd braved going downstairs straightaway when she'd first smelt something, then she wouldn't be stuck here.

Now she was on the third floor - too scared to open the door and go downstairs but too scared to remain here either.

Why did she come up here anyway? Why had she been so desperate to find that blue Prada dress anyway? Putting a collection of her less favourite clothes in one of the many spare bedrooms last year seemed a good idea at the time. She hated clutter. But then, thinking that one particular dress would be perfect for cocktails on the deck of a cruise ship at sundown, she was determined not to leave without it.

How she now wished that she hadn't.

Sofia banged on the window once again in a fruitless effort to get help. This bedroom was on the back of the house so no one would see her. She was so distressed and panicked even the fat tears rolling down her cheeks to leave tracks of black mascara in her thick foundation didn't faze her.

Then her eyes narrowed with a renewed rush of anger as the penny dropped.

Marco had failed her. He hadn't reached Diego in time and her bastard of a husband had come for her, just like she knew he would once he discovered the truth.

*Diego had set fire to the house.*

Sofia's eyes widened and then with the sting of smoke against her eyeballs she quickly screwed them shut. Diego set fire to the house knowing she was in it. *No doubt he was watching this right now!*

Breaking into a fresh round of hacking coughs, Sofia pressed herself against the window and peered through the blurred vision of her streaming eyes into the garden below. *If she could just open this, could she jump?*

Panic rolled higher. Of course she couldn't. Look how high up it was. She'd hit the ground and die.

*But then she'd die if she stayed here...*

'Diego, you bastard!' Sofia screamed at the top of her voice, which turned into a terrified scream as another loud bang of something else shattering and exploding downstairs.

Spinning back to the window, her sobs became hysterical. She couldn't burn to death, she just couldn't. It wasn't fair. It would ruin her face and...

*Wait! Was that someone in the garden?*

Sofia peered through the glass, sure the air in the room was getting hazy. The smoke was getting thicker which meant the flames were getting closer…

There *was* someone in the garden!

*Diego?*

*No! It was Marco! Oh, thank God!*

With a renewed sense of hope, Sofia pulled a reserve of energy from within and banged on the windowpane with both fists. 'Marco!' she screamed. 'MARCO!'

She knew he'd come. If he heard her; if he could see she was trapped then he'd rescue her for sure. She knew he would.

• • • •

THE COCAINE ALONG WITH the natural euphoria ransacking Marco's brain pushed him into the state of altered consciousness which he frequently fell into, lifting him to the top of the world. Nothing else existed aside from a neon-edged reality seen through the kaleidoscope of his faceted mind at times like this. Nothing seemed real, yet at the same time, everything possessed a lucid reality about it. Although it was enjoyable being King of the Universe, the strange things which materialised in his mind's eye were sometimes unsettling. And as gratifying as it was witnessing this house burn, knowing that at least two people he hated were trapped inside, he didn't like *that*.

His smile remained in place as he squinted up at the window on the third floor. It would be beautiful to see Diego or Zane melting as they got consumed by flames, but for a second, he was convinced the imaginary figure in the window was a woman.

Now, if it was Erin that would be fine, but this figure looked dark-haired, like Sofia.

Just thinking of that horrible scenario spoilt Marco's pleasure. When his visions got weird like this, he sometimes worried that the things he did in life made his brain fill with worst case scenarios as a form of karma. It was a good job he didn't believe in mumbo jumbo bollocks, wasn't it?

Wait! The figure was moving. It *was* someone.

Frowning, he stumbled further towards the house, his gaze still locked on the figure in the window, now partly obscured by smoke belching from a broken window on the floor below.

*It had to be Erin, not Sofia.*

Marco shook his head, the image still bothersome. He really did need to cut down on the gear. Or at least not take it when he was naturally wired because it pushed him over the edge and made him fucking hallucinate.

Sofia was safe, he knew that. She was at his house waiting. She'd told him exactly that when he'd called.

Marco shrugged. He'd go back there shortly. The vision in his mind of Sofia at the window had unnerved him, so returning to the only woman he'd ever loved became more pressing than ever. He'd seen about all there was to see here now.

'Hi Marco.'

Marco swung around at the unexpected voice. He was about to lose his temper with himself for hearing things as well as seeing them until he realised someone actually *was* standing next to him.

He blinked several times, weighing up whether this was real or not, his gaze flipping between the third-floor window where the figure still remained, back to the one in front of him. It *was* real. *And it was Erin...*

'Surprised to see me? I'm shocked you're leaving *her* in there though.' Erin nodded towards the house. 'Thought you two had a thing going?' She smiled despite the close proximity to the man who wanted her dead.

Marco wouldn't lash out at her at this moment in time. He'd made no snarky comments about her black eyes and smashed nose which provided a good indicator of his demeanour - the truth was sinking into whatever mess was left in his skull.

Marco blinked yet again. For Erin Langley to be standing in front of him and not in the house after all didn't seem real, yet he knew it was. He also now knew the person in the window - the one he thought he'd imagined, was...

A horrible, guttural sound escaped from Marco making Erin instinctively step back.

Marco lurched towards the house, still looking up at the window. *She was still there!* 'Sofia! It's me!' he roared. 'I'm coming.' *He'd get her. He'd sort this. He was Marco Morelli and he could do ANYTHING.*

Why Sofia had left his house and come here, he'd ask her later, but he'd get her out of there first.

Not remembering Erin or anyone else ever existed, Marco yanked open the back door. He wasn't losing Sofia - not now. Not now they had won.

Holding his shirt over his mouth, he burst into the rear hallway and disappeared from view.

• • • •

USING THE LOCKPICKING SKILLS learnt in prison, Zane quietly released Marco's front door. Both Sofia and Marco were somewhere in here and had to be taken by surprise.

His gaze darted around the reception hallway with doors leading off in every direction, as well as a large staircase - possibly one of two on the ground floor. And that didn't include the cellar...

'You take this floor and the cellar,' Zane hissed to Tiger and Leo. 'Me and Diego will take the upper floors.'

Leaving Tiger and Leo to carry on, Zane raced up the main staircase, Diego following and both with their guns at the ready. There was little further point in attempting to be quiet now.

Marco was here somewhere. If he'd been expecting their arrival, he'd be upstairs, barricaded into a bedroom, his gun trained on the door. Either that or the same difference, but with him being in one of the cellars. Both locations were equally weighted as traps. Despite this, there was no choice but to present themselves. It was the only way this could end.

At the top of the staircase, Zane turned left, Diego right. They booted the heavy, closed doors open and covered the areas inside with their weapons.

Sweating heavily, Zane cleared another room, his senses on full alert. He didn't want to die and if he'd misjudged this it stood a good chance he might. He wanted to meet his child. He wanted to marry Erin. He wanted to be a family.

He didn't want any of these men accompanying him here to die either. Nor had he ever wanted this last resort of having to kill Marco ever come to pass. *But it had.*

It had and he'd do it. He'd just have to learn how to live with breaking his strong code of conduct afterwards.

Zane moved along the landing, repeating the same action for three further rooms. His ears remained highly tuned for any indication from downstairs showing that Tiger and Leo had located someone, but there was nothing.

Diego met Zane around the corner of the split landing and shook his head. 'Nothing.'

Zane turned to the staircase leading to the floor above and raced up it. If Marco wasn't expecting him, then from what he knew of his brother, he'd be holed up in his bedroom, either preening himself, off his face or having sex.

He grimaced, only hoping for Diego's sake it wasn't the latter. The man didn't need to witness Sofia's adultery first-hand and up close. From the rooms they'd cleared so far, none of them, although grandiose, had the hallmarks of a master bedroom Marco would deem worthy to sleep in, therefore it had to be one of these up here.

Systematically checking each room on the top floor, Diego and Zane entered the last remaining room together, fully expecting both Marco and Sofia to be inside ready for the expected intrusion.

*But there was nothing.*

Flinging open the wardrobe and checking under the bed as a last-ditch attempt, Zane sagged into a chair and put his head in his hands. There had been no gunshots or signal from the lower floors either. *The house was fucking clear.* 'Fuck!' he hissed. 'We got it wrong!'

Diego's face twisted in rage as he picked up a pair of red lacy thongs between his thumb and forefinger, his blood pressure rising dangerously. 'They may not be here now, but Sofia has certainly been here. *I* bought her these!'

'So, where are they now?' Zane muttered, all but talking to himself. He snatched the lacy thong from Diego's hand and threw it onto the luxury carpet. 'Forget that thing. Where the fuck are they? Left the country? Where?'

He couldn't have this. He couldn't let Marco walk away this time. That his brother had succeeded in escaping only meant his family would be at risk for evermore and he wasn't allowing that any longer. 'I have to find him. Where the fuck do we look now?' *What if Marco had met up with Colt and amassed men already with promises of...*

Zane's head snapped up, his eyes blazing. 'The canning works!' That drop is due in during the night, so he'll attempt an overthrow! He's done that shit before.'

'It's feasible. Either that or he's at my house waiting for me to return so he can kill me.' Diego shrugged. 'I guess it depends which one he deems most important.'

Zane raked his fingers through his thick black hair. They'd walk into a trap either way because now Marco had the upper hand. Marco now had the bonus of seeing them coming, whereas they'd be going in blind.

Both men raced down the stairs to be met by Tiger and Leo.

'It's all clear down here,' Leo said, breathless. 'We've checked everywhere.'

'The gardens clear too. Everything's fucking clear,' Tiger

growled, fully immersed in locating the piece of shit he longed to see die, grateful that while something else was at the forefront of his mind it meant he couldn't think of what he'd lost.

Zane quickly recounted his and Diego's conclusion to Tiger and Leo. 'So, we need to check both places. I'm leaning towards him going to the canning works to intercept the coke drop out of the two. Especially if he has Colt with him.'

Tiger bristled at the mention of his treacherous brother's name. 'Then *I'll* go to the canning works!'

'It needs more than one of us there,' Diego said.

'Yes, it does. Knowing Marco's penchant for money, that's the most likely place. Three of us will go there and the other can check out Diego's.' Zane looked between all of the men.

'I want to be present at the place most likely the cunt will be!' Diego snarled, his face filled with wrath.

'That's everybody's general consensus I reckon,' Zane said, the irony of the situation not lost on him.

'I'll go to Diego's.' Leo held up his hand. 'Don't get me wrong, I want to see Marco get taken out as much as anyone, but you three have more personal involvement riding on his demise than me, so I'll do it.'

Nodding his approval, Zane left Marco's house with the other three men beside him.

# FORTY TWO

MARCO RACED UP THE first flight of stairs, grateful the door to the front half of the house remained closed. Although he could see raging flames licking around the edges through the small gaps of the doorjamb, it was a solid oak door so it should hold. He might have time to get Sofia out.

Correction. He *did* have time. There was no other way.

If he failed to save his one true love - the *only* true love - the only person in eternity he'd ever held in his mind and thought anything of, then his life was pointless. Everything he'd strived for; everything he'd lived for was pointless. All the shit he'd endured - the marriage to Hazel, all of that bollocks was equally pointless.

He'd done everything in his power to reach this point. Both Sofia and himself had yearned for it so it could not go wrong. Not like this. Not like anything!

But *he'd* screwed this up, for fuck's sake! *He'd* torched the fucking house but hadn't known Sofia was in there. *Fuck, fuck, fuck!*

He'd never have... *Oh Christ!*

That his plan might fail in this way was unthinkable, therefore nothing else was feasible. It would be fine.

Taking the back staircase three steps at a time, Marco concentrated on the end result rather than the acrid smoke filling his lungs. Racing up to the next floor he also ignored the heat searing his fingertips as he touched the walls. 'I'm coming, Sofia!' he screamed, hoping she heard him over the deafening noise of glass shattering and splintering, cracking wood. *He had to reach her. Had to.* 'I'll get you out of here.'

And he would. He *would*. He'd do it and then he'd kill the fucking cunt bitch who found it amusing to stand and watch from the garden.

He wouldn't waste time on that whore now.

Rounding the corner to the second landing, Marco stared in horror at a burning beam blocking the way. *That wasn't stopping him. Fuck was it!*

Marco leapt over the burning wood, the flames licking against his skin in searing agony. At this point it entered his mind, but only as a passing wisp, that starting this fire was the only thing in his life he regretted.

It was stupid thinking that way. Diego was dead, hopefully Zane too, otherwise he'd have caught sight of them in here by now. He'd get Sofia out. The bitch, Erin, would be dealt with easily enough afterwards.

Charging up the next staircase to the level where he'd seen Sofia at the window, Marco coughed and spluttered, his gaze darting up and down the landing. 'SOFIA!'

*The room she was in must be down here.*

He crashed along amid more creaks, cracks and bangs from below. His hands were burnt, he knew that. He could feel the skin blistering but that didn't matter. Nothing mattered apart from getting Sofia out.

Slamming his shoulder against the door of a bedroom, Marco fell through it, relieved to see Sofia.

But she was slumped against the window…

His heart lurched. 'Sofia?' he screamed, dread like never before swallowing him whole. 'SOFIA!'

Darting over, Marco pulled Sofia into his arms, not caring

that flaps of skin hung from his burned hands. 'Babe? Talk to me!' Hyperventilating with panic, he brushed the hair from her clammy forehead. 'I'm here. It's me - Marco!'

'Marco?' Sofia whimpered, breaking into coughs. 'You came?'

'Of course I did!' Clasping Sofia's face with his scorched hands, Marco studied every beautiful millimetre.

'Diego torched the house!' Sofia sobbed. 'He did it! I told you he would kill me. I told you!'

Pulling his jacket off, Marco tore at the sleeve of his shirt underneath. It was one of his best too, but never mind. He went to tie the strip of material around Sofia's nose and mouth. 'Here. Put this arou...'

'Don't do that!' Sofia squawked. 'I won't be able to breathe with that over my face! Did you not hear what I said? Diego did this! He's burnt his own house! He must have known I was in here. Him and your fucking brother!'

Marco's mind suddenly packed with loud clanging. *Diego hadn't started the fire, he knew that, but why did Sofia think tha...*

*Oh no. No!*

'You mean, him and my brother aren't here? They're not dead?' he choked, barely able to ask the dreaded question.

'Why would they be here?' Sofia screamed. 'They'd hardly stay inside a house after setting fire to it!'

All the shouting only aided further acrid smoke in filling her lungs. She coughed harder. 'You said you'd kill him! You said you'd sort everything and you didn't!'

'So, it's my fault?' Marco barked. Except it *was* his fault! *He'd* started the fucking fire, but he wouldn't mention that. He'd *never* mention that. But that Diego and Zane - even Erin, not being in here was as insult stabbing his brain. 'I told you to remain at my house, so why the fuck did you disobey and come here? Why the fuck didn't you do what I said?'

'What and leave my Louboutins?' Sofia screeched. 'Haven't I lost enough? I'm not leaving all of my decent clothes behind or...'

'We've got to get out of here.' Marco forced the strip of material around Sofia's mouth and nose, more of his skin coming away in the process. 'Stop struggling! I need to get you out!'

Sofia's eyes widened and her fingers tugged the makeshift mask. 'You don't expect me to go down there? Into *that*? We'll burn, Marco. Burn!'

'What the hell do you think will happen if we stay in here? There's still time to get out,' Marco panted, pulling Sofia to the door.

'NOOOOO! I can't! I *won't*. I...'

'I'll protect you. I promise we'll get out of here,' Marco said. 'And then I'll kill both of them!' Because it was Diego and Zane's fault he'd torched the house in the first place. If they hadn't had to be removed, he wouldn't have been forced to do this.

Pulling Sofia onto the landing, Marco stared in dread at the burning beam that had already wrecked his hands, the blaze now spreading along the landing towards them. He wrapped his jacket around Sofia's head and shoulders and ignoring her screaming protests, dragged her through the flames.

The jacket offered her enough protection whereas Marco gritted his teeth against the searing heat on his own skin. They had to be quick. If the downstairs back stairway was still closed off from the rest of the house there was every chance they'd get out alive.

*There could be no other outcome*, Marco thought, the hate for everybody and everything burning harder than the fire itself.

Lifting Sofia off her feet, Marco charged down the staircase overriding the screaming protest of his lungs. One more flight of stairs and they'd be out. And then he'd kill his brother, Sofia's cunt husband and that bitch in the garden with his bare fucking hands.

• • • •

ALL WAS QUIET AT the canning works. The guards reported nothing out of the ordinary and no one suspicious had been spotted around the general area. It was good that nothing had been flagged as worrying, but in Zane's present state of mind where anyone and anybody, including those on the inside might be a mole, did nothing to aid his conviction that everything was secure.

'My men are patrolling a square mile around here and have not seen or sensed anything.' Zane eyed the empty racks and workbenches, satisfied everything was in order, ready for the delivery. 'That aside, we know Marco and most probably Colt, are around somewhere waiting for a time to storm and we don't know how many men they've amassed.'

He looked at Tiger whose face painted a picture of rage layered over the most pain Zane thought he'd ever seen on someone whose closely guarded and invisible emotions were legendary. 'I am sorry about Alyson, mate. Leo told me you thought a lot of her.'

A grunt was all Tiger managed. That he'd thought a lot of Alyson was an understatement. If only he'd realised that before…

A nerve ticked in his neck, bitterness and hatred for his brother overstepping his rage for Marco. Whatever happened now wouldn't bring Alyson back, but if it was the last thing he did, he'd make Colt pay a thousand times over for what he'd done and prayed the cunt would show up here aiming to get his hands on the coke delivery.

Diego leant against the edge of a workbench, his big frame poised to strike. 'Marco and his flunkies are around for definite, but as no one was in my house, we have no choice but to wait for them to come to us.' His voice sounded more like a hiss of steam than words.

Zane nodded. Diego was right, but also knew the man was finding it difficult to hold himself in check. Diego hadn't mentioned Sofia and who could blame him after the stunt she'd pulled, but her whereabouts were also paramount.

And worse, who she'd pulled it *with*.

But not being able to reach Erin was still bothering Zane immensely. There was no way of finding out if Sofia was still with her at Harrods or even if she was all right. And that worry burrowed deeper in Zane's mind with every breath he took.

• • • •

'ERIN STOOD IN THE CENTRE of the lawn in exactly the same place where she'd taken the rash decision to approach Marco. Zane would go spare that she'd taken such a stupid gamble. Not only had she walked up to Marco but made a sarcastic comment too. It could have gone so very wrong.

She was angry enough with herself for taking such a reckless risk. Her ridiculous stubborn streak overtook logic, her own safety, as well as her baby's and that weighed heavily around her neck.

She'd clambered out of the safety of the bush and into that psycho's path before thinking of the possible repercussions. It was a trait which although she was better at controlling since bearing the responsibility of the life growing inside her, this ingrained stance still clung on.

Old habits died hard and Erin accepted she'd been fortunate her instinct of weighing up the situation had paid off.

But why was she still here? Marco had gone inside the burning building with other things on his mind, leaving her with a clear run to escape. Yet she was still here.

*Watching. Waiting.*

For what, she didn't know.

*Except she did. Maybe she'd known what that was all along?*

Remaining perfectly still, Erin was unable to move her gaze from the house in the throes of an out-of-control blaze. She'd trailed Marco's progress; seen his silhouette pass the small windows of the stairwells: the first floor, then the second and to give him his dues, he'd done well and moved fast. The fire was raging all around him, the heat blistering and the smoke must be choking from inside.

Squinting up, Erin saw Marco's silhouette at the window in the third-floor room Sofia was trapped in, but valuable seconds were being wasted because they weren't moving. She wondered whether their route out was now blocked, but then the figures disappeared from view once again.

Erin's gaze darted to the back door. There was a chance they could both get out. In what state, she didn't know, but Sofia and Marco could escape and they might live.

Hearing faint but distinctive sirens in the distance showed the brigade were on their way. The way the blaze had increased, they'd be too late to help Sofia and Marco if they didn't escape within the next few minutes. Whatever happened, they were definitely too late to save the house.

Suddenly seeing Marco's figure pass the lowest stairway window with something in his arms, Erin realised with a sinking dread they *would* indeed get out alive.

If only nature had taken its course and done the decent thing.

Despite everything, she knew Zane was dreading having to finish his own brother but would go through with it and live with the consequences. It would be perfect if there was no need for him to shoulder that additional burden.

Erin moved, her legs feeling like they didn't belong to her. She had to leave before Marco and Sofia got out of the building.

It was then she saw Marco at the back of hallway, his face burnt and red, carrying the woman who had earlier attempted to kill the unborn baby inside her.

She stared at the man who had ruined all of their lives and before she knew it, rushed forward towards the house.

# FORTY THREE

ALL TERROR AND PANIC swept from Marco as he met eyes with the fucking bitch watching through the glass pane in the back door. Seeing this diverted his whispered words of encouragement to the woman in his arms whose screams of protest had long since faded into wails of torment and agony.

Admittedly, Marco didn't want to see what was left of Sofia's beauty when he finally removed the jacket that had melted to her face during the long descent down the stairs. What had happened to him, he didn't care - he was past the point of pain because everything was neutralised by the sight of that cunt watching from outside.

Molten hatred slid through his veins to rival the heat around him. How he'd make that bitch suffer for this. How he'd make them *all* suffer.

If his fucking brother and Delgado thought they'd seen even *half* of what was yet to come, they were sorely mistaken. If Erin's baby survived Sofia's well-timed kicking, then once it entered this world, he'd track the brat everyday of its pitiful life and do whatever was required until it left this earth in an agonisingly slow and painful manner. Whatever inflicted the optimum grief in the bastard child's parents was the way things would roll.

'You'll regret every single breath you've ever fucking taken, Erin,' Marco sneered, his resolve to get out of this burning place into the open now more pressing than ever.

Rushing towards the door to salvation and Erin's demise, Marco began to flounder. Sofia weighed heavy in his exhausted, burnt arms and the raging fire closing in behind them seared the remaining skin on his back. 'We're nearly there,' he said to Sofia and also to himself.

Glancing over his shoulder, the fire was almost on top of them. *Come on! They had seconds!*

Turning back to the door, Erin's sneering face had disappeared from through the glass panel. *Probably run off if she's got any sense*, Marco thought, reaching for the doorknob.

He'd expected it to be hot. Maybe it was but his hands were so burnt it failed to register.

*Right. Now to get out of...*

*What the fuck?*

Marco turned the knob. And then he turned it again. He rattled it. He pushed and pulled. 'COME ON!' he roared, the fire now inches away.

The door was locked. How the fuck could the door be locked? He'd gone in this way. He'd closed it behind him, yes, but he hadn't...

*Erin!*

That bitch had locked the fucking door!

Roaring with rage, Marco placed a now unconscious Sofia on the floor. 'Okay,' he muttered, weighing up the advancing fire already licking at his ankles. 'Fucking come on! THINK!'

He'd smash his way out. That was it - the glass! He'd get Sofia outside through the panel and then get through it himself afterwards.

Using what little strength he had left, Marco smashed his elbow into the large pane of glass, quickly being reminded that this wasn't the best thing to do as the air rushed in, turning him and Sofia into human fireballs.

• • • •

HEART POUNDING, Erin kept up a rapid pace out of the road at the back of what had been Diego's house. She didn't go near the street at the front. It was awash with onlookers and the brigade had now arrived.

She'd find a payphone and call Zane. Even though her brain was mashed she should be able to remember his number or one of their numbers.

*But what would she say?*

Frowning, Erin hurried along the main road. She didn't know what she'd say just yet. Perhaps that she'd been getting asked too many questions in Harrods, so thought it best to leave? Or should she pretend she was still there when she called and say she'd make her own way back, as long as she knew where to come?

*Or she could tell Zane the truth?*

Whatever happened, Erin felt no remorse. If she hadn't locked the door and trapped Marco and Sofia in the house, they'd have killed her. They have killed *everyone* eventually.

Now that had been averted. Everyone was safe.

Plus, she'd taken the onus away from Zane of being the one to do it.

The opportunity was there so she'd grabbed it and it was done.

Given that choice, what other options were there?

*None.*

Spotting a phone box near to the High Street Kensington station, Erin darted into the road. She'd make that quick call, find out where best it was for her to go and then jump on a tube.

For the first time in a very long time, she felt lightheaded with relief. She was also elated. *It was over. Marco could not harm anyone ever again.*

With a wide smile on her face, Erin didn't even see the car that ploughed into her coming.

• • • •

WHEN HIS MOBILE BEEPED, Zane couldn't get out of his pocket fast enough, but his face fell seeing it wasn't from Erin. Opening the text, he sighed and stared up at the ceiling in desperation. 'It's the delivery driver! Christ! This is all we need!'

Taking the phone, Diego read it out loud, frowning as he did so. 'It says, "Delivery inbound. ETA 15:00". He looked at Tiger and then Zane. 'Shit! That's far earlier than expected! It's 2 o'clock now!'

Zane slamming his fist down on the worktop made everyone start. 'That's it! This is what Marco's waiting for! Storming the place as the drop arrives.'

'But how does he know? Is this contact of yours another mole?' Diego snarled, nodding to the mobile. 'Is it him?'

'It's not necessarily anyone new. Colt knew the drop was brought forward, therefore Marco does. He's laying low somewhere around here, watching and waiting for the lorry to show up.' But even that would be better than discovering new moles or plants within the firm. Any more of the bastards and he'd bin this whole fucking firm off himself.

He snatched his phone back up the second it beeped again. *Please let it be Erin this time.*

[Leo:]

I'm still not at Diego's. Traffic bad.

It's chockablock. Fire and accident apparently.

I'll be there as soon as poss.

Clocking Zane's face, Diego bristled. 'What is it now?'

'Leo's still not at yours because the roads are chaos,' Zane said, his stress levels growing. 'This will probably delay the delivery as well.'

'I'll see if I can find out what's happened,' Tiger mumbled. Pulling out his own phone, he opened the browser. There might be local news updates to give them a better idea of how long this would slow things up. And he was glad of something else to do other than wait and stew in his hatred.

• • • •

THROWING ANOTHER cigarette end out of the window, Leo drummed his fingers on the Transit's steering wheel. For Christ's sake! Out of all of the days he'd put up with gridlock on the London roads, this one had to be the most bloody frustrating. How the fuck would he get anywhere at this rate?

He gritted his teeth hearing the steady wail of further emergency vehicles arriving. Whether it was the brigade, the police or ambulance, he wasn't sure, but it was all he'd heard in the time he'd sat stationary along with what seemed like half of London.

Whatever had gone on had successfully snarled up the entire route around Mayfair. From the tail end of a snippet he'd caught on the radio news - as well as an accident, there were problems further afield too: something about a blaze. Whatever was going on it had better not be anywhere near where *he* was going otherwise he didn't stand a chance. He'd already texted Zane with the update but things needed to get moving!

Leo had to get to Kensington. However unlikely it was that Marco should choose Diego's house as his first stop, Leo had no qualms about being the one to put an end to the man and it would be perfect if *he* was there to take the fucker out. But nothing would happen at this fucking rate.

'Come on!' he roared, slamming his fist on the dashboard. There weren't even any side roads he could take to pick a back route out of here - the whole place was at a standstill.

'Ah, finally!' Leo cried when the cars in front moved forward. Slamming the van into first, he drove forward only to stop again several feet up the road. He craned his neck above the queuing traffic, spying the first hint of what was causing at least some of the problem.

Leo pushed his sawn-off further back under the left-hand side of the bench seat, not wanting anyone spotting *that*. Getting pulled in for carrying was the last thing he needed.

'Jesus Christ,' he snarled, turning the engine off. 'I'm not sitting here forever!' No one was moving so he might as well go and look himself. *Someone* must know how much fucking longer everyone would be held up for!

Jumping out of the van, Leo locked the door and strode up the centre of the road between the queuing cars. 'What's going on? Any ideas?' he asked an equally disgruntled driver chain-smoking out of his open window.

'Hell knows,' the man muttered. 'If you find out, let me know!'

Leo carried on towards the blue flashing lights up ahead. He picked his way through the chaos and reached the area blocked off by police cars and two ambulances, just about making out a group of paramedics around a body on the floor.

*Another shooting?*

A policeman blocked Leo's path. 'Sorry, sir, you can't come through here.'

Leo peered at the man, who in comparison to himself, was a dwarf. He could shove this copper out of the way and continue ahead if he saw fit, but getting himself and his Transit with guns in situ impounded wouldn't help. 'What's going on? I'm in a hurry and need to know how long we'll be stuck.'

'A pedestrian has been knocked down, sir,' the policeman said. 'We're doing everything we can to get things moving, but we can't open the road until medics have moved the victim.'

'Dead, I take it?' Leo muttered uninterestedly. *Bloody shoppers never looked where they were going.*

'I'm afraid I don't know the details, sir.' The policeman's arm moved in front of Leo reminding him to go no further. 'Now, if you'd just return back to your...'

'Hang on!' As a paramedic moved from his position crouched down by the victim, Leo caught sight of the shoes. He recognised those boots. Not many people had boots with a star on the side. *No! It couldn't be!* He lurched forward only to be grabbed by the policeman.

'Sir! I told you to please return back to y…'

'Fuck off!' Leo roared. Shaking off the man's grip, he pushed through to the group of paramedics, dread overtaking the threat of his vehicle.

# FORTY FOUR

'ANY LUCK?' Zane watched Tiger still busy thumbing through his phone.

'Not really,' Tiger muttered. 'A pedestrian's been mown down and there's a house fire, but as it's breaking news there's no further details.'

Zane sighed. That was no more information than what Leo said. 'I'll have to get word to the delivery driver and tell him to avoid the whole area.'

'Still no word from Leo?' Diego asked. 'He must still be stuck.'

'Yeah, it's getting ridiculous. Oh, wait! This is him now!' Snatching up his mobile, Zane paced the warehouse. 'For God's sake, Leo! Don't tell me you're still not th…'

Seeing the distinct and worrying change in Zane's stance, the colour draining from his face, both Tiger and Diego sat forward.

'W-What's happened? Is... is she...? You're going there now? Which...? Okay... I'll be there as soon as I can!' As Zane disconnected the call, the high-pitched whistling in his head became so overpowering that he stumbled forwards, his hands grasping for the back of a chair. Depositing himself with a thump onto the plastic seat, he put his head in his hands.

'What is happening, my friend?' Diego asked, exchanging concerned glances with Tiger. 'What has occurred?'

Zane looked up. His blue eyes brimmed with unshed tears that he swiped away with a trembling hand. 'It's... it's Erin... She's...' He could barely bring himself to utter the words. 'She's been hit by a car.'

'What?' Shock momentarily removed the twisted hate ingrained in Tiger's face. 'How?'

'The accident causing the traffic was my Erin. Some fucker has mown her down!'

'Is she...?' Diego stopped, the unspoken question hanging heavily in the silence.

Zane's horror turned to raging despair. 'I don't know anything. I don't even know how badly she's hurt or whether... whether...'

'You must go!' Diego pulled Zane from the chair. 'Go now! Go wherever Leo said she's being taken.'

Bewildered, Zane's eyes darted between Tiger and Diego, to the empty shelves on the rack. *Anything* but taking on board that Erin or his unborn child, might be dead. Perhaps *both* of them... Nausea formed a tight ball in his stomach. 'The delivery... I...'

'Fuck the delivery!' Diego barked. 'We'll deal with that. Just go to your woman. Go!'

'But...'

'Go, Zane!' Tiger repeated. Zane was skirting for a reason to avoid a reality he could not live with and Tiger prayed that what had happened to Alyson hadn't or wouldn't happen to Erin. The other unspoken words that all three men were thinking but hadn't voiced were the same: was what happened an accident in the *true* sense of the word or being as losing Erin would finish Zane completely, were Colt and Marco behind it?

• • • •

LEO SAT IN A ROOM TO WAIT. It was smaller than the main

waiting area, only containing a few other people, but at least it wasn't one of those tiny side rooms with nothing in there bar a couple of chairs and a box of tissues. Everyone knew what those rooms meant...

He glanced up at the television on the wall silently playing the news before looking away to stare at the floor instead.

At the scene the police had been about to cart him off when a WPC eventually listened to him saying he was a close friend of the woman lying on the ground. Able to tell the paramedics Erin's name and age, as well as giving the vital information about her pregnancy had secured Leo his ticket out of there. Getting a police escort to retrieve his Transit from the snarled-up traffic, he'd followed the ambulance to the hospital. Good job really because it wasn't like he could leave the van unattended with a shooter inside.

He'd called Zane on route. It wasn't the first time he'd had to break bad news about Erin to Zane. It wasn't the first time he'd been at the scene or first to arrive after something bad happened to her either. He was beginning to think he was some sort of fucking Jonah.

But this one was worse than them all because the baby inside Erin meant two lives might be lost. One was bad enough.

And there were so many questions which had, so far, gone unanswered.

No one was sure how the accident happened yet, aside from that Erin was hit at some speed.

*But Leo knew.*

His top lip curled into a snarl. *It had to be Marco.* Or something to do with Marco. That fucker had arranged for his own daughter to be killed, for Christ's sake, so what better way to hurt his brother than killing his wife-to-be and unborn child?

*The final stab to the heart.*

And, he thought with bubbling hatred, Marco had no doubt enlisted Colt to do the job. After killing Tiger's bird, Colt had disappeared and now it was obvious where to - the next hit on Marco's list. *Find Erin, follow her and mow her down.*

And the fucker had managed it.

Leo had seen Erin's smashed up face and her legs didn't look too good either. She'd been unconscious, but alive when she was loaded into the ambulance. Whether she was now and what the extent of her injuries were, he didn't know. Neither did he know if the baby was unharmed.

He stared at the double doors. They'd said someone would let him know what was happening, so why was he still none the wiser? Zane would be here any minute and there was nothing to tell the man.

*For God's sake, this was a nightmare.*

Leo leant back against the wall and took a deep breath. He didn't know why the other people in here were staring at him. Being here at all dictated there should be other fucking things on their minds aside from *him*.

Sparing the time to throw a steady glare around the room, triggering the other people's eyes to avert from his direction in record speed, Leo moved his line of sight back to the television.

The news was still on.

Even the fucking shopping channel would be better than the news.

His eyes then narrowed as the television filled with close-up footage of a raging fire, subtitles scrolling along the bottom of the screen:

Kensington fire remains out of control... Firefighters battle to extinguish blaze now threatening many homes... Roads remain closed in the area... Traffic backlog reaches gridlock...

*No shit*, Leo grimaced. So, that was the culprit then? Along with Colt and Marco's hit on Erin, a fucking fire had brought West London to a standstill? Now he was sitting in a hospital waiting room *yet again*, dreading the moment a doctor burst through the doors with news he didn't want to hear.

Unless he'd found a clear back route, it would take Zane

ages to arrive. But perhaps if he was on his motorbike, he'd stand more chance of...

'Wait a fucking minute!' Unaware he'd spoken out loud, Leo didn't notice all eyes immediately swivel back in his direction. Leaning forward to peer closer at the screen, he gasped as the film panned out.

*That was Diego's house, he was sure of it!*

And the proof of that came when the camera turned to the left. There, wedged between two fire engines was the Bentley Blower once belonging to Zane's father - the car which had kicked off this latest hideous chain of events.

Scrambling for his mobile, Leo scrolled through the contacts unsure if he even had Diego's mobile number.

'Shit!' he shouted, gaining further disapproving looks, which this time he clocked. 'What the fuck are you lot staring at?' he roared, glaring around the room. 'Mind your own fucking business or I'll...'

'Where is she?' Zane burst through the double doors. 'Leo! Where the fuck is Erin? Is she all right?'

Zane's gaze then fell to the television screen, seeing exactly what Leo saw. 'Oh shit!' he yelled, vaguely aware Leo was steering him in the direction of a chair.

• • • •

'IS SHE OKAY?' Tiger barely gave Diego the chance to disconnect the call. The look on the man's face didn't hint of good news - it warned of the very opposite. His heart clamoured like a drum. He'd already lost Alyson today, breaking a heart he'd thought had shut up shop forever. He couldn't bear to lose Erin on top of that.

Aside from not wanting Zane to feel anything like he felt right now, Tiger liked Erin Langley and had a lot of respect for the woman. What she'd done for the firm and for many of them personally would be difficult to repay. 'Diego? Is Erin okay? That was Zane on the phone, wasn't it, so…?

'Erin will live. She's got broken bones but she'll live.'

Diego looked up from the blank screen of the phone. 'They're operating now – she needs a pin in her leg, but they have to do more scans and tests to determine whether the baby is unharmed.'

Tiger nodded, disappointed the all clear hadn't yet extended to the child, but pleased that there was at least a positive starting point. 'By the look on your face I thought you were going to tell me that she was...'

If I look unhappy it's because I've also just learnt that my house is burning down,' Diego said casually as if he was stating a trivial fact. 'Looks like our "friends" got there after all.'

Tiger's face flipped back to ill-suppressed rage. *Marco and Colt. Again!* 'Fuck!'

'No one can tell me that is just a strange coincidence!' Diego laughed, surprising himself. 'But whatever they did, they fucked up because no one's there. I presume the overall plan was that there was supposed to be someone resident. Like me, for instance!'

Tiger shook his head in disbelief. 'You're taking it well, but you should go. The authorities will be trying to reach you, so you sh...'

'You want me to go to watch my house burn down and stress about a bunch of possessions I can't save?' Diego said, his voice calm. 'I can't save anything and furthermore, I don't particularly want to, so fuck it! Let it burn! That cunt has done me a favour!' Seeing Tiger's confusion, he continued, his voice now holding a distinct edge of resentment. 'That house and everything in it will only ever remind me of Sofia. And I don't need reminding!'

Tiger nodded. After what that woman had done, that stance made sense. 'What will you do about her?'

Diego frowned. That he was unsure about. Killing her along with Marco was preferable now there was no heir and never had been, but it was too soon to make a final decision on how he would deal with this. Processing there would never be a child had to come first. The embarrassment of clearing his throat to rid it of the forming lump was thankfully removed by his mobile ringing again.

Glancing at the display screen, he frowned at the Colombian number. He'd expected this, but not quite so quickly. 'Delgado. Ah, hola – buenas tardes... Sí... Sí, eso es correcto. Solicite ésa, información. Bueno. ¿Y estás absolutamente seguro de eso? Como sabes es muy importante. ¡Marailloso! Muy apreciado. Salud. Adiós.'

Tiger stared blankly at Diego. He wasn't guessing at that one. He possibly understood a couple of words and even they were probably wrong.

'Some information I requested has come in,' Diego smiled, looking up as a guard appeared through the door over the other side of the room. He nodded at the man who then promptly left. 'Looks like our delivery is here too. I'll go and deal with it.'

Striding across the warehouse. Diego seated his gun in his waistband leaving Tiger to ready his own gun in case Marco and Colt thought it sensible to undertake the next part of their expected operation.

# Forty Five

WATCHING THE LAST CRATE of cocaine being unloaded from the rear of the arctic from the back end of the lorry which had reversed right up to the open doors of the delivery bay, Diego dared to breathe a sigh of relief.

Well, almost.

He watched the sweating men hurry back and forth, working in a chain to unpack the tightly wrapped bales of drugs from the crates and stack them on the cleared racks. Next it would be weighing and cutting but he wasn't needed for that.

Diego risked a small smile. It was many years - too many to actually remember since he'd last physically overseen a delivery. In his position, he'd been party only to the arrangements, discussions and agreements - never the hands-on or even *present* during the physical work. He'd quite enjoyed being part of this side of the process, but he'd have enjoyed it more had the rest of the day been better, rather than proving his life had been ripped apart from the inside out.

The familiar thrum of adrenaline pulsing in his veins reminded him not to concentrate on that. It would get him nowhere. But the bereavement, because that's how it felt, of losing a child which had never existed, hurt in places he hadn't believed were part of him.

Sofia's betrayal was one thing, but to use a child...

Diego set his jaw determinedly. He would not think of that and instead concentrate on Zane, whose child was *real.* That baby's existence was not yet secured and the man must be going out of his mind.

Nodding his thanks to the delivery crew, Diego waited as the arctic pulled away and the iron shutters of the bay rolled back into place. His hand hovered over his gun, ready to pull it at the slightest notice. Now the delivery was successfully processed he should be with Zane offering solidarity. The additional news he had to share would help the man too, but he couldn't leave here whilst the threat of Marco was still at large.

Just even thinking of that bastard pushed Diego's blood pressure past the top limit of mercury. There had been no attempt to storm the building as yet, but that didn't mean there wouldn't be.

He walked out of the delivery area and into the room where men had already begun the huge job of weighing and cutting the coke. The radio blared as he made his way towards Tiger overseeing from over the other side of the room but was stopped in his tracks when Ian van Dahl's *'Castles in the Sky'* was interrupted by the news.

> *"The fire raging in Mayfair which brought much of the area to a standstill has now been extinguished and roads have been reopened... A full investigation is yet to be undertaken, further complicated by the discovery of two, as yet unidentified bodies on the ground floor of the property. It is thought the fire was deliberate and that the two victims - a male and female - may be the foreign owners of the house, known to be in residence at the time. Investigations will continue to determine whether..."*

Diego pulled Tiger into a side room. 'It's Marco and Sofia - the bodies. It's them.' A strange sense of peace washed over him. His wife was dead - he could feel it in his bones. Now he wouldn't have to decide when or if to do it himself. The same could now be said for Zane shouldering the burden of dispatching Marco.

'How can you be sure it's them?' Tiger asked. 'If they torched the place, why would they hang around?'

'Something must have gone wrong,' Diego shrugged. 'Stuck doors or windows, perhaps? Maybe the fire they started spread in the wrong direction, catching them out? I don't know, but it's them. No one else could have been in the house, so it's *got* to be them.'

Tiger nodded. It certainly was feasible, but this news was so unexpected he didn't quite know how to take it.

'This means we're free to leave here,' Diego smiled. 'Let's go to the hospital, tell Zane the news and see if we can be of any help.'

Tiger followed Diego out of the canning works. *Marco and Sofia dead from the fire they'd started themselves? What a shame...*

The only fly in the ointment was there hadn't been three bodies found – the third belonging to Colt.

But the authorities might find another body as they continued their investigation. Or maybe they wouldn't... If they didn't, then Tiger would have to continue watching his back for a long time to come.

• • • •

'SHE'S GOT TO BE out of surgery by now!' Zane had worn the laminate flooring bare from the amount he'd paced up and down, blind to the inquisitive stares from other people in the waiting room at the deranged, savage-looking man wearing biker garb.

Perhaps these people might have been more choosy about who they stared at if they were aware the man they were all so interested in speculating over had a loaded gun in his jacket and ran one of London's most infamous organisations that had just taken possession of millions of pounds worth of cocaine.

Zane turned to Leo. 'Will they ever tell us what's going on?'

'They did say they needed to operate,' Leo reasoned. 'Putting pins in someone's leg won't be a ten-minute job!' He glanced down at his own leg, the thought making his teeth curl.

'Even so, it's been hours!' Zane grumbled. Erin requiring her leg pinning was bad enough, but to still know nothing about the baby was crucifying him. His frustration gave way to the constant throb of pounding rage making it an ongoing battle to remain in this room rather than going after the culprits responsible.

They all knew who was behind mowing Erin down and it was no fucking accident.

Torching Diego's house and running off with the man's wife was bad enough, but for Marco to stoop so low to run over a pregnant woman - *Zane's* pregnant woman, was the epitome of everything!

Zane found himself staring at his grimy fingers which were shaking with pent-up rage and frustration, as well as pure dread. That Diego remained unscathed was Marco's only failure so far, but there was still adequate time to address that. And sitting here like a lemon with no one telling him a fucking thing was only aiding Marco in his quest.

'I shouldn't be here. I should be hunting those fuckers down. Every extra second gives them time to do something else and then escape.' *Robbing the coke from the canning works would be next.*

Even as the words left his mouth, Zane knew he couldn't go anywhere until he knew Erin and his baby were okay.

*And if they weren't...*

He shook his head to dislodge these downright terrifying thoughts. He'd stay here forever and a day if Erin and his child were safe and if that meant letting Marco win, then so be it.

'Come on, come on,' he muttered, resignedly plonking himself onto the chair next to Leo.

'They'll update us soon, I'm sure and...' Leo stopped, hopeful as the double doors opened, but his heart sank as a distressed man with his arm in a sling entered the room.

'Harry!' An elderly lady who neither Zane nor Leo had previously paid any attention to, jumped from a chair opposite to rush towards the man. 'Are you all right? I've been so worried! Have they said it's okay for you to go home?'

'I'm fine, Mum,' the man said. 'But I have to know about what happened to that woman and whether she's okay. She's in this hospital too. I won't rest until I know.'

Leo exchanged looks with Zane as the man sat down in a chair letting his elderly mother dab at the tears in his eyes, but before Leo could stop him, Zane rushed from his seat over to the distressed man.

'Was it you?' Zane barked.

'Zane!' Leo grabbed Zane's arm, worried he would lamp this bloke. 'He's hardly one of Marco's hit men! Look at him!'

Shaking Leo's grip away, Zane pressed on. 'The accident outside Kensington tube - was it you? Tell me!'

The man nodded. 'I-I didn't see her! The woman appeared from between two parked cars. She dashed out in front of me. I-I couldn't stop. I... Do... do you know her?'

'She's only the mother of my unborn child and the woman I plan to marry!' Zane spat. 'And being as you're so interested, I don't know whether either of them are okay either!'

'Oh God!' the man howled. 'She's pregnant? I'm so sorry. I...'

'What are you to Marco?' Zane snarled.

'Marco?' The man blinked, bewildered. 'I don't know anyone of that name. Is he...?'

'Forget it. It doesn't matter.' Zane shook his head and stared at the devastated figure in front of him, his rage transforming into relief. This bloke wasn't working for Marco, Colt or for any of them. It was obvious.

If tension could flood from a body out onto the floor there would be a pool under Zane's feet right now. What happened to

Erin was a genuine accident, not something dictated by his psycho brother. And as much as the end result was in no way good and could yet get worse, it *was* an accident.

'I really am so very sorry,' the man sobbed, tears now freely flowing down his cheeks. 'What can I do or say that could possibly make this any better? Tell me and I'll do it. I'll never forgive myself if...'

'It was an accident.' Zane muttered. 'Sometimes these things happen. Let's just hope they'll be okay.'

'Zane!' Diego and Tiger barged through the double doors. 'Any news? Because I have some for you.'

Leo followed Zane, Diego and Tiger into a corner of the room. He'd honestly thought Zane was about to rip that man's head off and make things more difficult, but he hadn't. That Erin's injuries didn't stem from Marco's instructions made an awful situation just that tiny bit less horrible.

# Forty Six

ERIN HEARD VOICES but they were muffled and didn't fit with what she saw. She turned in the direction of the voices - anywhere other than the scene in front of her, but no matter which way she looked, it was still there.

The crackling was loud and the sound of exploding glass deafening, but the smell... the smell of burning hair and stench of flesh burning and cooking was...

She flung her head in the opposite direction once more, but they were *still* there. Marco's ice blue eyes, so similar to Zane's, but with the gleam of psychosis making them colder than a deep freeze, were mocking even as strips of his skin fell away from his face, the fresh bubbling and sizzling in front of her eyes. And Sofia - her hair alight, her face blistering and post-box red, melting the woman's beauty in a pile of smouldering flesh.

Then the bodies dropped to the floor.

*Was that laughter? Was it hers?*

*No, it couldn't be.*

*More voices...*

*Another bang! The smell...*

Erin opened her mouth to scream but nothing came out. *Was she on fire? She didn't know. It hurt. It hurt real bad. But at the same time, she felt happy and relieved.*

Then it went black.

*And now...*

*Now she didn't know...*

The muffled voices and laughter increased in volume and became interspersed with flashes of writhing, burning corpses. Marco's face morphed into Sofia's before turning into bones, then returned to normal, before flipping into charred, blackened lumps. Then...

'Erin? Erin? Can you hear me? Erin?'

The faces were getting closer but now she could see the tube station. *That was it! She was supposed to phone Zane and ask where she should go. Did she still have stomach pains? No – it was now mainly her leg. Why her leg?*

'Erin? Wake up now, come on. Would you like a drink?'

*Drink? She didn't need a drink! She needed to get to the phone box. It's just over there, look! It won't take a second.*

*Oh shit!*

Erin's eyes jerked open to be blinded by a fluorescent strip light above her. Confusion, along with panic swirled.

'Ah! You're back with us! How about that drink of water now?'

Erin blinked, the room coming into focus. *A nurse? Why was there a nurse?*

The agony in her leg seared into Erin's mind while the burning faces of Sofia and Marco faded into the darkness to reveal the memory of stepping into the road. Not seeing the car until it was on top of her jolted into focus and her hands flew to her stomach. 'My baby?' she screamed. 'My baby! Is my baby...?'

'Your baby is fine.' The nurse patted Erin's shaking hands reassuringly. 'I can't say the same about your leg though. That will take many months to mend, but your baby is perfectly well.' Smiling, the nurse propped Erin's head up so she could sip some water. 'You were scanned during surgery and your little one has a healthy, strong heartbeat. Everything is intact and perfect.'

Relief coursed through Erin's whole body and she began sobbing with relief.

'Ah, now don't you fret,' the nurse soothed. Have ten minutes to get yourself together and then we'll take you to the ward. From what I understand, your partner and several others are waiting to see you.'

• • • •

ZANE FEARED THE WORST when Diego burst in saying he had news. Had the doctors got mixed up when Diego reached the hospital and given him an update about Erin and the baby instead? Had the cocaine drop gone wrong? Had Marco succeeded in overthrowing the canning works?

But it was none of those things. And what he *had* learned, Zane had conflicting emotions about.

Glancing around the other faces in the waiting room, checking once again there was no one in earshot, he rubbed his hand over his face, his stubble rough against his fingers. 'You're sure it's them?'

'As sure as I can be,' Diego muttered, his voice low, unsure whether to offer commiserations or get out the champagne. It was the same thinking of Sofia. Whatever she'd done, planned and very nearly succeeded with, she'd been his wife - someone who he'd believed would shortly become the mother of his longed-for child.

He shook his own conflicting emotions away. Sofia deserved no sadness over her passing. She'd made her bed and would forever lie in it. The same went for Marco. 'There's no one else it can be. The housekeeper left hours ago. I don't employ any men, so it could only be those two.'

Zane stared at his hands now resting on his thighs, barely able to believe it was over. Marco was dead. His brother was *dead*. There would be no further problems, no further payback, no more animosity, no nothing. *It was done.*

The relief of being spared from taking on the task of

removing his own brother from this earthly plane was bittersweet. Was he such a weak loser to find the prospect of doing that one particular job so uncomfortable?

No. He wasn't weak *or* a loser. He'd have done it. But the part which was glad he no longer had to, remained.

'So, it's over?' Leo said, as shocked as anyone. 'Finally over?'

'Apart from Colt,' Tiger muttered. 'My side of things is far from done, unless they find a third body.'

'If his body's not in my house then he'll be lying low, so you do not need to think of him for a while,' Diego said. 'I also have more news.' He glanced apologetically at Leo and Tiger. 'This relates to your father, Zane, so you might wish to speak privately?'

Zane shook his head. 'Whatever you have to say can be said in front of my men. However, I don't think there's anything left to discuss about that particular subject.' *He didn't need any reminders about it either.*

Diego adjusted his position in the uncomfortable plastic chair. 'What you told me before... I hope you don't mind, but I made enquiries…'

Zane bristled. *What he'd said was between the two of them, not to be bandied about.*

Sensing Zane's annoyance, Diego quickly put the record straight. 'I have not discussed you or your family with anyone, short of double-checking something.' Leaning forward, he lowered his voice further. 'What you'd been told about Guiseppe didn't sit right with me. As you know, I had no dealings personally with the man, but I was sure one of my father's associates worked closely with him. Do you recall a man by the name of Salvatore?'

Zane frowned. 'Salvatore? Yes, I remember him. He was a trusted member of my father's inner circle.' *The man was there on the fateful night of Marco's fourteenth birthday - the night Guiseppe ordered Shirley's rape.* His palms began to sweat and he gritted his teeth as his anger bloomed.

'Salvatore was my father's second cousin via marriage and I believe how the initial link between our families working relationship first developed,' Diego explained. 'Salvatore died some time ago, but I spoke to his son, who's the same age as me and was training his way up through the ranks of the Delgado firm at the same time. I asked him what he remembered about that incident and he got back to me today regarding it.'

Zane's skin crawled with a thousand insects, unsure if he could bear opening more cans of worms. If his father had been party to further unsavoury things than he was already aware of, it might just push him under.

'You're correct that Guiseppe knew what Marco did to the girl,' Diego said, 'but only afterwards.'

Zane looked up, confused. 'Afterwards? But he ordered for Marco to...'

'No!' Diego shook his head. 'Guiseppe instructed nothing. He walked in just as Marco finished having his way with the poor girl. That's how he knew about it. In no way did he order it.'

Zane laughed hollowly. 'Then why cover it up? Why pay off Shirley's family and force them out of the city?'

'You have to ask? Guiseppe was Sicilian. *You're* Sicilian. I am Columbian. Families like ours look after our own, regardless of what they do. That's what is drilled into us from the beginning - blood will out.'

*But how untrue was that half the time*, Zane thought bitterly.

Sensing Zane's reticence to believe his words, Diego pressed on. 'Your father would have done the same in any circumstance, but Salvatore's son clearly remembers his father, Guiseppe and the whole circle being stressed and revolted over the incident. What happened was a closely guarded, yet well-known issue within the inner circle.'

Diego could see Zane's mind processing this information for plausibility. 'Apparently, your father knocked Marco over a desk and launched him from his office for his actions. Why do you think your brother was never handed responsibility and kept at arms' length? Guiseppe succeeded in protecting his family name, but unfortunately to do that he had to extend that protection to Marco. But that's as far as it ever went. That's how things work in our kind of families, you know that.'

Getting up from the chair, Zane paced the small area the collection of big men sat in and Diego could almost taste the remaining questions hanging in the air. 'You are also correct that your father did not want you to have involvement with Shirley, but he did *not* instruct her ruination. Then, being as Marco was putting it about that Shirley had been having an affair with him and was easy, Guiseppe paid her family off in order to save the girl's reputation.' His face twisted with rage. 'It seems Marco never changed his way of getting what he wanted.'

Zane snarled at this additional information. 'Shirley wouldn't have touched Marco with a bargepole, given the choice!'

'But, and the *big* point here is that Guiseppe did not know the girl had become pregnant from Marco's act. I think you know as well as I do that had he known, things would have turned out very differently.'

Zane stared at Diego, his mind racing. 'Then why did Shirley backup what Marco said to be the truth?'

'Why do you think?' Diego shrugged. 'Because that's what she'd been told - most likely by *Marco*. And,' he added, 'everyone who knew about what Marco did, my father's cousin included, was sworn to secrecy. What I just told you was only confirmed because it was *me* asking about it on *your* behalf. I hope I haven't overstepped the line or betrayed your confidence in doing what I have done.'

Zane shook his head. No, Diego had not betrayed his confidence. He'd done something far different. He'd reinstated his faith and belief in his own father. To learn that the man hadn't ordered anything underhand brought astronomical relief.

A wide grin broke over Zane's face until the waiting room door opened. 'Do we have a Mr Morelli? A Zane Morelli?'

Zane rushed towards the waiting doctor. 'I am Zane Morelli. What is the news?'

# Forty Seven

THERE WASN'T MUCH ROOM in Erin's small private hospital room, especially with four large men crammed in there, but at least it gave them the chance to speak openly.

'I can't believe they're really dead!' Erin gasped, her act of being shocked to learn of Sofia and Marco's demise so good she would convince herself if she wasn't already well aware of what had happened.

'We'll know it's them for definite once they've been formally identified, but it's not possible for it to be anyone else,' Zane said, concentrating on the positives rather than the sight of Erin's broken nose and smashed leg. Erin would be fine and their baby was fine too, therefore it would *all* be fine.

Erin smiled. She didn't need to wait for formal identification to know those bodies at Diego's house belonged to Marco and Sofia, but her pact to keep that to herself remained. She turned to smile at Diego, Tiger and Leo. They were all here and all safe. Except... 'Wh-What happened to Colt?' she asked, not liking the glanced the men exchanged at this question.

'Don't worry about him. We know is that he wasn't behind what happened to you.' Zane nodded to Erin's leg suspended in a hoist. 'It was a genuine accident.' He certainly wasn't about to tell Erin that Colt was the only one they didn't know the location of.

'He'll be back though, won't he?' Erin's eyes darting to Tiger. 'He won't just walk away.'

Tiger swallowed uncomfortably with the weight of responsibility. Because of Colt, every second he remained here with these people he classed as family, he was putting them in danger. And that was not something he wanted to do. *Ever*.

'As I said, Colt's not someone you need to worry about right now.' Zane stroked Erin's cheek, hating the damage caused to her face. 'It will be dealt with as and when needs be. But on a different subject, I'm thinking about broaching further up north - to the Midlands.'

Erin's eyes widened. 'You want us to go back up there?' The thought of returning to the area which only held bad memories wasn't great, even if it meant her child would be safe from Colt. 'Oh, Zane! I'm not sure I...'

'I didn't mean *us*. This is to do with what you asked about opening a club and running somewhere above board starting with some of the girls who are ready to leave the Starbright.' Zane grinned. 'I expect you thought I'd forgotten? Well, I haven't!'

'So, you agree!' Erin exclaimed, already feeling better. 'That's brilliant!'

'It won't be another branch of this firm. I'm planning on setting up a brand new one. Myself and Diego will fund it, but that will be our only involvement.' Zane then looked to Tiger and Leo. 'I'm looking for someone to take it on. Interested?'

Tiger and Leo exchanged surprised looks. 'You want one of us to run a new firm?'

Zane shrugged. 'Why not? You're both more than capable of it, as I'm sure you know and have proved countless times.' Sensing the reticence in both men, he continued. 'Neither of you have to accept this offer. I know your life and home is here in London. Regardless of what you choose, you know you'll always be part of things here. That will never change. There are others we can put in charge, but myself and Diego wanted to give you both first refusal.'

'The other thing is,' Zane added. 'Is that now Marco is no longer, things won't be as, well, "interesting", to put it mildly.' A rare grin broke on his face. 'That, I'm glad about, but I don't want either of you getting bored!'

Leo frowned. 'And you're funding this new firm to set up but it wouldn't be yours?'

Zane nodded. 'That's correct, providing it is you or Tiger at the helm. Otherwise, me and Diego will remain as head and oversee whoever it running it remotely.'

Leo nodded. 'Running my own firm is one of my dreams, but no matter how tempting and a lifelong ambition it is, I couldn't be out of London. London's my life and all I know and I don't want that to change.'

Zane nodded in acceptable. 'Fair enough. And Tiger? Your thoughts?'

Tiger shifted his weight to his other foot, wondering whether leaving London look like Colt had won or was it the best thing to do? If he stayed here and Colt came after him once more, then remaining in the centre of Zane's life would put everyone at risk. Maybe it would be better all round to head up north? *And then there was Alyson...*

He took a deep breath. 'It's a very generous offer and a difficult call, but it's going to be difficult for me here now, what with the memories of Alyson. Then there's Colt. He clearly has an issue with me' His eyes fell to Erin. 'I don't want that impacting any more than it has done on any of you.'

'Alyson?' Erin looked around the room, realising by everyone's expression that Alyson had been yet another victim. Her heart sank. 'Oh God! Tiger, I'm so sorry! Wh...'

'Don't let Colt influence your decision, Tiger,' Zane interrupted. 'We'll deal with whatever comes along, you know that.'

'Yeah, I get that, but you guys are too important to me for

it not to make a difference.' Tiger shook his head. 'As for Alyson, Erin, I'm gutted, yes, but she showed me that I *do* still exist somewhere within myself, so something good has come from it. So, I'll do it. I'll miss all of you, but it's time to start afresh.'

Zane shook Tiger's hand. 'I'll get on with finalising the details and the premises. He then turned to Erin. 'I've got to ask you – there's something I can't quite work out about the accident… What were you doing outside Kensington station?'

Erin faltered. *Here it was - the question she'd been dreading.* She could never tell Zane that she'd been the one to finish Marco. It would make him feel like he'd failed her when that couldn't be further from the truth. 'I was trying to get to a phone box to call you,' she said. *Well, that was the truth - partly...* 'Sofia smashed my phone before she left Harrods and...'

Anger flooded Zane as he realised what Erin was saying. 'So, Sofia *did* realise we were onto her? I knew it! And this...' He indicated to Erin's face. 'This was her as well, wasn't it?'

Erin nodded. *She wouldn't lie. She just had to hope Zane didn't directly ask about anything else.*

'The fucking bitch!' Zane snarled. 'Good job she did get herself burned to fucking death, otherwise I'd...'

'Can we drop this subject now?' Erin smiled weakly. 'I'm okay, the baby's okay and we're all still here - *all* of us. It's finally over, so let's not go on about things we can no longer change.'

Zane's fury morphed into a smile as he took Erin into his arms. 'You're right. It's over.'

Erin nestled against Zane's warm chest and closed her eyes with relief. It *was* over and the part that she hadn't volunteered to mention would remain just that – something only *she* knew of.

# Epilogue

**Four months later…**

'AARRGH! This is so frustrating!' Erin moaned, struggling to get into the correct position for the next bank of exercises the physiotherapist had insisted she followed. 'I can't get myself into the right place!'

'The physio will go tits if you don't do your exercises properly, as will I!' Sitting on the sofa in the penthouse, his feet up on the coffee table, Zane wiggled his finger at Erin, a pretend stern look on his face. 'It can't be that difficult!'

From her yoga mat on the floor, Erin threw a cushion at Zane. It was true that she needed to follow these exercises to the letter in order for her leg to fully heal and to strengthen it up, but she had one now rather large disadvantage. *Not that she'd change it for the world.* 'You should try it with this spud in the way!'

Zane jumped off the sofa onto the yoga mat and pulled Erin into his arms. 'Ah, but he's an amazing spud!' His hands ran over the beautiful mound which had once been Erin's flat belly, the sight of her growing pregnancy never failing to fill him with awe, wonderment and excitement.

Lowering his head, he pressed his lips to the tight, bare skin exposed between her yoga leggings and cropped sports top, thinking she got more beautiful every day. 'I can't wait to meet him.'

Running her fingers through Zane's thick hair, Erin glowed with happiness. 'There's another two months before that happens, but I can't wait to meet him either!'

The child within her was definitely a boy. The horrible uncertainty following Sofia's beating and then the accident, meant it took time to fully relax and enjoy the pregnancy. But regular scans had gradually assuaged her fears and the latest had confirmed the baby's sex.

They'd already agreed on a name – *Guiseppe*. It was a fitting and apt name for their child - a silent tribute to the man Zane was now free to remember in the *correct* way, rather than Marco's skewed version of the man which, had it not been for Diego's actions, his memory would have forever remained another of Marco's casualties.

But Marco was gone, along with all the lies he'd told and gradually, most of the damage he'd caused would become less raw for all of them.

Zane stopped from trailing kisses along Erin's belly and raised his head. 'Did I tell you I heard from Tiger this morning?'

'No,' Erin frowned. 'Is everything okay?'

'It's more than okay,' Zane grinned. 'His firm is becoming well established already and the club is due to officially open next week. We've been invited to the opening.'

'That would be nice,' Erin smiled, glad that things were going well for Tiger up north. If anyone deserved a break and a bit of luck, it was him. 'And there's been no sign of...?'

'Nope. Colt's gone to ground, like we thought. Either that or he's back in Broadmoor!' Zane winked. 'Tiger's in a good place and seems upbeat. He still wonders what might have been with him and Alyson, but he's doing okay. He said that she gave him the gift of remembering he has a heart.'

'Tiger *always* had a heart,' Erin grinned. 'I'm glad he's

finally realised that!'

'Diego's planning to come over to visit once Spud is born as well,' Zane continued. 'I miss him being around so it will be nice to see him again.'

Erin nodded. Diego's side to this had panned out nicely too. Once the bodies were formally identified as being Marco and Sofia, things were fairly straightforward. It hadn't taken Diego much wangling to convince the authorities the arson attempt must have been from an unknown resentful of his success. No one had questioned Marco's presence at the house that day either. Thankfully, they had the sense when to stop digging. It meant Diego could return to Columbia and continue his life without the taint of scandal surrounding Sofia and Marco's affair, or the non-existent child.

On top of that, Zane's business was going from strength to strength. The association with Diego's firm continued as before and Leo was busy overseeing the majority of what went on at the canning works, freeing up time for Zane.

Erin smiled. It was strange how much time had been used up in defending against nutcase brothers…

'I still don't get why they didn't get out.'

Erin looked at Zane and frowned. 'Who?'

'Marco and Sofia. If they'd managed to get to the back door, I just don't get why they couldn't get through. It doesn't make sense.'

'I don't rightly know,' Erin said. Quickly taking Zane's hand, she snuggled against him. 'I guess we never will.' Zane had dealt with Marco's demise well. They'd hadn't spoken about it at length, but Erin knew he was relieved the death hadn't been by his own hand. And she wouldn't change any part of that by ever breathing a word about who was *really* responsible.

That was her secret and one she would forever keep.

# THE SCARRED SERIES

**MIRRORS NEVER LIE | THE PRICE OF BETRAYAL | TRUSTING BLOOD | THE HARD TRUTH | THE LAST PROMISE**

Disappointed to find out the promise of avenging his wrongful incarceration had already been carried out without him, Zane Morelli stepped out from prison. It didn't take long to realise that what he'd been told of the death of the man who had set him up was a lie.

A lie told by Zane's own firm.

A firm who had already overstepped the mark during his absence by scarring his face in retribution for their wrongful belief that he had betrayed them.

But the truth was now loud and clear. The man who had succeeded in getting Zane banged up was alive and so therefore, would be paying for what he did. This should be easy for someone like Zane, but there is another person with a grudge. Not only with Zane, but with his target.

And Zane hadn't thought Erin Langley would prove such a thorn in his side.

# More From This Author

## ALLEGIANCE SERIES:

**TAKEOVER | FALLOUT | VENDETTA | PAYBACK | JUDGEMENT**

Daddy's girl Samantha Reynold hadn't bargained on unexpectedly needing to step into her father's shoes and take over the family casino business.

Pampered and spoiled, Sam knows nothing about the rules of this glamorous but deadly new world. She has a lot to learn and even more to prove. But she won't let her family down, especially when it looks like they could lose everything to their biggest rivals – the Stoker family.

Eldest son Sebastian hasn't got time to pander to pretty girl Samantha as she plays at being boss. Rumours are swirling around the streets of Birmingham that have the power to rip the Stoker family apart and destroy everything they've built.

# More From This Author

## RETRIBUTION SERIES:

**AN OLD SCORE | FINDERS KEEPERS | THE FINAL TAKE**

**Three families... One prize...**

Teagan Fraser had no idea what she was getting herself into when she took on an assignment as a live-in carer for Dulcie Adams – a retired dancer from a Soho club. Dulcie has waited forty years for her lover, Michael Pointer, to return, but she's been living in hope for a time that never came and left looking after something important, which Jonah Powell and his firm want back.

In addition to the notorious Powell firm, there are others wanting to claim what they believe is rightfully theirs and they'll do anything to get it back. If only Dulcie wasn't around it would be a lot easier, but she's difficult to shift...

A lot can happen in a short space of time and Teagan might wish she'd never become involved.

# More From This Author

## HUNTED SERIES:

**THE STATUS DEBT | THE FAMILY LEGACY | THE TARGET OF LIES**

Lillian Morgan would do anything to regain the status she lost by marrying beneath her and to cover the sordid details of her husband's death. This includes blackmail and the hand of marriage of her own daughter.

Tori thought her life couldn't get much worse, but someone is not being honest and secrets have the power to rip everyone to shreds.

Especially when life is built on lies.

*** This series contains written depictions of graphic violence, sex and strong language. It also contains some themes that may be uncomfortable for certain readers.***

# More From This Author

## DOWNFALL SERIES:

**UNTIL THE END OF TIME | ESCAPING THE PAST | VENGEFUL PAYBACK**

Dive into Seth and Jane's train wreck of a life, where drugs, alcohol and obsessional love means this downright dangerous pair will do *anything* to ensure nothing gets in their way.

They do bad things. *Very* bad things and their promise to love each until the end of time turns into a war against each other.

A war neither of them can win.

*** This series contains written depictions of graphic violence, sex and strong language. It also contains some themes that may be uncomfortable for certain readers.***

# About The Author

Over the years Edie has worked all over the UK as well as in several other countries and has met a lot of interesting people - several of whom have supplied ideas for some of the characters in her books! She has now settled back in central England with her partner and children, where she is pursuing her writing.

Edie writes gritty gangland and urban fiction and her series so far include her latest – the *Scarred* series; the *Allegiance* series, the *Retribution* series, *Hunted* series and *Downfall* series.

When she isn't writing, Edie enjoys reading and is a self-confessed book hoarder. She also enjoys crochet and music as well as loving anything quirky or unusual.

Visit www.ediebaylis.co.uk for the latest news, information about new releases, giveaways and to subscribe to her mailing list.

Edie Baylis

gangland | crime | urban

THRILLER AUTHOR

# Connect with Edie

https://fb.me/downfallseries

https://www.goodreads.com/author/show/17153586.Edie_Baylis

https://twitter.com/ediebaylis

https://www.amazon.co.uk/Edie-Baylis/e/B075FQHWCZ/

https://www.bookbub.com/authors/edie-baylis

https://ediebaylis.co.uk/

info@ediebaylis.co.uk

https://www.fantasticfiction.com/b/edie-baylis/

https://www.instagram.com/ediebaylis/

https://www.tiktok.com/@ediebaylis

https://www.pinterest.co.uk/ediebaylis/

# Join Edie's Mailing List

Subscribe to Edie's mailing list for the latest news on her books, special offers, new releases and competitions.

**https://ediebaylis.co.uk/signup.html**

CWA MEMBER

# ACKNOWLEDGEMENTS

Firstly, special thanks go to the ladies (you know who you are) - who were brave enough to allow their names to be adopted by some of the characters in this story after winning a competition on Facebook. (I must point out that these characters are in no way anything to do with, or connected to, their namesakes in real life!) Just want to get that out there!

Also, many thanks to the people that kindly read my drafts of *The Last Promise*. I appreciate your time and feedback.

As always, thanks to all of the supportive friends and readers who give me the incentive to keep on writing. And, of course, love and thanks to my family.

Thank you for reading *The Last Promise*. I hope you enjoyed reading it as much as I did writing it!

If so, would you please consider leaving a review on Amazon and/or Goodreads. Reviews from readers are SOOOO helpful and especially important to us authors and without you we would have nobody to write for!

Thank you once again and hope you enjoy the rest of my books.

Edie xx

Printed in Dunstable, United Kingdom

65143989R00231